MUCH ADO ABOUT DYING

Guardians of the PHAE
Book Two

ROWAN DILLON

GREEN DRAGON PUBLISHING

Dedication:

I'd like to thank my fantastic critique group for all their help keeping me on-genre and for some tough love regarding too many points of view, especially authors Mattea Orr and MA Hoyler. And sincere thanks go to my editors and beta readers, including Ian Erik Morris.

I also dedicate this series to those who face prejudice, hatred, and bigotry in any form.

Pronunciation Guide

Below is a list of some of the words and names in the story that are in other languages:

Anú—(AHnoo) A goddess of pre-Christian Ireland. Sometimes conflated with Danú.
Balor—(BAHlore) A chieftain of the Fomorians
Bealtaine—(BELLtehna) "May" in Irish, also an ancient festival
Beannacht—(BANecht) "Blessing" in Irish
Bintou—(bin-TOO) A Malian name
Bláithín—(BLAheen) An Irish name
Bran mac Máelmórda—(bran mahk malMORdah) A 10th century Irish chieftain
Caoimhe—(KWEEveh) An Irish name
Cé a ghlaonn orm?—(CAY eh GHLAYon ORem?) "Who calls me?" in Irish
Ciara—(KEE-rah) An Irish name
Cú Chulainn—(koo KHUHlinn) A demi-god/hero of pre-Christian Ireland
Dáil Éireann—(DAWil YAIRinn) The Irish Parliament
Dáil—(DAWil) The lower house of the Dáil Éireann, the Irish Parliament
Dia 's Muire duit!—(DEEah smweerah ghwit) "May God and Mary be with you" an Irish greeting
Dia daoibh—(DEEah ghweev) "May God be with you" an Irish greeting, plural
Dian Cécht—(DEEun KAYecht) A healer god of pre-Christian Ireland
Draoí/Draoíthe—(DREE/DREEheh) Priest/priests of pre-Christian Irish religion
Dún Ailinne—(doon ALinyeh) A sacred site in Kildare, Ireland
Éire—(AYreh) Another name for Ireland
Éist—(EESHT) "Listen" in Irish
Emain Macha—(AWen MAHKah) A sacred site in Armagh, Northern Ireland
Ethniu—(ENyoo) A goddess of pre-Christian Ireland, mother of Lugh
Fomorians—(foeMOReeuhns) Beings who lived in Ireland before the Tuatha Dé Danann
Gaijin—(GUY-ZHEEN) "Foreigners" in Japanese
Go raibh maith agat—(go rahv MAH a-get) "Thank you" in Irish

Hiroki—(hih-ROW-kee) A Japanese name

Kami—(kah-mee) Spirit or deity in Japanese folklore

Kami—(kaMEE) Deities venerated in Shinto

Lugh Lámfada—(LOO lavFAHda) A god of pre-Christian Ireland, Lugh of the Long Arm

Lúnasa—(LOOnasa) "August" in Irish, also an ancient harvest festival

Macha—(MAHkhah) A goddess of pre-Christian Ireland

Manannán mac Lir—(MAHnahnahn mahk leer) A sea god of pre-Christian Ireland

Matsuri—(MAHTsooree) A prayer of gratitude to the ritual of Nature

Mo chroi—(mow KROY) "My heart" in Irish

Mo leanbh—(mow LANuv) "My child" in Irish

Oghma—(OWmah) A god of pre-Christian Ireland

Omoikane—(ohMWEEkaNEH) A Shinto god of wisdom and intelligence

Poitín—(pohCHEEN) An Irish alcohol, moonshine

Qacha—(KAH-chah) A Mongolian name

Ráth Cruachan—(rath CROOkhen) A sacred site in Roscommon, Ireland (Rathcroghan)

Róisín—(row-SHEEN) An Irish name (little rose)

Tá failte romhaibh—(taw FALLcheh ROWuv) "You're welcome" in Irish, plural

Taoiseach/Taoisigh—(TEEshekht/TEEsheeh) Head of government of Ireland (singular/plural)

Teachta Dála—(TYOKHtah DAWlah) An Irish legislator

Teachtaí Dála—(TYACKtee DAWlah) A member of the Dáil Éireann, the Irish Parliament

Tuath—(TOOah) A tribe or family group in Irish

Tuatha Dé Danann—(TOOha day DAHnen) Deities of pre-Christian Ireland

Uisneach—(ISHnock) A sacred site in Westmeath, Ireland

Wəlastəkwewiyik—(woolLAStwoWIig) "People of the beautiful river," native tribe in New Brunswick and Maine

Prologue

When the magnetic poles shifted, the world panicked, expecting electronic chaos. However, when the feared difficulties failed to manifest, everyone relaxed, much like the millennium bug in 2000. A few birds might have gotten confused when they migrated but, other than that, no one noticed any major changes.

At first.

After a few months, though, some people developed an increase in their special talents. A famed opera singer reached impossible octaves. An Olympic swimmer developed fins. A famous glass artist could manipulate molten glass with his mind.

People changed. They grew. They evolved.

In time, a center formed to care for and educate these people, dubbed the Unhidden. The Protectorate for unHidden Advancement and Education headquartered in Ireland combed the world, searching for those with new talents. Many of them came to PHAE to learn how to harness their growing powers. Anna, who had power over water. Max, who commanded the winds. Hiroki, with the power of persuasion. Komie, who could command plants to grow. Bintou, with the ability to read any language. And Qacha, who could control fire. They were welcomed by PHAE representatives Ciara, Paul, and Martin, and sent to the Byrne family farm for education. Colin and Michelle, along with their children, Róisín, Brendan, Fiona, and the twins, Liam and Hugh, helped them learn about PHAE and how to control their talents.

However, before they could finish their education, several groups against the Unhidden formed an alliance to fight their progress. The Pure

Earther Movement developed a plan, obtained weapons, and executed a multi-pronged attack on Ireland. Several bombs were planted in cities around the country. Those in Galway and Dublin were detonated, killing thousands of people.

In the aftermath, the Unhidden worked hard to heal those who survived the attack.

Chapter One

"The wound is the place where the Light enters you."
– Rumi

Róisín:

Róisín Byrne watched from the hallway while her brother Brendan mopped Anna's brow, his own furrowed in worry. Her cough had graduated into full-blown fever and, so far, even his constant attentions hadn't helped. Once her illness got worse, he'd brought her to Róisín's hospital.

Róisín had worked on healing Anna every day, which kept her from getting worse, but she'd been unable to get ahead of the disease, no matter how much of her energy she put behind her Unhidden talent. Eventually, she had to move on as she had a whole wing of patients who needed her attention.

Brendan prayed pretty much every hour, calling upon his faith to provide some solution. Their mam would have told him to pray to God, and he had. Many times. It broke Róisín's heart every time she heard him call upon St. Brendan, his own namesake. The patron saint of sailors ought to be appropriate, as Anna's talent involved water. He even called on *Manannán mac Lir*, the ancient Irish god of the sea, but she only heard him do that once. Better to stick with the Catholic entities. He'd gone through his entire litany of set prayers.

One night, she walked by as he started his prayers, and she didn't recognize it. He must have made one up from his own heart.

"Heavenly Father, it's so hard to watch Anna suffer. It doesn't seem fair for her to have to endure so much pain. I have no power to help, but I believe you are powerful and capable of stepping into this situation and completely altering the outcome. In faith, I believe you listen to our prayers

3

and those prayers can make her well. So, I am bringing my friend before you to ask for your healing touch in her life. Thank you for the forgiveness of sin and the promise of eternal healing, but I am asking you to provide healing for her on this side of heaven. Amen."

Róisín swallowed back her tears as she put a hand on his shoulder, making him look up as he sniffed away his congestion. She gave him a sad smile. "I finished up a bit early. Let me try to help some more."

He stood to give Róisín room to work. She put her hands on Anna's chest as the American woman shuddered and coughed. The painful, raw sound dug into Róisín's heart.

She thought not only of how much Anna meant to the PHAE, but how much she meant to her brother. They'd enjoyed a mentor/teacher relationship, but it had obviously blossomed into something much deeper, an understanding more intimate. Róisín envied them that closeness and wanted to do everything she could to keep them together. Brendan would be devastated if Anna never recovered. To lose her now would break his heart.

Róisín reached deep into the earth, to the primal center of her power. It flowed reluctantly after a long day of healing, sputtering and trickling where it should flow freely. Still, she managed to get a good deal of power into Anna. With a deep breath, she rose, glancing at Anna's face. She wasn't sweating as much, which gave Róisín hope.

She let out a sigh. "She's better. I'll stop by after each shift for another round. It might make the difference, but whatever's got hold of her is stronger than me."

Brendan swallowed, his eyes still glued to Anna. "I know you're doing as much as you can. Thanks."

She gripped his shoulder. "Brendan."

"What?"

"She's strong, and she's young. She'll make it."

His jaw muscles twitched as he ground his teeth. "How can you be so sure? Do you even know what she has?"

Róisín pursed her lips. "No. I thought I did, but I'm not sure now. But my talent doesn't need to know. It just heals. Look, I'll ask Dr. O'Shea to come by. Maybe he can diagnose her. At least make her more comfortable. We don't have much after the bombing, but he might have an antitussive."

He turned back to Anna as she fell into a fit of dry coughing. "She needs something."

"We'll get it for her. She's better than yesterday. Tomorrow, she'll be better yet. Have faith."

Róisín:

Galway

Róisín wiped the sweat from her patient's brow with the back of her hand, smearing the damp with grit. Ash still drifted all around from the explosions, even inside the makeshift hospital, despite being three days since bombs destroyed half of Galway. The stink of char fought with harsh antiseptics, blood, and other less pleasant hospital odors. "Did you want some broth?"

He shook his head, coughing into his hand. "No thanks, pet, but I've a fierce thirst on me. I'd love a drop of the hard stuff, if ye have it?"

"I'm afraid whiskey still isn't on your chart, sorry." She gave him a wry grin to take the sting from her words. As little as they had here, a bit of spirits might lift his mood.

A loud crash made everyone jump. Róisín glanced around wildly, trying to identify the source of the sound. Someone ran down the hall, paused, cursed, and kept running. She ran to the door and cracked it open, peering from side to side into the darkness. Only silence greeted her. Then another crash came and, this time, she could tell it was outside.

Róisín went to the nearest window, but she could find nothing that might have made the noise. She scanned the horizon, searching for plumes of smoke as she tried to calm her racing heart, even though the sound had been much too small to be another bomb.

She flinched as another sounded. This time, she spied someone rifling through the dumpster skips and slamming the lids when they were done.

Róisín heaved a deep sigh of nervous relief and wiped the sweat from her hands, grimacing at the grit. The ash and dust got everywhere, and she prayed to God for a heavy, drenching downpour to wash the ash away. Who would have believed any Irishwoman would ask for rain? But a good storm might wash the pain from the ruined city.

Harsh coughing behind her made her glance over her shoulder, but she could do little to ease that patient's suffering. For some reason, her Unhidden talent for healing hadn't helped the cough much. The new shipment of cough syrup hadn't arrived, and they were out of most of their palliatives. Operating a hospital, even a makeshift one, with so few supplies, had stretched the limits of their resourcefulness.

A baby cried, quickly shushed by a nurse. Róisín's swallowed against the tears pushing behind her eyes, knowing the girl's mother had died in the bombing.

The man coughed again. Another nurse urged him to drink some water. In a querulous voice, the patient demanded whiskey. Róisín chuckled under her breath, despite the grim scene. Trust Irishmen to want the cure that heals most things.

With a deep sigh, she noted her readings on her patient's chart and moved to the next bed. She'd finished her rounds in all three wards, and her long shift was almost over. They needed dozens more to cover all the work. Dublin promised to send medical personnel, too, but they'd also been bombed. Communication was sketchy due to damaged cell towers. Travel became difficult and dangerous. She couldn't even drive to her home near Limerick to be with her parents. Not that she'd consider leaving her duties here, not while she could be of help. She may not be a doctor, but as a trained veterinarian, she had many skills of use to the injured, as well as her healing magic.

With another quick prayer, this time begging for the health and safety of her family and friends, Róisín knelt beside the last pallet. She always waited to attend this patient until the end of her shift as working on her sapped the last of her strength.

Qacha Duar had been from the latest class of Unhidden at her family's farm, and she'd grown fond of the irascible Mongolian chef. The warrior woman had been integral in keeping Galway from being completely destroyed. Though this hero had roused briefly after the battle, she'd fallen back into a coma.

Róisín took her vitals, shaking her head at the high body temperature and rapid heart rate but knew they were typical for the woman. Perhaps Qacha's talent with fire accounted for the anomaly.

After sponging down Qacha's face and the few unburnt portions of her arms and legs, Róisín sat cross-legged at her side, placing her hands on the Mongolian woman's chest.

With a deep breath, Róisín closed her eyes and centered herself, pulling deep from the earth to tickle the power beneath her. Questing for that tingle, she sensed it, grasped it, and coaxed it from the ground and through her buttocks, her torso, and her arms. When it reached her fingers, her skin burned and itched. She'd grown used to that pain and welcomed it as a sign that her talent obeyed her command.

As the power flowed through her hands and into Qacha's chest, Róisín cracked open her eyes. The illumination was a new phenomenon, and she liked watching her hands glow with healing power.

Róisín had always been able to heal her own minor cuts and bruises. After the magnetic pole shift, though, she could heal others. Broken legs. Deep cuts. But even those required time and intense effort.

Healing injuries as deep as Qacha's demanded more power, and Róisín rationed her strength each day. Róisín wasn't even certain she made a difference. The small improvements might be the woman's natural healing, but at least Róisín didn't make things worse, and she must try.

As a wave of exhaustion swept over her, Róisín slumped over the Mongolian woman. The other attendants knew the routine and let her recover on her own. She concentrated on her breathing. In and out. In and out. Slowly drawing in the energy of the earth to restore her own exhausted supply.

Once the tingling faded, Róisín pulled her arms off the other woman's pallet, dropping them into her own lap. She stared at her hands, seeing nothing but a beige blur. Sometimes, her mind took longer to recover than her body.

Now that her shift was over, she could sleep. Oh, how she craved sleep, and yet it frightened her, too. The nightmares came so strong, torturing her nights with screams and blood, and her unable to help anyone's pain.

Letting out a shuddering sigh, Róisín dragged herself to her feet. After she made notes in Qacha's chart, she shuffled toward the break room.

She bunked with the other volunteer doctors, nurses, helpers, and clean-up crew who worked to clear away the destruction. Perhaps they found silent comfort in staying in one room, in one of the few places of order left in the city.

There would be no returning to normal after two bombs, but they all worked hard on survival.

Róisín ached for a shower, but the water system had been destroyed by the blast. She considered walking out to the shore, but she didn't have enough strength. Even though they set up the makeshift hospital on the outskirts of town, with crews working hard to get the water and power back, they must stay close enough to help the injured. They originally set up in the National University of Ireland Galway buildings, but that was destroyed in the second blast.

They'd shifted across the street to the University Hospital. Without water and electricity, everything was improvised, but at least they had proper equipment and tools. Most of the equipment needed power, but they hadn't found any undamaged generators.

With a sponge and a tepid bucket of water, she washed the stinkiest parts of her body, changed into fresh scrubs, and sat on the bench with her head in her hands. At least they had plenty of scrubs. A medical supply depot across the street had donated everything they had.

Her mind swam with snippets of information, swirling around like a confetti whirlwind. Róisín couldn't make any sense of it. She pushed herself to her feet and shuffled down the empty, dim corridor toward the dormitories. Ten large patient rooms had been converted for the staff to use, dark rooms with no windows.

Despite her aching muscles, Róisín knelt by the bed and sent a silent prayer for the speedy healing of her patients, her family's strength, and her own stamina.

Even as she laid in her cot and closed her eyes, her mind buzzed with more half-formed ideas, shreds of screams, and the stink of fear and blood. She rubbed the grit from her eyes for the thousandth time since the blast, praying she could erase the pain and terror from her memory.

Eventually, giving into the anguish of her soul, she fell into a fitful slumber. Róisín's breathing melded with the other sleeping forms to create a symphony full of fatigue.

Róisín:

As she fought to emerge from the depths of her dreams, Róisín stretched her entire body, wincing at the ache. For a wonder, she actually felt rested. She'd never describe herself as bright-eyed or bushy-tailed, not since the bomb. However, she must have gotten some much-needed rest. She rose, wiped herself down, and brushed her hair. She wished the supply depot had a store of toothbrushes. Instead, she scrubbed toothpaste on her teeth with her finger, and rinsed from the potable water bucket. It was odd how much she relied on modern conveniences, only missing them when they were absent.

After detangling her shoulder-length, honey-blonde hair and plaiting it into a tight French braid, she gazed at her image in the mirror. Hazel eyes stared back at her, complete with dark circles. Still, she almost felt human.

A doctor stumbled into the large bathroom, and Róisín waved at her. "Hey, Mairé."

The doctor barely raised her hand, grunted, and scrubbed her face with the washcloth and bucket. "Hey."

"Is your shift done?"

The doctor nodded, barely glancing up. Róisín left Mairé to her ablutions and decompression. Time to start her own day again.

With over a hundred critical patients and two hundred more needing care, the staff of twenty got spread incredibly thin. That came out to about fifteen patients per person, three times the normal load, and without essential equipment. Because of her healing power, she carried twice that many. They only had enough hours to work, rest, and wash.

Other makeshift hospitals were being set up around the destruction zones here and in Dublin. So far, begging for more doctors, nurses, or aides hadn't worked. Hell, she'd even be happy for an intern.

Róisín had just started her veterinary career when her natural talent burst into force. Along with many others across the world, the magnetic pole shift heralded changes in her abilities, intensifying her power of healing.

Even as a child, cuts on her own hand disappeared overnight, headaches would go away. Once the change came, though, she experimented on her brothers and sisters, discovering she could heal them now.

At first, she could only heal small things, but over the last seven months, her powers had grown. She paid a price for that power, as healing someone else sapped her strength.

So far, a good night's rest restored her flagging energy. Still, Róisín suspected that effort took a deeper toll, especially her work on Qacha. She didn't mind, though. Róisín had grown to like the prickly woman, admiring her honor and fortitude.

In the meantime, Róisín had to check on thirty of the most injured people, make sure they were clean and fed, then update their vitals.

Anita O'Sullivan had been a schoolteacher, a young woman of just thirty years old. She taught at a Catholic primary school, as she told everyone when the workmen brought her in. A sunny personality, full of positivity and strong faith. She asked after her children every day. Róisín promised to try to find word of them but, so far, hadn't gotten any information.

The first blast had hit her school, and as she shielded two students, concrete blocks fell on the lower half of her body, crushing both her legs. She'd never walk again. Prosthetics were her only chance and, until they got water, that chance got further away each day. It took daily work to keep the incipient infection at bay.

Róisín always visited Anita first, because the infection grew stronger overnight. She'd promised herself not to let the rot win, and she prayed for strength. "Anita, how was your night? Any problems?"

The short, dark-haired woman gave her a sunny smile. "Oh, no, my dear. Everything was lovely. I could even see the moon peeking out from the clouds in the night. Is it a full moon? The ward lit up with lovely blue light. If we were out in the country, we'd surely see fairies dancing in the mushroom circles."

Róisín grinned as she took her blood pressure. "Your heart rate is doing well, and it looks like the infection hasn't gotten worse. That's great news. Have you eaten yet this morning?"

She waved away the rations. "No, no, save that for someone who needs it. Water is enough for me."

Róisín gave her a stern expression. "You need to eat in order to heal. The IV gives you nutrition, but you need bulk, too. Don't fight me on this, now."

"Ah, well, you know best, dear. Is it the protein bars again?"

"It is, I'm afraid."

"Well, that's the lot of life. Hand it over, and I'll do my best to pretend it's a proper Sunday roast."

Róisín grinned, wishing she could bottle Anita's good nature and administer it like a drug to her other patients. Maybe she'd even sneak in a sip of it herself. When Anita coughed several times, she said, "Don't cram it all at once, now! You can savor it. You have all the time in the world."

Anita didn't stop coughing. Róisín put a hand on her shoulder, concern blooming in her heart. With a quick quest of power, she closed her eyes. Moving her hand on the woman's back as she hacked, Róisín sent her talent into the teacher's chest, trying to suss out what caused the cough. A simple cold? Smoke in the lungs? Coughing was a new symptom in Anita, though many in the ward had been coughing from smoke inhalation.

Róisín sensed something wrong, something other than the virulent infection poisoning Anita's blood. That was old, familiar, a natural enemy she'd fought for days. No, this was something she hadn't felt before, something prickly, powdery, and malevolent.

With soothing sounds, she coated Anita's lungs with her power to ease friction and irritation. The coughs eased but didn't cease.

Róisín placed a hand on her patient's forehead. "Have you been aching, Anita? More than usual?"

Anita raised her eyebrows, and Róisín realized the idiocy of her question. *Usual* meant nothing right now. What was *usual* to someone who'd be an amputee?

"The cough is new. My chest does feel tight. Do I have a fever?"

Róisín grabbed an old-school thermometer, thankful they had a supply, and placed it under Anita's tongue. Thirty-nine. Definitely a fever.

But the disease didn't *feel* like a fever, at least not one she'd dealt with before. She pushed at the fever with her healing, but it refused to budge.

"Róisín…" Anita's face grew pale as she frowned. Róisín hadn't seen that expression on the cheerful woman's face since they'd brought her in. Without further warning, Anita spewed half-chewed protein bar all over Róisín's chest.

Anita coughed, spittle dripping as she wiped her mouth with her sleeve, horrified at her lack of control. "Oh, oh, Róisín, I'm so sorry. I don't know what came over me. I just felt so ill…"

Róisín forced a smile. "It's fine. Let me find you a bucket, a new protein bar, and something to wipe everything down." And some acetaminophen, perhaps. Something to bring down the fever since it hadn't responded to her talent.

As she turned away from Anita's cot, she slammed into a man standing behind her. She stumbled back and slipped on a spot of vomit, but he caught her. "Whoa, there. I've got you."

Róisín looked into the doctor's blue eyes, and then down at her scrubs, covered in disgusting spew. She let out a rueful chuckle. "This isn't my best look, Dr. O'Shea. Sorry."

He grinned back. "Par for the course, Róisín. Do you need help?"

Róisín kept her voice low, with a glance back at her patient. "Where can I find a bucket? And some acetaminophen. Ms. O'Sullivan has developed a fever, and I don't want it getting out of hand in her condition."

"I'll fetch the meds. The bucket'll be in the closet just outside that door and to your right. Bring it back, but then go get yourself cleaned up."

She hurried away, careful not to slip again. The slick floor and the mess on her shoes presented a challenge, but she made it to the maintenance closet and back again without further embarrassing herself. Once delivered, she escaped to the washroom.

As she scrubbed her clothing, she mulled over the symptoms. Fever and ache. The texture of the illness still bothered Róisín. But as she returned to her rounds, the enigma faded. She must keep her head clear to attend each patient.

As she worked her rounds, Róisín checked for hints of the wrongness she sensed in Anita. A few might have something, but she just couldn't tell. She cursed her power for being too weak, too vague, and that she really didn't understand how to use it best. Even amongst the Unhidden, healing powers were rare. Maybe with proper instruction, she'd be able to figure out what Anita had, or if she'd had a medical degree for humans, but she just lacked the nuance needed.

By the time she made her way to Qacha hours later, she was almost too drained to try another healing session. However, Róisín knelt by the woman and pushed energy into her.

The edge of a memory flickered against her questing power, and she trained her attention on it. It flitted away, like a summer butterfly. Exhausted, she tried again but couldn't pin down the anomaly. With a sigh, she withdrew and stumbled toward the dorms.

When Róisín checked in on Anita the next morning, she seemed better, and the fever had receded. Róisín performed her morning fight against the infection, feeling proud of her progress. However, this morning Anita had a new complaint. And as she seldom complained, Róisín paid close attention.

"Something feels like it's sitting on my chest. Like a fat cat or something."

Róisín narrowed her eyes and grabbed her stethoscope. "Can you take a deep breath?"

"I can, but only with effort. See?"

Her lungs rattled as if she had pneumonia, but Róisín had felt no pneumonia in Anita's lungs. "Right. Let me see if I can find a battery-powered pulse-ox."

Róisín spent at least a half hour searching for this unicorn. While she found an electric pulse-oximeter, that did her no good. She needed to test the oxygen level, or at least lung capacity.

Róisín clenched her fists in frustration and, in the relative privacy of a dark and empty hospital hallway, pounded them against the wall in anger. How could they do anything without real equipment? Over and over, she banged on the sickly green wall, wishing upon wish that they had the tools they needed. Or at least water and power.

A door opened down the hall, and she pushed away from the wall. The person went in the other direction, though, and didn't notice Róisín and her guilty expression.

With her head hung in defeat, Róisín returned to Anita's bedside.

The schoolteacher looked pale and, when Róisín put a hand to her forehead, she felt drenched in sweat. "Doctor O'Shea!"

The doctor rushed to her side, glancing at her IV bag. Just as he prepared his stethoscope, Anita seized.

Róisín and Doctor O'Shea held the patient on her side, exchanging a glance of deep concern. He furrowed his brow. "Was she like this earlier?"

"No! No, she was having trouble breathing deep, but she was lucid and joking. She had a temperature, but no sweats."

As the seizure passed, they let her back down, and Dr. O'Shea pressed his lips into a thin line. "She's not responsive." He glanced up, as if expecting a full emergency crew to come at his beck and call, but only Róisín stood beside him. The other staff were either sleeping or in other wards. Other than the twenty patients in their cots, they were alone.

He gave Róisín a bleak look. "There isn't much we can do for her in these conditions."

Róisín set her jaw. "That can't be true! She's a fighter, Doctor. She's a good person! We can't just let her go."

He placed a hand on her arm. "We have very limited resources. If we had what we needed, we'd have already amputated her legs and removed that part of the infection risk. We can't waste time or medicine on someone who won't benefit from them, Róisín. I know you want to help, but…"

Anita moaned, and Róisín shoved the doctor aside to place her hands on the injured woman's chest. "I'm here, Anita. I'm here. Hold on, do you hear me? Don't give up. We've got you."

The schoolteacher's head moved back and forth as if watching a tennis match behind closed eyes. Róisín reached inside and yanked hard on her healing power. Deeper, into the earth below her feet, she drew upon all the energy she could grasp.

As a conduit, she channeled the power into Anita. The woman screamed, her throat raw from coughing, her eyes flying open. Doctor O'Shea tried to yank Róisín away, but she kept her hands firmly on Anita's chest.

Finally, the doctor wrenched Róisín from the injured woman, both of them falling to the slick hospital floor. Róisín skinned her hands as they skidded to a stop.

The doctor stared at her. "Jesus, Mary, and Joseph, Róisín, what did you just do?"

She shook her head free of the cloud of confusion and power, trying to get a grip on herself. "Whatever I could."

A sound from the cot made Róisín scramble to her feet to rush back to the woman's side. Anita opened her eyes, a wan smile on her face. "I'm not feeling very well, Róisín. Could you get me some water?"

With a triumphant smile, Róisín turned to fetch her a cup, but her vision clouded as gray swirled in her mind, and she collapsed.

"Róisín!" Doctor O'Shea knelt beside her, slapping her cheek. Then he pulled her prone. "Róisín, open your eyes!"

His voice grew tinny as if he spoke down a long, metal tube. It faded in and out, gray and cloudy. Róisín wanted to answer, but her voice refused to obey. She drifted through a shrouded forest, full of misty shapes. Someone else called to her, someone bright and beautiful, someone full of answers, full of power. She was drawn to this strange person, reaching out to touch them. They had no features, just general benevolence and love radiating like sunlight. As soon as her hand touched them, they disappeared. She cried out as the ache of loss gripped her heart. A dark hole in her mind swallowed her.

When Róisín finally battled her way out of her mind fog, she opened her eyes. She moaned, placing a hand on her head. It ached so much, throbbing with waves of pain.

"Are you awake?" Doctor O'Shea's voice cut through her sleep fog.

"Doctor?"

"Shush, don't speak. What did you think you were doing? Don't you know better than to burn out your power?"

"How's Anita?"

"Anna, the girl with scales? She's fine, remember? You were finally able to heal her a few days ago and your brother took her back to Cork."

"No, not Anna. Anita."

"Oh, the teacher? She's grand. Still a cough and a fever, but better thanks to you. You almost killed yourself, you know? If you ever, and I mean ever, try a stunt like that again..."

She'd done it. And she'd do it again, if she must. Slowly, Róisín let slumber tumble over her once again.

She fell into the arms of Morpheus. Róisín nestled into those warm, familiar arms as if digging into the earth. The comfort of the land surrounded her with stolid succor.

Something called her name. Something familiar. That shining shard of sunlight, warm and welcoming.

With great reluctance, she pulled herself from the reassuring embrace of the earth toward the light. She wiped the dirt from her thighs and stumbled toward the sound. Róisín didn't recognize the voice, but it sounded like home. Someone she knew from childhood, or a forgotten relative who kept sweeties in their pocket. Someone who offered an extra shawl or sang her favorite song. The epitome of nostalgic contentment.

Shapes rose from the ground. Not angry or frightening, but curious. Creatures who wanted to know who she was and why she was here.

Something shone behind them. Tree trunks spread out in a spiral from this central light, an ancient pattern older than time itself, a kada of healing, a life-giving rune. In the center of this labyrinth, a being stood. Róisín couldn't make out their face as the brightness amongst the gloom made her squint and look away. Who could look upon such brilliance and escape unscathed?

That bright, shining presence reached out, caressing her face. Their hand felt warm and soothing, soft and strong at the same time. She placed her hand over theirs on her cheek and shut her eyes. They felt like a dear lover, someone she'd known for years, comforting her when she cried.

A feeling she'd ached for all her life.

This wasn't the comfort of a loving family. She had that in spades. Her parents, her four siblings, they formed a close-knit and supporting group. No, this felt sensual and full of promise. She didn't want to wake up and lose that sensation.

Something dragged her away from the shining presence, something inarguable, strong, and cruel. "Róisín, wake up! Come on, Róisín, open your eyes."

With intense reluctance, she creaked her eyes apart, ripping away from the homely comfort of the shining one's caress.

She blinked several times, trying to make sense of Doctor O'Shea's worried face. Tears choked her throat as she instantly missed the shining one, that loving presence she'd abandoned. Swallowing to banish the pain of separation, she flashed the doctor a shaky smile.

He let out a deep sigh. "Oh, thank the good Lord. Your heart rate and blood pressure grew dangerously low."

The warmth of the glowing being still suffused her blood. "I feel better now, Doctor."

"After all we've been through, can't you call me Sean? I've asked several times."

Her shaky smile fell. "Not in the hospital, Doctor."

The corner of his mouth quirked up. "Fair enough. I've set you up with an IV. You're to stay put for as long as you can. Do you understand?"

Róisín glanced around the ward. "We're already spread so thin. You can't do without my help."

"A family of veterinarians came in from Roundstone last night. They're a bit rough around the edges, but with three well-grown lads and their mother, they'll be a huge help. You rest. That's an order."

She allowed herself a chuckle. "Very well, Doctor. Thank you."

Once he left the ward, Róisín hugged herself, trying to bring back that amazing sensation of warmth and love from her dream. Was it a dream? A vision? A wish? She didn't know. Did it matter? Whatever it had been, it had restored her.

Róisín had been so mentally and physically strung out, thinking beyond the necessary routine became difficult. Now, she felt as if she'd just taken a two-week vacation on the Costa del Sol. Her fatigue had simply vanished. Almost as if she'd healed herself, except she'd never had that much power. She could fight someone's infection, or heal a clean break, but even those took time, working every day, layer upon layer of healing energy, like painting varnish on a deck. Róisín's power had grown since she first discovered it, but still never came close to what she'd just experienced.

Her skin tingled, and her hairs stood on end all along her arms. Róisín rubbed them, hugging herself again. If she closed her eyes, could she make out features on that too-bright face? Róisín fell back into that comfortable slumber, sinking into bliss, but a harsh, painful cough roused her. She struggled to sit up, glancing around the ward. How long had she slept? Anita's infection must have gotten worse.

Carefully, Róisín rose, wheeling her IV stand behind her. The metal wheels squeaked along the tile floor. Once she reached Anita's bedside, she flashed the schoolteacher a tired smile. "That sounds like it hurts. Would you like more water?"

Anita shook her head, her face drawn. "No, it'll just make me cough again. Doctor O'Shea said you saved my life."

Róisín let out a laugh, echoing in the quiet room. "He's exaggerating greatly. I just did some healing work. It looks like you could use another session. Can you lie back, please?"

She placed her hands upon Anita's chest and closed her eyes. That wrong feeling permeated the patient's body, stronger than before. Róisín quested with her talent, trying to discern the shape of the disease. It tasted… raw. Nasty. No disease tasted nice, but some held a familiar pungency. This one held a rotten edge.

Anita still had a fever. Not dangerously high, hovering around thirty-eight. The infection hadn't moved, but Anita's clothes felt damp. "Have you been sweating a lot? Or is this from yesterday?"

"On and off. I'm either too hot or too cold, it seems." Her voice lacked the spark of life and humor she'd held onto for so long. Anita coughed again, a hacking, harsh cough, dry and unproductive. The schoolteacher held her forehead with a moan.

A memory niggled at the back of Róisín's mind. A horrible idea bloomed as she recalled something she learned about in veterinary school. It clicked with other memories, frightening newscasts from another part of the world, a time in America filled with fear and terrorism.

She swallowed, glancing out the window to the still-smoldering ruins of Galway City and prayed she was wrong.

*Latest **CNN Update**: "We'll go now to George Tallin, reporting to us today from Houston, Texas, where the Pure Earther Movement organization is holding a rally."*

"Thank you, Nadine. It looks like they're getting ready to open the doors here, and let the crowds in. I estimate about four thousand

people are waiting in line to see the chosen speakers. Their new leader, a businessman named Tiberius Wilkinson, is slated to be the keynote."

"George, can you give us a bit of background on Wilkinson?"

"Sure, Nadine. He was a minister in the West Village Baptist Church for a decade before he retired from that position, but he is still a member. As you may recall, they have been a strong force behind the organization of the PEM, and one of their loudest voices, even louder than the Alliance of American Klans."

"Do you have any insight to what he will say today?"

George shakes his head. "Not yet, but I can guarantee you, it won't be kind on the Unhidden. He seems to have made it his personal crusade to campaign against them."

Róisín:

Frustration warred with anger in Róisín's voice, but she modulated her volume as they still stood in the ward next to Qacha's bed. "Doctor O'Shea, please, consider the symptoms. They all match!"

The tall Irish doctor shook his head. "But it can't be, Róisín. What about her bloody sputum? That symptom doesn't fit."

Róisín clenched her jaw. "I don't know. Maybe it's from smoke inhalation. But I swear, the others all point to one thing. I've seen it before!"

He crossed his arms and glared at her. "You've seen it before. Where?"

Rolling her eyes, Róisín sighed. "In cows."

"In cows."

"Is there an echo in here? Yes, cows. Where else do you think I'd see anthrax?"

The doctor shook his head. "It doesn't make sense. Anthrax isn't contagious. There must be another explanation."

Róisín glanced at the other end of the ward, where Anita's coughs grew louder. "Will you at least do some tests?"

He turned on her, his voice loud. "How am I supposed to do any tests, Róisín? In case it's escaped your attention, we still have no electrics, no fresh running water, and no specialized lab equipment. Oh, wait, hold on. What's this in my back pocket? Oh, it's a serology lab. Fancy that!"

Taken aback at his vehemence, Róisín retreated several steps, barking her shins on Qacha's cot. She spun around to reassure herself she hadn't hurt the patient.

A raspy, ruined voice whispered, "Come closer."

Her argument abandoned, Róisín knelt by the burned woman. "Qacha? You're awake! Oh, thank Mother Mary you're awake!"

Róisín bent down, but Qacha shook her head. "Not you. Him."

As Dr. O'Shea bent obligingly to Qacha, she clutched his arm in a fierce grip that belied her weakened body. "Listen to her, you fucking idiot."

Róisín took Qacha's hand, taking care not to touch the damaged skin. Ignoring the doctor spluttering behind her, she poured her power into the woman, willing her to remain awake.

To his credit, Dr. O'Shea came around to the other side of the cot, checking oxygen levels and heartbeat as Róisín worked her talent.

Qacha whispered again, "Doctor."

"Yes, Qacha?"

"Stop arguing. Listen to her. She is correct."

Doctor O'Shea furrowed his brow and frowned. "How could you possibly know that?"

"I know her. She wouldn't lie."

He shook his head with a condescending smile. "I'm afraid that's rather lacking in scientific method. Now, you rest, Qacha. You've been through a great deal. I'm thrilled you've come out of your coma, but we must get you…"

Still whispering, Qacha nevertheless put steel into her voice as she dug her fingers into his arm again. "Listen. To. Her."

"I *am* listening to her, Qacha. But she can't be right."

The patient turned to Róisín. "He's a fool. Go over his head."

Qacha closed her eyes, and Róisín searched frantically for the woman's consciousness with her talent, but she only fell into a normal sleep. Róisín let out a sigh and folded Qacha's hands over her chest.

Dr. O'Shea raised one eyebrow at her. "I think you'd best get back into bed yourself, young woman. But keep an eye on her. In fact, I'll move your cot next to hers so you won't be tempted to do other rounds."

Once he shifted her bed, he left, and Róisín realized she hadn't gotten him to agree about the anthrax. Cursing under her breath, with a silent apology to her mam for cursing, she created a plan.

She'd prepare a list of possible symptoms and create a correspondence table with their patient's symptoms. Then she'd calculate the probability and compare it with any other diagnose candidates. And if he still refused to listen, Doctor O'Shea may be the ranking doctor on site, but when reinforcements came from Dublin, she'd be bending their ears.

If reinforcements came from Dublin.

Chapter Two

"Jealousy is never satisfied with anything short of an omniscience that would detect the subtlest fold of the heart"
– George Eliot

Anna:

As Brendan drove north, Anna stared out the window at the rolling hills and lonely shoreline of Connemara. Anna didn't like Galway, but the area just outside the city seemed a lonely, beautiful place. Maybe when this was all over, she'd find a cottage along the coast.

When this was all over. She laughed to herself. What did she imagine the world would look like after this? Would the Pure Earther Movement back away from their demands for eugenics? She highly doubted it.

She didn't want to go back to Galway itself, filled with fire, ash, and death. But if PHAE called her back, she must obey. She began to think Max had been right to resist being recruited, but even Max had shut up after the attacks began.

Anna shivered and hugged herself, unwilling to let her anxiety take over. Not this time. She concentrated on her breathing and tried to focus on something to derail the attack. Nothing but trees showed outside the window. This section of road had no scenic farmsteads or rolling hills. Anna felt somehow cheated, as if being in Ireland guaranteed her constant bucolic landscapes. When had she grown so cynical?

As they drove through a village, she rubbed her arms, her scales smooth and cool under her hands. She couldn't see any sign of the explosions this far away, but she remembered them. Qacha's heroic actions, her own futile attempts to help, and the cries of those burned and dying. Tears burned behind her eyes, and her mind grew fuzzy with fear and panic again. She bit her tongue to keep from falling into despair. She bit too hard and let out a yip.

Brendan sent her a sidelong glance from the driver's seat. "Are ye okay, Anna? Did a brownie bite you?"

"A what? Oh, no, I just, uh, bit my tongue."

He raised his eyebrows. "But you weren't eating anything?"

"I'm talented that way."

He chuckled and returned to watching the road as a roundabout came up.

"What's the name of the place we're going again?"

"A town called Westport. Lovely place. You'll fall in love with the charm. PHAE is moving their western offices up there. And the village we're to help is Keel, on Achill Island." He glanced out the window at the suburbs, untouched by the Galway bombing. He must have had friends in the Galway office, folks who'd been killed by the bombs her brother had planted. The incipient panic threatened to take over again.

She'd fallen in love with Cork. She'd fallen in love with the Byrne farm. She may have even fallen in love *at* the Byrne farm. Anna stole another glance at Brendan, his shoulder-length black hair mussed from the open window. Anna swallowed and forced herself to stare at the landscape again. Her stomach growled, but she hoped Brendan didn't notice.

The Irish man had held her hand when she needed to cry. He'd assured her that he liked her, and they'd shared more than a few kisses. Still, Anna didn't want to push herself on him. She didn't want to risk him rejecting her. Safer just to let things develop naturally. But that meant she analyzed every move, every sound, and every glance, and that was exhausting in the best of times. These were far from the best of times.

After several hours of delving into her innermost thoughts, Anna felt more than ready to escape the car and her own psyche. They pulled into a town just as charming as Brendan had promised with a canal running through the center of town, flanked by hanging baskets of purple and white flowers spilling over the sides. He parked in front of a row of attached houses.

As Brendan went to the trunk for their luggage, Anna stepped out onto the wide sidewalk, gazing up at the Victorian façade. Red brick, blond stone arches, and iron work decorated the front door. Brendan nudged her with his elbow. "Will you be gawking there all day, or will you come in? Sure, and they promised to have lunch ready."

Her stomach growled in answer to his question, and she rewarded him with a grin. "Lunch? Yes, please!"

As they walked along the narrow entrance hall, the hardwood floor echoed with their footsteps. Someone called from another room, "Brendan, is that you?"

A young man with loads of brown curly hair, brown skin, and a disarming smile poked his head around the corner. "Soup's on!" His American accent had a touch of Spanish.

He ducked back into the dining room. They left their bags in the hall as Anna breathed in the savory odor of her favorite, lamb stew. Loaves of Irish brown bread, fruit, and a huge tureen sat on the sideboard.

Anna wanted to waste no time in loading up a plate. However, Brendan held her arm. "Anna, have you met Carlos? He came to us from Miami."

Forcing herself to smile and not look at the sideboard, Anna put out her hand. Carlos blinked a few times at her white gloves but gave her a firm handshake. His smile made the skin around his eyes crinkle. "Welcome to my place! Well, sort of my place. I've been running it as a B&B, but things have changed, as I'm sure you know. Electricity is out for the moment as EirGrid was hit pretty bad in Galway."

Anna glanced to the sideboard. "How'd you make the soup, then?"

"Gas stove."

Brendan frowned. "I thought you had turbines here?"

Carlos laughed, but his expression turned sour. "Sure, plenty of turbines north of here. But the blast screwed up the delivery system. Donegal has plenty of power, but they route it to us through Galway, and that channel is cut now. Idiotic system. But you must be starving. Dig in!"

Her stomach answered with an imperious growl. Anna's eyes grew wide, horrified with her body's betrayal, but both Carlos and Brendan laughed. Swallowing her shame, she sent Brendan an accusatory glare and grabbed a bowl. The lamb stew and thick slabs of soda bread did much to ease her embarrassment and her hunger. Sweet, farm-made butter spread upon the slices dipped into the savory stew healed many ills.

"So, Anna, Brendan tells me you're from the States. I'm from Florida. Grew up in Miami. What about you?"

Anna swallowed her bite and coughed into her arm before nodding. "Upstate New York. I just got here, what, a month ago?" It couldn't be so recently, could it? She felt like she'd been in Ireland for years already.

"Well, I've been here four months. Do those gorgeous scales reflect your talent? They look iridescent."

Unconsciously, Anna pulled her sleeves back down, horrified they'd shown. "Yeah, sort of. I've got a water talent."

Carlos nodded, taking a long drink of his coffee. "Good stuff, that. My talent is in computers."

She narrowed her gaze. "You do magic on computers?"

He gave a casual shrug. "Sorta. PHAE aren't certain if it's an Unhidden talent or just brilliant hacking skills, but they're assuming the former. Who am I to argue?" Carlos opened his hands and shrugged. "If it gets me out of Miami and to Ireland, I'm game with however they want to classify me. Besides, the scenery is stunning here." He stared at her, and Anna shifted her eyes to her stew. She tried to quell the butterflies taking up residence in her stomach.

Brendan cleared his throat. "So, Ciara told us to stay here overnight, but then you're to join her in Dublin."

Carlos raised an eyebrow. "Ciara said that, did she? Hmm. Funny, she didn't tell me. I just talked to her last night."

The Irishman cocked his head. "Oh? Your phones are working here?"

"They are not. But I've got battery packs and my own hotspot, so I got through."

Brendan looked distinctly uncomfortable. Anna concentrated on eating her lunch, but it had become a congealed lump in her stomach.

Anna:

As Carlos cleaned up lunch, Brendan insisted Anna rest. "You're still recovering from whatever you had. Róisín did her best, but she said you needed to finish the rest, and you ran yourself ragged this last week. You need all the recovery time you can get."

She let out a sigh. "A nap does sound lovely."

Brendan gestured down the hall. "C'mon, we'll find you a room. I'll get your bags."

As they entered the Victorian-style bedroom with a nine-foot ceiling, he lifted her bag onto the luggage rack. "I'll leave you to settle in, but we're off to Achill Island tomorrow."

"You said Carlos is going to Dublin. Are we going with him?"

"Not that I know of, why?"

She sat on the bed, clasping her hands in her lap, and stared at them. "I sort of want to find out what's going on with Joel."

He answered with silence, clenching his jaw several times. Finally, he said, "You don't need to worry about that. Joel's in PHAE custody."

"I *do* worry about it. He's my brother."

He took her hands, worry clear on his furrowed brow. "Anna, I don't understand. *You're* the one who told us he'd planted those bombs. He's killed hundreds, maybe even thousands of people."

Her throat clenched, and she pulled her hands out of his grip. Joel was a jerk and a traitor, but he was still her brother and the only family she had left. He'd always wanted to be famous. Maybe he planted the bombs because he felt slighted that she went to Ireland first. Maybe he did it to get his name splashed across the headlines. It hadn't worked, had it? No one knew about his betrayal but the PHAE, and they weren't broadcasting the news.

Brendan tried to take her hands again, but she pulled away. With a sigh, he said, "Look, I'm sure he'll be treated with respect and honor. He's a human being, and PHAE are not monsters. He'll be held and questioned. They'll charge him for his crimes and put him on trial. But Ireland doesn't have capital punishment. You know that, right?"

Anna glanced up, the tears in her eyes making his entreating face blurry. "But Ireland isn't trying him. *PHAE* is. Does PHAE even have a policy on capital punishment yet?"

Brendan didn't answer. He probably didn't know. PHAE was such a new organization, they surely didn't have all their policies in place. How could they? The magnetic shift occurred less than a year ago. Anna had worked at a college and knew any bureaucracy took time to get policies in place.

The Irish man let out a deep sigh and gave her a tired half-smile. "There's nothing we can do to help him right now. Please, it's best if you just put him out of your mind."

"He's my brother. You come from a large family. Surely, you can understand the duty I have for him, even if we don't like each other much."

"I *do* understand the duty. Believe it or not, I don't always like my own siblings."

Anna gave him a sidelong glance. "None of your siblings are prime-A jerks like Joel."

Brendan chuckled. "Sure, and that's the truth. He is a particular nob. But, yes, he's still your sibling. I understand you must watch out for him, especially with your parents gone. That being said, I'm asking you to leave it alone. For now."

She clenched her jaw as her spine turned cold. "Is that an order from PHAE?"

His eyes shifted away, staring at the door. "I suppose you could say so, yes."

"Fine. I won't ask you about it anymore."

"For now."

She walked to the window, gazing out on the back garden. "For now."

Hiroki:

Hiroki Kubo rested his forehead in his hands as he studied the document in their Dublin bunker office.

After his successful speech on PHAE's behalf and the PEM signing non-aggression agreements, Hiroki flushed with confidence. However, as much as his confidence had grown, he detested this aspect of his job. The treaties, agreements, and contracts were housed in such complex English, he had to read and re-read each one several times before extracting the true meaning from the bureaucratic language.

Why must lawyers make everything so complex? They delighted in using seven words where one would work perfectly fine. Perhaps it was built-in job security. If no one else could read contracts, then they were assured of more work.

Still, Masaaki helped him with the thorniest issues, along with Bintou. None of them were well-acquainted with idiom, slang, or casual expressions, so Hiroki kept a running list, asking Martin or Ciara for their true meaning. Eventually, he'd be fully fluent in the language, but not yet, not even after four years. He didn't have a talent for it, like Bintou.

Luckily, these agreements didn't use idiom. However, they used a fresh set of phrases, legal jargon, and confusing connotations. Hiroki started a new list.

He glanced up as the door rattled. Ciara strode in, her face pale. Hiroki stood, his brow furrowed. "Has something occurred, Ciara?"

She pulled out the chair between his desk and Bintou's. The Malian woman glanced up from her work. "Ciara, you look unwell. Would you like some water?"

"What I need is a shot of whiskey."

Hiroki's heartbeat raced. Ciara normally stayed cool and collected, the perfect picture of elegant calm.

Bintou shook her head. "We have no alcohol."

Ciara waved her apology away. "No worries." She walked to the filing cabinet and reached behind it, her eyes rolling up as she moved her arm. A smile spread across her face as she extracted a silver flask. "I thought Martin had stashed one here."

As the tall Irishwoman unscrewed the top and knocked back a long draft, Hiroki exchanged a glance with Bintou.

"Ah! That's grand, that is." She let out a sigh and sank back into the chair.

His heartbeat wouldn't stop racing. "Ciara, what has happened? How can we help?"

She glanced at Hiroki, and then to Bintou, and let out another sigh. "It's nothing I can talk about, I'm afraid. I just needed a safe space to lose it for a moment."

Bintou cocked her head to the side. "Did you come in for the alcohol? Or did you have another purpose? Not that we don't enjoy your company, but we usually only see you at the morning briefings."

Ciara took another swig from the flask and replaced it behind the filing cabinet. "Aye, there's another reason I'm here. We've been assigned a mission."

Hiroki swallowed and blinked. "A mission? More speeches to write?"

She shook her head and clasped her hands together, her lips pressed flat. "No. This time, you're taking the show on the road. You, Bintou, Masaaki, and I are to take a tour around the country. A series of speaking engagements, live, so your talent has a chance to shine. While the populace gets the news from internet, television, and radio, many places still lack infrastructure after the attacks and, besides, your talent is stronger in person. Personal reassurances are much more effective and will boost morale. It'll also keep rampant misinformation down to a minimum."

Bintou sat back in her chair with wide eyes. "When do we leave? What is our itinerary?"

Ciara stood and paced. "Tomorrow, and we head north first. A stop in each county."

Furrowing his brow, Hiroki said, "Aren't there thirty-two counties in Ireland? That is many speeches."

"Twenty-six in the Republic of Ireland, and six in Northern Ireland. We're only speaking in the twenty-six as our treaty with the UK isn't final."

Bintou straightened the papers she'd been reading and asked in a nonchalant tone, "Will Martin be coming as well?"

The Irish woman gave her a knowing smile. "Yes. He specifically asked to be part of this mission. We'll have a few other assistants, and at least two offensive talents for protection."

Hiroki's throat caught. "Protection? Will there be danger?"

Ciara shrugged. "Not necessarily. But much of the country is still in chaos after the attacks. The terrorists hit Dublin, Belfast, and Galway, three of our four largest cities. Cork only escaped because of Anna and Max's protection. Power grids and other infrastructure were damaged. Wi-Fi is intermittent throughout the countryside, as is power. Clean water is easier to fix, as most of that comes from local sources, and nowhere in Ireland is far from a stream. But Galway still needs major work to be livable again."

Hiroki clenched his hands out of sight, beneath the desk. "I do not understand. How will our speaking help their power get fixed?"

"It won't, Hiroki. But you can reassure each group that the PHAE and the government of Ireland have things under control. That repair crews are working around the clock to get power back to the country. That we've signed agreements to keep this from happening again. We need our people to feel safe."

Hiroki swallowed. "But not all of that is true. Some may be true in a few weeks, or in a few months. And something may happen to keep it from coming true at all."

Ciara pressed her lips together. "Nevertheless, you must make sure the people believe us."

She left before he could argue further, but their conversation grew heavy on his soul. As Hiroki packed that evening, he weighed his options. If he convinced the populace that everything would be fine, what happened if they discovered the lie? What if the PEM broke their agreement? What if they'd planted another bomb not yet exploded? What if the infrastructure repairs took months, even years? Any credibility he might have would vanish.

Lying had no honor. He'd lied in the past to test his talents or to save a friend but, in those cases, fibs felt necessary and sometimes the kinder option. Lying to the entire population of a country, to make the PHAE appear more effective, bothered his conscience.

The next morning, Hiroki joined the others at a minibus with great trepidation. They all kept their own counsel as the bus drove out of the city. Their first stop would be County Meath, northwest of Dublin. Their arrival must have been announced beforehand, as the Navan GAA stadium was packed when they entered.

Hiroki had never spoken to such a large live audience. He wiped sweat from his forehead as he stared at the crowd from behind the center dais.

Bintou and Masaaki had helped him prepare his notes. Clutching his ePad, he touched it to ensure it hadn't shut down or deleted anything. It blinked on reassuringly.

Hiroki tried to process the snippets of crew conversation as they finished arranging the dais. Rumors of illness and overflowing hospitals seemed too extreme to be coincidence. Róisín mentioned respiratory cases in Galway.

As Ciara announced Hiroki, his talent kicked into gear. His skin tingled, and he pasted on a smile. When the applause subsided, he drew false confidence and power on like a suit of armor. "Today, though I am a visitor to your country, I join you in mourning those lost in the devastating attacks on Ireland's beautiful cities."

Hiroki continued with his crafted speech, imbuing his words with his talent and urging his listeners to believe his sincerity. By the end, he almost believed it himself.

He did believe the PHAE regretted every life lost to the attacks. Hiroki also believed they'd do everything within their power, with the willing assistance of Ireland's government, to restore power and fundamental services. What he didn't credit, and what he must make his audience embrace, was that these repairs would be quick, and that no further attacks would be made. That the disaster had passed, and they only needed to move forward from here.

Hiroki didn't believe that part.

He had no good reason *not* to believe it. He had a poor grasp on this country's resources or capabilities. But the rumors swam in his mind, niggling the back of his conscience, and his ingrained optimism took a severe beating.

The bombing of Dublin had been the most frightening day of his life, even including the mob who attacked him in Tokyo. Hiroki didn't know if they'd be buried alive forever in that entombing warren of tunnels. He'd spent way too many hours imagining their food and water running low, their air growing stale, and their lives seeping away.

Despite his father disowning him, he still grasped tightly to his last shred of remaining honor. He'd promised the PHAE that he'd serve their organization to the best of his ability, and he must honor his vow.

Hiroki just wished he didn't have to lie to so many people.

Bintou:

Bintou unpacked in their latest B&B, placing her new clothing into the press. They'd visited fifteen counties with eleven to go, and Bintou already felt exhausted from the brutal pace. She was no stranger to travel, even across continents, but this was all driving and performing. Very little time was given to relax or decompress.

She wished her cough would settle. Her throat felt raw, a ring of pain that irritated whenever she swallowed. And because she thought of it constantly, she swallowed often, testing to see if it felt any better.

She'd gotten used to carrying throat lozenges for the constant tickle, and tissues for her congested nose. Bintou's head felt three times larger than normal. Pulling out a tissue, she blew hard, trying to dislodge the massive plug in her sinus cavity. She moaned and held her forehead as the pressure readjusted.

She'd ask Ciara to sit this presentation out. Hiroki had his speech down pat by now and no longer needed her support. While she'd miss watching him, she needed to rest. Bintou rarely got ill, but when she did, it hit hard, as if making up for the times her immune system fought the good fight.

The latest throat lozenge didn't seem to help. Perhaps their hosts could make some tea for her. After she put away the last piece of clothing, she climbed down the narrow stairs. Ciara chatted with Martin in the sitting room, but when Bintou's foot caused a stair to creak, they halted. Had they been talking about her?

She reached the landing and poked her head into the room. "Ciara, may I ask you a favor?"

"Of course! Whatever I can do. Are you feeling any better?"

Bintou shook her head. "No, I can't say that I am. In fact, I think it would be wise to remain here today and rest. Do you have any objections?"

Ciara glanced at Martin, who shrugged. "If you like, I can stay here with her. That way, if she needs anything like soup or tea, she won't have to navigate the stairs."

With a smile of pure gratitude, Bintou nodded. "That would be delightful. If Ciara agrees?"

"Sure, we'll be grand. We know the routine by now, and Hiroki already suggested you stay here today. Heal well, my friend."

Bintou climbed back up the stairs and changed into her sleeping clothing. To sleep during the daylight felt surreal and gave her a pang of guilt, so she closed all the curtains. The lacy white things did little to block the light, so she turned her back on the window and closed her eyes, hoping to get some rest. The satiny gown slipped smooth on her sensitive skin as she slid under the covers and let out another cough.

After her tenth time sitting up to cough, sip water, and cough again, Bintou sighed and wished her Muslim beliefs allowed her alcohol. Many of her new friends waxed poetic on the efficacy of a sleeping draught of whiskey. Perhaps their host had some medicine. Scripture did not forbid alcohol in actual medicine.

She pulled on a robe and padded downstairs, her bare feet cold on the hardwood floors. Ciara still spoke with Martin in the sitting room, so it must not be as late as she thought. She halted when she heard Joel's name, and she stilled, trying to make out their words.

Ciara sounded more upset than Bintou had heard her before. "I really don't think they're adhering to the conventions, though. They've got Hafsia on him, and you've worked with her. She's not gentle by any stretch of the imagination."

Martin responded with a harsh tone. "*Not gentle?* That's a rather understated way to describe torture, even for you."

Bintou disliked Joel intensely. His harsh treatment of Anna made Bintou and many of the other Unhidden angry. However, that didn't mean she approved of torture. Despite his cruelty, he remained a human being and deserved the dignity and duty of care required of them. Torture did not fit into that duty of care.

With a start, Bintou realized she'd lost track of the conversation. Her mind was muzzy with her cold. They seemed to have moved to another subject.

Ciara's voice filtered around the corner to Bintou's straining ears. "Are you certain? You've only known her a few weeks."

"More certain than I've ever been in my life. Her intelligence amazes me, and I'm happy just being around her. We complete each other's sentences. Whenever she smiles, my heart melts."

The Irish woman let out a snort. "That's lovely and poetic, but not very practical."

"Feck being practical. I've lived my entire life being practical. What's wrong with wanting to grasp magic when it literally steps into my life? She's everything I've ever dreamed of."

Bintou plastered herself to the wall, willing her throat to remain silent. She had a fantastic crush on Martin, and she prayed to Allah that he spoke of her. Of course, the tickle clutched her at once, defying her need for stealth.

"What about Ibrahim? Didn't she come to Ireland to be with him?" They *were* talking about her. Her heart raced as she stopped breathing to hear better.

"I admit, that's kept me from saying anything. I don't want to barge in on their relationship. It must be her choice, not my pressure. If she has feelings for me…"

Ciara chuckled. "I can't believe she doesn't. She asks to be with you every chance she gets."

"That's as may be, but I can't leave this to chance. If she likes me, is that a rebound from Ibrahim? Will he show up in a few weeks and win her back? Will she fall into his arms, having loved him all along?"

"Oh, come on. You sound like a trashy romance novel. This is the real world."

He let out a low chuckle, his baritone voice like liquid. "There's plenty of romance, drama, and anger in the real world. Even if you've risen above them most of your life, the rest of us wallow on a regular basis. Some of us even enjoy it. I'd rather have more romance and less drama, myself."

"Well, staying here and caring for her will help, I'm sure. She needs pampering. I could hear her hacking all the way down here."

Knowing this would be an ideal time for her entrance, Bintou stepped on the creaky stair. She rubbed her eyes. "I'm so sorry to ask, but do our hosts have any cough medicine? I haven't been able to soothe my throat enough to fall asleep."

Martin's face lit up as he jumped to his feet. Bintou watched him leave the room, perfectly aware that Ciara studied her reaction. Her affection for him was genuine, and she didn't care who noticed it.

Róisín:

The next day, Róisín lay in her cot, more frustrated than she'd been in years. Qacha slept peacefully and naturally. Her patient wasn't the problem. Her frustration lay with the ability to heal herself. For the first time in her life, her own healing talent wouldn't obey her.

She'd already made three attempts. Róisín dug deep into her heart a fourth time, just like she'd always done. She pulled out the healing magic she *knew* she possessed. The Unhidden talent used on countless others in the months since her power grew. The talent she'd drawn on over and over again. What was she doing wrong this time? Why couldn't she heal herself?

The persistent cough and aching fatigue might be stymying her effort. Or she might just be burnt out with the work she'd done since the bombing. Did she have a finite limit on her healing power? Not just until she rested, but a grand total to how much she could heal? Had she used up her healing?

Róisín refused to believe that. How would that work? It would be so inconsistent for her power to run out. She understood fatigue and temporary draining. Mathematics described a lot of things, including the logarithmic rise of the Unhidden talent strength, but to describe a finite limit where it just cut out rather than leveling off made no sense.

She must operate under the assumption something blocked her power. Maybe she couldn't heal herself? But even before the magnetic shift, she'd healed her own cuts and bruises, even a twisted ankle, though that had taken time.

The only other factor she could think of was her illness. Whatever she'd contracted could be inhibiting her talent.

And thus, her intense frustration.

Despite repeated arguments and Qacha's support, Doctor O'Shea still refused to consider her diagnosis of anthrax. But if she was right, they needed the right antibiotics. From what she remembered, anthrax had a human death rate of about twenty percent, without treatment, but had a much lower rate with the proper medication. They had a few weeks, maybe even a month, before they'd pass the point of no return. If they waited too long, people might die needlessly.

But if both she and Anita had it, that couldn't be coincidence. Anthrax wasn't contagious between humans. They must have been infected from a common source.

Róisín glanced outside again. The edge of a broken concrete wall jutted into sight, still coated with dust from the blast. What if those bombs contained more than explosives?

She sat up suddenly in the throes of a coughing fit, her throat raw. Finally, she lay back, utterly drained of all energy. She could barely lift a hand to her chest. Dizziness and nausea swept over her, making the room spin.

Róisín swirled into a hole of illness and fever dreams.

Komie:

Nokomis Nicholas hadn't left the Byrne farm area since she arrived. With great interest, she stared at the karstic moonscape as Colin Byrne drove her and Fiona north across the Burren and through the suburbs of Galway. They didn't go all the way into the city. Instead, Colin chose a farm along the bay, too far from Galway to have been damaged by the bombs, yet close enough to supply food.

The farmers, an older woman and her two sons, peered at Komie with skeptical hope. "You say she can help? The crops wilted with all the ash, and then it floated down and near smothered the wee things. Sure, and Irish potatoes can grow well enough with many cloudy days, but this wasn't clouds bringing rain. This was ash blocking the sun without benefit of the water. We could use some rain, right enough. Can she make that happen, too?"

With a half-smile, Colin answered, "I'm afraid not, Mrs. Kearney. We do have a rainmaker, but she's busy elsewhere. It's an odd time indeed when we wish for rain in Ireland. Which field would you like us to start with?"

Komie, Colin, and his ten-year-old daughter, Fiona, followed the Kearneys to the back forty, filled with potatoes and turnips. The wilted vines seemed so pitiful. Komie pulled up her sleeves, looking forward to touching their sprouting energy.

With a nod to Colin, she dug her hands into the soil at the edge of one field. Sending a tentative prayer to the Irish land spirit, she asked for their help, but didn't hold out much hope. She didn't need their help, but she could do more if she received it.

Back in Limerick, Komie had worried about working with this Irish goddess of the land, Anú. It felt disloyal to turn her back on her own ancestral spirits in Maine. For thousands of years, her people had a tradition of honoring their ancestors.

However, when she'd moved out to the western desert with her son, she learned that while the Great Spirit is the same throughout the world, other lands honored other faces of the spirits. The land there had always fought her power, in the arid and unyielding desert. But when she moved to Ireland, hints of familiarity filled in the soil. The names of these ancients might be strange on her tongue, but they were still earth powers, aspects of the Great Spirit.

Colin helped her build a sweat lodge, and she spoke to her ancestors. They gave their blessing for her to work with these Irish spirits. With that blessing in mind, Komie bent to her work.

Deep, deep, deeper into the earth she quested, her tendrils of power curling around stones and roots, tickling the worms. As she pulled the energy toward the surface, it glowed and throbbed with the heartbeat of the land, a living, breathing thing. Into each potato root she guided her power, letting it lick the sluggish growth into verdant life.

Still deep in the earth, Komie sighed when the earth answered. She'd grown used to the comforting voice, the female goddess she believed to be Anú herself. The voice, full of spice and heat, felt as comfortable as a crackling hearth fire and a warm woolen blanket. Danger hovered behind the power, that of a mother bear protecting her young. Komie had no wish to rouse that anger. She only asked for help with feeding those who lived on this island.

The glow of her power shot up, stronger than anything Komie could summon herself. It coated the farm in an orange glow, sparking as if on fire.

The farmers cried out, and Fiona gasped. Colin put a hand on Komie's shoulder, but whether to help her or to stop her, she didn't know.

The glow faded, falling gently back into the earth, a dying firework. As it disappeared, the greenery perked up and grew at least half again as big as before.

With exclamations of wonder, the Kearneys helped Komie to her feet, patting her on the back, and asking all sorts of questions. Their voices faded into tinniness as gray fog wrapped around Komie's head. She normally didn't get so dizzy when the goddess helped her, but this had been stronger than usual.

Fiona must have noticed her shakiness as she pulled the native woman from the farmers' well-wishes. The younger girl led Komie to a bench near the barn and sat beside her. "Are you okay, Komie? Do you need some water?"

"I'm a bit wobbly. Do you have any juice?"

Fiona dragged one of the Kearney's sons into the house and returned with orange juice. Komie drank it and grimaced, used to the thick, pulpy juice she'd get in America. Still, the sugar gave her strength, at least enough to stop shaking.

She'd never felt this weak after the goddess helped her before. Had she done something wrong? She walked through each step but could remember nothing out of place. "I need to rest before I try again. Where are we staying tonight?"

The Irish girl exchanged a look with her approaching father. He clapped Komie on the shoulder. "There's a house just down the road. The owner belongs to PHAE, but they're in Belfast, so we can use it. D'you need to eat?"

"I will, but that can wait until we're settled." She held out her hands and Colin lifted her to her feet. She leaned heavily on his arm as they returned to the car.

Once at the house, Fiona went immediately to the kitchen and made them sandwiches, thick with slices of ham and farmhouse cheese. Komie chewed hers thankfully as her soul smoothed back into her body. Food grounded the soul and anchored the body.

When she stumbled toward a guest room to sleep, Fiona followed her. "What happened today, Komie? Did something go wrong?"

With a sad smile, Komie nodded. "Something, but I'm not sure what. Maybe I'm just getting older. The magic is a strain on my body. Anú helped me, and usually that means I don't have to use as much of my own magic. She bears the brunt of the power."

The girls' eyes lit up. "Anú answered today? Was that the glowing?"

Komie raised her eyebrows at the girl. "Have you ever seen my power glow before?"

"Never. Wow, Anú. What was she like?"

Komie chuckled. "We didn't have tea, child. She spoke. Not with words, just her voice. The sound carried the magic up through me."

Fiona stared at her hands. "I wish I could meet a goddess."

The older woman placed her hand on the girl's head. "Perhaps you will someday, child. Perhaps you will. For now, though, I need to rest. Today drained me much more than it should have."

The Irish girl stood, but hesitated at the door, turning back to face her. "Komie? Do you think...do you think I might be able to learn what you do? I don't mean the magic part, though that would be so awesome. I mean the spiritual part. Talking to the land. Honoring nature and the goddess and the ancestors and stuff."

With a half-smile, Komie asked, "Aren't you and your family of the Catholic faith, Fiona?"

The girl dropped her gaze to the floor. "Yes." She looked up again and spoke in a rush. "But I talked to the priest, and he said that there were so many ancient pagan beliefs mixed in Irish Catholicism that it wouldn't be a sin if I talked to them."

Trying to stifle a chuckle, Komie nodded with solemn wisdom. "It was wise to seek the advice of your priest. However, I'd need your parents' permission, too."

Her eyes widened. "Da said it would be okay! I asked him this morning before we came here."

"It seems you have done your homework. Very well. Starting tomorrow, I will teach you about the land and the spirits I honor. But you must promise to be an attentive student and treat the knowledge with respect."

Fiona bounced up and down on her toes, her face lit up with radiant joy. "Thank you, Komie! Thank you, thank you, thank you! I will, I promise!"

Komie:

Komie sat cross-legged along the edge of Flannigan's beet farm, within the stone wall. Fiona sat beside her. Hiding a smile, Komie placed her hands, palms up, on her knees. "Now, the first thing is to close your eyes and breathe deep."

"And then what?"

"Just that. Do nothing else. Pay attention to your breath."

For a flash, Komie remembered teaching her son to honor the land. He'd been more interested in female pursuit than spiritual pursuit. She'd dreamed of teaching her granddaughter someday, but her daughter-in-law had destroyed that plan. Komie sent a brief prayer of safety to Tansy, hopefully safe with Old Tom and his son, and out of Yamka's toxic care.

Instead, this young girl wanted to learn. Komie needed to pass her knowledge onto someone. Fiona had a stubborn streak and might have enough fortitude to learn properly. Komie hoped she'd prove a good enough teacher.

"Komie?"

"Yes, child?"

"My mind keeps thinking of other things."

"That's fine and natural. As each idea comes to you, tell it you'll pay attention later. Then breathe again."

"But what if more come?"

"Do the same with each idea. You aren't doing it wrong, but it takes practice to keep your mind clear."

Komie concentrated on her own breathing, focusing her mind upon the act of drawing breath in, then letting it out. Pulling it in, letting it out. Pulling it in, letting it out.

As she did this, her chattering mind fell away, and her world narrowed to her body, the air around her, and the dirt beneath her.

Pulling it in, letting it out.

She spoke in a low voice. "Now, Fiona, I want you to take that focus, and push it into the earth below. Gently, a little farther each time you breathe, like waves on the incoming tide. Count each breath. When you draw it back in, bring a bit of the power of the earth with you. Not a lot, just enough to heal any nicks in your own soul, like sanding a piece of wood. Draw it back in, and then push down a bit more. Repeat until you aren't counting anymore. Keep your focus on the movement into the earth and back into your body."

Komie quested down into the earth with her mind, not her power. Each time she breathed, she dipped further into the loamy soil of the farmer's land. She could sense Fiona's own tentative touch, frightened and unsure. But it dipped with each breath, as she'd described. Fiona was a quick learner.

Her mind tickled spindly roots, pebbles, and insects. The native woman caressed each of them as she withdrew her attention and then returned again, deeper each time.

Something powerful touched her. Komie pulled back, not wishing to rouse anything with Fiona near. As she opened her eyes, she placed a hand on Fiona's arm. Startled, the girl's eyes flew open, then she shook her head like a dog after getting wet.

"That's enough for today, my dear. What we just did is called grounding, letting your mind be friends with the earth. It's good for relaxation, gaining back lost energy, and getting confidence. Can you feel that?"

Her eyes wide, Fiona nodded. "I feel sort of tingly all over."

Komie smiled. "That means you've drawn some healing power of the earth into yourself."

"It makes my skin feel weird. Good, but weird."

With a chuckle, Komie rubbed her back. "Energy from the land is coursing through you. You'll learn to relish it and to use it to restore your own body and mind."

"But you're always tired afterward. Why doesn't it restore yours?"

"I do more than just commune with the land, Fiona. I channel its power, along with the Unhidden talent within me, to help the plants grow. That takes both my energy and that of the land. When the goddess helps me, I don't have to use as much of my own."

Except yesterday. Komie felt reluctant to try today, after being so drained at the Kearney's farm. Whatever she touched in the earth proved something waited for her, whether to help or harm, she wasn't certain. And yet, the countryside must heal from the attacks, and she had the means to help it heal. The smothered land cried out for help, a constant pressure on the back of her mind. She had to try.

Directing Fiona back behind the stone wall, Komie bent to the ground and dug her hands into the earth for today's healing session.

As soon as she quested with her Unhidden talent, the blast from the goddess' power almost shoved her out. She reeled with dizziness, yanking her hands away as she fell against the stone wall. Had she offended the goddess?

Gray enveloped her. Even sitting down, Komie lost her balance and fell to one side as her world blotted out.

Chapter Three

"Stab the body and it heals, but injure the heart and the wound lasts a lifetime."
– Mineko Iwasaki

Anna:

Anna rose, feeling physically refreshed but still emotionally drained. She'd dreamt of Joel. Nasty dreams that involved every single government torture scene from every spy movie she'd ever seen. Since her dad had loved James Bond movies, she'd watched a lot of them, though the torture scenes were never very believable. Still, her subconscious added governmental reports of techniques like waterboarding, more apocryphal acts like thumbscrews, and other medieval delights.

Her imagination made things worse because *she'd* been the one to turn him in, so anything he suffered felt like her fault, despite the fact that he'd been the one doing the betraying. He'd pretended to be one of them, got access to the PHAE headquarters in Galway, and murdered hundreds, maybe even thousands, of people. Anna only discovered his complicity after the fact and told on him.

Snitches get stitches.

Where had she heard that line? Maybe in elementary school, when being warned not to tell on the bullies. Maybe from some mob movie. Now it chanted within her mind on a constant loop.

Anna dug her nails into the palms of her hand until little half-moons of red showed on her skin. Then she took a deep sigh, washed her face, and changed her clothes. This gave her an artificial feeling of being brand new. She wandered down the hall to the dining room.

Carlos sat at his corner desk, working on a computer. Brendan might have been resting in his own room.

Their host rose as soon as she entered. "Anna! Did you get good sleep? Have a seat. Can I get you some tea?"

"Tea would be great, thanks, Carlos. Milk and sugar?"

She watched him as he opened the sideboard, taking down two cups before he walked into the kitchen. He must have had an electric kettle on, as he returned with two steaming mugs and a tray with teabags, milk, cream, sugar, and fake sugar. "Sweets for the sweet."

Giving him a sarcastic half-smile, she chose chamomile while he prepared a mint tea for himself. "Thanks."

"Anytime. It's literally what I'm here for. Well, that and *creative computing*."

"What were you just working on?"

He glanced over at his desktop computer. "Just data mining at this point. Trying to scrape the deep web for some information on the PEM and their plans. They've been pretty canny so far, laying false trails all over the place and planting fake news. But I'm beginning to learn their favorite patterns, so I can filter out the known false positives."

Most of that went over Anna's head, so she nodded, sipping her tea. As the warmth washed the rawness down her throat, she cradled her hands around the steaming cup. "Brendan said you had to go to Dublin?"

The Hispanic man frowned. "He *said* that, but I don't know that I believe him. Ciara's my boss, not him. I won't be going until she gives the go-ahead. I'm safer out here, away from the Capital. Most of the people they've got on network tasks are scattered around now, to keep them from getting hit. Like…like Galway." His expression turned bleak, and he stared into his tea.

She placed a hand on his arm. "Did you lose someone you cared for there?"

With a shrug, he shook his head, making his curls bounce. "I don't know. I've only been here a few months, so I haven't made any close friends, but I went through training with a guy there. We kind of connected. I haven't heard from him. We weren't super close. But he was the only person I really knew in Ireland. I know Ciara, but she doesn't count. She's my boss."

Anna squeezed his arm. "Well, you know me, now. We're supposed to be here a day or two." She swallowed and glanced toward the hallway, but it remained empty. "I'm sort of searching for someone, too."

He glanced up, his dark eyes strained. "Oh? Did they get lost in the blast?"

She swallowed, trying to stick to the truth without really giving any details. "Not in Galway, but I think he's in Dublin. I heard it's been pretty crazy there, too."

"Yeah. Their bomb exploded in the harbor rather than the city, but it disrupted a lot of systems. Who're you looking for? Maybe I can find some information." He gestured toward his computer. "Uh… your boyfriend?"

Anna glanced at the hallway again with a frown. "No, no, not my boyfriend. My brother. His name is Joel. Joel Taylor. Would you really look for him?"

She felt incredibly guilty flanking Brendan like this. But she hadn't promised not to ask about Joel, just not to ask *Brendan* about Joel. What could it hurt for Carlos to poke around? Besides, he seemed eager to help. Maybe helping her find Joel could help assuage his worry about his own missing friend.

"I'll find out what I can. It might not be quick, though. Do you have a cell phone? I can text or call when I get something. Well, when the phones come online again."

She frowned, thinking about her phone and the huge crack across the face. "Sort of. I mean yes, I have a phone, but it's on its last legs. It got pretty cracked up and won't hold much of a charge. And it's a US phone.

Since I got here, I haven't even thought about getting a new one. I don't have a lot of money, and until I get an actual job, I don't know how to get more."

A huge grin spread across Carlos' face. "I can help you there!" He jumped up and scooted to his desk, shoving things around in the lower drawer. He came up with something in his hand and a triumphant "Aha!"

Handing her the cell phone, he pressed the button, opening it. "It's set to my thumbprint. I can show you how to change it. It's a PHAE phone, but I have several, so I can give you one. Besides, it's legit for you to have one. You aren't earning yet, so you're allowed to requisition needed equipment. Consider it requisitioned. I'll fill out the paperwork later."

She stared at the proffered phone, one of the newer Samsung models. "Are you serious?"

He gave her a charming half-smile and pressed the phone into her hand. His skin felt warm on hers. "Dead serious. Remember, I'm on the tech team."

Anna narrowed her eyes. "Why do you have several PHAE phones?"

He winked at her. "I only have one PHAE phone, officially."

"And that's not shady in the slightest."

Carlos shrugged. "Shady is relative. I'm not stealing anything, I swear. Just bending rules here and there. I collect bent rules."

He walked her through changing the thumb print, shifting the settings to her preferences, and setting up a password. "There. All yours. And I already have this number stored in mine, so let me text you so you can get hold of me. My hotspot should work."

Her new phone buzzed, and she added him as a contact. It made her feel a little less lost to have something of her own, something new, something unbroken. And it boosted her flagging independence to have something not given by the Byrne family. She gave him a heartfelt smile. "Thank you."

His answering grin almost melted her heart. "Anything I can do to make you smile. Though, if you keep doing that, I'll have to go take a cold shower."

She giggled at the offhand compliment, and her cheeks burned.

Footsteps down the hall made her shove the phone into her pocket. Would Brendan notice the new phone or ask questions? She didn't know and didn't want to find out.

Brendan appeared in the doorway, yawning and stretching his arms. "Hey, Carlos, at the risk of sounding like a demanding guest, have you any supper? I'm fair starved."

"Just soup or sandwiches. Unless you want a fry-up. I usually don't serve three meals to my guests, and there's the power issue on top of that. But I can take you to the market."

Anna cocked her head. "The market? Like, a supermarket?"

Carlos shook his head. "Not without electricity! No, the locals have been setting out tables like a farmer's market each day. Some of them have barbecues and propane fryers, making street food. It's like a festival."

He must have remembered the reason and frowned. "Except not as merry. But still, people gotta eat, and people growing food need to sell it to pay their own bills. So, the need creates the means."

Brendan's mouth pursed. "It feels sacrilegious to enjoy ourselves when there's work to be done, but our assignment starts tomorrow. So, to the market we shall go!"

Despite the summer season, the wind blew cool as they stepped outside. The Irishman crooked his elbow out for Anna to take. With a guilty glance at Carlos, she took it. Without missing a beat, Carlos offered his arm on the other side. Thus, a little awkwardly, they left the B&B and strolled down the wide sidewalk.

As they passed one darkened pub, live traditional music filtered out and Anna held back, trying to peer into the gloom. She desperately wanted to get the full pub experience she'd always heard about. But Carlos pulled her forward. "Matt Molloy's is a fantastic place for music, but they don't do food, even when there is power. I thought you were hungry. We can stop later if you're still interested."

Reluctantly, she let him lead them a few blocks to a central square. Cloth-covered tables lined the edges, each with piles of fruits, vegetables, cheese, bread, honey, and cured meats. A few tables had trays with Sterno cans beneath, hot food ready to eat. Food trucks parked on each of the radiating side streets.

Overwhelmed with the choices, Anna suggested they do a full walkaround first.

Brendan cocked his head at Anna. "You haven't actually eaten out in Ireland yet, have you?"

Carlos' eyes widened. "How long have you been here?"

"About a month."

With a raised eyebrow, he glanced at Brendan. "This one's been keeping a short leash on you? What gives, dude? Trying to keep her all to yourself?"

Brendan's arm muscle tightened against hers.

Anna didn't know whether to laugh or get angry. "I've been on Brendan's family farm. Not much night life there."

With pursed lips, the American man nodded. "Sure, I can see how the rustic life might be fun. But city life has its benefits, too. Even a city as small as Westport. It ain't Miami by any stretch of the imagination, but it has its charms."

They stopped to check out a fish fry booth, the aroma of fresh-fried chips covered in salt and vinegar making her mouth water. Then Carlos pulled them to the next booth, with fresh clams and oysters. Then Anna spied someone with samosas.

The next place grilled hamburgers and ribs. Carlos' grin widened as she took in a deep sniff. "Let me lend you the benefit of my worldly experience. The fish and chips in Ireland are fantastic, much better than in the States. The burgers are on par, depending on where you go. Stay away from regional American specialties, though. Never order anything Cajun, as the Irish translate it into 'burnt to a crisp.'"

Brendan let out a snort. Carlos shot him a glare. "It's true! Beware of ribs and any other sort of barbecued delight. Again, the sauces will leave you sorely disappointed. Nothing like at home."

The Irishman scowled. "She doesn't come from Florida, Carlos. She's from New York. They're worlds away."

Carlos poked Brendan in the side. "Not when it comes to spareribs, amigo. Ribs are an American staple. And I've never, I mean never, come across an Irish plate that comes close. I will admit, seafood is great here, even compared to Florida, but stay away from orange juice." He wrinkled his nose in an expression of disgust.

That last example seemed out of place. "Orange juice?"

"I'm from Miami, so I *may* get a bit snobbish about my orange juice. The stuff here tastes like watered-down Tang."

Brendan scowled at him. "Watered what?"

With a wrinkled nose, Carlos answered, "Tang. It's a powdered drink from the eighties."

"Powdered orange juice? What the hell's your problem, Carlos?"

Anna extracted her hand from their now-tight grip. "Guys! Come on. Let's pick a place to eat."

By the time they'd checked out all the options, Anna returned to the first place, with fish and chips. They each got an order and retired to a picnic bench to devour their meal.

Carlos took a bite of his still-steaming fried cod and closed his eyes in sheer delight. Anna did the same, burning the roof of her mouth. She sucked in cool air to relieve the heat. When she finally finished her bite, she nodded. "You're right, Carlos. This tastes unbelievably good."

"Yeah, better than anything in Miami, even down in the Keys. If the Irish can do one thing right, it's fish and chips."

Brendan sent him another glare, but as Carlos had complimented Ireland cooking, he could do little about it. The Irishman salted his chips and chewed on a few before clearing his throat. "So, I used your phone to talk to Ciara before I took my nap."

Carlos lifted his eyebrows. "Oh? Anything more on that mysterious trip to Dublin I'm to take?"

With a prim look, Brendan shook his head. "No, she doesn't need you anymore. Instead, Anna and I are off to Achill Island tomorrow. The fishermen there are having issues with their catch, and Ciara wants Anna to find out what's going on. They used to get a decent haul each day, and now absolutely nothing."

As he swallowed a bit of fish, Carlos snorted. "Lazy fishermen looking for a handout?"

"Ciara said no, these are honest, reliable folk, people who have been vocal in their support of the PHAE. A few of them even have talents. They can't find a single fish in any of the regular spots."

Carlos cocked his head. "*Curiouser and curiouser.* Well, if Anna's got water power, then she's obviously the best person to send."

Brendan clenched his jaw. "Yes, she is."

The two locked eyes and practically growled at each other. Anna ignored them and licked salt off her fingers.

Anna:

Dawn arrived so early in Ireland in the summer, the sun had risen long before Anna woke the next morning. They ate a cold breakfast, scones and cereal, but Carlos handed her a thermos of tea. "For later. Are you sure I can't come with you?"

She glanced at Brendan, but he shook his head. "No, you're to stay here in case Ciara calls."

Carlos pressed his lips together. "Didn't you claim she wanted me in Dublin? Make up your mind, dude."

"I must have misunderstood her." They exchanged tense glares.

As Brendan took their bags out to the car, Carlos spoke to Anna in a low whisper. "I've put out some feelers about your brother. I promise if I find any information, I'll let you know."

"Thank you. You don't know how much this means to me."

He stared into her eyes as he squeezed her hand. She had to pull herself away from his compelling gaze as Brendan came in for her. She clutched that nugget of information close, like a special gift, not daring to hope he'd find something, and yet afraid to think of the alternative.

As they drove out of Westport, Brendan glanced at her. "Carlos seemed to like you a lot."

Anna shrugged. "He was just being hospitable. Isn't that how a B&B host is supposed to act?"

He frowned and concentrated on driving. Awkward silence lay heavy on her shoulders, but she didn't know what else she could say. She had no control over how someone else acted, did she?

Clouds hid the sun, but soft light bathed the bay as they drove along the coast. Wind picked up when they crossed the bridge to Achill. As they drove through Keel and passed the strip of silvery beach, Brendan kept glancing at the sky. Anna followed his gaze to angry-looking clouds speeding by.

The sheltered pier had about twenty boats lined up along the marina, rocking from the wind. As Brendan parked and helped Anna out, a grizzled older man approached them. "Oi, we've got no fishing tours today, lad."

He flashed the older man a reassuring smile. "PHAE sent us to find out why. Are you Mr. McNamara?"

The man's lined eyes widened as he glanced between Brendan and Anna. "Sure, and I am. They didn't mention they were sending a couple of weans, though! How're ye going to find that out, then?"

With a pat on Anna's back, Brendan gave a jaunty grin. "This young lady is going to ask."

As Mr. McNamara watched with black, shining eyes, Brendan led Anna down to the sand. "Are you ready for this? Do you want to rest first?"

"No, let's find out what we can."

They both removed their shoes and socks and waded into the sea. The cold water shocked her into a gasp, but it subsided quickly enough. Her skin warmed as it got used to the temperature, and her legs flashed under the water. Though her scales hadn't grown as fast as those on her arms had, her skin itched less in the sea. Anna still had nightmares about growing completely scaled. She rubbed her arms as a wave rocked her back.

Brendan curled his arm around her shoulders. "It'll be grand, Anna. Let's see if these waves will speak to you."

She turned to the deep ocean and asked in her mind, *Are you there?*

Where else would we be? Hello, friend. We've missed you.

Anna almost lost her balance in the sand. Brendan squeezed her shoulders. "Are you okay? Another strong wave?"

"I'm fine, I'm fine. I just didn't expect them to answer so quickly." Or that they'd remember her. Or that they'd actually *speak* to her in words. She'd only received images before, but Max could speak words to the wind. Maybe this was her talent evolving?

Brendan squeezed again. "Can you talk out loud? I want to hear at least half of the conversation."

She watched Brendan's face as she spoke both in her mind and with her mouth, "Uh, I've missed you, too. But I need some information. Can you help?"

What do you want?

"I'm trying to find out where all the fish went. Did they go away?"

They are afraid.

Her blood turned cold as she swallowed. "What are they afraid of?"

The Son. The Storm.

Anna furrowed her brow, glancing up at the clouds. They were gray, but not foreboding. "Sun in the sky, or a child? A Son of the Storm? Is there something coming?"

Far out in the biggest current, a storm comes. The Son of the Sea warned the fish to hide.

She blinked, staring at the horizon, trying to make out anything beyond the overcast sky. "Brendan? Can you look up the weather? They said there's a big storm coming."

He shook his head. "Cell towers are still wonky. I can ask in town. Someone's bound to have a radio. Fisherfolk always keep an eye on the weather. There's certainly wind and dark clouds, but that just means it's a Tuesday in Ireland."

She gazed up at the clouds. "They don't look that bad, do they?"

Brendan tugged on her arm. "Come on, let's find Mr. McNamara."

"Give me a few moments more." Waves caressed her legs as the water reached her knees. She took another step, and they licked the top of her thighs. They danced around her skin like silken handkerchiefs in an exotic dance.

Anna closed her eyes to enjoy the oddly comforting sensation. She didn't want to get out of the water yet. It felt so welcoming, so wonderful to no longer itch. Her fear of deep water faded next to her need to be part of this kinship.

"Anna?"

With a sigh, Anna left the new camaraderie of the ocean, her feet squelching on the white sand of the idyllic beach. She cast a backward glance at the waves as they filled her rapidly disappearing footprints.

As soon as she emerged, her skin burned with itching. She had to stop and scratch. Brendan waited but looked impatient.

Within the pier office, Mr. McNamara picked up an ancient rotary phone and dialed. "Aye, what's it say for later today, Mick? Are ye sure? Fair enough. *Go raibh maith agat.*" He turned to Brendan. "Mick's got one of them fancy solar-powered weather stations at his place on the point. I've just got the barometer, but even that has pressure dropping to the floor. Between the two, I'd say there's a big blowup coming, sure enough."

McNamara turned back to Brendan. "Weather might make the fish harder to catch, but the fishing is usually fine before and after a storm. Did the lass find anything else out?"

Just as Anna's shoulders tensed, Brendan put a protective arm around them. "*The lass* can answer for herself, Mr. McNamara."

The older man cleared his throat. "Aye, fair enough. Apologies to ye, lass."

"No offense taken, Mr. McNamara. They mentioned the Son of the Sea, but I think they just mean a big storm coming in with the current."

He rubbed his stubbled chin. "Aye, well, we'd have normally gotten word about any hurricane coming across the Gulf Stream. But with the bombs…" He stared at the horizon through the large plate-glass window, making growling noises in his throat. "The Son of the Sea? That sounds like something from our lore. But how would the waves know about our stories? Well, if there's a big blow coming our way, we'd best prepare the boats."

Several grunts behind her made Anna turn to discover three other fishermen crowded into the doorway. They cleared off with a wave from Mr. McNamara, presumably to secure vulnerable craft.

He pointed toward the village. "My sister runs a B&B, The Bervie. She said to come by for a hot bowl of soup. Ye're welcome to stay the course, if ye like. In fact, I'd appreciate it if ye did. If the storm isn't the only answer, we'll be needing help after, most like."

Brendan nodded. "We can do that, Mr. McNamara. Thank you."

Max:

Max eyed the plane from his vantage point.

It wasn't a model he was familiar with, and a far cry from his old, reliable Boeing-Stearman biplane in Coober Pedy. Still, he'd taken several lessons from Kieran flying back and forth to Galway. He should be able to translate that new knowledge to flying this craft.

Ciara'd told him to stay put. Without new orders, he *should* stay put. That didn't mean he had to like it.

With everyone called to Galway, they'd left him pretty much on his own. He'd finessed his friendship with the local winds into an early warning system, so he didn't have to be on watch 24/7. A lone watcher became practical, along with the electronic backup at the lighthouse.

Other people worked at the fort. The place was huge, after all, but it was a tourist spot, not a functioning defense structure. Its vantage offered a great view of the surrounding waters, but no modern weaponry. He must rely on his friendship with the wind for any defense.

They'd been lucky to keep electricity in Charles Fort. The renovated 17th century bastion had its own generators, so they didn't need to rely on the national grid. While the PEM planted bombs in Galway and got past defenses at Dublin and Belfast, Max's efforts, along with Anna, had kept them from hitting Cork.

Despite that, the Wi-Fi signals were intermittent, at best. Information grew scarce. Max had never owned a mobile, and while the tourism office had a land line, they hadn't gotten much information, either. He fretted about the safety of those few people he knew in Ireland. Hiroki, Róisín, and Qacha hovered at the top of his mind, three of the other Unhidden talents he'd met at the Byrne farm. Folks who had actually treated him like a friend, despite his abrasive self.

PHAE sent Hiroki and Bintou to Dublin, to work on the trade agreements, and hopefully head off further military engagements. Róisín and Qacha had gone to Galway to handle their defense. Qacha had prevented the spy drones from gaining a foothold, but Anna's brother, Joel, had smuggled bombs into the city. The resultant explosions had destroyed the place.

Despite their initial antagonism, Max respected Qacha loads, and her injuries after the explosion filled him with rage and regret. He wanted to punch Joel over and over, inflicting the murdering bastard with every pain he'd given to Anna, Qacha, and most of all, Róisín.

Max swallowed, thinking about the carnage. He failed in Galway. He ran from death and burning skin, the horrible memories stirred in his psyche, and headed straight for an abandoned pub. With all the liquor he could drink, he descended into a drunken debauchery that would have made Bacchus proud.

Róisín hadn't been proud of him. When she found his dead drunk self, reeling from alcohol poisoning, she nursed him back to health, but she refused to speak with him beyond her healing.

When he recovered, PHAE sent him back to Cork to guard his post. Róisín only gave him a disappointed glare as a farewell.

Cork, at least, had become familiar ground. His chest puffed up a bit in pride at his success. He didn't have many successes in his life, but this time, Max had actually saved lives. Not like the last time. He deflated as Trina's beautiful face flashed in his memory.

His gaze strayed once again to the plane. It was parked on a private airstrip. A person owned that plane, not the government of Ireland or PHAE. If he took it, he'd be a thief. But he could find Róisín and talk to her. Her disapproval ate at his conscience.

He snorted. Since when had he gotten a conscience? He'd lived sixty years without needing one of those bloody things. But the soldier in him screamed against disobeying an order.

Letting out a sigh, Max glanced back toward the plane. He ached to be up in the air. The only time he felt truly alive, when his heart soared, was when he flew. He still stewed about Hiroki promising they'd give him a plane if he came to Ireland. They hadn't made good on that promise.

An overly cheerful voice intruded on his misery. "Hey, Max! We got news from Dublin!"

He spun to find Pat, the kid who worked the tourism desk. The twenty-year-old barely weighed ninety pounds soaking wet, skinny and freckled like a typical Irish bloke. "What news?"

"The PEM signed the agreement! They're pulling back!"

Max let out a long breath and clapped the young man on the back. "That's bloody fantastic news, mate."

Pat staggered from the impact but grinned wide.

"Any news from Galway?"

The boy's face turned sour. "It's pretty bad there, still. No power, no water. The PHAE hospital is filling fast. I heard…"

With a clenched jaw, Max gestured for Pat to continue.

"You've got a friend out there, right? The Byrne girl?"

Max narrowed his eyes. "I do. What about her?"

"I heard she got sick."

Max's heart skipped a beat. Róisín had taken care of him. She was a good soul, one of the best he'd ever met. "Sick?"

"Aye, lots of people are getting sick. Some sort of nasty cough. She works in the hospital, right? She must have gotten it from one of the patients."

If she died…

Something in his expression must have changed. Pat's face turned pale, and he pelted back down the stairs.

Max's gaze returned once more to the plane. The PEM had signed the treaty. They wouldn't attack again. This was no longer an urgent watch. That meant they weren't at war any longer. They didn't need him on this post. Technically, he wouldn't be deserting.

Anna:

By the time they got to the B&B, Anna's energy had drained. She stumbled through the red-painted door, almost falling on her face. Brendan kept a firm grip on her arm.

When their hostess showed them inside, she gestured for them to sit on the chintz-covered settee in a knickknack-filled room. Anna squeezed into the narrow seat next to Brendan, incredibly conscious of their thighs touching.

Their hostess nodded as if approving of their existence. "A wee bit of tea and some choccy biscuits will help. I'll add a dollop of whiskey and honey. Good against the cold wind."

Anna croaked out, "Please, no honey, I hate it."

She pursed her lips. "Aye, well, the whiskey'll do, I'm sure."

Brendan went to fetch their bags, wrestling them up the stairs and into their guest room. By the time he returned, Anna had her tea, and her strength seeped back.

"See? A wee bit of whiskey always cures what ails ye. Now, Mac said ye'd be here a few days. Can I help ye with some information about the sights?"

Brendan munched on a biscuit, crumbs falling on his shirt. "I'm afraid we aren't here for holiday, Mrs. Barrett. We're with PHAE, and we're helping your brother discover what happened with the fishing."

"Ah, well then, I'll leave ye to what ye need to do. Just ring that bell should ye need anything. There're sandwich makings in the dining room down the hall if ye've a hunger on ye beyond the biscuits."

Anna's stomach growled at the mention of food, and Brendan brushed his crumbs away. "I guess I know what the answer to my next question is. Let's go see what's on offer."

After they'd stuffed themselves with coronation chicken sandwiches and apples, Anna made more tea. They moved to their room to relax, and she let out a sigh of relief at the sight of two beds and a bookshelf stuffed with books. When Brendan said there was only one room, she'd gotten worried. Her arms itched again, which set off her legs so, to distract herself, she grabbed a book on local legends and curled up into a chair. Brendan settled in the other chair, clasped his hands across his belly, and shut his eyes.

She'd almost gotten used to the itch, this relative constant in her body over the last weeks. It only really hurt when she couldn't stop, scraping her skin raw. However, that pain always disappeared in the ocean, even when she only stood knee-deep. An intriguing detail to keep in mind. How long could she actually stay in the water?

All her life, Anna had been terrified of murky water. Chlorinated water posed no problem. If she saw the bottom, she could verify no creatures waited for her.

Anna still didn't particularly crave the wild water, but increased time in the sea while testing her talents blunted the sharp edge of her fear. For a moment today, she felt warmly welcomed by the ocean, like being hugged by her mother. Her throat caught in sudden, painful grief.

Before her mother died.

Before Anna had known about her talent and left everything she knew for Ireland.

A wave of nostalgia slammed into her. Nostalgia for her old job as a swimming coach, for upstate New York, for her parents. Even after that, for the idyllic time at the Byrne farm, learning how to harness her new powers. For a moment, Anna railed against the unfairness of these past two weeks. She should still be there, with Brendan teaching her to control her talent. Instead, she'd been thrown into a battle against an insurgent attack in Cork, then to Galway to clean up after another, and after only a few days' rest, now to help against a hurricane.

Fuckabiscuit.

What the hell had these people done before they had Unhidden talents to fix things?

She chided herself for uncharitable thoughts. Brendan explained the Irish had been under the heel of the English for nine hundred years, that's what they'd done. The nation had only freed itself a hundred years ago, finally rebelling against their overlords after centuries of theft, oppression, and outright genocide.

Now, just as they emerged as a stable world power, this wave of Unhidden talents hit the world. And as more of its population demonstrated these talents than anywhere else, Ireland became the natural world headquarters for the PHAE. Which meant any groups organized to eradicate what they considered abominations attacked the tiny island country.

The luck of the Irish.

Anna snorted, making Brendan glance up from a semi-doze. She waved off his inquiring look and he settled back in the lounge chair. Anna considered telling him he should lie down, and then decided she should do so herself. If she was going to fight a hurricane, she'd need all the rest she could get. Mr. McNamara had gauged the storm to be about five hours out. A few hours' sleep would do her good.

If she *could* sleep.

She drained the dregs from her teacup and rinsed it in the room's sink. Then she kicked off her shoes and crawled under the covers, self-conscious with Brendan still in the room. He looked adorable with his head canted to one side as he snored. His shoulder-length black hair fell in front and blew out as he exhaled.

Her heart grew warm that he felt comfortable enough to sleep in the same room as her. Despite her deep attachment to the Irish man, Carlos' delightful grin as he teased her flashed in her mind. And with Carlos' American voice, homesickness washed over her. As much as she adored Brendan's Irish accent, someone from the States would be nice to talk to.

Anna shoved the thought from her mind. She hadn't come here on some reality dating show. She needed to learn her talent and use it to protect the people of Ireland and the PHAE. If she didn't pull her head out of the clouds, she might get distracted in a disaster. Her affection for Brendan, and for Carlos for that matter, had to wait until they had more leisure time to explore it.

Anna pictured a gentle, lapping ocean on a white sand beach, much like the one outside, in an attempt to quiet her mind for sleep. The even rhythm of the waves matched her breathing and soon, slumber embraced her.

A klaxon dragged her awake, clanging loud and echoing against the cliffs. Next, a siren wailed, an ululating cry bouncing in her brain. She leapt out of bed, her legs tangling in the covers. She fell to her knees and whimpered from the impact.

Brendan jumped from his chair and extracted her from the blankets. They both rushed out to the sitting room.

Their hostess tugged on her mackintosh. "I've a few extras on the hooks if ye don't have any of yer own. The storm's arrived, and we usually gather in t' pub in case we're needed to help out."

Brendan grabbed a yellow raincoat and handed it to her, then chose one for himself. They donned hats and followed Mrs. Barrett outside.

The rain slashed at them sideways. Anna had to lean into the wind to make any progress. Brendan took a firm grip on her arm, and they pushed through, following their hostess. As they stumbled step by step, she saw nothing but rain and the yellow slicker.

After an indeterminate time fighting the wind and the rain, they made it to the pub. In reality, it was only a half-block away. Once they escaped the weather, Anna tripped, so used to bracing against the wind. Brendan steadied her as they peeled off their outerwear.

When they walked to the bar, a steaming drink appeared before her. Anna glanced around, certain there'd been a mistake.

Mr. McNamara's laugh boomed out and clapped her on the back. "It's a hot whiskey, lass. Drink up. Ye'll need the warmth in your belly if we have to go out with the sandbags. High tide's in about an hour. That's the dangerous bit."

Brendan got a hot whiskey as well. Anna sniffed hers, smelling lemon, cloves, and whiskey. She took a cautious sip. It traveled straight down to her belly, a warmth of alcohol and lemon. She grinned and took a deeper sip.

She raised an eyebrow at Brendan. "I think I need these all the time."

He chuckled and toasted first to her, then to the gathered villagers.

They returned it, and then fell silent as the battery-powered radio crackled. "Johnnie reported a tree fell across the Dooagh Road, big enough it'll need chainsaws in the morning."

Mac wrote in a notebook. Anna spied several lines of scrawling black letters. He must be making a tally of repairs to do after the wind stopped.

The radio squawked again. "The sea wall near Keem's been breached near the pier. Concrete broke but no one got hurt."

Mac made another note.

A motor whined and another man bent down behind the bar. Suddenly a background noise ceased, and Anna sighed in relief. The wind outside still howled, and the rain pelted the windows but, with the generator off, a layer of oppressive sound lifted.

Mrs. Barrett turned to Anna, her own hot whiskey already half-drained. "Once we secure the boats and get everything else tied down, we all stick together. That way, if one of our houses gets hit, we aren't in them. This pub has weathered many a fierce storm and has stood for a hundred years or more. We're all safe here. There'd be music, if we didn't have to listen to the radio."

His reassurances notwithstanding, a large crash outside made everyone flinch. With solemn footsteps, Mac strode to the window, peering through the rain. Something slammed against the pub wall, and he sprang back. He shook his head. "Might be a buoy flung up from the sea."

Anna swallowed her heart and sipped her hot whiskey.

Another heavy object slammed against the pub, and a few locals exchanged worried glances. Anna found Brendan's hand and squeezed it. She tried to drink more but couldn't get the whiskey past the lump in her throat.

Brendan placed his empty glass on the bar. "Anna, I have an idea."

Her eyes grew wide. She suspected she wouldn't like his suggestion.

"Do you think you can talk to the storm?"

Fuckabiscuit. That's exactly what she was afraid he'd suggest. Anna stared at the gray window and swallowed. "I need to be outside to do that. Wait, do they have a back door? Facing away from the wind?"

Mrs. Barrett nodded, her brow furrowed. "Aye, just behind the bar, near the bathrooms. It'll be relatively sheltered. But do be careful, lass."

Brendan kept a grip on her hand. "I'll keep a strong hold on her, I promise."

Mac grunted before nodding. "Wear the macs, both of ye."

Anna grabbed them, handing Brendan one. The fishermen all watched as they exited the back of the pub. Once outside, the storm hit them with all the fury of unleashed nature, despite the pub shielding them from the worst.

Anna closed her eyes and quested out with her mind, searching for the water to answer her call. Nothing came. She tried a second time, with only silence as an answer.

She shouted in his ear. "I think I have to take off the raincoat, Brendan!"

"What? Why?"

The wind whipped her hair across her eyes in a stinging slap. "To be in contact with the water!"

Brendan hooked an arm around a pillar on the back porch and linked his other arm in hers. "Tell me when to pull you back in!"

She nodded, her throat easing again. Arm firmly hooked on Brendan's, she laced her fingers together and tried again. "Can you hear me?"

The wind whistled and moaned around her, a freight train rattling her bones.

"Will you speak with me?"

A low groan filled her ears, followed by a chorus of tinny voices. *Why?*

"Because I am asking you to." She breathed a sigh of relief that they finally answered. The wind must be pulling water from the ocean as it churned.

What do you want?

"For you to slow down. Your winds are hurting us."

We don't care if we hurt you. We are the wind. We are eternal. You are only ephemeral creatures.

Crap. This was Max's area, not hers. "The ocean is my friend. Is the ocean part of you?"

They didn't answer at first. They only howled more loudly. Her fingers slipped from their interlacing, but she adjusted. Brendan tugged, but she shook her head.

We are playing with the ocean.

"Wonderful! I love the ocean. The ocean speaks to me often."

The storm didn't answer.

"I would be grateful if you stayed over the water. Or slowed down."

We don't care if you are grateful.

A sudden gust ripped around the corner and yanked her away from Brendan. Her locked fingers slipped apart. Falling on her hip, the wind tugged her across the parking lot. She slid away from the pub as concrete ripped her skin and tore her scales. Stinging rain pelted her cuts.

With a panicked shout, Brendan ran after her, but the winds pulled her faster.

Anna screamed. "Stop!" Her throat turned raw.

The wind ignored her.

Her body only stopped sliding when she hit a low stone wall, which divided the pub parking lot from windswept fields and the open ocean beyond. When Brendan finally reached Anna, he sheltered her body from angry winds. He draped the raincoat over her, but the winds blew too strong for him to pull her back to shelter.

A gust of wind almost pulled Brendan from her, slamming him against the stone wall. He let out a grunt but held on tight to her. His hands dug painfully into her waist, but she didn't care. She just wanted to survive the storm.

They huddled against the stone wall for an eternity. When the storm finally eased, they disentangled. Brendan helped her to her feet. Anna's skin felt raw and painful from her slide across the parking lot as they stumbled toward the pub. Several fishermen came out to search for them and helped them inside.

Her body, from head to toe, was covered in road rash and scrapes. Mrs. Barrett brought her a thick, fluffy towel, and she carefully patted her skin dry. She shivered violently, despite a second hot whiskey, and a third. She didn't stop shivering until she sat in front of the peat fire for a full hour. Angry coughing racked her entire body until her throat grew too raw to speak.

Her skin throbbed with damaged nerves. Brendan never left her side, his brow knitted with worry.

When Anna felt able to brave the stumbling trek back to the B&B, she gazed out at the ocean, transfixed by its undulating beauty. The one place where her itch went away, and her body didn't feel the constant pain.

Chapter Four

"In a mad world, only the mad are sane."
– Akira Kurosawa

Qacha:

Qacha faded in and out of intense, dangerous nightmares. She rose from the mire to bright lights, acrid odors, and unbelievable pain. Her skin burned with fierce fire. Being unable to scratch the itchy, healing skin drove her to shake, struggling against her restraints during her brief, lucid periods.

What had her life become? For the thousandth time, she wished she'd remained at the restaurant in Ulaanbaatar. At least there, she held a measure of control over her body and her future. Here, in this far away island full of rain and white people, she'd always be an outsider. She'd done her best to save their city, to be rewarded with a ruined body. If she stayed like this much longer, she'd go mad.

Had she already gone mad? That was entirely in the realm of possibility. Was she here, in this rustic hospital ward? No lights worked. No machines beeped. Qacha may have constructed this hell from her own fears. Unable to move, unable to live. The tubes and wires snaked from her arms, bringing her fluids. She'd never been in the hospital before. Shouldn't she have more machines attached if she had this many injuries? The movies always showed beeping contraptions and graphs measuring her heart rate, blood pressure, and the gods knew what else.

Where was she, in truth? Still buried under the rubble of a destroyed city? Struggling with her beloved fire, trying to siphon hell into a reluctant ocean?

Qacha's throat ached, itched, and burned. She wanted nothing more desperately than to drink cool, creamy milk to ease the pain. She'd even choke down fermented mare's milk if she had nothing else. She'd never cared for the traditional Mongolian drink, but at least it would ease the burning.

Her mind swirled again, transporting her far from the shuffling sounds of the makeshift hospital. She stood on a windswept prairie. Qacha's grandfather's yurt hulked next to her, the tent flaps flicking in strong wind. Her waist-long black hair whipped against her ears.

Something pulled at her shoulder. She glanced at it, eyeing the leather strap of her quiver. She should ride. A Mongolian horse archer must ride, take aim, and hit her mark, all at the same time. Her grandfather had been a champion.

Qacha would never be as good as him. Even if she'd started young, even if she'd devoted all her time to practice, even if she felt it in her heart as he did, she'd never measure up.

He'd told her as much the night before, as they prepared for today's final competition. She'd yelled at him, accused him of leading on her hopes. His jaw had clenched at her disrespectful words. Then he turned and left her without a word.

She'd slept alone in the competitors' yurts.

Would he watch her compete? Or had she poisoned his mind forever against her?

For a mad moment, Qacha wanted to throw her grandfather's bow and quiver on the ground in front of his yurt. To stalk away, never to return. She might wander the plains, as her ancestors did, living off the land.

With a snort, she shook her head. She'd never survive the harsh land. Qacha had no training, supplies, or instincts for the nomad life. It took groups of people working together to be proper nomads, to live and thrive in this unforgiving environment.

Instead, she marched to the horse stalls, gentling her mare with low whispers and calming pats. The beast acted nervous, with a storm brewing on the horizon. But the beast had been well-trained and would perform as she should. Qacha had no fear of that.

As she mounted her horse, the earth below her exploded in a burst of violence, dirt, and rocks. Chunks of turf flew through the air.

Qacha turned her mount from the explosion, cantering toward the competition grounds. Another blast to her left made her swerve. The horse, now completely panicked, reared as a third one burst on their right.

She couldn't gain control of her horse. In a moment of panic, Qacha rolled off the saddle, curling herself into a ball, trusting the mare to find her own way to safety.

When she rose again, chaos surrounded her.

Qacha hated the earth. It smothered her own talent of fire. She couldn't fight against this.

Just as the thought pierced her mind, she realized this was a false memory. This had never happened. Qacha the child didn't yet know of any talent with fire. The adult Qacha, recognizing this memory as a dream, remembered no such event to mar her competition day. And yet she couldn't withdraw herself from this surreal nightmare.

"Qacha? Qacha, wake up!"

The gentle yet persistent voice intruded as her body shook uncontrollably. She curled up in a ball again, to keep the blasts of earth from injuring her.

"Qacha! You're screaming, wake up!"

As if she swam through treacle, Qacha yanked herself from the terrifying vision and opened her eyes.

Her throat ached as if scoured by sandpaper. A pretty young woman with honey-blond hair stood over her, worry etched on her drawn face. Her name tickled Qacha's brain. "Róisín."

"Yes, Qacha, it's Róisín. You screamed in another language, Qacha. Are you alright?"

"I am not."

Róisín's brow furrowed more deeply. "What hurts?"

Qacha rasped her answer through her parched throat. "My throat. My skin. My bones. My mind." She hated this place. The healer did what she could, but the hospital made her feel like a prisoner, an inmate who'd never escape her bonds. She pulled against the restraints on her wrists and ankles, but they held fast.

The Irish woman placed a cool hand on her arm. "I have been working every day to heal your body, Qacha. But I can't heal your mind. You must do that. We don't even have a psychologist here. But if you want to talk to me, I'm happy to listen."

The older woman growled. "No talking."

Róisín had plenty of good intentions and her healing abilities. But Qacha needed someone wiser than herself and from her own culture, like her grandfather. And he'd died long ago. She no longer spoke to her parents, not for years. She had no family. She had no friends.

This nightmare had been the latest installment in a series of terrifying episodes. Each one felt real, an honest memory from her past, until events took a left turn and became a horror movie.

She shook her hands. "Restraints."

"Are you certain? You were pulling against them in your sleep. I don't want you to hurt yourself from what was obviously a nightmare."

"Off."

Róisín let out a deep sigh. "Very well. I'll take off the leg restraints. If you don't hurt yourself by tomorrow, we'll try the wrists. Okay?"

Qacha tried to nod, but the blocks to either side of her head limited her movement.

"Grand."

As the other woman ripped open the Velcro around her ankles, Qacha rolled them with delightful freedom, lifting her legs up one at a time. Her muscles ached, unused to moving. Her skin remained tender and healing from her massive burns.

She'd been covered with burns. Anyone else would have died from so much charred flesh. But Qacha's own immunity to fire, while overwhelmed, simmered beneath the damage. It healed her burns, albeit slowly. Róisín's talent bolstered her own. Together, they'd reduced most of her damaged skin to scabs and scars. Eventually even those might fade.

In the meantime, she must gain her strength.

After Róisín left to finish her rounds, Qacha used her new-found freedom to exercise, discreetly, from her bed. Leg lifts, twisting her torso, as much as she could stand before the pain grew too bad.

Painful exercise was better than sleeping. Sleeping brought the nightmares. Nightmares brought screaming. Screaming hurt her throat.

Qacha:

After two weeks of intensive work, Róisín told Qacha she'd made considerable progress. The Irish woman helped her to walk around the ward several times a day. Still, Qacha got little sleep in those weeks. What rest she grasped came between disturbing dreams. She hadn't allowed Róisín to hear her scream in her sleep again. The Mongolian woman waited until Róisín wasn't on shift to sleep.

At least the healer had been able to nurse Anna back to health. Qacha's path wouldn't be so easy. She stared at her face in the mirror, aghast at how haggard she'd become. She'd never carried extra flesh, always being tall, lean, and wiry. Not once had she ever considered herself pretty. However, now she looked positively cadaverous. Her skin seemed so thin as to be translucent, despite her swarthy complexion.

She traced her fingers along her strong jawline, down the jutting neck tendons and her protruding clavicle. She might play a famine victim in a film, someone from the concentration camps of Nazi Germany.

Well, she'd never been vain, and she had no reason to begin now. Once she healed, then what? What would be her place in this land? She had control over fire, but her true talent lay in cooking, and chefs were in demand everywhere. As a foreigner in this country, finding a new kitchen might be challenging. She'd never been the easiest person to get along with, and her new scars would do her no favors.

Maybe she should return to Ulaanbaatar. At least she'd have one less barrier to deal with. Two, as her English wasn't perfect.

All the dying people in this hospital sapped her hope. She must go elsewhere. Somewhere the nightmares couldn't find her. Galway had been the center of so much pain and death, destruction on a grand scale. If she were alone, she wouldn't have to worry that her nightmare screams bothered others.

Qacha longed for the windswept plains of her home, the steppes of Mongolia, where she'd traveled with her grandfather as a child. The memories dredged up by her nightmares, before they turned to horror, had brought an incredible longing she must obey.

She couldn't get to Mongolia right now. She didn't even know where her things were; her purse, her clothing, anything. At least her grandfather's antique bow and her beloved cat, Manol, were safe at the Byrne farm. Fiona, the youngest child, had promised to care for Manol. She remembered those details. Every other recollection had been swept away by the explosion.

If she could get away from this antiseptic temple of fatality, she might find some peaceful spot in the surrounding countryside, a place like home. Ireland, from what she could tell, had plenty of lonely places. Not as many as Mongolia, but there were places away from people. It lacked the open plains she craved, but something near the sea might suit her. The ocean wind might drown out her screams.

As she returned to her cot, Róisín helped her in. "Doesn't it feel nice to be able to use the bathroom on your own now?"

Qacha nodded. Her throat still felt too raw to speak gratuitously.

"I'll fetch you some cold soup for your tea. I've also some milk. You said that helps."

With a rare show of affection, Qacha placed her hand on Róisín's arm and squeezed. Róisín's mouth quirked up on one side. "Anything for a friend. Besides, Fiona told me I'd better take good care for you, or she'd tell Manol."

Manol. Qacha's heart prickled with guilt. If she fled to the countryside, she'd have to leave him in Fiona's care. He'd always been an indoor cat. But she couldn't return for him. Not yet. Not until she got her mind under control. She wasn't fit for others in this state. Manol would be in better care at the Byrne farm for now.

Róisín returned with soup and milk. The cool potato soup did soothe Qacha's throat. She wished she had a thermos to carry more. She must forage for food as she could. While Galway itself had been destroyed, it would offer ripe looting. She'd have to leave after Róisín's shift, once dusk came. She'd search the ruined stores before heading to the countryside.

As twilight spread across the hospital, sounds faded to silence. No electricity meant only hearth fires and candles for light. Flickers of life shone from dozens of windows, people too stubborn to leave the ruins, and sparkled through the hospital windows.

Qacha crept from her bed, retrieving scrubs and shoes from the supply closet. Without a backward glance, she exited the hospital, stumbling once outside. The rubble on the streets had been shoved aside, but not cleared. Months, perhaps years of work would be required to return this city to its former glory, if it ever recovered.

Carefully picking her way through narrow alleys, Qacha searched five half-standing buildings, each one already picked clean or empty, until she found something useful. Not food but clothing. She took a large bag near the cash register and stuffed it with warm weather gear, underclothing, and everything in between.

The next three buildings held nothing of value, though she did find a bottle of whiskey. Qacha kept that for medicinal purposes, in case she couldn't suppress the nightmares.

Finally, she found a small general store, one of the corner types that sold candy, newspapers, produce, and canned goods. The produce had all gone rotten. Mice and insects flocked around it, and the stench was incredible. Pushing past that, though, she found soup, crackers, canned meat, and other staples. The chef wrinkled her nose at the tastes she must endure, but gourmet food seldom had a long shelf life. She'd survive, but she wouldn't enjoy it. This realization fit her grim mood and determination.

Water, peanut butter, anything with carbohydrates and protein. Qacha glanced warily at the metal shopping carts. One would be useful, but the racket as she dragged that through the city streets would be disastrous. Instead, she fashioned a backpack from a laundry sack in the storage room and wrapped things in clothing and plastic in case it rained.

Hefting it on her back, she hissed as it hit her still-tender burnt skin. With a final glance of disgust toward the pile of rotting produce and vermin, she limped out of the store with a bottle of water in her hand.

The sky had lightened while she looted the store. Her scavenging had taken all night and dawn would break soon. Perfect. She'd prefer some light to tramp the countryside, and there would be fewer people to see her outside the city, but she must leave now.

Qacha glanced left and right, unsure which direction to head. The sun rose in the east, and she wanted to travel west, along the coast, among the wild and rugged Connemara coastline. There, she might find the solace she needed to heal.

Adjusting the straps of her makeshift backpack, Qacha set herself a swift, steady pace toward the disappearing darkness.

Latest **CNN Update:** *"Here is your evening update on news of the world. Ireland has fallen into chaos as nightly riots erupt from formerly peaceful demonstrations. Shortages of food, supplies, and medical care have turned the previously wealthy nation into a dangerous island. The governments of the Republic of Ireland and Northern Ireland, as well as the PHAE, have urged their people to stop hoarding supplies, but their pleas have evidently been in vain.*

"Some are comparing the current situation to that of the historic Great Famine from the 19th century, a time when English landlords siphoned food from the island for profit, reducing the Irish farmers to eating only potatoes which rotted in the ground.

"Now the future might balance upon the effectiveness of the current government to placate the masses.

"Communities are being torn apart, as they blame the attacks upon Galway, Cork, Dublin, and Belfast on the so-called Unhidden talents. Those Irish who do not possess these special talents want their country back, and who can blame them? Some believe if they eject these Unhidden, their world will return to normal.

"Some of this might be a faint hope, but the sentiment has been fueled by rumor, media reinforcement, and conspiracy theories."

Qacha:

The storm lashed against her face, but Qacha didn't mind. Step by step, through the driving rain and the fierce wind, Qacha kept her head down and stared at her feet. Chilly rain cooled and quenched her ravaged skin and kept people from noticing her. Still, the backpack grew heavier with every step and her energy had long since been sapped. The skin on her back felt like it was sloughing off with chafing and friction. But Qacha kept walking.

The sun had risen, but twilight ruled the soggy landscape beneath the thick, gray clouds. They clung to the hillsides like candy floss, caressing the curves and hiding the details from prying eyes. Qacha kept walking.

Farmhouses dotted the road, firelight flickering in the windows. She ached to go inside and warm her sodden skin. But stopping meant resting and resting meant sleeping and sleeping meant nightmares. Qacha kept walking.

Without being able to see the sun, she couldn't gauge how long she walked. It must have been hours with that huge soggy stone of a backpack digging into her shoulders. Several times she considered abandoning it, but the rational portion of her mind won, so far.

She'd finally reached a place where houses disappeared, and the ground rose into rocky outcroppings. Green grass clung to the edges, lush in the low light and glistening with rain.

Something bright caught her eye on the hillside. Curious, she climbed an old trail to get a better look. White taunted the edge of her vision and she climbed further.

When she finally spied the creature, the white sheep ran behind a cottage. Glancing behind her, Qacha realized it was well-hidden from the road.

A stone farmhouse with a thatched roof peeked up over the hill, but no light flickered inside. Perhaps, just perhaps, this was an abandoned place.

With a weariness she felt down to her bones, Qacha climbed the incline, slipping on the rocks and cursing frequently as her new-grown skin scraped. She approached the weathered wooden door with care in case someone dwelled inside.

Nothing stirred.

The rain masked sound, so she rapped timidly on the door. Qacha rarely did anything timidly, but if someone lived there, she must flee quickly, and she had no energy to do anything quickly. No one answered.

She knocked again, just to be certain. When no sound emerged, she cautiously turned the knob.

The inside seemed as dark as Tam, the Mongolian version of a punishing afterlife. Qacha had searched the stores for candles but found none. She could control fire but hadn't tested if she could create it from nothing. So, she'd stuffed several lighters from a countertop display.

She must gather kindling to start a true fire, but right now, she just needed light. She took out a lighter and after a few tries, the tiny flame illuminated the interior. As she turned around, she noted the dank, dirt floor with a few flagstones, the remains of a rotted wooden bed frame, empty shelves, and the reek of sheep dung. Exactly what she needed.

Qacha didn't particularly care for the scent of sheep dung but, in an odd way, it reminded her of life on the steppes. Since trees grew scarce, the nomads burned animal dung and bone for fire. She could do the same here, once she got some rest.

That's what she needed now. Sleep. With no one for miles to hear her scream in the night.

Max:

Under cover of the night, Max snuck out of the Charles Fort and jogged along the road toward the private airstrip, his backpack knocking against his back with each stride. He'd never be a marathon runner, but his lean build and long legs ate up the distance quickly.

It hadn't been difficult to get into the plane. While the small craft had a lock on the door, the trusting owner hadn't bothered using it.

Panting and sweating, despite the cool summer evening, Max pulled himself up into the plane. As he climbed into the cockpit, Max patted the door. "You are a true beaut, aren't you, darlin'? I'll take good care of you, never fear."

They weren't foolish enough to leave the keys in the ignition, though, so Max would have to get creative.

This wasn't the first time he'd had to do this. A few panels removed here and there, and Max found the wires he needed. Hopefully, this one had no prop locks. He didn't see a throttle lock, so he might just be in luck.

He considered leaving a note for the owner, that he'd return the plane as soon as he could, after checking on Róisín. But that would be too much bother. Besides, where would he leave a note? And they'd know exactly where to find him if he did that.

He must find Róisín first.

What he thought he could do to help her, he didn't know. But she'd been there for him when he needed her, so he felt duty-bound to return the favor.

Max didn't love Róisín, not in the romantic sense. But he'd developed an almost obsessive need to watch over her, like a daughter. Or a granddaughter, to be fair. Lovely, kind, and talented, much too fit for anyone like him, even if they'd been the same age.

Regardless of their relationship, his mind filled with the need to find her.

The engines finally fired up, but sputtered out just as quickly. Frowning, Max fiddled with the wires again. *Planes hadn't changed so much in the last few decades, had they?* Another sputtering start, and then nothing. He dredged his memory for anything Kieran had taught him about starting these newer planes, but nothing came to mind.

Max punched the instrument panel in frustration. "Bloody fucking hell!"

He glanced out the windscreen into the clear night sky. A full moon lit up the land like a movie set. The germ of a plan formed in his mind.

Before he could chicken out, Max called to the wind. "Oi! You lads out there or what?"

We are here.

"I've got another favor to ask of you."

We are listening.

"Can you…can you lift this craft in the air? Can you blow under the wings? Gently, mind you! And lift it up so it flies?"

No answer came, but the plane shuddered as winds danced around it, testing, trying, tasting.

That is possible.

Not exactly the rousing confidence he hoped for, but it'd have to do. Before he sat back in the pilot's chair, Max rustled in the cabinet for a parachute. Once he found it, he considered putting it on now, but that would be annoying. Instead, he plopped it on the co-pilot's chair within easy reach.

"Right. Let's go! I need to get to Galway. If I picture the coast in my mind, can you find it for me?"

We can.

"Bloody brilliant, you are. Let's do this!"

The plane jumped forward, wiggled, then jumped again. One wing went up as the craft accelerated along the runway, then it dipped down. Gripping hard on the throttle, Max tried to steer as the winds picked the plane up like an enormous toy. Max had to clench his sphincter and suddenly wished he'd waited for daylight to try this trick, but he was stuck now.

The plane wobbled and rumbled and whipped, but still hadn't left the ground. Just as the edge of the runway rushed into sight, with the ocean glittering beyond it, the wheels left the ground, touched twice more, and then glided away.

Max let out his held breath, calmed his heart, and steered, but the plane reacted horribly. The winds held up the wings rather than the wings cutting through the air. Everything felt off, and his stomach didn't like it one bit. He had no control. The wind had him at their mercy. If they wanted to dash him onto the coastal rocks jutting up at the ocean's edge, they could kill him with impunity. He had no way to stop them. He glanced at the co-pilot's seat but even his parachute would be useless at this low altitude.

With great difficulty, he hugged the coast, finally gaining enough altitude that he chanced breathing again.

Now, the land below him sped by in black, blue, and occasional bits of shining white as the full moon reflected on a pond.

Max was in the air again, and it felt glorious. Sure, every minute shift in orientation was wildly inaccurate. He didn't even want to think about how to land this thing, especially at night, or even where. He shivered but didn't let himself think about that. He'd get there, he'd land, and he'd find Róisín.

Less than an hour later, he spied the tiny Aran Islands below him, dark spots in a bright ocean. Galway Bay should be just ahead. Time to land this sucker.

From his lessons with Kieran, he knew about the airstrip in Rossaveal, used for planes to the islands. Max told the wind to bring him down in that area, due north.

"I need a long flat place, mates. Like the one the plane was on when we left. That way the plane has enough room to roll to a stop. There should be one along the shore. Can you find that for me?"

You don't need a long place. We can put you down wherever you want.

Bloody hell. He didn't know if his colon would survive that sort of landing. Max shivered, but then had a bonzer idea. "Right. Let's have a contest. How gently you can put me down?"

The plane pitched and shook. Max gripped the yoke so hard his hands ached as the ground loomed. He might be better off with a water landing. At least he'd hit softer if they mucked it up.

Max held his breath as the darkness of the night-clad earth rose to meet him. He had to trust the winds at this point. Well, mostly trust them. They had no concept of the fragility of human life. If he crashed into the ground, they would happily toss the fragments of his plane around in the air for a lark.

His new friends had assured him they'd land him without a runway. Max swallowed and gripped the throttle, as if that would do anything at this point.

At least the plane didn't need to hit the ground at landing speed, so the damage would be light even if they made a shemozzle of this. Having the wind carry his plane, rather than pushing the plane through the air with enough speed to hold it up, had been a novel experience. Max wasn't certain he ever wanted to do it again.

"Right. Let's see what you've got, mates."

As gently as a butterfly's kiss, the winds set the plane on the rubble-strewn parking lot next to the marina. Max let out a huge breath of relief, dizzy from holding it. "That was right proper, mates! Thank you!"

We don't like this place. It stinks.

"Oi, you can stick around, can't you? I've got more to do!"

We don't like this place. We are going back.

Max let out a sigh. At least he'd already worked with the local winds during his defense of Galway. "Well, thanks anyhow."

Goodbye.

Max didn't remember them saying goodbye before. Perhaps they were becoming actual mates, after all. Or learning how to act polite. He let out a snort at the idea of polite winds.

Jumping out of the plane, Max glanced around to get his bearings. Róisín was in a hospital, but which one? In the city itself? On the outskirts? Now that he'd made the mad trip to Galway, he had no bloody idea how to find her.

With a deep breath, he chose a direction. He'd find someone and ask where they took the wounded. Max didn't like the idea of talking to anyone, but he needed information, and the wind couldn't help with this one. Or could they? He quested out with his mind. Those who had brought him here left, but the locals might still remember him. "Are you there, mates?"

We are here. But you were not. You left.

"Aye, humans do that now and then. But I'm back, aren't I?"

You are.

The winds wouldn't know where Róisín was, but Max gave it a shot. "Right. Hey, I'm looking for a place with sick people. Do you happen to know where it is?"

What is sick?

Max rubbed his temple. "Uh, people who are bleeding. The red stuff that comes out of our bodies. I'm looking for a place with lots of those folks."

No answer came for several minutes. They must have gotten bored and buggered off. He shrugged. It had been worth a try, but he had to get to the city regardless, and so he started walking.

However, just as the sun peeked over the horizon, they spoke in his mind again, **We found this place.**

"Can you show me where?"

Follow the whirlwinds.

Max glanced down to see bits of trash and leaves swirling in front of him. "Right, mates! Lead the way!"

He followed the little whirlwind of debris down several alleys, around a pond, over a crumbled wall, and between two crashed cars. However, when it tried to lead him over a two-story ruin, he balked. "I can't climb that! Take me around."

Humans are so limited.

"Aye, we are, at that! Just show me a path on the ground, will you?"

The whirlwind hovered for a moment before leading him to the right, through a swampy park. His feet squished in the mud. Max made a face but had to admit he'd literally asked for that.

When the complex of buildings came into view, illuminated orange by the rising sun, Max paused, panting, his hands resting on his thighs. The whirlwind had set a brutal pace, and he was still more used to arid desert air than this humid Irish crap.

People stirred inside and candlelight flickering in the windows. He passed a sign for the National University of Ireland, Galway. "This is it? Where the sick people are? In a university?"

We don't know the human name. We know humans inside have leaks. The strongest smell comes from the biggest building.

"Well enough. Cheers, mates."

Max strode toward the nearest door. When he entered, his footsteps echoed on the tile floor. Someone in scrubs turned a corner into the corridor, and he asked, "Oi, mate, I'm looking for a friend of mine. Róisín. Do you know her?"

Startled, the man shook his head. "We've got lots of patients. C'mon, I'll take you to reception."

Reception? In a bombed-out city? Max shrugged and followed the guy to a desk next to a large window. The morning sun lit the area up brighter than any fluorescent light would have done.

An older woman filling out paperwork glanced up as they approached. "May I help you?"

Feeling foolish and surreal in this odd combination of normal business and disaster-area, Max sat in the plastic chair. "I'm looking for a mate of mine. Her name's Róisín. She's a healer, but she may be a patient now."

The woman gave him a sad smile. "Oh! Sure, we all know Róisín. I'll take you to her ward. Such a shame about her."

As they both rose, a chill ran down his spine as he grabbed her arm. "A shame? What do you mean a shame?"

With a quelling look, she jerked her arm away. "That she's fallen sick, that's all. But you knew that."

"Aye, but I have no details as to how sick or if she…"

As she led him to a set of double doors, she gave a shrug. "She's likely got the same respiratory illness everyone else has. Horrible coughing, nausea, dizziness. People *have* recovered, though."

Reading between the lines, Max realized that meant some hadn't. He swallowed and entered the ward. Searching the cots for Róisín's smiling face, he spied her honey-blonde hair spilled around her head on the pillow. She was hooked up to an old-fashioned mechanical IV. She looked so pale that her skin seemed blue. He rushed to her side.

With cold, clammy hands, Max took Róisín's. Hers felt flaccid, like a limp ragdoll. She moaned, her head tossing.

He squeezed her hand. "Róisín! Róisín, it's me, your old pal, Max. Wake up, Róisín!"

Her eyes fluttered open. Then she sat up, racked with a horrible, raw cough. When she settled back again, she gifted him a wan smile. She croaked out, "Hey, Max."

"Oi, you. You don't look so good."

She shrugged. "I have good and bad days. What about you?"

Max swallowed. "I have…days."

The Irish woman took his other hand and closed her eyes. This time, Max felt her questing into his brain. "Oi! What're you doing?"

"Shush. What I've always done. Just relax."

The intruder poked in his mind, soothing prickly bits and cooling burnt parts. "No! No, get out!" He jerked his hands from Róisín's grip and scooted his chair back.

She opened her eyes and raised her eyebrows. "You don't want me to heal your pain?"

"No! I mean, not like that. You're already so, I mean, I don't want… I just…"

A doctor wearing a frown approached. Róisín quickly fell back, exhaustion clear on her expression. She closed her eyes again, but whether she actually fell asleep or faked it, Max couldn't tell.

The doctor tapped him on the shoulder and spoke in a whisper. "Be gentle. She needs all the sleep she can get. The cough takes so much strength, the more she can avoid it, the better."

Max turned to the doctor with rage, confusion, and despair warring in his mind. "What can we do to help? What're...what're her chances?"

The other man's eyebrows rose. "And you are?"

"I'm Max Hurley. She's my friend."

"Well, *friend* Hurley, even in the middle of a war, we only discuss patient care and condition with relatives. However, I can show you to the waiting room."

Max pulled away from the man's offered hand. "No, I don't bloody want to bloody wait for anything! I need to know what's going on, and I need to know how to help!"

The doctor hissed, "Mr. Hurley, keep your voice down. We have patients trying very hard to rest and heal. If you must argue, let's go into the hall."

Max resisted as the doctor pulled his arm. He glanced down at Róisín, her eyes shifting beneath her lids as if in a dream. She groaned but didn't open them despite him silently begging her to.

Reluctantly, he let himself be led to the hallway. The doctor crossed his arms. "Now, Mr. Hurley, what do you need to know?"

"What's wrong with her?"

"You mean what illness does she have? We aren't certain. We're doing everything we can to treat her with palliative measures. Do you understand what those are?"

Max stared through a small, foggy window in the door, keeping Róisín in sight. She moved but didn't wake. He waved his hand dismissively. "Yeah, yeah, treating the symptoms. I get that. But what're you doing to find the cause?"

"Our testing facilities here are limited without electricity. It's a severe respiratory ailment. We understand how to treat that."

The Australian man glanced at the doctor. "And how successful has that been, so far? People have died, right?"

The doctor clenched his jaw. "That's true enough. However, other factors have contributed to the mortality rate. Injuries from the bombing. Broken bones, severe burns. It's difficult to determine the cause of death with our current equipment limitations. She has none of those, so her chances are stronger."

Max spun, his face two inches from the doctor's. "I don't give a flying fuck about your equipment limitations! My friend is in there, perhaps dying, and you can't figure out why?"

The doctor pressed his lips tight. "Calm yourself, Mr. Hurley. Do you really think we're not doing all we can to help one of our own healers?"

Not knowing how to answer, he turned back to stare through the foggy window. The mention of burns dredged up a memory. "Burns. Is Qacha here? She was at the bombing site. She bloody saved the city from the fire. How is she? I need to see her."

Chewing on his lower lip, the doctor refused to meet his gaze. "Qacha *was* here, yes. And as far as I know, she's still alive."

Max turned back to the doctor. "'As far as you know?' What the hell does that mean?"

The doctor gave a shrug. "She disappeared one morning. She took supplies, so she might have headed into the countryside. No one's been able to find her."

Max slapped the wall hard in frustration, making his palm sting. "What the fuck kind of hospital is this? You can't heal the healers, and you lose your patients in the middle of the night?"

The other man put his hands on his hips. "This kind of hospital is a makeshift one. We're trying to extract a center of healing from the rubble of a bombed-out city, Mr. Hurley. We've had challenges. We will overcome them. And your interference is making that task more difficult. If I've answered all your questions, I have patients who need me."

As the doctor strode toward the door, Max inserted himself in his path until their chests almost bumped. "That's *not* all of my questions. What can I do to help Róisín?"

The doctor took a step back. His face clouded red with anger, and he threw up his hands. "Do? You? Nothing! You can do exactly nothing, Mr. Hurley, except leave her in peace to heal. Unless you can heal whatever virus she's contracted, you have no medical training, no empathy, and obviously no patience. With your attitude, I wouldn't even trust you to empty the bedpans. Now, get out of my way!"

Max stood his ground, wishing he could call on the wind to help him, but that wouldn't work indoors. The doctor growled and shoved him back into the door. Rather than stopping his movement, the door flung inwards, and Max skidded along the tiles on his butt.

"Oi! What the fuck?"

The doctor marched past him, ignoring his outcry.

Scrambling to his feet, Max rushed the doctor, rage filling his mind. The doctor turned at the last minute and shoved hard to his chest. Max staggered back and clenched his fists.

The doctor pointed to the door. "Mr. Hurley, leave. Now. You're no longer welcome at this hospital. If you won't leave on your own, I'll have you removed."

Two burly men dressed in scrubs stepped up behind the doctor, their expressions grim. Max glanced between them and found no sympathy in their eyes. For a moment, Max imagined how much sympathy they might find if he threw a bloody hurricane in their smarmy faces.

He held up both his hands and took a few steps backward. "Fine, fine, I'll bloody leave."

This wasn't the first time he'd been kicked out of a place, and it wouldn't be the last. He gave Róisín's prone form one last, lingering glance before stalking out the door.

Once Max got outside, he clenched his fists and flung his head back, letting out a primal howl of frustration. He sounded feral, like a wild animal let loose on the countryside, but he didn't care.

The countryside. He was no use in civilization, not right now. Why should he stay here? He could go anywhere he bloody wanted. Maybe he'd find Qacha and enjoy a drink with her.

Max marched toward where the plane had been dropped by the wind, but then pulled up short. What did he need the plane for? If the winds could carry that bloody heavy thing on their own, why couldn't they just carry him?

"Oi, are you there?"

We are here.

Why wouldn't they be there? Max never knew if he talked to the wind, the air, or some sort of elemental spirit. He supposed it didn't really matter, so long as they listened to him. "D'ye remember back when I was standing on the lighthouse and you lifted me up to dance?"

What is a lighthouse?

Bloody *hell*, he hated when they did that. "That tall, round building on the water, out that way!"

We remember. You did not wish to dance.

"Right. Well, now I do. Can you lift me? Gently, mind, not too high?"

They swirled around him. Gulping, Max glanced at the ground. He'd already risen five meters. "Oi! Slower, slower. I don't want to be so high that I'll hurt myself if I fall."

What is hurt?

"This body of mine, this solid thing? It's fragile, mate. If it hits the ground, it can break or leak, like those blokes in the building back there. That would be painful."

What is painful?

Max rolled his eyes. He couldn't deal with philosophical arguments just now. "Painful is bad. I'll explain later. Look, can you move me out of the city? Someplace in the country, where I can be alone?"

What is the country?

With a long-suffering growl, Max pointed west. "That way. Can you move me that way? I just need to get away from this bloody place."

As the wind rushed him westward, Max stared over his shoulder at the dwindling building where Róisín slept. He couldn't do anything for her, and that frustrated the hell out of him. His normal reaction to frustration was a bottle, but he had no bottles.

The wind grew icy as it dragged Max through the air, faster and faster. The ground below, ruined from the blasted city, blurred in the morning light. "Oi! Slow down, mates. I'm not in that much of a hurry!"

His progress eased just as suburbs faded into farmland. Isolated farms and silos flashed by, punctuated by rocky outcroppings.

Up and down over the rising hills the wind pulled him until his stomach roiled in protest. "Mates! Can you pull me along the road? This up and down isn't good for me."

We enjoy dancing along the hills.

"Right, well, I don't. Not just now. Maybe later, aye? For now, let's follow the road."

Very well.

The landscape glowed orange as the sun peeked out from behind the eastern cloud cover. Like some post-apocalyptic movie scene, complete with dramatic lighting and rugged coastline. Of course, it wouldn't surprise him in the least if some ocean monster rose from the sea, intent on the destruction of civilization. An Irish Godzilla.

Water monsters made him think of Anna. Where was the American girl now? Last he'd heard, she'd gone north on assignment with Brendan. At least the bloke would take care of her. She needed caring for. Too sweet and innocent for this harsh world.

Komie, on the other hand, though she had a sweet soul, had experience with the world. That one would survive on her own. She was made of strong stuff. Hiroki and Bintou should be safe in those Dublin bunkers, working on their magic words.

Which brought his thoughts back to Qacha. Where had she gone? With a twinge in his stunted sense of guilt, he realized he hadn't learned more about her state of healing. She'd been hurt badly in that final battle. Burned inside and out trying to control the fire from the blast, and certainly traumatized by the event.

Max knew about trauma. He'd dealt with his own over the years. Or not dealt with it, more to the point. He slapped a hand to his forehead. He hadn't gotten *any* supplies for this jaunt. Going off to live in the countryside? He had no food, no clothing, no water, and most importantly, no drink. He didn't immediately crave a shot, but he would eventually.

"Oi! Mates! I forgot something. I need to go back."

Without a word, his body reversed hard, knocking the breath out of his lungs. He still faced west, so he couldn't see where he was going. This kicked his stomach into high nausea, and he struggled to turn. It felt like swimming in treacle, but he finally wrestled his position so he could face east.

The rising sun burned his eyes through the morning mist.

Once he'd looted some blasted stores, including several pubs, Max told the winds to carry him west again. He fought off the déjà vu and the feeling he was making a huge mistake.

With a snort, Max shook his head. If he ever refused to do something just because he thought it'd be a mistake, he'd never do anything. He'd just do what he wanted because nothing else mattered. And right now, he wanted to be on his own. Someplace he could howl with rage and frustration whenever he wanted. Someplace alone.

Rocky crags rose as the wind carried him, cave entrances peeking out like hungry mouths. Would any be livable?

He shouted as something smacked him in the face in a flurry of feathers. He batted it away and rubbed his forehead. "Bloody bird!"

Someone below glanced up, pointing to him. Max considered waving, but it was just a farmer. The bloke'll probably convince himself he'd imagined it. Still, he should head away from the road now that the sun had fully risen so fewer people would see him.

After a few suggestions to the wind, he climbed up and over the nearest stone hill. A farmhouse appeared just behind the outcropping, a lone figure outside. They stood, a bucket in their hand, their mouth open. They yelled something, their hand waving frantically at him. The sound reached his ears as a faint echo.

"Max!"

He recognized that voice. *Bloody hell.*

"Take me down! Take me to that woman!"

The ground rushed toward him.

Qacha:

Qacha woke, her throat parched and raw. She stumbled from under her coat in a defensive crouch, unsure of her surroundings. The dirt floor felt cool against her bare feet, despite her skin burning.

She coughed and her meager energy slipped to nothing as she untangled herself from the blankets. Then she grabbed the old bucket she'd found in the cottage and shuffled outside to the well, looking at her arms in the light. The red lines along the veins on her arms must be a permanent feature. She didn't mind, as the pattern looked rather striking.

Just as she drew the full bucket up, something caught her eye in the air. A bird? No, a human flying in the sky! Qacha knew only one person who might ride the winds.

She dropped the bucket, water splashing across her feet. Jumping up and down and waving her hands, she yelled through her raw throat, "Max!"

He must have heard her, as the figure changed direction and headed straight for her. He stomped his foot in the air, as if applying the brake on a car, but it did no good. His foot touched the earth, pitching him forward into an uncontrolled roll, tumbling along the grass until the cottage wall stopped him.

She pulled him to his feet, and they stared at each other for a moment before sharing a fierce embrace. Then she broke contact and glared at him. "Where have you been? You're a mess."

The Australian man raised his eyebrows. "You're one to talk, love. You look like you left a rummage sale with all your worldly goods on your back."

She wrinkled her nose and rewarded him with a rare grin. Despite his rudeness, she enjoyed Max's company. At least, more than anyone else's, which was a very low bar. "Come. I have food."

"Let me refill your bucket first."

As they entered the cottage, Max looked around. "Well, it's cozy enough. Bet the wind's cold during a storm. I'd think you, of all people, would have a fire going, though."

Qacha nodded. "I have found little fuel for a fire. My body stays warm without it. I've worked on filling the gaps in the thatch, but there's still much work to be done."

"Why'd you come out here, then?"

She clenched her jaw, anger jumbling her mind. "They kept me in restraints in the hospital. I will not be restrained. And I didn't wish others to hear me scream in my sleep."

His gaze slid away from hers to lessen the impact of the confession. "Aye, well enough. I found Róisín in the hospital but didn't see you. I'm glad you're out here, and not...well..." He swallowed, suddenly uncomfortable.

"I am not dead. Nor am I badly injured any longer. I heal more quickly than they can credit. I am here now, and I will remain here." Walking to a wooden shelf, she drew down a tin of sardines, handing it to him. She grabbed one for herself, as well as a sleeve of crackers to share.

He pulled out a bottle of rum and offered it to her, one eyebrow raised. She flashed another smile and took a swig before handing it back. "Thank you."

"So, what's the plan, mate? Just stay out here for the rest of your days?"

"I will remain here until I have completed healing. Then I will retrieve Manol and my grandfather's bow from the Byrne farm. From that point, I have not yet planned."

He slipped a sardine on a cracker and popped it into his mouth, chasing the treat with rum. "Then you're not interested in serving our esteemed PHAE masters anymore?"

She shook her head. "I am not. They are too controlling for my taste. What are your plans?"

"I'm still not sure. Haven't really thought that far ahead. But I definitely need to be on my own a bit, aye? Well, as on my own as I am now." The image of Róisín thrashing around in a nightmare on her hospital bed made him press his lips into a thin line. Max had to admit, even to himself, that the doctors would care for her better than he could, even if he hated the idea of leaving her to their tender mercies.

They finished their meal in silence, except for the howling wind outside.

Just as Qacha placed the empty tins in her midden pile out back, she heard a female voice. Her hands itched to hold her bow, which might be a visual deterrent to any curious neighbors. Qacha re-entered through the back door and peered through a front window.

Max had already positioned himself at the other. "How many do you see?"

"I count five. I recognize none of them."

He glanced toward her as more appeared over the hill. "Me, neither. Neighbors?"

"I do not think so. They do not walk like farmers."

By the time the group reached the top of the hill, ten people radiated out in a single line. Each wore a grim expression and fatigues, and each carried a Kalashnikov. Together, the two Unhidden walked out the front door. Qacha stood with her feet planted apart and her arms by her side, her skin tingling with unspent fire. She'd never used her power on a human before, but everything had a first time.

Max stood next to her, also in a power stance. They didn't even need to exchange glances. "Oi. What do you want?"

The center man took a single step forward, his chin raised. "Are you Maximilian Hurley?"

"Who wants to bloody know?"

Instead of answering, he turned to one of his companions and nodded. "That's him, all right. Move in."

Qacha clenched her jaw so tight it ached. She raised her hands as if shooting a bow. Back before the bomb in Galway, she'd destroyed spy drones by directing her fire energy like a shot arrow. If she must do the same to protect them, she would.

Max held up his hands. "No need for all that, mate. What do you want?"

"We've been sent to find you."

"And if I'm not interested in being found?"

"We have our instructions. And if that is Qacha Duar, we have instructions to fetch her as well."

The intruders took a step forward in unison. Qacha's heartbeat raced, but she held her ground. So did Max.

Her Australian companion let out a howl of laughter. "You and whose army?"

The breeze picked up, swirling around the spokesman. It spun so fast, his top button unsnapped, flapping in the wind. He stumbled and windmilled up into the air, his arms flailing as he lost balance. The man next to him grabbed his leg and they both rose in the air.

The entire line rushed forward with a shout. Qacha took aim at her closest attacker. She pulled deep inside for the spark of fire constantly burning within her blood. As she let go of her visualized arrow, she aimed for his knee. Her target's clothing burst into flame. The heat burned through the fabric, and he jumped back, frantically patted his leg.

Qacha let a slow smile creep across her face. Her flames weren't so easily quenched. She aimed at the next person and dealt them a similar shot. Then the next.

She counted four of the intruders floating in the air like a line of paper dolls. Three rolled on the ground, trying to smother their flaming clothing. The remaining three glanced back and forth, assessing their chances.

Just as they looked ready to flee, a sound behind her made her spin. Three more attackers rushed toward her from behind the cottage. More ran toward Max from the other side. She turned to blast them, but only a few sparks hit the front man. Her power needed time to recharge.

Qacha only had enough time to register Max's attackers flying into the air before someone tackled her. She gasped as all the wind rushed from her lungs. She jabbed her fingers in his eyes, but he held on even as he screamed.

She brought her elbow sharply into his ear. Qacha kicked at his groin, but he twisted. When she knocked his forehead into hers, he grunted but held tight. By this time, two more had reached them, piling on like an American football game.

Knowing hair burnt easily, she concentrated hard on the man with arms in a lock around her waist. He screamed but, to his credit, kept a tight grip. She hit the other two, but they concentrated on putting out the first man's hair. Now, she must wait to recharge again. If only she had an external source, like a hearth fire, to draw from. But she'd found no fuel to burn on this lonely, rocky shore. Frustration ripped through her, morphing into a rage which trampled any bits of rational thought, destroying her sanity like a rampaging wildfire.

Somewhere in the periphery of her vision, Max flew into the sky. He disappeared into a dot on the horizon.

As the remaining invaders wrestled her to the ground, Qacha screamed. Her voice cracked across the raw tissues of her ravaged throat, but she couldn't stop screaming. Her screech echoed across the lonely green hills.

Róisín:

A week later, when Róisín finally emerged from her fever dreams, she felt like someone had stomped on her body. Every single muscle ached from her illness. It took a week of physical therapy before she could even walk a block without collapsing from exhaustion. However, with grim determination, she pushed herself further each day.

When Dr. O'Shea signed off on her recovery, he glared at her. "Mind you, no work for you yet. You're to stay off your feet for at least two more weeks. We've finally gotten more medical personnel in from the county, so we don't need you." He flushed with the phrasing. "I mean, sure, you're needed. And you're always welcome in my ward, no question. But you need to take care of yourself, and we're finally in a position where we can insist. Do you understand?"

Glancing down at her hands, still clasped on her lap, she nodded. "Aye, that's fair play, Doctor. I had an idea on how to help without a lot of physical effort. I wanted to help trace the progression of the disease, if that's sufficiently sedate for you? There's a clinic in Athlone doing research." She arched an eyebrow.

He gave her a half-smile, signed her discharge paperwork, and clapped her on the shoulder. "That'll do, Róisín. I mean it about coming back when you've recovered. We can use a nurse with high empathy and your talent."

She glanced up and got caught in his ice-blue eyes. "Thank you. I'll think about it. I'm not sure yet if I'll fall back into veterinary work or not. Animals have one advantage over human patients. They don't talk back." She gave him a wry smile.

He chuckled and rose, handing her the paperwork. "Regardless, check in after a week. I'd like to check on your progress."

When he left, Róisín made no move to get up. She held her discharge papers like a life-vest, clutched close to her chest. She'd made it out of the hospital alive. For a long time, she didn't think that would happen. Her brief moments of lucidity were interrupted by the torment of terrifying nightmares, night sweats, and intense pain. But she'd made it, instilled with a determination to help others before this illness did the same to them.

When she was a child, she'd always been fascinated by mysteries. From Nancy Drew to Sister Fidelma to Sherlock Holmes, little Róisín had devoured every clue. Now, she might be able to funnel that passion into identifying the disease, where it came from, and how it was spreading.

Doctor O'Shea had given her the latest news from the epidemiological department in the Health Research Board, but their findings were tentative, at best. She needed to be in the middle of it to see all the clues spread out before her.

But first, the hard part, telling her parents she wasn't coming straight home. She may be an adult, but her parents still held tight upon all their children's lives.

When she called her mother, Róisín began with asking about the farm and the family. However, just before she asked about her father, her mother asked, "When can I expect you home?"

Róisín hesitated, but then blurted out. "I'm not coming home, Mam. I've taken a position at the Health Research Board."

Then she held her breath as silence greeted her. At first, Róisín thought the mobile had dropped the call. "Mam? Are you still there?"

"I'm here. Róisín, we need you home."

"What for, Mam? You don't have a new group of students, do you?"

Her mother let out a snort. "No, of course not. In this chaos? No, we need you here, for us. We're worried sick."

Róisín rolled her eyes. "Mam, if I came home, what would I do? Cook and clean? Help you weed the garden? I can do work, real work, important work, out here. Brendan's out doing things with Anna. Are you calling him home, too? Or just your daughter?"

Her mother's voice grew even chillier, if that was possible. "Brendan isn't part of this discussion, young lady."

"That's what I thought. Mam, I need to do this."

"I don't like it."

Róisín's heart pounded. Taking another deep breath, she kept her tone firm. "Mam, forgive me, but I'm not asking your permission. I'm letting you know my plans."

A long pause came before her answer. "I see."

Even at twenty-seven years old, she'd always be a child in her mother's eyes. She must be strong and determined if she ever wanted to live her own life. "I'll call you when I get to St. Vincent's, Mam. Give my love to Da."

When she put down the phone, Róisín let out a long, deep breath, squared her shoulders, and strode out of the hospital.

The trip was rough, in the back of a farmer's truck. Regular train and bus service remained spotty at best. Róisín clutched tight to her overnight bag, filled with donated clothing and a few basic toiletries. She questioned her decision a dozen times during the journey, but when she arrived at the Athlone research facility, her heart soared.

Róisín had trained as a veterinarian, and she truly loved healing both people and animals. But research had always fascinated her. She looked forward to getting back into the thrill of solving a puzzle. And if she could solve this puzzle, her work would help all Ireland, not just the few people she might heal with her talent.

Doctor O'Shea had called ahead, so the team enfolded her as a long-lost colleague. They set her immediately to several tasks. Sure, they gave her the mind-numbing, tedious tasks none of them wanted to do. That's the way being new on a team worked. But the simple tasks left her mind free to study the entire problem.

Each day, she absorbed all the data and analytics performed so far, comparing lists, correspondences, symptoms, and flowcharts.

Each evening, she trudged to the dormitories happily exhausted, still not at full strength.

Each night, she dreamt about what she read, what she discovered, and what she might yet find. She rode through a sea of possibilities, with an amorphous, shining guide showing her the hidden places under massive leaves or improbable stones.

Each morning, she woke up with a new idea about the disease source, symptoms, or vectors. So far, none of them proved true. But she kept reminding herself that this was how science worked, to try every idea until one works. So, she kept trying.

By the time she'd been there three days, they'd created a chart, tracing the known cases across each county and the country. As she munched a sandwich, Róisín studied the chart, frowning when she noticed some odd clear spaces, including one in the middle of the island.

She glanced back at the team second. "Blá? What's going on in this spot?"

Bláithín didn't look up from her paperwork. "What spot?"

"This area west of Mullingar. They don't have any cases at all?"

Pushing her red bangs out of her eyes, the other woman squinted at the map and shrugged. "As far as we know, they have none. But that presumes people are reporting data. Likely, there's just no one calling in."

Róisín examined the map with new eyes, finding bald spots near Armagh and south of Navan. Something about those places tugged at her memory, but she couldn't pull up the connection. Taking another bite of her sandwich, she took a few steps back, looking at the map as a whole. She shut one eye and covered each spot with her hand in turn, trying to remember why they seemed so familiar.

More bare spots showed near Kildare, east of Tipperary, and near Castlerea in the west. Tracing the path with her finger, she sketched out an oblong circle, with the Mullingar spot roughly in the center. The shape triggered a memory.

Her father's voice spoke of the ancient tales, his words echoing in her ears. "Long ago, our ancestors held certain places to be sacred. They'd hold fire festivals to honor the gods. These sites are still rumored to be full of magic, the ancient royal seats of each traditional province. *Emain Macha* for Ulster, *Dún Ailinne* for Leinster, *Rathcroghan* for Connaught, Tara in Meath, and *Uisneach* in Westmeath, the central hub."

She gasped and took several steps back, knocking into Bláithín's desk. "Hey! Watch where you're going!"

"Blá, there's something going there. This can't be coincidence. I need to call my da."

Róisín tapped her fingernails anxiously as the phone rang twice, three times, four times. Finally, on the fifth ring, it clicked.

Her mother's voice whispered, "Hello?"

"Mam? It's Róisín. How are you?"

Her mother didn't respond right away. "I'm well enough."

The awkwardness slammed Róisín in the chest. It was very much unlike her mother not to ask after her own health. "I'm well, too, Mam."

"That's good to hear." Her tone remained flat, with clipped words. This wasn't going to be an easy conversation.

"Is Da around? I have a question for him."

Another pause. "He can't come to the phone."

Róisín let out a deep sigh. "Mam. You're mad at me, aren't you?"

"Not mad, Róisín. Disappointed, yes. But not mad."

Bláithín walked in with a cup of tea, raising her eyebrows. Róisín shook her head and pressed her fingers to her temple. Her head ached so easily. "I'm sorry I've disappointed you, Mam, but we're making real progress here. Can you ask Da to call me back?" Again, that strange hesitation, then a sound in the background. A growl? "Mam? What was that?"

Her mother let out a sigh. "That's your Da. He's fallen to your illness. If you were here, you'd know that. If you were here, you might heal him."

Róisín's heart jumped into her throat. She almost dropped the phone. "Da's ill? Feck! Why didn't you say so?"

"Language!"

"Sorry, Mam. I'll be there as soon as I can. How bad is he?"

"Bad enough. I've got to take him his tray. Be quick, Róisín."

She ended the call and blinked at Bláithín. The older woman nodded with an understanding half-smile. "I heard. Go, do what you need to do. Sure, and family comes first. I'll take care of things here, aye?"

A lab tech offered to give her a ride. The whole ninety-minute trip to Limerick, horrid scenarios flicked through Róisín's mind. Her father, lying in his deathbed, unable to say he loved her. The twins and Fiona falling ill next. A row of new gravestones in their beautiful garden. She could barely breathe as the car sped along the motorway.

As her ride approached the farmhouse, her anxiety kicked into high gear. What if she was too late? What if he'd already died? She'd never forgive herself for putting her own desires above her father's health. What was she even thinking? Why didn't her mother tell her right away?

Róisín tumbled out of the car, barely giving a wave to the lab tech. She'd have to send him a thank you card later. Barreling through the front door, she searched wildly for someone, anyone to assure her she arrived in time.

Fiona popped her head in from the kitchen, her eyes lit with delight. "Róisín? I thought you were in Athlone?"

She dropped her purse and overnight bag in the hallway. "Where's Da?"

Her little sister's smile melted. "In his room. Mam's there, too."

Pelting up the stairs, two at a time, she rushed into her parents' room. Her mother sat on a chair beside the bed, a wet washcloth in her hand. When she looked up, the worry lines were clear on her face.

Her father's skin had turned pale, almost matching the cream-colored sheets. Panting, she put a hand to her chest. "Da?"

Her mother's mouth hardened into a thin line. "He's unchanged."

Róisín knelt on the other side of him and took his hand, clammy and limp. He moaned, sweat glistening on his face.

With all the power she possessed, Róisín dug deep into the earth, pulling the healing energy up through her body. She didn't bother with the subtleties like pacing herself or trickling her power. She let loose like a firehose, shooting the energy out of her hands and into his body, willing it to fix everything.

An eternal voice behind her eyes answered her question. What question? She never asked, she just took. She had no time to deal with mysteries. She must heal her father.

As the power flowed through her, everything buzzed. Like a million bees flying under her skin. When Róisín finally ran out of power, she collapsed over her father's chest, his hand still in hers. When she raised her head, utterly exhausted, he still hadn't woken.

Her mother wiped his brow with a cool cloth. "What did you do?"

"Everything I could. Was it enough?"

Staring at her father's closed eyes, her mother shook her head. "I don't know."

Róisín pushed herself to her feet, gripping the bedpost to keep her balance. "I'll try again after a nap. Over and over until it works." The world swirled and turned gray as she collapsed.

Chapter Five

"Worry is itself an illness, since worry is an accusation against Divine Wisdom,
a criticism of Divine Mercy."
– Said Nursi

Bintou:

Hiroki hadn't wanted to go on with the lectures without Bintou. He wrung his hands when she mentioned staying behind. "You give me much more confidence just by being there than anyone else does."

Bintou squeezed his shoulder. "You've been brilliant, Hiroki. You'll do fine without me, and besides, Masaaki will be with you. How many times have you given this speech now? You can practically do it in your sleep."

He glanced down at his hands. "I feel strong while I speak, but afterwards, all my insecurities rush back."

"Can you keep hold of your power when you're done? Like a maintenance level. Think of someone singing a song at the top of their lungs for a concert, but then humming slightly afterward."

He glanced up at her, a puzzled expression on his face. Then he gave a half-smile. "That sounds like a good idea. Very well, I shall try that. Thank you."

"Just don't try too much at once. Are they giving you enough time to rest between speeches?"

Hiroki gave a shrug. "Since we arrive and rest a day after each travel, and then give the speech, I feel rested. And each county seat is only a few hours away. Ireland is small, like Japan. Traveling from County Town to County Town is quick. I just wish we had time to visit places."

"Visit?"

He looked down at his toes. "Ever since I was a child, I dreamed of traveling. Now, I'm traveling, but I see nothing. I don't get to enjoy the traveling."

She coughed into her elbow and nodded. "I don't imagine your childhood dreams had this situation in mind. There will be time for visiting the sites someday, Hiroki, a chance to enjoy the beauty of this country. Just make sure they continue to keep your strength in mind. Maybe we'll join you before you're done."

They embraced before Hiroki, Masaaki, Ciara, and the rest of the troupe departed, leaving Martin and Bintou alone in Letterkenny. As she watched them leave, a part of her felt bereft of their companionship.

Bintou had never been a solitary person. While she found joy in perusing the dustiest of ancient manuscripts, she also found joy in being with friends, of shopping, of exploring, and of learning. Since she arrived in Ireland, those joys had been few and far between.

But the events of the last months had necessitated drastic actions, and she felt proud to have been an integral part of their team. To split the team felt wrong, despite her own insistence on its wisdom.

A week later, Bintou sprang up, a racking cough gripping her entire body. Martin rubbed her back as she spasmed in miserable pain. Days and nights slid together as she grasped what rest her body allowed.

When the cough finally eased, he urged more hot tea. "I added honey and lemon since you won't take whiskey. Are you sure that wouldn't be considered a medicinal use? Sure, you aren't drinking to get drunk. It's strictly to help you rest."

She shook her head, unwilling to talk and set off another coughing fit. Sipping the warm liquid, she closed her eyes as it trickled down, honey coating and soothing ravaged tissues.

Martin stood, his hands on his hips. "I'll be back with more soup, my dear. You stay sitting up." He cleared his throat as he left the room, gently shutting the door.

She fluffed up her pillows. The seven pillows he'd brought formed a great ramp for her torso to remain upright. Bintou had never been good about sleeping on her back. She much preferred lying on her side, curled in fetal position. However, whenever she got sick, she had to sleep sitting up. This meant light, fitful sleep, even without the added complication of a raw throat.

Luckily, her cough had grown productive, a sure sign of recovery. Martin agreed, though, when he coughed, she insisted he take just as much doctored tea as she drank. He had no qualms about adding generous dollops of whiskey.

When her illness abated, she resolved to walk to regain her strength. Her body felt like rubber. She'd lost weight. Martin assured her she still looked beautiful, but she knew he'd preferred her curvy.

Martin returned with a tray. The two bowls of steaming pureed soup, soda crackers, and a bright yellow flower in a slender vase made her smile.

He gave her a stern look. "I thought I told you to lie back and get some rest?"

"You did, but I can't eat soup lying back, now, can I?" She couldn't resist a wide grin as he sat next to her.

"Fair play. Here, let me get your lap tray set up."

As he fussed over her, Bintou studied him with a faint smile on her face. His skin was lighter than her own, though his ancestry came from Jamaica while she was from Mali. His family had immigrated a few generations back, and his accent sounded as Irish as Ciara's. Still, his features comforted her, despite being so many generations removed from Africa. He would look at home in Angola or Tunisia, with those features and medium-dark skin.

As he lifted her spoon, she raised her eyebrows. "You needn't feed me, Martin. I can do that myself."

Abashed, he handed it to her. "Fair enough. Make sure to eat the entire bowl." He turned and coughed into his elbow. The cough sounded as harsh as hers had.

Bintou gave Martin a wry smile. "Perhaps you ought to lay down instead."

Latest CNN Update: "Reports are coming in of seemingly isolated incidents of arson at businesses known to be owned by Unhidden in several cities across American. There is a strong concentration of these incidents near Houston, Texas, the new home of the PEM, Pure Earther Movement. While we weren't able to gain press access inside their headquarters, we did get an interview with their spokesperson, Tiberius Wilkinson. We join George Tallin in Houston now."

"Thank you, Nadine. Mr. Wilkinson, thank you again for agreeing to speak with us today."

"Absolutely my pleasure, Mr. Tallin. I'm happy to speak with the press any time."

"And we appreciate that. Can you tell us some more about the rising violence in Houston?"

Wilkinson let out a hearty laugh. "Violence in Houston? Son, I love my home city dearly, but it's always been wilder than a peach orchard boar here, know what I mean?"

The reporter blinked before answering. "I suppose I do. And what sort of involvement does the PEM have in these cases?"

"None at all, son! None at all. But I'll tell you, if these damned Unhidden don't hightail their way out of my city, they'll only have themselves to blame if things get hotter'n Hell. You get my drift?"

Joel:

As his captors drove through the countryside, Joel stared out of the window, not seeing the green hills rolling past.

Joel hadn't had a great day. Disastrous would be closer to the truth. At the same time, he'd succeeded in his assigned task, and that, at least, made him feel proud. He still resented that Anna's power had shown up first, despite him being the eldest. This made up a little bit for that slight.

And God *damn* Anna for ratting him out. She was his sister, for God's sake. He never could hide his feelings from her, no matter how hard he'd tried. That fact added to his bitterness toward her over the years. His best weapon had always been to make her angry, so he could read her just as easily. His beloved sister became an open book when she got pissed.

Joel still couldn't understand why she loved this mad cult. They seemed so sappy, so saccharin. He couldn't stand them. Well, he'd completed his assignment and maybe they'd stagger for a while. And while he hadn't expected a ticker-tape parade from the PEM, he should at least get some recognition. If he ever escaped PHAE and returned to reap his rewards.

Staring at the back of his driver's head, Joel tried to conjure up some fire power, but his talent was with water. Maybe he could make the guy sweat so much, he pulled off the road. He tested the zip ties around his wrists again, but they just cut into his skin. Water didn't do much against plastic and even if he did make the driver crash, he'd be tied. And where would he go?

You'd think, for Ireland, a guy with water power would be spoiled for material. He stared out at the depressingly dry day. He couldn't even make the road slick. It made him want to scream in frustration. Maybe that would startle the driver out of concentration. The realization that Joel might also get hurt if they crashed kept him from trying.

His driver glanced in the rear-view mirror. "You need a pee, mate?"

"I'm not your mate."

With a shrug, the driver said, "Suit yourself."

Joel did, in fact, need to use the bathroom. However, he'd wet himself before he gave this guy the satisfaction. He tested the zip-ties for the thirtieth time since they left Galway.

The drive should be about two hours, but traffic on the highway looked bad. People fled Galway in droves, thanks to his own actions. That made him smile. He'd actually *done* it. The guys back in New York hadn't thought him up to the job, but he'd *done* it. He'd proved himself, despite their doubts.

Now they'd *have* to give him a command. Not a large one, of course, just a few specialists. A small task force for important missions. The theme tune for *Mission Impossible* started running through his mind.

If he managed to escape these idiots.

Joel's jaw ached from gritting his teeth. He stared out the window again.

His briefing had told him about the bunker in Dublin. If they took him there, his chances of escaping would dwindle to nothing. He had to make a break before that. He only had the driver to deal with. Joel didn't even know the guy's name. Some PHAE pawn, corralled into transporting an unexpected Prisoner of War.

Prisoner of War. That sounded significant. Noble. Honorable. Someone written about in history books. What would Anna get? A footnote on the PHAE Wiki, at most. Joel straightened his back and held his head high. No matter what met him in Dublin, he'd hold strong. His legacy depended on it.

As they drove into the city, he noted the route, in case he needed to run through the streets. The driver pulled behind a nondescript warehouse near the marina. Even better. If he came near the water, he'd use his talent to hide, escape, or fight.

In fact, he might get his chance as soon as he got out of the car.

They pulled in front of a mirrored glass double door, and seven people emerged. Joel cursed. No matter. The water was only a few feet away.

He reached out to the inlet, pulling on the water itself, urging it to rise in a powerful wave and shove his would-be captors over. Then Joel would run to the pier and jump in. The water ignored him. Not even a blip.

Joel scowled and tried a second time, pushing harder. Still, nothing happened.

A female voice behind him curled in his ears. "Don't bother a third time, Joel. It won't work."

He turned to see the tall Irishwoman, Ciara, with her arms crossed. "What are you talking about?"

"I can feel you trying. It's adorable. But I never told you my own talent, Joel. I can block other people's Unhidden talents."

With a heartfelt growl, he spat out one word. "Fuck."

"Precisely. Now, it seems as if you will be our guest in Dublin."

He set his jaw, his eyes flicking again to the water. "Not a willing one."

"That's as may be. I'm in charge of your accommodation. We don't want you in the bunker. However, we do have another option. Normally, we'd send you to Portlaoise, to maximum security. In light of recent events, we need you in Dublin. Therefore, you'll be staying in Mountjoy."

Joel suspected Mountjoy wouldn't be a posh hotel.

Ciara nodded to a swarthy, older woman in a smart pantsuit. "Hafsia will accompany us, and once you're settled, will become your best friend. Back in the car, Joel. Don't worry, I'll be with you every step of the way." She gave him a sarcastic grin. Joel tried one more desperate call to the water. The estuary stirred, but no wave of justice rose to rescue him. The only result was his desperate need to pee.

With poor grace, he ducked his head into the back seat. Hafsia entered the other side.

Their destination lay well inland, behind the obligatory high fence, complete with razor wire. Joel's hopes for an easy escape sunk further as they entered the complex, past several layers of security. They led him past a central circle to an underground basement landing.

Down several hallways and past empty classrooms, they brought Joel to a cell about ten feet wide in each direction. It held a bed, a toilet, a sink, and a tiny television.

The corner of Joel's mouth quirked up when he spied the sink, but Ciara let out a short laugh. "I'm afraid they've had some problems with the plumbing in this cell. I'm sure you'll understand. No running water. Also, you have no neighbors. This is part of the Separation Unit and has been unused for several years."

Her smile deepened as this registered on Joel's face. She exited the cell, locked the door, and turned to Hafsia. "He's all yours, love."

The click of Ciara's heels echoed in the empty, metallic halls. Hafsia, her arms crossed again, stared at Joel. He returned the favor. She was a solid woman with strong shoulders and a sour expression. Dark hair, skin hinting at middle eastern origins, and glittering dark eyes that would cut crystal.

He shifted his balance. "Hey, listen, would you turn around? My bladder's about to burst."

She stared at him.

"Uh, do you not speak English? I gotta pee, lady. You know, psssssss?" He made a gesture with his hand as if using his penis as a garden hose, spraying all around him.

When she didn't move, Joel shrugged and turned his back, dropping his pants to take care of business. He tried to flush, but the handle just rattled. At least they provided toilet paper to wipe with, but he couldn't wash his hands. "Can you at least get me some wipes or something?"

She spoke with a strong Middle Eastern accent. "You will not be permitted access to liquid."

He gestured at the toilet bowl. "What the hell do you think I just peed out? Cheese puffs?"

"You will be given dry food. Any liquid will be carefully monitored and removed if not consumed immediately. Do you understand?"

Crap. Joel glanced up at the walls, but his cell had no windows. He couldn't even hope for a rainy day.

That Hafsia woman kept staring at him. Did she want something? She just wanted to unnerve him. Well, she was doing an excellent job. He sat on the thin mattress, staring at his hands.

She still wouldn't leave.

Oh, wait. She'd asked a question. Maybe if he answered, she'd go away. "I understand."

After a moment, the woman gave a single, sharp nod and stalked off. Joel let out a deep sigh. His stomach grumbled. He hadn't eaten since before he set the second bomb. That quick sandwich grabbed on the way out of the lighthouse had been what, yesterday? Time sort of melded together now. He couldn't even tell if there was daylight in the bowels of this place.

Footsteps echoed in the hall. Maybe she brought food. When she came into view, Hafsia held an apple, shiny and red. Joel's stomach growled again.

"You are hungry."

This didn't seem like a question, so he didn't answer.

"If you agree to answer my questions, you can have food."

Double crap. Joel had expected interrogation. His trainer had warned him. They'd laughed when he asked for a cyanide tooth, though. Evidently that was all Hollywood spy crap. Still, they cautioned that if he gave up vital information, and he somehow managed to escape, he wouldn't live long. That was reason enough to keep his trap shut.

They hadn't promised to rescue him if he was caught, but said they'd do their best. That's all he could hope for. Delay, deflect, lie, resist. He'd use that as an internal chant to keep his purpose focused.

He clenched his jaw in defiance as his stomach growled audibly.

"When did the PEM contact you?"

Idly, Joel wondered if he might extract sweat from her skin. Probably not. She didn't look like she did anything so human as sweat. And that wouldn't yield enough water to do anything offensive with, anyway.

"When did the PEM contact you?"

Maybe if he added his own sweat? He might gather some over time. But where would he keep it?

"When did PEM contact you?"

How much water did he need to create a weapon? Maybe a waterpik style jet of water in the eye? That wouldn't do much damage. A minor inconvenience at most. *Delay, deflect, lie, resist.*

"When did the PEM contact you?"

Would she just keep asking until he answered?

"When did the PEM contact you?"

"I don't know! I didn't keep a stupid diary!"

"When did the PEM contact you?"

Joel let out a deep breath. *Delay, deflect, lie, resist.* They probably knew the answer, anyhow. Anna would have told him, the sneak. "Fine. It was, maybe, a day after Anna came by my place."

"How many were there?"

That apple looked juicy and delicious. His stomach rumbled again. *Delay, deflect, lie, resist.*

Joel:

A week later, the apple no longer looked juicy and delicious. It looked…fragmented. It swam in Joel's mind like a jewel, always floating just out of reach. He couldn't focus on the single object now. He discovered that while he might resist saying anything, he was unable to lie to this woman, and even keeping his mouth shut was difficult.

After the second day, Hafsia informed him she had a talent for forcing the truth. And she didn't mean she was a good negotiator. This was her Unhidden talent. What an insidious power for an interrogator. He'd given up far more information than he'd wanted to before she told him. Intending to lie, to redirect, to obfuscate, Joel had instead blurted out the bald truth time and again. Who contacted him, when, how they communicated, how frequently they spoke, and how he obtained the bombs. So much for *delay, deflect, lie, resist.*

Each truth earned him five bites of food and a sip of water.

Finally, after spilling all that information, Joel finally worked out how to keep his mouth shut and say nothing at all. Not even shaking his head or nodding, as that also became the truth despite any plan to lie.

He felt like a wet towel, wrung out and stomped on. Luckily, he'd been unable to give details of how the bombs were made from the simple strategy of not having a clue. His trainer had given him the packages and told him to plant them in two places in the city of Galway. That was the extent of his instructions. He didn't even know how they'd managed to get the bomb ingredients into Ireland. After that, they left him on his own.

Being on his own truly sucked.

Through the course of the questioning, Joel collected every drop of liquid which came his way. His own sweat became his best source, as well as his rare urine. The few sips of water allowed made him dehydrated, and therefore a lean source. Hafsia didn't sweat much. Perhaps her sultry skin meant she'd grown up in a warm climate, and therefore used to the heat. He didn't dare remove any liquid from his grudgingly won sips of water. He needed every drop she gave him.

He might extract liquid from other living things, but so far, he'd only found a fly and a spider in the cell. *Not even a decent rat visitor, damnit.* A rat would yield all sorts of bodily fluid. Saliva, urine, even blood after he killed it. Maybe he should take on the codename Renfield after this.

Blood. Could he extract water from blood? From someone still using the blood?

He'd just about decided to cut himself to experiment when Hafsia's footsteps marched down the hall. It must be time for his morning question session.

Joel lay down on the cot, pretending to be asleep, though he suspected Hafsia saw through that deceit. Regardless, it gave him a small illusion of control, and he needed every scrap he could grasp.

"I have your meal. You will answer my question. What was inside the incendiary devices?"

Playing on an idea he'd had earlier, Joel covered his head and shook like he'd seen Anna do when she got an anxiety attack. If he could convince Hafsia he had some mental issue, he might find a chink in her armor.

"What was inside the incendiary devices?"

Whatever she'd brought him to eat smelled incredible. Bread? Bread always smelled amazing, even when he wasn't surviving on ten bites of food a day. His stomach growled, so he let out a moan to mask the physiological betrayal.

He shivered, his skin suddenly breaking out in goosebumps. Maybe his shaking hands weren't a lie, after all.

Did Hafsia have empathetic or telepathic powers, too? If she read his mind, even his emotions, he'd need to throw up a shield of confusion if he wanted to appear out of control. He remembered reading that people would recite poems or mathematical formulas to keep their mind away from focusing on something. Perhaps that would work for him. *Mary had a little lamb, his fleece as white as snow.*

Joel conjured scenes from his childhood, interspersed with music videos, movies, snippets of songs, and for added spice, images of roiling, boiling mud. Because, why not?

Suddenly, he couldn't keep hold of the mud scene. Joel formed another image, one of a million butterflies bursting from a tree. He'd seen that in a video. Then he made it a million flies, but his mind wouldn't cooperate, and it grew static.

Was she suppressing lies within his brain? Now, Joel shuddered in earnest.

He stuck to things he'd seen or heard. No sense trying to form images if she blocked them. With a violent shake, he dug his fingers into his hair, clutching his scalp. Sure, it was a Hollywood image of madness, but even that must be based on some truth, right?

More footsteps came down the hall. *Hafsia was leaving?* Joel's heart leapt with victory, but the footsteps grew louder. Someone else was coming. This would be the first other person he'd seen all week. Joel's performance almost slipped but he pushed on by running through *Psycho* scenes. He didn't remember the whole film, but he could pull up famous images.

Ciara's sharp tone cut through his invented confusion. "Hafsia, what in the name of Mother Mary are you doing to him?"

After a moment of judgmental silence, Hafsia snapped, "I will explain elsewhere."

Two sets of footsteps faded away, but Joel didn't relax. He didn't trust them. He hadn't found any cameras, but with modern technology, one could easily hide behind the stone wall.

When footsteps returned, so did the incredibly enticing aroma of fresh-baked bread. Joel could taste it, warm and delicious. His mouth watered. He saved the saliva.

Since he had no vessel to store his tiny supply of water, a small part of him must control it at all times. After a few sleeps, he figured out how to maintain the tiny globule under his bed as he slept. Now, it stayed strong throughout the night. Joel still had no idea how he might use it. Maybe he could fashion an icepick to unlock the cell? He remained in the heart of a high-security prison. Not as high as SingSing, but maximum enough to make escape unlikely. Especially as he had no chance to check out the security measures.

Still, the place sat inside a city, so he wouldn't have to cross vast empty fields to reach cover. That was something. If he could ever get out of this cell.

Hafsia's harsh voice cut into his musings, "What was inside the incendiary devices?"

Hiroki:

Despite Hiroki's resolve to stay true to his conscience, five counties and five speeches later, Hiroki realized his resolve melted away bit by bit.

So far, he had lied to approximately four thousand people. To their faces. Each day, his honor slipped farther and farther away. Each day, he died a little inside.

When he'd discussed his worries with Masaaki, he didn't see it as a big issue. "Haven't you read any history? Governments always lie, Hiroki. The only difference is how much they are willing to be seen as liars."

"I am not willing to be seen as a liar."

He closed his eyes with a nod. "I appreciate that, Hiroki. But you're a mouthpiece for the PHAE, a governmental body in all but name. Therefore, you must tell their truths, even if you do not believe in those truths. Can you say, without hesitation, that they will *not* make their repairs as fast as they promise?"

His head hung low, Hiroki sighed. "I cannot say, for I do not know."

"Then you need to do as they ask and continue your lectures."

"What if I am not telling the truth? What if they aren't able to fulfill my promises?"

He placed a hand on his arm. "Then we will all have a lot to worry about, and the people will forget your promises."

They'd both chuckled, though with a tinge of sarcasm in the laugh. "You'll get through this, Hiroki. I have faith in your honor, no matter what. The very fact that you're worried about your honor proves you have it. Don't you see that?"

"That cannot be true. Many people lose their honor despite good intentions. I have seen it in Japan."

"But not you. Bintou would tell you the same, just ask her. You have such a strong sense of honor, it's painful!" He smiled to lighten the mood, but Hiroki felt his comment as a stab in the heart.

Maasaki had glanced toward the door. "Did you hear Ciara on the phone? She was talking with someone at headquarters about your speech."

His spine tingled with apprehension. "What did she say?"

"She praised your delivery, and that your ability grew stronger. It's hard not to believe you, even though we know your talent."

"What else?"

Maasaki shook his head. "Something about someone named Hafsia. She mentioned food and water. Her words grew heated after that, and she lowered her voice. I could hear her, but not make out the words. I thought I heard her mention Joel."

He straightened his spine. "Joel? Anna's brother? She spoke to him?"

"No, no, but she may have talked about him. Do you know where they took him?"

Hiroki clasped his hands together. "Masaaki mentioned a prison in Dublin, but Martin wouldn't verify it. He said that Joel would be kept in isolation until his trial."

Maasaki picked at his lip. "A trial. Food and water. Do you think they're starving him? Trying to make him talk, like in the movies?"

Hiroki:

Hiroki entered the B&B sitting room. Maasaki and Ciara hunched over the coffee table, speaking in low tones, and glanced up with guilty expressions. Ciara cleared her throat and sat back, teacup in hand. Masaaki sat up more slowly with the flicker of a frown.

He hesitated in the doorway. "Have I interrupted something? Would you prefer me to return later?"

Ciara held up her hand. "No, Hiroki. Please, stay. Have some biscuits and tea. What I just told Maasaki, you should know as well."

Hiroki's hands clenched as he sat, taking an offered biscuit just to have something to do other than fidget. He liked the ginger biscuit, but the hard, crumbly treat exploded with crumbs as he bit into it. With a couple of coughs into a hastily grabbed napkin, he cleared his throat.

Maasaki also coughed, perhaps in sympathy, perhaps in an effort to shift attention away from his mess. Either way, he felt gratitude for his friend's effort.

Ciara swallowed and took a deep breath. "Maasaki has a serious concern. I cannot, with all honesty, verify the details. Even if I knew them for certain, my position forbids me to share them. However, I also can't deny the truth of his allegations."

She clasped her hands in her lap and glanced at Maasaki, who sipped his Coke.

Hiroki's friend shrugged. "It seems that I stumbled into the truth, somehow, though Ciara very carefully can't confirm it. Officially."

Hiroki brushed his crumbs from his lap into a napkin, his hands shaking. Had something happened to one of their friends? To someone in the Byrne family? "The truth about what?"

"The truth about Joel."

The lump grew larger, and he poured some tea. As he moved through the ritual of adding sugar and cream, he tried desperately to swallow past the lump, without success. "What is the truth about Joel?"

Maasaki clenched his jaw and glanced at Ciara. "Joel is in prison, and there's a real possibility, even a probability, that his food and water is being withheld. He's being interrogated. That much the PHAE has sanctioned. The methods of his interrogation may be more extreme than legally allowed."

Ciara held up a finger. "More than legally allowed by Ireland. The PHAE have not yet signed the International Covenant on Civil and Political Rights or the Convention Against Torture and Other Cruel, Inhuman, or Degrading Treatment or Punishment. The Republic of Ireland has, but PHAE has not. Yet."

Maasaki nodded. "Just so. Therefore, though technically illegal, Joel may be being tortured to get information on his activities with the PEM and his bombs."

Hiroki took a sip of his tea, now cooled enough that he didn't scald his throat. Grateful for the warmth which soothed and pushed through the lump, he sighed. "Do we know for certain that he planted them? It wasn't a mistake?"

Ciara frowned. "He admitted it to Anna and has said nothing in the meantime to disabuse that notion. While I'm not privy to his actions since being placed in custody, if he had proven his innocence, I would have been told."

If they were torturing Joel, the PHAE approved this action. Hiroki's heart shrank. He glanced up at Maasaki, and he looked just as uncomfortable as he felt. At a loss how to react, he fell back on the formality of his culture. He bowed his head and clasped his hands. "This news brings me sadness."

Maasaki pursed his lips. "It brings both of us sadness, too, Hiroki. Ciara tells me the PHAE wasn't founded on these principles."

Ciara sat up again. "I detest this. It warps our original purpose. Torture should be forbidden on any human, especially an Unhidden, one of our own."

Maasaki turned to Ciara. "What can we do about it?"

Now Ciara smiled with grim determination. "I have some thoughts about that. I have a plan, but I'll need your cooperation."

Hiroki suspected he wouldn't like the plan.

Chapter Six

"He has to be knocked silly before he comes to his senses.
Only torture will bring out the truth. Only under torture does he
discover it himself."
– C. S. Lewis

*Latest **CNN Update:** "We come to you today from the city of Waterford, Ireland. On the ground, our reporter, Tom Ballin, has some disturbing news."*

A tall, blonde man came on the screen, a line of buildings behind him. He spoke in a posh London accent. "This is Tom Ballin, and I'm here in the lovely city of Waterford, an ancient city on the southeast coast of Ireland.

"The last time Waterford was attacked was during the Cromwellian conquest of Ireland in the 17th century, but now they are preparing for another. There have been several attacks on the island, including bombings in Galway and Dublin. Reports are spotty out of those regions, as communication is strictly controlled by a recently organized group known as the PHAE, the Protectorate for unHidden Advancement and Education. This group represents a small percentage of the total population of Ireland, formed of those who show strange powers.

"The aftermath of these attacks has resulted in increased security measures. These measures have caused controversy, and I'm here to ask the local residents their thoughts on the matter."

He stopped a pair of older women, scarves tied on their heads to combat the breeze. "Excuse me, ladies, but would you have a moment to speak about the recent attacks on Ireland?"

One woman shook her head and tried to keep walking, but her companion grabbed her arm. "I do! It's a disgrace, these attacks. We Irish are good, Catholic folks! We don't want these magical jobbos coming here and attracting bombs. Do we, Agatha?"

The other woman shook her head again but said nothing. She stepped away from the camera as her friend continued. "And another thing, they're taking over our government, they are! I see them on the telly, meeting with the Taoiseach and the Dáil. They are not welcome here! And you can tell them that for free!"

The interviewer turned back to the camera. "There you have it, folks. The Irish don't want the PHAE taking over their country."

Joel:

Footsteps approached in the darkness. He'd imagined steps several times, only to discover he imagined it, so he pinched himself to ensure he was awake.

Could a sound be a hallucination? Or was there a better word? He itched to look it up, but he hadn't had his phone since he was taken into custody.

He didn't see melting walls or monsters emerging from his dry toilet, but he heard things all the time. Creaks as the building settled, chittering mice running along the walls, or other, less identifiable sounds. Sometimes voices teased his ears, but no one came near. Planes roared outside, which morphed into symphonic music.

Music played in his mind a lot. Whether his memory created the sound or if it existed in reality, he had no idea. Sometimes the music turned to laughter, which haunted his dreams.

Hafsia's questions had wrung him completely dry. Joel had no strength to resist her, even if she hadn't used her Unhidden talent. He'd told her absolutely everything. He just spilled it all out, despite all efforts to keep silent. He hated his weakness. *Some agent I turned out to be.* Just a failure at everything, like his father had always said. Anna had always been the good one, the shining child, excelling at everything while he just tried to keep up. Well, the look of shock on her face when she realized he'd planted those bombs had been almost worth it all.

Lack of food made him dizzy. That woman gave him just enough to keep him going, a few bites each day of some disgusting fortified mush. A few swallows of water. He fondly remembered the crisp, sweet apple he'd gotten to eat once.

His skin cracked and bruised easily. When he brushed his fingers through his hair, it felt like thinning straw. He shivered constantly. He'd tried to keep his strength up with daily stretches but had little energy for any exercise.

Footsteps came closer. They sounded real. A different gait from Hafsia. Someone trying to keep quiet.

He sat up on the bed and faced the bars. Was it Ciara, the woman who had put him here? Anna come to find him? Maybe she came to gloat over his imprisonment like the self-righteous jerk she was.

The footsteps slowed. Whoever came for him, they didn't know where he was. Not Ciara, then. Joel cleared his throat, a rough, raspy sound.

A male voice he didn't recognize whispered loud in the silence. "Joel? Joel Taylor?"

He swallowed and licked his lips. "That's me, buddy. Who're you?"

"My name's Carlos."

Joel crossed his arms, though it was too dark for the other guy to see him. Youngish, deep voice, American with a hint of Spanish accent. "Yeah? And what's that to me?"

"Anna sent me."

Joel gritted his teeth against a sudden surge of hope and tears, suddenly ashamed of his earlier thought of Anna's gloating. "She did?"

Sure, he'd always given his sister a hard time. They never really got along. They'd grown apart after their parents died, especially when he talked about their dad's abuse. Anna never wanted to hear it. Once, she literally covered her ears and started singing "lalalalala" when he described what their dad had done to him. After that, he wrote her off.

To hear that she sent someone for him made his heart thaw. Not much, but a little bit. "Alright, you have my attention. Where do you know Anna from?"

"Do you want a complete personal history, or do you want to get out of here?" The man bent, examining the lock with a tiny flashlight. "This is both mechanical and electronic."

Joel straightened his spine at the man's attitude, but he had a point. "No shit, Sherlock. I could probably break the mechanical bit, but the electronic has me beat. The housing is too tough to break off. Trust me, I've tried."

Carlos stood, shining the penlight into Joel's eyes. "You can spring the mechanical lock? Do it."

Joel narrowed his eyes. "It means using up resources that I'm hoarding. Why should I trust you enough to waste them?"

Exasperation colored the other man's voice. "Because I'm here to get you the fuck out of here, man. Do you want out or not?"

It didn't take Joel long to weigh his options. He'd tried everything he could think of to escape, and nothing had worked. He needed help, even if it galled him to admit. "Yeah, fine. Move over."

First, he walked to the stone divot where he kept his carefully hoarded water supply. Then he formed an ice lockpick. He wished he could shield his talent from Carlos, but working from inside the bars, he didn't have the best angle.

With careful movements, he wiggled the pick into the keyhole. After a few seconds, he changed the shape, then again, and again, until it clicked. The hasp fell halfway open. He pulled the icepick out and melted it into his mouth. If he didn't have to hoard the water any longer, he could enjoy the treat. Joel savored the sweet moisture as it trickled down his throat.

Carlos let out a snort. "Right. Seems you and Anna share some talents. My turn." The other man bent to the electronic half of the lock and pressed buttons. Then he wrapped his hand around it and hummed.

Joel could see better now. Dawn must be coming. Hafsia usually came an hour after dawn. "Uh, hey, Carlos…could you speed things up a bit? I don't want my morning torture session to start while you're still here."

"Take a chill pill. Be just a bit more." His hand and the lock glowed as he hummed louder. A click, and he let out a satisfied "Aha! Gotcha!"

The hasp fell the rest of the way open. Joel backed up as the door swung in. Joel scooted out of the cell, anxious to leave this hellhole behind him. Carlos led him down the dim hallway.

As their footsteps clicked on the tile, Joel asked, "How did you get in here? Can we get out the same way?"

"Sort of. I came in delivering laundry."

Joel let out a snort. "That never works. That's just a movie thing."

"Yeah, but the Irish must not have seen those movies. Or I got lucky. I've been delivering the laundry for three days. Never been searched. I'm part of the background, now."

Joel pursed his lips, but he had to admit he was impressed. This guy did some planning.

As they crept through the empty hallways, out into the early dawn, Joel took a deep breath of fresh air. It tasted sweet, despite being in the middle of a city.

Carlos tugged on his arm. "C'mon, you idiot. Don't stand their huffing all day like an angry bull. The laundry van's this way."

Would Anna be waiting for him outside? For the first time in a long time, he really wanted to see her.

Qacha:

Qacha fought the firebeasts, raining fiery arrows upon each one. They exploded in a shower of sparks, yet still they swarmed. No matter how much she increased her power, no matter how many times she triumphed, more formed in the background and bore her to the ground. She screamed for help until her throat turned raw. No one came. She begged for mercy, but her pleas fell upon deaf ears.

When Qacha finally dragged her mind from her nightmares, her entire body shivered. Even when she opened her eyes, she found nothing but inky darkness. With tentative movements, she touched what she lay upon. A bed. Had she never left the hospital? Had she imagined that entire time at the country cottage, Max's arrival, and their battle with invaders?

Memory of her capture jumbled into her mind. They overwhelmed her, despite her Unhidden powers. Someone hitting her on the head. She gingerly touched her temple, finding a sore bump. That must be why her head pounded. Her skin, hot to the touch, felt dry and cracked. She needed moisture. Water.

Qacha sat up, peering around to discern the extent of her space. Not a glimmer of light. Could she create a light from nothing? Even for her, fire needed fuel, and she didn't want to burn her bed.

She felt around the bed and gripped an edge of the sheet. With a grunt, she tore a strip away. She couldn't even see it when held directly in front of her face, the darkness was so complete. With one hand on each end, she pulled deep inside her to find the fire and sparked the edge.

A flame flared so bright, it hurt her eyes. Qacha turned away and calmed the flame to a smolder. The fire ate the cloth quickly, but it didn't take long to discover the limits of her prison. The room looked three meters wide by three meters long, and the same height. The one stone door resisted all her attempts to open it, long after the flame died. Metal fittings held it fast against the stone wall. The mattress sat on a thick plastic frame. The only flammable items were her clothing and the bedding.

Metal and stone didn't burn. They'd found an effective cell.

Qacha banged her fist on the door, shouting for help, but with her throat still horribly ravaged from the fire, her shouts came out as strangled croaks. No one came. It seemed she must be content with her own company.

She sat on the bed and counted. When she tired of counting, she sang songs in her head. She wasn't particularly enamored of any popular tunes, and her traditional music, the throat-singing her grandfather had practiced, had no words. Her damaged throat would never be able to perform that sort of singing.

Next, she recalled the stories Colin told over each evening gathering. Tales of Irish gods and goddesses, heroes and legends. Qacha didn't remember her own native gods. Her grandfather hadn't been keen on mythology and didn't pass those stories on. She'd never developed an interest in them herself, but now she mourned that lack of curiosity, simply for want of some stories to recount in her head.

She returned to the Irish stories, her most recent exposure to something, anything, to keep her mind occupied. When she ran out of stories, she repeated them. Perhaps in time, she'd memorize them.

After countless hours, Qacha's stomach growled so loudly, it echoed in the empty space. Would they feed her? Or had they shut her away forever, to slowly starve to death? She'd take her own life before allowing that to happen.

A sound caught her attention. Footsteps? She sprang to her feet, hissing as her muscles screamed at the sudden movement. She tensed, looming next to the door.

Qacha expected the door to open but, instead, a small section along the bottom edge creaked aside. Someone shoved a tray in. Before she could react, the opening slammed shut.

Fuck a goat.

She knelt to examine the delivery. A plastic tray and spoon, a plastic bowl with warm soup, and a cup of water. Nothing metal, nothing she could fashion into either a weapon or a digging tool. Not that she could dig through stone.

She might whittle the plastic spoon into a point, but it seemed too flimsy for an effective weapon. As her stomach growled again, Qacha sighed and perched on her bed to feed her body's needs. At least the soup tasted good. Not up to her standards, but better than the bland offerings of most institutions.

When she finished, she returned to her internal recitations. Perhaps that would keep the nightmares at bay. Her body grew fatigued, and she'd need to rest soon, but she dreaded the inevitable nightmares. She *must* keep hold of her sanity, if she could.

After the third meal, Qacha struggled out of terror-ridden dreams. Each time, rising from the quagmire became more difficult. Each time, a bit of madness took residence in her mind. This time, it took the form of visual hallucinations. Her eyes still flitted to each corner of the room as *things* moved in the shadows, small and fast, running circles around her. As it got closer with each circuit, she lifted her feet back onto the bed, like a frightened child. She let out a scream, her throat aching with pain, and collapsed on the bed.

Disgusted with her pitiful terror, Qacha forced herself to place her feet back onto the cold stone floor. The shadow flickered again. If she closed her eyes, it would disappear. But then, within the darkness of her imagination, it grew wings and reached for her, claws out, sharp and menacing.

To escape the imagined raptor, she opened her eyes, only to catch the glimpse of the tiny creatures in her cell.

Qacha covered her face and let out a moan. She couldn't scream, she couldn't sleep, she couldn't escape them, whatever they were. They haunted her, awake or not.

A warmth called to her from the darkness. A flickering flame of hope, a woman's strong voice, one which wrapped her in a blanket of warmth and home.

Qacha didn't recognize this voice, but she ached to be in its embrace. This voice held some kinship, despite its unfamiliarity. This voice helped to keep the nightmares at bay. This voice burrowed into her soul.

Qacha sought the darkness now, just to hear that wonderful, liquid, powerful voice. A voice which soothed her jagged edges. A voice which caressed her ruined soul. A voice who finally spoke a word, "Qacha."

Hearing her name seemed a strange thing. Qacha hadn't heard it spoken in eons. "Who are you? *What* are you?"

"I am fire."

Qacha was a creature of fire, so why wouldn't fire call to her? "Do you have a name?"

"You may call me Brigit."

Bintou:

Bintou shot a worried look toward Martin's room and wished Róisín had joined them, but she had no way of contacting the healer. Though the land line still worked in the B&B, their cell phones got incredibly spotty service, and no calls went through to Galway.

She tried to call PHAE headquarters in Dublin, but they'd been less than helpful. Across a crackly connection, Paul told her to stay in the B&B. "Things are a mess in Dublin. More people are getting sick every day. The hospitals are straining at the seams. You're much safer up there, in the wilds of Donegal."

"We aren't exactly in the wilds. We're in Letterkenny. It's a decent-sized city"

"That's as may be, but you're away from the worst of it. Galway is a chaotic mess. Dublin isn't much better. Even Cork's cases are rising, and Belfast is running out of hospital beds daily. Whatever it is, it's spreading across the country with alarming speed."

Alarm bloomed in her heart. "Isn't it just a bad flu? I was sick about two weeks, but I'm fine now."

Paul hesitated as the line crackled, and for a moment, Bintou thought the line had died. "Bintou, are you where anyone can hear you?"

She glanced down the hall, but their hostess was busy in the kitchen, water running as she did the washing up. Martin remained in his room. "No."

Paul let out a deep sigh. "It's not the flu. We're having a hard time determining the exact pathogen, but it's bad. Really bad. People are dying."

The alarm morphed into panic, and she swallowed hard. "Dying? People are dying of this?"

"Aye, and we don't have a treatment. Palliative measures help, but if the cough gets too bad, chills and dizziness turn into a high fever. It's mad contagious, too. Keep Martin well away from everyone."

She glanced toward the kitchen. "What about our hostess? She's been cleaning the room, the dishes…"

"That's why I asked if anyone could hear."

Bintou clenched her jaw. She didn't like deceiving her hostess, a lovely older woman with a cheerful smile. But if she mentioned being contagious, they'd have to move. They shouldn't move Martin, not in his condition, even if the hospital had space. "What should we tell our doctor?"

"Tell him to keep the fever down however he can. That's all we've got at the moment. I'll call if I learn more. And Bintou?"

"Yes?"

"Stay safe yourself. Oh, Ibrahim is grabbing my arm. Will you speak with him?"

Ibrahim? She steeled herself against a flash of anger. Ibrahim, who dumped her after college. Ibrahim, who made her heart laugh with his voice. Ibrahim, who lured her to Ireland under false pretenses. Resentment and rage warred within her before she shut them away, chiding herself for petty childishness. Now was not the time to nurse grudges, despite their past, so she gritted her teeth and faked a smile. "Put him on."

The voice on the other end changed from Paul's midland Irish accent to Ibrahim's velvety Malian voice. "Bintou? Are you feeling better?"

"I am, Ibrahim. You?" It sounded so banal to exchange pleasantries in the middle of this growing disaster, but pleasantries were the oil that kept the machinery of polite society moving. Where would they be without the necessary small talk? Speaking of uncomfortable truths and baring their souls. No one wanted that in any day or age.

"I'm wonderful. I want to come help. What's the name of your B&B?"

Her shoulders tensed. Bintou didn't want him here, not with her heart pledged to Martin. And yet, having a familiar face around might be a comfort.

Panic crept into Ibrahim's voice. "Bintou? Are you there?"

"I'm here, I'm here. I don't think it's a good idea for you to travel right now. You should stay at headquarters."

He murmured to Paul, and then said, "Stay safe, Bintou. Be careful."

"And you as well. I'll call with any news."

As she hung up, she stared at the old-fashioned phone with its curly cord. Then Martin coughed again, the hacking, awful sound ripping at her spirit. She rushed up to sit by his side.

The next day, Bintou rose and indulged in a hot shower. She closed her eyes as the steaming water sluiced down her body, reveling in the delicious heat. This northern clime chilled her bones, even in the summer. The B&B had central heating, but the hostess laughed when she asked about it. "In June? Are ye mad? We don't turn it on until at least November. Ach, but it's a lovely day outside. Would ye like me to bring you your breakfast out on the patio?"

Bintou shook her head. "No, I'll eat with Martin. Do you have his porridge?"

"That I do. It'll be good for his throat, it will. Now, I've the tea and honey, with a wee tot of whiskey in it. He does take the whiskey, aye? It helps a treat."

She took the tray with a grin. "He does, thank you." Just as Bintou reached the landing, the front door opened. She half-turned to see who had arrived.

Ibrahim.

With a gasp, she almost dropped the tray as her ex-lover's eyes darted around the entrance, finally alighting on her. He opened his arms wide, a joyous smile filling his face and eyes. "Bintou!"

Her throat closed. She felt both immensely relieved to see him and angry that he had come despite her insistence that he remain in Dublin. But he'd always listened only to his own counsel.

She'd been at university with Ibrahim. For two delightful years, they'd been lovers, equals in intellect and body, but then parted when he took a job in Ireland. They hadn't spoken for two years when he contacted her out of the blue.

It was Ibrahim who convinced her to visit Ireland under the guise of renewed romantic interest. If the invitation hadn't come just after a row with her supervisor, she might have dismissed it out of hand. Perhaps she should have anyway, but throwing caution to the wind, Bintou closed her flat and flew to Ireland, ready for a new adventure.

When she arrived, she discovered he'd really been tasked with recruiting her to the PHAE and had used the prospect of rekindling their romance as bait. When Bintou exposed his duplicity, she refused to talk to him. However, she'd joined the PHAE after all, thanks to Róisín's intercession. Bintou hadn't regretted that decision. Perhaps she'd consider forgiving him someday. But ignoring her wish for him to stay away didn't help his cause in the slightest.

Now was not the time to discuss his actions nor her opinion of them. She only cared about Martin's health at the moment. With a tight grip on the tray, Bintou's eyes flicked from the upper floor to Ibrahim, unsure what to do. Martin needed his breakfast, but Ibrahim, with his velvet, deep voice, offered her comfort and respite, and it would be rude to leave him immediately.

Their hostess clicked her tongue. "I see you two know each other. That's grand! Well, come into the parlor, young man, and I'll fetch you a spot of tea. You must be weary from your journey. Have ye had your breakfast? Bintou will be down directly after she's tended to Martin."

Flashing their hostess a smile, Bintou gave Ibrahim one last look before she climbed the stairs to Martin's room.

Bintou sat as he moaned in his sleep. The doctor had given him some paracetamol and recommended keeping him warm. Bintou snorted at that notion. Martin had probably sweated out ten pounds in the last two days. Still, he had four blankets on hand if the chills replaced the sweats.

She didn't want to wake him. Rest was difficult and fitful. The aroma of the tea might rouse him. His arm had slipped out from under the duvet. Bintou stared at the red spots bright on his dark skin. When had he developed a rash? The spots looked like angry blackheads, infected and painful. She touched one to test if it felt hot.

Martin moaned again and coughed himself out of sleep. He sat up, the fit scraping his throat with raw, painful hacking. His skin had grown so pale, he almost looked white. His curly hair felt like straw. Concerned, Bintou pulled down his night-shirt, discovering more sores on his neck, creeping up to his jawline.

Swallowing down on her rising fear, she sat back as he opened his eyes.

"Bintou?"

She took his hand. "I'm here, Martin."

He reached for her hand, squeezing it tight. "I'm frightened."

To hear a grown man admit fright shook her to the core. Martin never showed fear. His height and build made him a rock. She'd been able to lean on him in her own moments of weakness. "I recovered. You will, too. I'm sure of it."

He shook his head, setting off another coughing fit. "I don't think so. I think...I think I need to say this..."

Her throat caught. "Say what?"

Staring into her eyes, he whispered, "I need to tell you I love you."

Tears welled up, dropping onto their clasped hands. If she didn't tell him now, he might never know. "I love you, Martin. And do you know what that means? It means you are not permitted to die. Do you hear me? I won't allow it."

He gave her a sad smile and shook his head again. "I'm afraid we don't get a vote."

When his next coughing fit subsided, a knock at the door made Bintou glance up. Their hostess stood in the doorway. "How can I help, dears? Should I call the doctor again?"

Bintou nodded. "Yes, please. Tell him Martin's gotten much worse." She glanced at the sores again. "And we have a new symptom, one I never had."

As the woman left, Martin subsided into a restless doze, his head tossing back and forth. Bintou held tight to his hand. His skin radiated intense heat, turning crepey and thin. The veins on the inside of his arm distended.

Footsteps came up the stairs. When Bintou turned, hoping to find the doctor, Ibrahim stood in the doorway. He looked tense, a fresh tray of food in his hands. "I thought you might be hungry yourself, Bintou. May I join you?"

She swallowed and glanced back at Martin, still groaning in his broken sleep. "It might not be wise. You heard what Paul said about limiting exposure."

"I've already been exposed, just by being in this house, haven't I?"

She let out a sigh. "Come in, Ibrahim."

He carried a chair from the next room and sat beside her, massaging her shoulders. He said nothing, for which she felt gratitude. Bintou had no energy to make niceties. She still hadn't forgiven him for deceiving her.

"Here, I brought sandwiches. You need to eat." When she opened her mouth to protest, he held up a hand to forestall her words. "If you fall ill again, you won't be able to take care of him."

She had to admit, he had a point. Her stomach answered him, and they shared a weak smile.

Ibrahim handed her a half sandwich. "Our hostess had mutton. I remember you love lamb and peanut sauce, so I made a peanut sauce. It's not the same as home, but it is tasty."

Bintou flashed him a grateful glance and took a bite. She didn't taste it. Instead, she chewed and swallowed to quiet her traitor stomach. Martin moaned again, and she put down the sandwich to wipe his forehead with a wet cloth. His skin burned.

As she reached for the thermometer, the doctor arrived. Ibrahim squeezed her shoulder before leaving the room.

The doctor peered at the patient. "Right. What's happened to change things, Bintou?"

Standing so the doctor could examine Martin, she clasped her hands. "He's got a new rash on his arm and up his neck."

Martin rose again in a coughing fit. He wheezed, unable to get enough breath between dry coughs. Just as it eased, he vomited nasty, black blood on the duvet. He didn't even have enough energy to look ashamed as he coughed again.

The doctor called down their hostess, "Call 999! Now!"

As they waited for the ambulance, he turned to Bintou. "You'd best wait here."

"I will not leave him, doctor. I've been by his side since this started. If I haven't caught this by now, I won't. Besides, I fell ill first. It's far more likely that I gave him this. But I didn't get those sores."

"He might not have gotten it from you. Different symptoms have been showing up in different people. We don't even know if this is one disease or several." He glanced at Bintou and back to Martin just as the latter seized, his entire body tensed in a rictus of pain. She fell to her knees next to him, aching to take his pain away.

The doctor barked out, "Help me get him on his side!"

Once they moved him, he looked at his watch, timing the seizures. Martin's entire body shook. He coughed again, bringing up more dark blood.

Just as Martin gazed at her with pleading eyes, they turned blank, and he seized again. Bintou could barely breathe as his muscles locked. After the seizure passed, he fell limp and unconscious. The doctor checked his breathing and glanced frantically toward the door. "Jaysus! Where's that bloody ambulance?"

Pushing Martin onto his back again, he laced his fingers together and placed his hands over the patient's chest. After a few ineffective shoves against the too-soft bed, they pulled Martin to the floor to continue.

Bintou scrambled back, giving the doctor room. Her own breath came in gasps. Hands on her shoulders made her glance up. Ibrahim must have meant his smile to be reassuring. It wasn't.

The paramedics finally arrived, their boots pounding on the stairs. Their hostess directed them to Martin's room. Bintou cowered in the corner as they shifted Martin to the stretcher as the doctor performed chest compressions.

Once they left the room, Ibrahim helped her to her feet and guided her down the stairs. "I'll follow in my car. You need to be with him."

Bintou wasn't allowed in the ambulance, as she wasn't a relative, so Ibrahim drove her behind the medical vehicle barreling through the streets of Letterkenny toward St. Conal Hospital. She clasped and unclasped her hands, wiped the sweat off on her skirt, and stared at the ambulance doors as they drove through red lights, around corners, and past pulled-over cars.

When they finally arrived at the hospital, Ibrahim pulled in and slammed the brakes. "Go. I'll park and join you."

With a grateful smile, she jumped out of the door and followed the paramedics pushing Martin's gurney. They went straight into a room in the A&E, one medic still doing chest compressions.

They shut the doors, but she watched through the window. A nurse touched her arm. "Miss? Are you a relative?"

She shook her head, not taking her eyes off Martin's still form as they shoved a tube down his throat. "No. I'm a friend."

"You can wait over here, miss. They'll come with any news."

Bintou didn't want to leave. If she left, she sensed Martin would give up. She gripped her hands so tight, her nails bit into her palms. If only she had some useful talent. Healing, rather than reading moldy, ancient documents. If only Róisín was here. If only they'd stayed in Dublin, which surely had more state-of-the-art equipment and the best doctors. If only, if only, if only.

Just as she allowed the nurse to lead her away, above the cacophony of other noises, a machine beeped a long, single note. Bintou turned back, her heart in her throat.

The doctors and nurses in the A&E room weren't frantic, but they obviously worked as quickly as they could. Someone had heart paddles in their hands. The nurse tugged on her arm. "Please, miss, it's better if you sit. You need to back up at least to here, to keep the door clear. You look pale. May I get you something to drink?"

She shook off the woman. In an emotionless voice, Bintou said, "I need to see."

Ibrahim appeared beside her, his arm around her shoulders. A cup of something warm appeared in her hand, but she didn't drink it. The warmth felt good, leaching through the waxed paper cup to her hands. The hospital was chilly.

It might have been a few minutes. It might have been an hour. The doctor looked at his watch and spoke, but she couldn't hear. Everyone stopped.

A single beep cut through the relative silence.

As the doctor pulled off his gloves and pushed the doors open, he caught her eyes. She knew what he'd tell her. Her breath caught in a sob. Bintou buried her face in Ibrahim's shoulder as he drew her into an embrace.

Anna:

As Brendan rubbed a greasy balm along her scaled, scraped leg, Anna batted his hand away. "Stop it! That hurts!"

The Irishman held his arm up, frustration clouding his face. "Would you rather apply the salve?"

Anna shook her head. "It doesn't help anyway. I just need to be in the ocean. That's the only time the pain goes away."

He frowned, glancing out the B&B window. The storm remnants still lashed the windows. "I don't want you going out in this until you're healed, much less into the ocean during a storm."

She just needed to be in the salt water. Anna gave him a scowl. "You aren't my dad! I'm a grown woman. I can make decisions for myself!"

He stood up, crossing his arms. "No, I'm not your dad. I thought, though, that we had an understanding."

Her eyes grew wide as her temper flared. "An *understanding?* Is that what they call it in Ireland?"

"Fine. A relationship, then. An affection. What do you want to call it? Or did you develop more *affection* for Carlos in the five minutes you talked with him?"

She glared at him. "Really? You're pulling out the jealousy card? I didn't take you for the jealous type. It's not a good look on you. Don't even go there. Don't even bring Carlos into this."

"Fine, I'll leave him out of it, if you do!" He let out a deep breath and closed his eyes for a moment. When he opened them, he lowered his voice. "Listen, I received a message this morning to go north to help Qacha with something. You probably want to stay here, near the ocean. But promise me you'll actually stay here, in this B&B, and not go up to Carlos' place, okay? In fact, I'd rather you not visit that B&B again. If you need to leave here, go back to Mam's farm. Understand?"

"How the hell am I going to do that, fly? I control water, remember? Not air. I don't even have a stupid driver's license."

She pouted as Brendan rolled his eyes. "You can call PHAE, and they'll send transport. Or call a taxi, and Mam will pay for it when you arrive."

Anna hated the idea of being a passive partner, captive to her husband's whims. She'd always feared that fate. Housewife was never something she'd aspired to. That was one reason she'd gotten her degree, to be independent.

Brendan was sounding more and more like he wanted a compliant girlfriend, someone to support him but not have ideas of her own. Well, she wasn't about to fit herself into that mold for him. Squaring her shoulders, she clenched her jaw. "In case you hadn't noticed, I'm not a child. I am thirty years old. I'm not yours to command. If I wish to visit Carlos, I will. Isn't he official PHAE? Why shouldn't I visit him, except for your mad jealousy?"

His tone rose again. "I'm not jealous!"

She pursed her lips and crossed her arms. "Sure as hell looks like jealousy to me. To quote Shakespeare, *'I had rather hear my dog bark at a crow, than a man swear he loves me.'* Listen, right now, this is between you and me, no one else. And I don't want to call it, whatever *it* is, whatever *we* are, *anything* at the moment. I just want to ease this pain. It feels like it's eating into my skin. I want to scratch it and scratch it until it stops!"

"Into your scales."

Anna scowled at him, clenching her fists. "Fine. It's eating into my *scales*. Whatever! You can't seem to get past how I look."

"How you look? You look beautiful! I love the way you look."

She scowled. "I'd rather you loved me for myself."

Brendan threw up his hands. "You know what? I can't win. You seemed worried about your looks, so I assured you I love the way you look. Then you complain because I love the way you look. I don't do these sort of crappy games, Anna!"

"Fine, whatever. I just need to be in the ocean. Here's another quote for you, *'Let me be that I am and seek not to alter me.'*"

He glanced at the window, still being pelted with raindrops. "Going out right now is not a good idea. Can't you at least wait until the storm stops?"

Anna ground her teeth in frustration. "It's been three fucking days! This storm is eternal. My legs are on *fire!* Did you not hear that part? I can't wait for your precious Irish weather to stop because Irish weather *never fucking stops!*" She pounded her fists on her thighs. She instantly regretted it. The previous fire erupted into small explosions of pain with each strike. Brendan placed his hands on her shoulders, but she shrugged out of them. "No. No more placating. No more calming. Will you take me to the shore, or will I walk alone?"

He stared at her for a few seconds before pulling on his coat. "Fine, I'll go with you."

She let out her breath, thankful despite her angry words. The pain drove her to distraction, and she just needed a break. Instinctually, she knew being in the water would help. Bath water helped slightly, but she needed the sea to truly ease her pain. Some subliminal truth, a voice low and deep in the back of her memory, knew this.

Anna didn't bother pulling on a coat. A coat would defeat her intent. She must feel the water on her skin.

As they closed the B&B door behind them, the wind drove icy needles into her face. She loved it. Her legs already felt better. She couldn't wait to immerse herself in the embrace of the blessed salt water.

The sand irritated the bottoms of her feet. She hadn't even bothered with shoes. They walked the half-mile to the beach in silence. Brendan refused to let her hand go until they reached the water's edge. "Will you let me come in with you?"

Anna arched her eyebrows. "I'm going all the way in, Brendan. Are you coming swimming, then?"

Emotions warred on his face, flickering between concern and determination. Finally, he kissed her hand and let it go. "I'll be right here. Call for help, and I'm diving in. Understand?"

Anna gave him a sad smile. "I understand. Thank you. Sorry I've been such a bitch."

His half-smile made her heart melt, despite her anger. "You haven't been a bitch. You're in pain. I know that. I hope this helps."

She swallowed back an angry retort about his jealousy. That wouldn't help anything.

As soon as her scales touched the water, an icy hand caressed the pain away, as if someone peeled her skin off, leaving nothing but delicious bliss. Anna shut her eyes as she slipped deeper, until nothing but her head remained above water. The rain still drove sharp into her face, but the pain disappeared for the first time in three days.

The ocean caressed her skin and scales. The silky-smooth embrace sent a delightful chill up her spine. Anna shivered in sheer pleasure, a wave of excitement pulsing through her body. The beckoning plea enfolded her. A low, liquid, velvet voice without words, calling to her like a siren.

Anna resisted at first, but she must find out who called to her in the sea. Was it someone like her? Someone growing scales and learning to love the water?

"Anna! Anna, you're swimming too far!"

She glanced back. Brendan stood in the surf up to his knees, waving his arms. But she didn't see the Brendan who cared for her. She saw the jealous Brendan. The man who wanted to keep control over her. Submissive housewife. Angry. Controlling.

The voice called. She turned to gaze at the distant whitecaps waving for her to join them.

"Anna! Come back!" She looked back a second time to see him shoving through the water toward her, his eyes growing wide. "Anna! Please! I love you!"

As she looked back the third time, her throat closed with tears. That was the first time he'd said it. And yet she couldn't deny the summons of the ocean.

Brendan's voice faded as she swam toward the song of the sea.

Chapter Seven

"When everything goes to hell, the people who stand by you without
flinching
-- they are your family."
– Jim Butcher

Róisín:

Fiona shook her awake. "Róisín! Róisín, Da needs you."

As her little sister left, Róisín dragged herself up from the gray bliss of sleep. After glancing at the alarm clock, she rubbed the grit from her eyes. The digital numbers said eight pm, so she'd only gotten three hours of rest. She needed more than three hours! But if Da needed her, she must go.

After splashing chilly water on her face, she pulled on her bathrobe and shuffled to her parents' room. Her mother must be down in the kitchen, as she could hear dishes clacking together. Fiona's voice drifted up, but Róisín couldn't pick out the words, only the questioning tone.

She sat beside her father's bed. He wasn't drenched in sweat, so that was a good sign. His skin felt warm and dry, but not too warm. Even better. She grasped his hand and reached into the well of her soul for her healing power.

Only a faint flutter of power answered her call. She'd emptied herself a dozen times over the last two days, in between periods of hoarded rest. After a session with her father, he'd improve for a few hours, only to fall back into the clutches of fever-dreams. Róisín's efforts kept him from getting worse, but she couldn't seem to bring any lasting improvement.

Her mother didn't want to hear that she couldn't do more. And for once, Róisín agreed. She just didn't have the power. Róisín rarely wished for more than she had, but now she prayed with all her heart for the ability to heal her father.

Perhaps because she made this prayer with her power conduit wide open, the plea had more power. Perhaps someone just happened to be listening. Perhaps God granted her his grace. Whatever actually happened, someone answered her. A voice itched in the back of her brain, **"I can help you."**

The healing energy which had trickled from an empty cup, barely a dribble, now rushed like a tidal wave, sweeping past her and into her father. Buzzing flowed into her blood, her skin, her head, and out her arms. Sparks teased the edges of her vision as her father's chest rose once with one massive heave.

His eyes flew open as he bolted upright, gasping for breath, making Róisín jerk back, both startled and a little frightened. The harsh sound echoed in the quiet room and footsteps pounded up the stairs. Her mother flung open the door, staring at her husband as he drew in harsh breaths, clutching at his chest.

She dropped her dish towel and ran to his side. She grabbed his hand. "Colin? Colin!"

He gasped several more times before he became aware of his family. "Michelle? You're here! Oh, thank all the gods, you're safe!"

Róisín's mother pulled him into an embrace. They gripped each other tight and sobbed with relief. Róisín sat back and calmed her heart, trembling with the power still tingling in her veins. The voice tickled the edge of her mind. **"You have done well."**

Róisín retreated to the hallway. Checking to ensure Fiona wasn't in earshot, she whispered, "Who are you?"

"I am a healer."

That answered nothing, but the evidence didn't lie. Still, she wanted to know who helped her. "What is your name?"

Only silence answered her. Had she imagined the voice? She couldn't have imagined the power, the flowing river of healing energy that brought her father back from death's door. Róisín shook her hands to get rid of the remnants singing in her blood. She glanced back over her shoulder. Her mother still sobbed in her father's arms.

Róisín slid into her room and closed the door. She asked again, "What is your name?"

Nothing answered. Was her imagination playing tricks on her? Had her lack of sleep caused a hallucination? She couldn't shake the feeling that something watched her, so she shut her curtains, cinched her robe tight, and crawled back beneath her covers. The familiar warmth of her childhood bed embraced her, nostalgic comfort at maximum. Even with whatever help she'd gotten, the healing had drained every ounce of energy she had left. Still, despite being utterly spent, she tossed and turned a long time before she slept.

When she finally woke again, sunlight streamed in the window, warming her face. She propped herself up on her elbows, frowning. Hadn't she closed the curtain? She rubbed her face and staggered to the bathroom, pausing at her parents' door. Low voices rumbled through the wood. Her mother chuckled.

She hadn't heard her mother laugh since before the attack on Galway. Róisín grasped that sound close to her heart as she showered and dressed. When she padded barefoot into the empty kitchen, she comforted herself with the familiar morning routine of making tea and toast. Fiona shuffled in just as she finished, so she added two more slices for her little sister.

They sat together in familial silence as birdsong filtered in from the garden. All seemed peaceful in the world. For just one perfect moment, Róisín felt content with life.

A scream shattered all tranquility.

Róisín jumped to her feet, ready to tackle whatever threat attacked them. The scream was followed by a young boy tearing through the kitchen, holding a toy car and singing at the top of his lungs. "You can't catch me! You can't catch me!"

A bare second later, another screech ran through the kitchen, trying to catch his twin. Róisín glanced at Fiona, who rolled her eyes at their brothers' antics. In a tone too old for her years, Fiona rolled her eyes and said, "Boys." They shared a chuckle and finished their breakfast.

Her mother called for help, but it wasn't a call filled with desperation and worry. This time, she just needed help getting her father to the bathroom. She supported him under one arm with her mother under the other. After her mother washed him, Róisín brushed his hair. Then he dressed and they practically carried him down the stairs. He'd healed but remained incredibly weak. Despite that, he shuffled into his study to be amongst his books, replete with tea and breakfast.

Once he recovered from the trip, Róisín sat across from his desk, peering at him with curious eyes. "Are you really better, Da?"

"I am, *mo leanbh*. This last week has been mostly a fog, but I knew when you helped. Your healing felt like a beacon in the misty morning."

She rolled her eyes. "You, Da, are a hopeless romantic."

"Fair play, I'll grant that with pride. Now, grateful as I am that you returned to heal your dying father, you've something else on your mind. What is it?"

Róisín wasn't sure she wanted to share what happened as she clasped her fingers in her lap and stared at them.

"Róisín, speak to me."

"I didn't heal you, Da."

He raised his eyebrows. "Available data would indicate otherwise."

Shaking her head, she met his gaze. "I tried but didn't have enough strength to do more than keeping you from getting worse. I tried for *days*, Da. Finally, I had nothing left and prayed for help. Someone…some*thing* helped me."

"I see." He sat back in his overstuffed leather office chair and steepled his fingers. "Did this something speak to you? Like Anú has with Komie?"

She nodded, her gaze dropping back to her hands.

154

"What did they say? Did they give a name?"

"Just that I'd done well. I asked their name, twice, but they didn't answer. I don't know if they left, or lost interest, or didn't want to answer."

"Hmm." He stared at his bookshelf for several moments before he spoke again. "Well, is this something you want to find out more about?"

"I don't know if that's wise. I mean, it's not like I don't have other work I should be doing. In fact, that's something I wanted to ask you about. I'd called Ma, but that's when she finally told me you were sick."

"Well, I'm better now, thanks to you. What did you want to ask?"

"So, I'm helping with a research project at Bioclin in Athlone, to study the disease's vector. And I really ought to get back. I sort of abandoned them. But I found something you might be able to help me with."

He leaned forward, his expression suddenly eager. "What did you find? Something important?"

Róisín swallowed, trying hard not to get excited about her next question. "I think so. But it's just a hunch. And that's why I called you, to check on this hunch."

"Daughter, if you don't stop skipping around the question and ask, I'm going to pour this tea on your head."

She laughed, and it felt wonderful, like a new day had dawned. His eyes sparkled as she rose, stepping to the large wall map of Ireland. While the map was modern, it had been drawn in an ancient style, with brown lines and parchment-style deckled edges. She pulled a pushpin from the edge and placed one each on the Hill of Tara, Emain Macha, and Rathcroghan. Her father rose to join her, his finger touching each one as she added pins to Dún Ailinne and Uisneach.

She stepped back, staring at the map. "These areas have reported no cases of the illness."

His eyes grew wide. "Are you certain?"

With a shrug, she turned to her father. "No, of course not. There may just be a lack in reporting structure. But this pattern is worth investigating, don't you think?"

They both stared at the map for several silent moments before he burst out laughing so hard, he had to sit, holding his side. "Well, at least we know who to contact to help you find out!"

Colin:

Colin felt frayed. His home, the farm he'd built for his entire family, seemed echoingly empty. His eldest daughter, Róisín, had gone back to Galway just when he needed her here.

After he left Komie with that priestess, Caoimhe, Fiona kept asking after the native woman. Colin didn't want to think about her. As much as he liked Komie, he wanted his family back home and safe. Sure, Hugh and Liam remained home, and his lovely Michelle. But his heart ached with emptiness for his older children.

He kicked himself for foolishness. Did he think they'd live at home forever? Someday, they'd find their own lives. But not yet. Not yet. And not like this, in the middle of a national disaster.

His eldest son, Brendan, had been brought to University Limerick Hospital, ranting with a high fever. They'd taken him straight to the Intensive Care Unit. Ironically, if Róisín had been with them, she could have helped heal her brother. They only let him visit once a day, but he called every few hours. The last time, the nurse had told him firmly that they would call when anything changed, so he decided to visit instead.

Amidst the antiseptic halls of the hospital, Colin sat by his son's side. He dipped a washcloth in cool water and placed it on Brendan's forehead, hoping to keep his son's core temperature down. He'd sweated through the hospital gown, thrashing around in fever dreams.

Whenever Brendan woke enough to speak, he asked for Anna.

When Colin first saw his son, half out of his mind with grief, Colin couldn't make head nor tail of his grumblings and cries. All he knew was that Anna had left him for... what? The ocean? That didn't make sense. Brendan said she was still alive, so she hadn't drowned. The girl had an affinity for the sea, but as far as Colin could remember, she didn't care for the deep water, where she couldn't see the bottom. However, before Colin could get more information from his son, Brendan fell back into fever dreams.

Michelle pulled the hospital curtain aside. She brought in a bunch of flowers from their garden, arranging them in a plastic vase by Brendan's bedside. "Any change?"

Colin shook his head. "Nothing."

She sat next to him, leaning her head against his shoulder. He squeezed her shoulder in a hug.

When visiting hours ended, the nurse shooed them out with a kind smile. They traveled home in silence. Not until they entered the house did Colin gather the energy to speak. "You look tired, darlin'. You should sleep."

Michelle shook her head. "I've still got to clean the boys' room. You'd think a tornado struck, the state of it."

"Tell them to clean it. They need to learn."

"I don't trust them to do it right. Have you seen what they consider 'clean?'"

"Leave it tonight. It won't kill them to sleep in a messy room. Go rest."

She swallowed and stared at Brendan's bedroom door, painted bright red. Michelle's jaw clenched and she looked more frightened than Colin had ever seen her in his life. He hugged her again. "It'll be grand, Michelle. I promise."

Suddenly, she pulled away from him, glaring at him like she did with Fiona at her worst. "How can you possibly make a promise like that, Colin Byrne? After all that's gone on? There is no way on God's green earth that this will all be anything resembling grand. The world has changed, and we're getting the dirty end of the stick. Such an Irish thing that is, too. I've had it with smiling and pretending things are grand. I've had it with always doing my best, while the wolves chew on my ankles. I've *had* it with the platitudes. All we've done is wait around and hope for the best. Well, I'm done with that. We have to *do* something."

"Michelle! Keep your voice down. You'll wake Fiona!"

"And what if I do? It'll keep her from whatever dream is making her moan and cry. Won't that be a shame!"

The fire in her eyes made him pull back. She so rarely lost her temper with him.

Suddenly, she deflated into his arms. "I'm sorry, my love. I didn't mean to snap at you. But I just feel so frustrated, so helpless."

"So do I, *mo chroi*. So do I."

Qacha:

Inside the frantic darkness, the voice called. Not the voice of comfort, the voice of fire she'd heard before, but a new voice. A familiar voice, though she struggled to attach a name to the sound.

It seemed like an eternity since the shadows left her in peace. They screamed at her constantly, whispered in the back of her mind, called to her from unfathomable distances. But this one seemed different.

This one held a glimmer of the familiar, a tiny shard of solace. A splinter of memory.

"Qacha! Qacha, can you hear me?"

A male voice, with an Irish accent. Not Brigit, then. The Fire entity had returned each time Qacha slept, and sometimes when she woke. She'd forged a bond with the fire goddess, almost a friendship, a comfort in her madness.

Was Qacha still in Ireland? She'd traveled to hell and back within her mind. How had she returned to Ireland?

It must be yet another illusion, something else to drive her mad. Losing patience at the constant barrage of insanity, she threw fire at the voice.

Her stone prison and her lack of strength resulted in a few bare sparks which died against the walls.

"Qacha! I have food for you. Real food."

She didn't need food. She needed light. She needed structure. She needed…human contact. Was this a human voice? Or another figment of her imagination?

"Qacha! Please, I need to come in. It's Brendan. Do you remember me?"

Brendan. The name tickled her memory. It flew around her mind like a blue butterfly, alighting upon a maze of hedges. She couldn't grasp hold of the memory of his face. Young man. Tall with long black hair. He liked the ocean. Why did water come to mind? She didn't like water. Water quenched her fire.

Qacha paced around her cell. By now, countless days into her imprisonment, she knew well the dimensions of her space. She paced four times in each direction, barely brushing the cold stone walls. She tried to call Brigit, to ask her advice, but the fire entity remained silent. Qacha must be on her own.

Suddenly, flashes of life at the Byrne farm bombarded her, forcing her to her knees. The large dining room laden with home cooking. The kitchen gardens filled with herbs and root vegetables. The rustic outbuildings. Her beloved cat, Manol. Her grandfather's antique horsebow.

Tears pricked the back of her eyes and burned in her throat. Something snapped inside her, and she crawled to the door. Chilly stone scraped her knees. In a hoarse whisper, she croaked, "Brendan? Brendan? Is that you?"

The door clicked and clunked. Then, for the first time since she'd arrived, it opened. Painful light flooded into the small space, and Qacha let out a cry, covering her eyes with her arm. She scrambled into the corner, hiding her face and moaning.

"Qacha, don't be afraid. It's just me."

Brendan's amorphous form transformed into a monstrous creature, bursting with tentacles and angry teeth. Qacha cowered in the corner, away from the attacking beast. Anger and shame at her own cowardice filled her but left her powerless to act.

The creature retreated. The door closed. The blessed, comforting darkness enveloped her. Qacha moaned and rocked, hugging herself until she fell into a fitful sleep, still huddled in the corner.

If it had been Brendan who visited her, he left her alone again. Had he even been here in body? Maybe only his spirit visited her. He must be floating around the Otherworld.

Over the next few sleeps, he returned. Sometimes, she could speak with the visitor. Other times, she lashed out, trying to destroy the intruder. Each time, she begged for help from Brigit, the only reliable comfort left in her universe. Sometimes, the goddess answered. More often, she remained silent.

Qacha hated herself. How had she become so helpless? How had she turned into this craven, cowardly creature? So dependent upon another person for protection? But Brigit wasn't a person. She was an entity, a goddess, a living flame.

The next time her mind crawled out from the madness, Qacha examined the visions. Was any of it real? Or had she created this torture from her own distorted imagination?

Qacha tried to piece together her memory of events. She'd been at the cottage. Had Max found her? Or had the illusions already begun? Max stood by her as invaders rushed them. She defended herself. Had she killed someone? The events ran into a blur. She couldn't piece reality from the muddled impressions. The white-washed cottage wall. A gloomy morning light piercing through the clouds. Soldiers rushing toward her. A spark of light hitting someone's face. The smell of scorched hair. Plastic cutting into her wrists. Pain.

That's all she could dredge from her shattered memory. No matter how hard she tried, she couldn't extract more. She must have been captured and hurt several people. She'd only defended herself, but they threw her in a prison. Had there been a trial for her guilt?

Memories, true or false, swam in a maelstrom. Qacha slept, woke, and ate. In a moment of lucidity, she stared at the plastic bucket in the corner, which never got full. Someone must be entering while she slept.

Was her visitor real? Or simply earlier memories from the Byrne farm translated into her madness? Surely the fire goddess wasn't real. Qacha must have created Brigit from Colin's stories, the ones she recited to herself over and over to keep the insanity at bay.

The flame intruded into her thoughts. **"I am real."**

The voice had never before spoken to her waking mind. Qacha grasped the straw and pulled. "What are you?"

"I am Brigit. I am a daughter of fire, as you are. I command the flames of inspiration, of creation, and of vengeance."

Qacha stood, trying to discern any shape in the darkness. "Are you physical? Or are you in my mind?"

"Yes."

She gritted her teeth. "Did you have me captured?"

"Those who follow me obtained you at my bidding."

Her mind must be lying to her, as it had so many times before. "Show yourself!"

Something burned against the far wall. Qacha narrowed her eyes to keep from being dazzled. A bright glow, a rip along the stone wall. It widened and sparked until it reached from floor to ceiling. This rip widened, and a woman stepped out.

And what a woman.

She smoldered with radiance, with hair so bright red, it hurt Qacha's eyes, even half-shut. A powerful woman, with broad shoulders, muscular arms, and a severe expression on her face.

Qacha fell to her knees, despite fighting the urge. Her eyes burned from the image before her.

"This is Myself."

She couldn't breathe. Though her throat had healed during her time in prison, it still scratched when she spoke. It caught with uncontrollable wonder. A true goddess. This was a creature from legend, in her cell. This was power.

This was Herself.

Qacha's heart flooded with unaccountable humility before Brigit.

"Rise, daughter of fire. Be one with me."

Finding herself on her feet, with no recollection of having risen from her knees, she rushed to the goddess. They embraced with no thought for her own safety or the wisdom of touching a fire goddess. Instead, the warmth licked her skin with delicious ecstasy. Qacha wanted nothing more than to surrender herself to this fiery bliss.

"Qacha! What are you doing?"

Brendan's voice sounded frightened and confused. Qacha turned to confront the young Irishman. He stood in the open door holding a tray of food. The warmth behind him flashed brighter, scorching Qacha's skin with an embrace.

"This is Brigit."

He dropped the tray and backed away, his eyes wide with horror. "No, it can't be!"

She stared at the Irish man. "Why are you here? Did you assist in my capture? Is this the PHAE that have imprisoned me?"

His eyes flicked to the door. He swallowed and lowered his voice. "No, not the PHAE. It's a group who worship the old gods, and they've gone off the deep end lately. I had some contacts, so convinced them I was joining, so I could get to you. I'm working on a way to get you out, so please, be patient!"

Qacha didn't believe him. He was probably just another illusion, anyhow. She turned away from his image and stepped toward the beckoning flame.

"Qacha, get away from that! You'll be killed!"

Qacha cast a disdainful glance toward the younger man. "No, she's a protector. A patron. She won't hurt me, Brendan."

Brendan's hair glowed. At first, Qacha thought sunlight must be streaming in behind him, surrounding his hair with a liminal light. But no, it was her beloved fire. Then his clothes glimmered with sparks. He let out a scream as he ripped his burning clothes from his body. The smoldering scraps of cloth blazed as they ate into his tender skin.

Qacha was torn between terror that this young man, this friend, was being consumed by fire, and delight at the beauty of the sacred flames.

She turned to Brigit, whose intense smile engulfed her into fanatic pleasure with the burning flesh. She must save Brendan. She couldn't watch him burn to death.

Drawing the fire into herself and away, as she did in Galway as it burned, Qacha siphoned the heat away from Brendan's skin. The flame scorched Qacha's blood, licking hungrily to consume. The Irish man still screamed. Qacha echoed that scream.

Brigit clutched her shoulders, a painful, vice-like grip. **"Let him be a sacrifice, Qacha. A fitting offering for your ascendance. The price you must pay."**

A sacrifice to a goddess. Something out of ancient legend. Brigit expected her to give all of herself to this legend. And Brendan.

A scrap of memory slammed into her. Her family's honor. Qacha had never been a servant, a supplicant. Her strength defined her, not her servitude. Her grandfather had taught her that. If she were to be herself, she must make a stand. "No! I cannot! He is innocent!"

She needed to save the boy. Not only to satisfy her own honor, but for her own sanity. He must live. He must tell the others about these dangerous gods. He must warn them all.

Qacha wrenched more flame from Brendan. *Too much!* She couldn't digest that much fire, but she didn't care. The Irish man must be saved from Brigit.

The searing heat burned into her veins, ripping apart the delicate structures in her arms. Flickers of Anna's smile as he spoke to her flashed through her mind. This man was loved. He had a family, young love, and a talent of his own. He had his life ahead of him. How could she possibly make the decision to save herself over him?

Blood burst from her arteries as she screamed, pulling more fire from the young Irish man. Harsh to her own ears, her voice turned to a gurgling screech as her legs failed her. Qacha fell to her knees, still shielding Brendan from Brigit's deadly blaze.

The flames finally consumed her, mind, body, and spirit. The last sound she heard was Brendan's whimpering cry as the eternal darkness enveloped her into an echoing silence.

Qacha swam in a sea of fire. How long had she been screaming? She couldn't recall a time without it. Nothing existed in her memories of another place. This was her life now, pain and burn and horror. A voice whispered in her ear, a voice too quiet to ignore. It asked her to become one with the goddess. Each time, Qacha denied the voice. A wave of disappointment and regret swept across her, sinking her soul into despair. And she burned again.

A vague memory of someone else flitted through her mind. The Irish boy, Brendan. Had he escaped? Had he survived? Qacha hoped so. Or had this all been an illusion, a glamor created by the goddess or her own mind's madness? She hoped whatever Hell she'd created for herself had at least succeeded in saving his life.

Now she must fight for her own survival. If she could call this survival. If she wanted to survive with this horrid pain. Almost worse than the physical pain was the emotional pain. Why had her beloved fire betrayed her?

Latest CNN Update: "*The Republic of Ireland has declared a state of national emergency. Reports of an uncontrolled epidemic within the country has forced the government to issue a travel ban to all countries. This travel ban includes the Northern Ireland portion of the United Kingdom. There is to be no travel to the island at all. This ban will be strictly enforced for both air and boat travel.*

"In related news, the PEM, or Pure Earther Movement, has signed several treaties and trade agreements with the PHAE and the Republic of Ireland. The PHAE have announced their intention of honoring these agreements and looking forward to a more peaceful relationship. However, rumors abound in social media channels of a new organization forming, with some of the same leadership of the PEM."

Komie:

As Komie opened her eyes, Fiona's red hair bobbed into view. Her entire body ached, and her head pounded, but the aroma of bread roused her.

"Oh! You're finally awake! I'm so glad. Do you need help to the toilet? You must be bursting."

165

Just as the Irish girl mentioned it, Komie needed the toilet very much indeed. She swung her legs to the side of the bed to rise. Every muscle in her body protested the move and she let out a moan.

"Here, let me get my shoulder under your arm. It's just across the hall."

After taking care of the bodily necessities, Fiona helped her stumble back to the bed and turned to the tray on the side table. "Are you up for bread? We just made it fresh. I brought soup, too."

Komie put a hand to her aching head. "How long did I sleep?"

Fiona swallowed. "Not so long, really. You must have been really tired."

With narrowed eyes, Komie tore a piece of bread off. "How long, Fiona?"

The young girl heaved a sigh. "About two days. But Da said you did a lot of work!"

Her mouth set in a firm line, Komie shook her head. "I need to learn how to pace myself and my use of power. I can't keep collapsing."

"Maybe you can…ask for help? Didn't you say Anú helped you?"

Komie raised her eyebrows. "I'm not in the habit of begging the gods for their help. I believe that is more of a Christian conceit."

"I don't mean begging! But asking. Like, working as a team. This is her land, too. She's our mother goddess. She'd want things to grow."

"Hmm." Komie chewed her bread and took a sip of the steaming tea. Fiona had a point. Perhaps she *should* request aid from the local manifestation of the Great Mother.

A twinge of guilt shot through her pounding skull. She shouldn't be working with an Irish goddess. She should be working with the spirits of her own land, her home, and her ancestors. But she'd asked them before, in a sweat lodge at the Byrne farm. They'd given her permission to work with Anú, but Komie longed for their familiar, empowering presence.

With decisive energy, Komie put her cup down. "Fiona, how do you contact your goddess? You saw my sweat lodge. What do the Irish do?"

"Uh…" Fiona glanced toward the door. "I'm not sure. I mean, we go into church to ask God for help."

"That would be for the Christian God. Who might know about asking Anú?"

"If it were God, I'd ask a priest. But I don't know about the ancient ones. Maybe…we can find a priest of the old religion? Do they have priests? Da might know."

Komie nodded. "Then we shall ask your father. Is he still here? Or has he returned to your farm?"

"No, he's still here. He wouldn't leave without us."

After she'd eaten, dressed, and descended to the family room of the B&B, Colin embraced her tight. "I'm so glad you're feeling better, Komie. Fiona said you had some questions for me?"

"I do. I'd like to contact Anú. Can you please connect me to a priest or priestess of the native Irish religion?"

He cocked his head. "Native Irish? You want a pagan priest?"

"I do. How can I find such a person?"

He frowned and glanced at the ceiling. "That's a fine question. I'm not sure, but there's a Spiritual Centre in Limerick. They're Jesuit, but they'll know the locals. They'll be able to point us in the right direction."

At first, the priest at the Spiritual Centre didn't take them seriously. Then he took them for tourists. Eventually, Colin convinced him of their intent, and he sent him to a place in the Gaeltacht near Spiddal. "There's a woman there who leads ceremonies at the stone circles and dolmens in Connemara. She'll be your man."

Komie snorted at the phrasing but thanked the priest. She hoped this priestess, Caoimhe, would be willing to help. She foresaw another hurdle in convincing the woman of their sincerity.

As Colin, Fiona, and Komie arrived at the Celtic Journey Maze and Gardens, Komie narrowed her eyes at the Disney-esque sign, promising spiritual journeys and tours. However, the Jesuit priest had assured her they were genuine in their beliefs.

They entered the gift shop, filled with books in the Irish language, Brigid's crosses made from many materials, crystals, and jewelry. A clerk behind the check-out counter glanced up with a bright smile. "*Dia daoibh, agus tá failte romhaibh!*"

Colin grinned and replied in kind. "*Dia 's Muire duit!* And thanks for the welcome. We've got some questions about Anú and were directed to ask for Caoimhe. Can you help us?"

The clerk's eyes widened. "Sure, and we can! Would you like me to take you to meet her?"

As they followed the clerk in through a charming café and a set of French doors, Komie noted the subtle designs in the décor. Triple spirals and Celtic knotwork had been painted on the walls, carved in the back of chairs, printed on the tablecloths and napkins.

Once outside, they walked through a wicker arch into the formal gardens. The same triple spiral had been crafted into a waist-high hedge maze.

Bright colored fabric peeked out from behind a hedge, and as they approached, the person turned around, a frown played across her lined face. "Yes?"

"Caoimhe, these good folks wanted to speak with you about Anú. Have you some time?"

Caoimhe narrowed her eyes at first Colin, and then Komie. She didn't even look at Fiona. With a deep sigh and a roll of her eyes, she snapped, "Fine. Follow me. We'll have tea, and you can ask your questions."

They followed her back to the café. She had a confident stride, helped by long legs and a lean frame. She held her back straight and she'd braided her long, graying hair tightly against her scalp.

The priestess gestured toward a round table and disappeared into the kitchen. When she returned five minutes later, she bore a tray with a teapot, four cups, and the typical milk and sweeteners.

The priestess took her own cup with none of these. Komie filed that away as another clue to her personality.

Caoimhe's gaze bore into Colin as he poured tea for Fiona. "Now, Anú. What questions do you have?"

He shook his head. "Not I. Komie here has the questions."

Raising one eyebrow, the woman turned to Komie. "And what would *you* like to know?"

Komie stared at Caoimhe for a long moment before answering. "I would like to contact Anú. Have you a ceremony to do so?"

After a quiet heartbeat, Caoimhe burst out laughing. She pounded the table with the palm of her hand several times before she got her howls under control, the tea things jangling with each impact. When she finally quieted, she wiped the tears from her eyes. "Did Tommy put you up to this? It has to be Tommy."

Komie pressed her lips in a thin line. "I assure you, no one has 'put us up to this.' I am sincerely searching for a way to contact the earth goddess known as Anú."

The other woman glanced first to Colin, then to Fiona, as if searching for the truth in their eyes. Seeing no smiles, she shrugged. The echo of a smile still played across her lips. "Well, that's that, then. Why do you think you want to contact her?"

Komie grew tired of this woman's dismissive language. "I do not *think* I want to contact her. I must contact her. There is no question. She has contacted me several times, and I require information on her intentions."

Caoimhe's face clouded over. "Her…intentions? Anú isn't some young man coming around to court you. You aren't even Irish, not with that skin and accent. Why the hell would *our* goddess be contacting *you*?"

Komie fought to keep her temper in the face of such rudeness, but Colin placed a hand on her arm. Then he turned to Caoimhe. "Komie has recently moved to Ireland, because she is one of the Unhidden. She has an earth power and, as such, has been working with growing things. I believe Anú contacting her is a natural consequence of those workings. She would like to form a strong relationship with Anú to ensure what she does continues to honor Ireland."

Instead of answering right away, Caoimhe sipped her tea. She muttered to herself several times, while Komie exchanged glances with Fiona and Colin. Finally, the other woman rose, her hands on her narrow hips. "Well. Let's go see what we can. Komie, is it? Follow me. The rest of you will stay here."

Colin rose, his mouth open in protest, but Caoimhe pinned him with a glare. "I will not eat her alive. I will, however, determine if she is mistaken, or worse, presumptive. Either way, we shouldn't be more than two hours. Drink your tea."

She strode back through the arch, into the gardens. Komie gave a shrug to Colin and followed. The other woman's legs were long, but Komie didn't hurry to keep up. She refused to be baited into supplicant behavior by default.

Eventually, they came to a tall stone jutting out of the earth. Caoimhe said, "Wait here. Don't touch it."

As the other woman disappeared behind a hedge, Komie studied the stone. Unlike the rest of the gardens, this construction seemed old, ancient as the hills. Carvings in the stone formed the same spirals which decorated every flat surface. Just as she bent closer to examine them, the other woman returned.

She now wore a flowing blue robe, a diadem of delicate silver, and held several candles and bundles in her arms. She deposited them with no ceremony on a nearby stump, then arranged the candles in a circle. All this time, she muttered under her breath, but whether she complained or cast ritual words, Komie had no idea.

Caoimhe stood, holding her arms up in a V formation, muttering in a monotone. Komie couldn't understand the words and guessed the priestess spoke Irish. The woman processed slowly around the ancient standing stone, a candle in her right hand. As she passed Komie, she didn't make eye contact. She gestured with her head for Komie to follow.

Three times they walked sunwise around the circle.

After the third circuit, Caoimhe marched to the stone itself, holding the candle up, to each side, and then down, still intoning in Irish. As she finished, she stood to one side. "Come forward, Komie."

Komie took a step, pulling deep into the earth for stability and connection.

"Stop that! Not yet. Do only as I say."

Caoimhe must have sensed her power. Either she had a genuine connection or had some Unhidden power herself.

The other woman spoke in Irish again. Komie wished she understood the words. She disliked meeting spirits blind. Still, she'd come to ask a favor, and she must accept whatever form the answer took. She'd never been good at languages, but learning Irish might be a survival tactic in the future.

Rumbling beneath her feet made her glance down. Caoimhe hadn't moved her head, but she did shift her feet wide into a power stance. Earthquakes were uncommon in Ireland. She knew that instinctively, having worked with the land. This was no earthquake; it was the earth answering Caoimhe's call.

Bubbles burst forth from the surrounding grass, like boiling water. Komie resisted the urge to step aside and avoid the blisters.

"Who calls me?"

The words weren't in English. They weren't in her head, either. They boomed across the gardens in several tones, as if three voices spoke at once in different registers. The sound made her skull itch.

"Your priestess, Caoimhe, calls you, Anú."

"Why?"

"I have one here who would be your student. Will you accept her?"

Komie wasn't certain she wanted to commit to being a student of anyone or anything. She just wanted to talk to Anú, to find out how to honor her adopted land. But neither Caoimhe nor Anú gave her any time to redirect the statement.

"Touch me."

Caoimhe gestured for Komie to place her hands on the stone. The ancient stone that now glowed the deep, intense green of moss growing beneath an oak tree in a northern forest.

Komie gripped the spiral pattern cut into the stone with both hands. The stone screamed. Vital lifeforce sparked through her body, from her hands, up her arms, down through her torso and into her toes. Her head almost exploded with writhing things, bursting with verdant power, but she didn't let go.

Komie screamed with the stone. Her body twisted, trying to escape the pain, but her hands remained stuck to the spiral cut pattern. Growing tendrils formed in her fingers and toes, questing out into the world. Her hair danced like Medusa's snakes, green shoots thickening her gray locks.

Finally, the pain subsided and Komie slumped against the ancient stone, sliding down to the blessed ground.

As the blackness enveloped her, Caoimhe crossed her arms. "Huh. I guess she really did want you."

Chapter Eight

"If you can, help others; if you cannot do that, at least do not harm them."
– Dalai Lama XIV

Róisín:

Róisín looked forward to seeing Komie again. She hadn't spoken with the native woman since she left the farm. That seemed like ages ago. Had it only been a month? She couldn't even keep track any more. The days swam together. Ever since her recovery, her head ached at random times and her brain fogged with confusion.

As they approached the Celtic Journey Maze and Gardens, her father clapped her on the shoulder, pointing at the sign. "I know it looks like the absolutely worst tourist tat, but this woman's the real thing."

Giving her father side-eye, she pursed her lips. "If you say so, Da. I don't imagine Komie would have any patience for someone faking it. You say she's been here for a while?"

"We left her here before I fell ill. She sent word that she's been learning a great deal."

As he led her in through the brightly lit gift shop, nodded to the clerk, and emerged into the ornamental gardens, Róisín let out her breath as the lush greenery enveloped her like a cool embrace. At least this was a true healing space. Her energy surged just stepping on the path.

As they passed a lone hawthorn tree, she got the sudden urge to stop, laying her hand on the bark. An electric thrill shot through her arm, making her jerk back. "Ow!"

A sharp, female voice came from behind her. "Touching that tree isn't a good idea."

Róisín whirled to confront the snide tone and came face-to-face with an older woman, her graying hair pulled back in a waist-length braid. Her crossed arms and her severe frown reminded Róisín of the nuns in school.

Komie stood behind her but stepped in for a hug. "Róisín! Oh, it's a delight to see you again."

Róisín held the older woman tight, infusing a gentle healing into her trembling body. She felt even more exhausted than Róisín.

The other woman's voice cut through their hug. "Stop that, right now! If you're going to enter my sanctuary, I'll have no unasked-for workings here. Is that understood?"

Guilty, Róisín dropped her arms and her gaze. Komie turned, her hands on her hips, standing between Róisín and the other woman. "This is my friend. We have greeted each other in the manner acceptable to both our cultures. She is a healer, so it's natural for her to lend me strength. If you consider that interference, then we will both leave immediately. If you can't accept basic courtesy, I have no use for your help, even with the gods."

The strength in Komie's strident words gave Róisín heart, and her father clapped her on the shoulder. "It seems you're in good hands here. Caoimhe, may I leave my daughter with you? She has some questions similar to Komie's. I need a good cuppa. I'll be in the gift shop if any of you need me."

Róisín didn't like the older woman and wanted to beg him to stay. But she knew he needed rest, so she contented herself with a wave, then straightened her spine to face this new person.

The priestess in question glared at Komie, but the native woman gave no ground. Finally, the Irish woman nodded once and spun on her heel, striding deeper into the gardens. Komie glanced back at Róisín and gestured for her to follow. "She's caustic as hell but knows her stuff. She's helped me forge a bond with Anú. I've learned so much through that link. It's worth the rudeness."

Róisín wasn't all that certain she could deal with the rude woman without slapping her, but for Komie's sake, she'd give it a try. She rubbed her aching eyes. Where had that thought come from? She'd never slapped anyone in her life. She must still need more rest.

Caoimhe led them past a complex labyrinth hedge, a firepit surrounded by rough wooden benches, several fragrant herb gardens, and through three wicker arches dripping with vines and flowers. The only sound reaching this sanctuary was the soft soughing of wind through the trees and the sweet caress of birdsong.

A large roundhouse, in the manner of iron age dwellings, stood in a clearing surrounded by rhododendrons. The woody stalks rose around the edge, cradling the area like a protective wall.

The place looked lived in, with a firepit outside, and a half-cut animal hide on a wooden bench. Primitive tools lay around the fire pit, as if the artisan had been interrupted in their task.

The priestess ducked through the low doorway. When Róisín followed, she had to blink to accustom her vision to the dim light. Benches surrounded a central hearth, with tables and fabric-walled alcoves around the outside. Their guide gestured toward the benches as she fetched a pitcher and wooden cups.

After she poured each of them a drink, she stared at Róisín. "Well? What's your question?"

Cradling the cup in her hand, Róisín took a deep breath. "I tried to heal my father but wasn't making any progress."

"That isn't a question."

Róisín pressed her lips together. "I hadn't finished."

"Get on with it. I don't have all day."

Trying not to crush the cup, Róisín breathed out and closed her eyes before continuing. "Everything I did only kept him from getting worse. Finally, out of desperation, I asked for help, like a prayer. A voice answered me."

"What did it say?"

She swallowed, her gaze flickering to Komie. "They said, 'I can help you.' Then a flood of power rushed through me, and Da instantly got better."

Caoimhe took a sip from her cup and Róisín did the same. She almost choked on the powerful spirits. It wasn't whiskey, or anything so refined. Had the priestess distilled this herself? The roughest of *poitín*, then.

"What else?"

With liquor-roughened voice, Róisín continued. "When I asked them who they were, they said 'I am a healer.' But when I asked for their name, they said nothing. I don't know if they'd gone away or just didn't want to answer."

Caoimhe tapped her fingers on her cup. "Interesting. Interesting indeed. First *Anú*, now *Dian Cécht*, if I don't miss my guess. He's always been the swift one." She chuckled as an enigmatic half-smile spread across her face.

The *draoí* stared into the unlit firepit, tapping over and over again. Róisín glanced at Komie again and the native woman shrugged. Caoimhe rose abruptly, slamming her cup on the wooden table. "Right. I don't see any way around it. We must go to *Uisneach*. You're lucky it's almost *Lúnasa*. I'll gather the others."

The Hill of Uisneach, one of the spots she'd identified on her father's map. The spiritual center of Ireland. A massive hill with ancient tombs, mounds, and standing stones. Likely a few holy wells sprinkled on top. Local pagans held annual *Bealtaine* festivals there. She'd seen photos and videos from the celebrations, full of bonfires at twilight.

A cold shiver ran down her spine as she crossed herself. What had she gotten herself into?

Róisín:

After they arrived at Uisneach, Róisín trudged up the hill, halting frequently to mop the sweat off her forehead and cheeks. This hill was steeper than it looked, hidden behind hedgerows and a deep tree line. They'd already passed several standing stones, like avenue markers. Now a huge, amorphous stone loomed on the hill's crest. When they reached the top, Komie leaned against a tree, her hands on her knees, panting heavily. At least Komie had the excuse of being sixty years old. Róisín needed to catch her breath, too, and she was barely thirty. She felt so weak and out of shape.

Caoimhe ignored their distress and pulled supplies from her backpack. She laid out a circle of white pebbles around the large standing stone. Someone else shouted from down the hill. The priestess waved at them without looking up from her task.

Three more people arrived up the path. As they arrived on the crest, Róisín noted their appearances, two with beards, and one more androgynous. They exchanged bare nods with Caoimhe as they pulled items out of their own bags. None of them greeted either Róisín or Komie.

The four Irish *draoíthe*, or priests, gathered in a small knot, exchanging words, while Róisín's heart finally calmed to a normal speed. Komie no longer breathed heavily. One *draoí* glanced at the bright, clear sky with a grimace while another set up an altar with a bowl, goblet, and herbs.

Róisín turned to her friend. "You said you've learned a lot from Caoimhe. How do you deal with her attitude?"

The native woman shrugged. "I've dealt with people's attitudes and arrogance all my life. Their behavior is not a reflection of my worth. Once you embrace that, it makes little difference to your own actions. Now, if

Caoimhe acted inappropriately to Fiona, for instance, I would take her to task, just as I did when she was rude to you. However, her knowledge has been worth dealing with her manner."

Their behavior is not a reflection of my worth. Róisín resolved to keep that phrase close and remind herself of it often. "Thank you, Komie. I'll try to do that."

They exchanged a secret smile as the older woman touched her shoulder.

Caoimhe approached with long strides. "You both wait here and enter the circle when told."

The other *draoithe* stood in a semicircle around a crackling firepit. When had they lit a fire? Róisín had no recollection of that. Had they smuggled up a flamethrower?

A camp table stood next to the fire. Upon it lay a wooden bowl with fruit, a whiskey bottle, and a Brigid's Cross made of wheat sheaves. One *draoí* sprinkled herbs on the fire, releasing billows of fragrant smoke. The odor caressed them, sweet and cloying. Her nose tickled as the sky swirled above. One poured whiskey into the fire, making it flare and crackle.

The four *draoithe* marched around the fire three times, clockwise, taking their original positions again. Caoimhe stood at the north edge of the circle, her head thrown back and arms raised to the sky.

Beannacht nime, nél-beannacht,
Beannacht tíre, torad-beannacht,
Beannacht mara, íasc-beannacht.

Éist lenár nglao, Anú.
Éist lenár nglao, Dian Cécht.
Éist lenár nglao, agus tabhair d'eagna dúinn!

Róisín didn't understand most of her chant. Her Irish was rudimentary, to her father's eternal frustration. She could ask for the bathroom or carry on a simple conversation with memorized phrases. All Irish children learned that much in school. But anything beyond that slipped away from her memory like sand through netting.

Komie leaned over and whispered, "What is she saying? I recognized Anú's name, but nothing else."

With a shrug, Róisín shook her head. "I don't have a lot of Irish. I heard Dian Cécht. Dad has some tales about him. I know *Éist* is 'listen,' and *beannacht* is 'blessing,' but I don't know the rest."

They repeated the chant a dozen times before they regrouped and returned to their bags. They came back with more offerings. One carried a small clay pot, which they poured over the fire, producing a thick, amber-colored liquid. The scent of burnt honey hung in the air. Another carried something made with feathers. Evidently, they had to up the ante.

This time, they chanted with more fervor, a staccato rhythm, almost shouting the words as fire swirled sparks into the late afternoon sky.

After a dozen more repeats, Caoimhe frowned, glanced at the other *draoíthe*, and heaved a deep sigh. She stepped toward the firepit and pulled out a short, wicked-looking dagger. Before Róisín could protest, the priestess sliced her left thumb, squeezing drops of blood into the crackling fire.

It spat and hissed. A cold wind cut across the hill, making her shiver. She rubbed her arms to smooth the goosebumps. The previously bright sky grew dark. Róisín and Komie exchanged a glance and then stared at the dark, angry clouds spinning above. Komie sucked in her breath and Róisín fumbled for the other woman's hand, squeezing tight.

Thunder roared across the hill. Forked lightning struck the fire with a nerve-shattering *crack*.

A voice boomed behind her eyes. **"Cé a ghlaonn orm?"**

Róisín shivered and clutched harder at Komie's hand.

Caoimhe spoke in a strident voice. "I am Caoimhe, *Draoí na Ráth Cruachan*. I call you."

"What do you offer?"

Her blood chilled and her knees didn't want to work. A sudden, horrid thought intruded on Róisín's mind, with echoes of bad horror films. Were they a sacrifice? Scenes from horror movies flickered through Róisín's memory and she swallowed, trying to soften her dry throat. At least whatever answered them had switched to English, though the heavy accent was difficult to understand.

"We offer you gifts." Another *draoí* lifted the four-armed Brigid's Cross, a complex weave of braided wheat sheafs. Róisín remembered making them each November with her father, but nothing this big. A third *draoí* lifted the bowl with apples, berries, and sunflowers. The fourth sang out in a clear, sweet alto, their wordless voice holding a single note. As the note died, silence grew heavy upon their shoulders, the only sound left being the wind of the storm.

"Your gifts are acceptable. Ask your question."

"These women seek counsel of the gods. One is called to Anú. One is called to Dian Cécht."

Panic gripped Róisín and she wanted to scream *No, I'm not!* But her body refused to move, much less shout. She didn't want to be called to any god, certainly not some ancient god she'd barely heard of.

"Step closer."

Caoimhe moved aside and gestured toward the fire. This must be their time to enter the circle. With a nervous glance at Komie, Róisín approached. The flames warmed her face as the storm whistled behind her. The faint spray of rain made the hair on her arms stand up. Komie stepped next to her, back straight and chin up.

"Nokomis Rayne Nicholas, honored grandmother of the *Wəlastəkwewiyik*. You have traveled far from your ancestors' land."

Komie's shoulders tensed as the older woman answered with steel in her voice. "I have already received their blessing to work in foreign lands. It is not for you to judge me."

Booming laughter ran around them like a pack of circling dogs. **"You may stay. Anú will not come, but I shall."**

The native woman glanced up at the storm clouds. "By what name shall I call you?"

"You will call me Macha."

Róisín may not recall much of Dian Cécht, but the name of Macha wove through many of the ancient tales. Her father's voice echoed in her ears, telling of the goddess of war, of magic, of sovereignty. A goddess of dark stories, tragic battles, and dangerous magic. A goddess she never wanted to meet.

Da's going to shit himself. As she stifled a giggle, Róisín schooled her expression. Thinking of her father helped steady Róisín's nerves. She squared her shoulders and lifted her chin, as Komie had done. So what if the goddess of death, destruction, and blood wanted them?

"Róisín Sarah Byrne of the Ó Brioin, descendant of Bran mac Máelmórda, King of Leinster."

All of her resolve fled the moment Macha spoke her name. Bran mac Máelmórda? She vaguely remembered that name from history class, the founder of the Byrne family a thousand years ago. It took every ounce of bravery to not turn tail and run away from this booming thundercloud calling her name.

"Come closer."

Her knees locked, but Komie placed a hand on her shoulder and whispered, "Be the strong woman you are."

She stepped closer, her face now blazing with the heat of the bonfire.

"You interest me."

Róisín's breath caught. What would she do if a goddess wanted her for herself? How could she fight a goddess's will?

"But you are not to be mine. Another claims you. You are the chosen of Dian Cécht. He answered your call and accepted you as his acolyte."

Thunder crashed again, a double-forked bolt of lightning striking the flame. The bonfire was quenched in an oily cloud and the sky cleared, leaving only a trail of smoke and the acrid odor of charred wood.

Róisín's knees finally buckled, and she fell to the ground. Darkness embraced her. After some time, a rough voice intruded on the gray. "Wake up, girl. What are you playing at?"

Róisín groaned and held her aching head. When she opened her eyes, Caoimhe's angry face glared at her. "What in the name of Anú's green earth are you about, fainting in front of Macha? Are you so eager to be a sacrifice?"

"Wh-what?"

The *draoí* rolled her eyes, pulling Róisín up to her feet. "You can't show weakness! This is not the time nor the place to play the fainting princess."

Clouds still swirled above, but the metallic taste in the back of her mouth had disappeared, and the scent of ozone no longer filled her nose. "Is she gone?"

"Aye, and lucky for you. She might have just taken you, and you with no way to stop her." The priestess strode to the table, where the other *draoí* packed their items away.

Róisín wrinkled her nose. "Like I have any power to stop her when I'm awake?"

Caoimhe whirled on her. "You can fecking say no, you stupid girl!"

Komie held up her hand. "You will not speak to Róisín in that manner. I will not permit it."

"What in the name of the gods do you have to do with it, Komie? Do you think because Macha chose you, you can wield some power over me? I've been her priestess for a dozen years."

The native woman raised her eyebrows. "Length of service does not give you the right to abuse others."

She threw up her hands. "For the sake of all the gods, I'm *not* abusing her! I'm trying to protect her, and us with her. If she can't handle herself around the gods, I can't save her from her own folly. Sugarcoating it would do neither of us any favors. I don't have the patience, and *she* doesn't have the time."

Time. Time swirled around Róisín's mind like a scrap of paper in a whirlwind. She kept trying to catch a glimpse of it, but it danced at the edge of her vision.

Caoimhe hesitated with the Brigit's cross in her hand. "No, she didn't answer the call. I don't need to toss that into the fire." She shoved it into her bag. The fruit, however, she placed within the stones lining the firepit, next to the empty honey jar.

Róisín tried to shake the cobwebs from her head. "What about time? Why don't I have any?"

Caoimhe turned on her. "Dian Cécht. He'll come for you. Maybe in two minutes, maybe in two days. But he's accepted you. He might not be as imperious as Macha, but he's bloody demanding and fast. If you can't keep up, you'll die trying."

This seemed like a dream conversation. The words didn't make sense. Róisín couldn't think straight. "Die? I already almost died. I don't need to do that again."

The priestess let out a humorless snort. "Then Dian Cécht has already attended you. He'll be back, mark my words." She turned to the native woman. "Komie, you aren't getting Anú. Macha has tagged you, and one doesn't argue with Macha's choices. Do you want to continue instruction with me? While I've honored her for decades, she's only rarely spoken to me in the past. You've just graduated past my skill set."

Caoimhe's arrogance faded, and she dropped her gaze. Perhaps Macha's appearance cracked her priestess persona. However it happened, Róisín liked her more. Well, at least disliked her less.

Komie shrugged. "A wise woman knows when she's out of her league, and I need any help you're willing to give. I'm unfamiliar with the Irish pantheon, their traditions, and their folklore, despite Colin's endless stories. I need to know what I'm dealing with and what not to do. If you're still willing to help, I'd be honored to learn from you."

Caoimhe gave a single nod and turned to Róisín. "I can teach you, as well. However, Dian Cécht keeps his own counsel, and his healing magic is far more specialized. Since you're a healer, you'd quickly outstrip my poor knowledge. Your father is a folklore scholar. Have you grown up on the tales, at least?"

Róisín gave a startled nod, swallowing against the apprehension welling up inside her.

"Then you should know how to deal with the Other Crowd. I can teach you little else."

Róisín stared at the sky. How would this god contact her? She didn't want him calling her as she drove on the highway. Maybe he'd come in her dreams.

The *draoithe* finished their packing and descended the hill. Komie took Róisín's hand. "We'd best follow. Caoimhe drove us here, remember?"

Róisín:

Róisín and Komie returned to the Byrne farmhouse. The kitchen was empty, but she heard someone upstairs. Suddenly starving, she opened the breadbox and pulled out a half loaf of brown bread, slicing herself three. Her mother just poked her head in as she asked, "Komie? Would you like some?"

Before the native woman could answer, white-hot pain flashed in her mind. She grabbed her temples and fell to her knees. Her mother rushed to help her, but Komie held her off. "The *draoí* said a god would contact her. This might be their first contact."

Shaking the older woman off, her mother knelt by Róisín. "The *draoí*? What are you talking about? Róisín, what's wrong? Has your illness returned? Talk to me."

The world swirled gray. Autumn leaves spun around her, a whirlwind of crackling color. A voice boomed in her head. **"You are to be mine."**

Róisín's forehead pounded with a thousand drums. The voice dripped of familiar comfort and yet set her nerves tingling. "Who are you? Will you tell me now?"

"You know who I am. The *draoí* told you."

She didn't like his evasive answers. "Tell me your name. If I'm to work with you, you must tell me."

A low chuckle came as her answer, warm and sticky like a treacle tart. **"You have strength. You will need it."**

That sounded ominous. A scrap of memory flashed. "Tell me your name. I ask you three times."

Róisín instantly regretted asking, as he let out a booming laugh, the sound bouncing in her head. **"Your mind has been befuddled with false tales and silly rumors. I have no obligation to grant your request, but I shall, in the interest of working together. As you have been told by Macha's pet, I am Dian Cécht, healer of the *Tuatha Dé Danaan* Father of Cu, Cethen, Cian, Miach, Airmed, Étan, and Octriúil."**

"I didn't ask for your genealogical chart. I asked your name."

Another chuckle. **"You amuse me. Now, we must begin."**

She didn't want to begin anything, not with her head pounding like a Japanese Kodo drum troupe. "If you want me to be any help, you'll stop hurting my head, immediately."

"I do not take commands from humans. However, your request has wisdom. You will learn more easily if you do not have pain. I shall heal you."

As her head stopped throbbing, Róisín wanted to scream. Her father would be so disappointed in her folly. She'd just accepted a favor from the Fae, without hammering out the details. How could she be so stupid? She put her idiocy down to pain. She could think more clearly now that it had disappeared.

From somewhere far away, her mother's voice called her name. She followed it, turning her back on Dian Cécht and his booming laughter.

"You must stay here. We are not finished."

Róisín spun around, her lips set in a firm line, and her mother's voice sprang from her lips. "Yes, I want to learn from you. No, I will not ignore my life and family for you. Are these terms acceptable? If not, go away and find another apprentice."

For a frantic moment, Róisín considered praying to Jesus Christ and Mother Mary to rid herself of this demanding, arrogant ancient entity. As a good Catholic, she had faith prayer would banish the pagan god. But what if he held the secret to healing this plague? How could she balance the cost of her own soul against millions of lives? This time, it would be her mother who would be disappointed in her. She hadn't been raised to be so selfish.

Instead of calling upon Jesus, Mary, and Joseph, Róisín took a deep breath. "Do you agree to my terms?"

"We are agreed. Attend to your family until sundown. I shall return then."

She swallowed and nodded. "So be it."

Max:

As the winds carried him into the sky and him away from Qacha, Max clenched his fists. He wished he had enough power to save the Mongolian woman. He might punch one attacker and convince the wind to blow down two or three others. But sixteen? He didn't have the strength for that many.

Qacha had incredible resources and sharp intelligence. She'd realize he had to get away without her. He hoped. As prickly as she was, she was the only person whose opinion he actually cared about.

Except Róisín.

For a brief moment, Max fancied asking the winds to carry him back to the hospital. Maybe even let her do whatever she'd tried to heal in his brain, if she'd healed by now. But they'd kicked him out once, and he had no doubt his own stunning talent for diplomacy would earn another ejection.

No, this time he must truly go off on his own.

He cursed when he realized all his hard-stolen supplies were piled in the cottage. "Take me down behind that hill until they're gone."

The ground rushed at him. He instinctively raised his hands to brake as they dropped him. This time, they brought him more gently than when he tumbled before Qacha, but it was still too fast for his comfort. He was sure to get bruises all over his hips and shoulders. *I'm getting too bloody old for this shit.*

Max climbed an outcropping to get a clearer view of the abandoned cottage. Movement out of the corner of his eyes made him freeze. Black forms crawled the hill, and under his breath, he counted the intruders. Sixteen, seventeen, eighteen… how many in total? Did they leave anyone? He remembered ten at first, then three more ambushed them, but then he'd lost count.

Three carried Qacha's limp body. Had they knocked her out? Her power should have roasted them. They must have been warned about what she could do. Three men sprawled on the ground. Others picked them up. Were any of them dead?

Along with Qacha, Max counted twenty people climbing or being carried toward the road. He waited for a half hour before emerging from his hiding spot. He crept up to the back of the cottage, listening for sounds. Nothing but seagulls crying in the distance and the wind howling around the hills.

He listened at the front door. Nothing stirred inside. Holding his breath, he entered. A sharp pain, a flash of light, and everything went dark.

After swimming in the gray for some unknown time, Max groaned and opened his eyes. His head ached like the devil. Why did it pulse with pain? He tried to touch his scalp, but his hands were tied. Someone had hit him and tied him. The invaders must have left someone behind after all. So much for his finely tuned senses. *Bloody hell.*

In the dim light, a shadow stirred. "Good morning, sunshine."

The accent sounded, Australian and for a moment, a wave of homesickness washed over him. He couldn't tag the voice as male or female. He craned his neck to see who spoke. Only the darkness stared back, until they smiled. "Who the fuck are you, mate?"

A figure stood, towering over him. A powerful person. He still couldn't discern any gender. "I'm Ash. You're coming with me on a mission, Max."

Dark skin. Aboriginal. Deep voice, but in the range of some women. Strong shoulders, slender waist. Max tried to see what their arms looked like but couldn't see details under their thick sweater. "Like hell I am, *Ash*. Why am I tied up?"

They crossed their arms. "Don't worry, I'll let you loose as soon as I have your word you won't fly away. Also, if you look around, you'll notice I've shut both the windows and the door. No wind is allowed inside this charming hovel until I say so."

Then they knew his power. *Damn.* "And why should I promise *you* anything?"

"Because I have a proposal for you. Also, I brought whiskey."

Someone had done their bloody homework. "Right, mate. Well, tell me your proposal, then. And pour me a shot."

As Ash poured two shots, Max searched for more clues to his captor's identity. They wore a simple shirt and jeans. Hair pulled back tight offered no clues. He mentally shrugged and stared at the shot as Ash held it out. "How the hell do you expect me to drink that with my hands tied?"

They flashed him a grin and held the cup to Max's lips. For a moment, he considered refusing until they untied him, but he really needed that drink. Maybe it would ease the pain shooting through his skull. They must have walloped him. He'd have one hell of a goose-egg in the morning, to add to all the bruises from falling. He tipped his head back, and Ash poured the liquor into his mouth.

Not being in control of the drink, he almost choked and coughed, but that would be a waste of whiskey, a true crime against nature. He swallowed, relishing the burn on his throat. A burning throat reminded him of his friend. "Where did your mates take Qacha?"

"She'll be cared for. They won't hurt her."

Max didn't believe any assurances from this person.

They sat cross-legged across from him. The dim light still didn't reveal details, but their accent was familiar and soothing. "So, this proposal. We need to go to England."

"England? Bloody hell. Why would I go to England? I can barely stand it in Ireland."

"The PHAE needs information about the PEM."

Max let out a bark of laughter. "Isn't that what hackers are for? Look, I know I'm a dinosaur, but isn't paper more old-fashioned than I am? Who uses paper nowadays?"

They shrugged. "We have hackers on the problem, but the PEM are canny, especially since Tiberius Wilkinson took over. They've kept a lot of their records on paper, for that reason. We need those records."

"Why?"

They rolled their eyes. "To keep them from bombing us again, for one thing. What are you, thick?"

Max ignored the insult. "What'll they do with these records?"

"I haven't been given that information. Neither will you be. We have our mission."

"You're a bit light on details, luv. Why don't you pour me another shot as you flesh them out?"

Ash obliged with another shot, much to Max's satisfaction. Maybe, if they talked long enough, he'd get pleasantly drunk.

"So, we've got a flight booked…"

Max shook his head. "Stop right there, sunshine. No can do. I don't do well with commercial flights."

They rolled their eyes. "I've read your history. If I need to get you dead drunk for the trip, I will."

He thought about offering to take them both via the winds, but he didn't feel like letting anyone else in on that particular trick, and wasn't certain he could get across the ocean, anyhow. He clenched his jaw. "Fine. What next?"

"We find the records complex for Britain First, extract what we need, and return the information to the PHAE."

Max furrowed his brow, enjoying the growing buzz the shots had given him. "What the hell is Britain First?"

"One of the many far-right organization who support the PEM. We need membership records and recruitment data."

"Right. Correct me if I'm wrong, but won't there be a bit of security?"

Ash grinned, their teeth bright in the gloom. "I have some talent to help with that."

He narrowed his eyes. "Right, what talent's that? And why me?"

They shrugged. "You'll discover that in time. As for why you, well, you've proven your abilities to think on your feet, protect others, and you can keep doors shut with the wind. Given your rep, I asked for you."

That, he couldn't believe. If anyone read about his past, they'd realize he was far from a reliable person. Hell, he'd worked bloody *hard* to be as unreliable as humanly possible. And he'd excelled at that mission. "Why the hell would you do that?"

Another grin flashed in the darkness. "You're already a legend in Australia, Max. Clips of you destroying that boat in Cork are all over the net. You've gone viral."

He drooped. Fame was the last thing he wanted. "Bloody hell." Max chewed on his lip. If they sent this person, they knew his capabilities. They'd found him readily enough. Had they tracked his progress here?

Is that how they found Qacha? Was she captured because of his own incompetence?

He'd have to discover more about that. For now, he studied his erstwhile companion. They seemed capable, stable, and intelligent. He appreciated those qualities. He also liked that they didn't pry or get emotional. He decided he could work with this Ash if he had to.

And it seemed he had to. He might escape again, into the wild, but he must find out first if they had a tracker on him. If they would just find him again, flying away would do bugger-all.

He'd help Ash, and then reassess. He meant to discover some answers in the meantime. "Right. Pour me another shot, luv."

Anna:

Anna reveled in the delicious saltwater currents as she slid through the waves. She'd never felt so free before in her life. Not in the swimming pool at the college she used to coach for. Not in a thunderstorm. Not even when rushing downhill on her bike. All of her worries shed away from her body as her scales glistened and shone in the light every time she surfaced.

She stole a glance back to the shore. A sole figure stood there, waving his hands. Her mind supplied the name, as if of someone long-forgotten, an ancient memory from another life. *Brendan.* The name tugged at her, but another name pulled her back.

Manannán mac Lir. The god of the sea.

Anna must answer this call, even if she never did anything else. Only answering his demand would allow her to live her life to the fullest, the way she must live. The way she was born to live, upon the undulating waves of the ocean.

The last dregs of the storm disappeared as she swam further out from the shoreline. Soon, she couldn't even see the land any longer. It didn't matter, as she was home. Finally, after thirty years, she found someplace she actually felt was her home. Her place. Her family.

The call brought her further to the south, and she followed it willingly, eager to discover what was waiting for her when she arrived.

A wave rose above her, and she shot through the middle, laughing with glee and the freedom of no expectations, no clock, no students, no responsibilities, and no stress.

And still he called.

For a moment, she rebelled, and didn't want to answer his summons. She had freedom, why should she shackle herself again with responsibilities? But Anna knew she couldn't resist forever if she wanted to live in his realm. So, she headed toward the source of the voice, thrumming through the sea water and into her mind.

As she approached the three lonely islands off the coast, seals barked a welcome. She came to a sheltered cove with a sea cave, a sandy beach, and a tall headland overlooking them both. People would find it difficult to access this spot from the cliff above, which would make it an ideal retreat.

She pulled herself onto the rocks and caught her breath after the long journey. While she loved just being in the sea, she basked in the sun next to a few young seals, soaking up the warmth. The waves still splashed upon her skin every few moments, so her skin never grew dry enough to itch. She might live here for a while, if she could get food.

"What I wouldn't give for a big, greasy slice of pizza right now." The sea was lovely, but her stomach growled loud enough to be heard over the surf.

At the mention of food, one of the seals barked and slapped his tail against the rock. Two others dove into the water.

Just as she wondered if they had somehow either understood her words or heard her stomach rumbling, something gurgled beneath the ocean surface. A great whirlpool formed, white water at the edges forming a tempest in a teacup.

A bubble formed, pale aqua, rising larger and larger in the center of the whirlpool. Anna struggled to sit up to face whatever this new threat was. Suddenly, the top burst forth in a spray of seawater, revealing a man.

As the water sluiced from him, Anna realized she was mistaken. He wasn't a man. Sure, he had a man's form, but he stood at least eight feet tall with skin of pale blue. Where a man would have hair, he had seaweed, flowing in the ocean breeze. Where a man would wear clothing, he wore scales, similar to her own.

Is this the form she would eventually take? Was she looking at her own future? As much as she loved the water, a shiver ran down her spine. She didn't want to be an eight-foot-tall blue sea creature.

He spoke, his voice filled with the rushing of the tide on a moonlit beach. **"You have come."**

Komie:

After Róisín explained to her parents what happened on the Hill of Uisneach, answered her father's eager questions, and quieted her mother's worries, they returned to the Celtic Journey Maze and Gardens. Komie and Róisín followed Caoimhe back to her iron age roundhouse. Despite the early evening hour, the *draoi* collapsed on the sleeping pallet and waved the other two women away. "I need rest after that. Go play in the plants. Give me at least four hours."

She turned her back, pulling a rough-woven wool blanket over her shoulder.

As Komie and Róisín left the roundhouse, the older woman crossed her arms. "Well, I'm certainly not tired yet. We've got sleeping quarters next to the gift shop, unless you'd rather return to the farm. Would you like a tour of the gardens? It's really a lovely space. I've been helping them grow while refining my powers."

"I would love that! But I'm starved. Can we get tea at the shop first?"

Sandwiches and tea calmed her nerves after the ordeal on Uisneach. Would Macha contact her here? Or would she need to go through all that again to secure the goddess' attention? Komie didn't really want to work with this strident goddess. Macha seemed like Caoimhe, powerful but imperious. Komie didn't do well with imperious. Her own grandmother had been imperious, and they'd fought often. She preferred the gentle voice of Anu, the few times she'd spoken. Nurturing, protecting, and very mother-like.

The gardens, designed for tourist traffic, had spotlights shining along each winding path. Despite the late hour, they could see well enough to explore.

Róisín cradled a yellow and white flower in her hand. "Do you think Caoimhe would be upset if I harvested some of her feverfew? It's useful in healing."

A voice boomed across the clearing. **"You are never to steal from my garden. If you would take supplies, you must receive my permission first."**

Komie took a step back, glancing up to the starry sky, her eyes darting back and forth to identify the source of the voice. Róisín clenched her jaw. "Is that you back again?"

"We had a bargain. You had your freedom until dusk. It is now dusk."

Róisín turned pale but held her head high. "Very well. Let's discuss how we will work together."

A bright light flashed at the end of the path, so bright Komie had to shade her eyes. It grew as it came closer, resolving into a human form. When her eyes finally adjusted, the figure took shape. A tall man with long, brown hair and a strong jawline strode toward them, his shoulders back and his spine straight. A multi-colored cape fell to his knees, and he wore a white tunic, belted at the waist.

Róisín's mouth dropped open as he strode to her. He gripped her shoulders, staring straight into her eyes. His voice boomed in three echoes. **"You are my apprentice. You will learn from me. You will heal others."**

The Irish woman fell to her knees with a cry, her gaze still locked with his. Róisín's body trembled but seemed unable to escape his spell.

Anger rose in Komie's blood. How dare this entity take control of her friend? Komie grabbed his arm, trying to pull his hand off her shoulder, but his arm felt like rock. He spared her the barest glance and then his gaze slid off her. He returned his attention to Róisín. **"I will teach you the magic of the gods."**

Róisín let out a strangled cry, as if trying to speak through a paralyzed throat.

Komie clenched her fists. "And what if she doesn't want to learn?"

Dian Cécht spun on her again, his eyes narrowing. **"You are not to speak, woman."**

Her eyes grew wide. "The *hell*, you say! I won't permit my friend to be bullied by anyone, not even the likes of you. What if she doesn't want to learn?"

"She already requested it. I have accepted her request. The bargain is sealed."

That sounded far too final for Komie's taste. Róisín found her voice, waving her hand at Komie, her eyes glued on the healing god. Her tone sounded flat, but the words came clear. "No, it's okay. I want to learn! I dreamt of this."

Komie growled under her breath, her gaze shifting from Róisín to Dian Cécht, but she stepped back. If this was what the younger woman truly wanted, she had no call to interfere. Dian Cécht locked eyes with his apprentice and some of his brightness flowed into her. Róisín gasped, her back arched. Her hair spread out as if filled with static charge. The Irish woman opened her mouth in a silent, painful scream.

Komie stepped toward them again, ready to push the god aside.

Another voice called behind her. **"They are not your concern, Nokomis Rayne Nicholas."**

Spinning to confront this new threat, Komie spied another shining figure emerging from the night. This one stood as tall as Dian Cécht, but with long, black hair tightly braided against her skull. Leather armor covered her body from shoulder to toe, not an inch of skin showing other than her face and hands. An enormous raven rode her shoulder, glowing black against the garden lights. The raven cawed, the raucous sound echoing through the gardens.

"I'm guessing you're Macha."

"You need not state the obvious. You will be mine to teach."

Still stung with Dian Cécht's arrogant attitude, Komie crossed her arms. "I didn't ask for your help. I asked for Anú's help. I'm told you are a goddess of battles. What do you know of plants and the earth?"

A slow smile spread across Macha's face, her black lips stretching over white teeth. **"That is for you to learn."**

The girl from the gift shop poked her head out, her eyes wide at the shining strangers. "Uh, Komie? Phone call for you."

Who would be calling her here? Colin?

"What is this message?"

She glared at Macha. "A telephone call. A conversation from far away. And this is my personal business. We can continue when I'm finished."

The goddess scowled and the raven cawed, but she gave a single nod and faded into the gloom. Komie suppressed a shiver as she hurried to the gift shop. When she reached the phone, the crackling voice had a southwestern American accent. "Komie? It's Tom."

196

Her heart pounded as she asked, "Is everything alright? How's Tansy?"

"Calm yerself, woman, everything's fine. I just thought you'd like to hear something." As Komie breathed in deep from relief, a shuffle sounded and she heard a baby's voice say, "Gamma!"

Komie's heart ached to hold her granddaughter, a half a world away. "Hello, my sweet baby. I love you so much!"

She sniffed the tears away as Tom returned to the phone. "I thought ye might want to hear her latest word. She says it whenever we show her yer photo. She's a smart little girl, no doubt about it."

"Thank you, Tom. How is everything else there? Any news?"

As he regaled her with the gossip from her former home, Komie held her granddaughter's voice close to her heart, determined to keep the sound like a talisman against future trials.

When she returned to the garden, Macha had disappeared. So had Dian Cécht. Róisín lay curled up asleep on a stone bench. Komie woke her and helped her stumble to their room behind the gift shop.

As she tried to sleep that night, Komie couldn't get Macha's words out of her mind. *You will be mine to teach.* She didn't like that notion at all. Belonging to someone else had horrible connotations. Her people hadn't experienced as much enslavement as those stolen from Africa. But generations of native children stolen and forced into white schools left her with an intense hatred of the notion of human chattel.

Yes, she wanted to learn to control her power. The memory of what she'd almost done to those men at the Byrne farm still haunted her in the dark hours. At the same time, choosing the right teacher meant everything. Anú, a goddess of the growing things, would have been the best match. She felt this in the depths of her spirit. And yet, Anú, supposedly a being with power and knowledge beyond her own, had sent Macha instead. Had Komie done something to anger Anú? Or had Macha simply been more willing to manifest? Or was there a deeper purpose to the match that Komie didn't have enough information to see?

Over the next few days, Komie and Róisín worked in the gardens, taking basic instruction from each of their mentoring gods. Macha pushed Komie through a series of minor exercises. Folding and unfolding flowers. Curling leaves. Enriching soil. She appreciated the subtlety and precision of her tasks. Before, she'd thrown everything she had into her talent. Now, her power developed finesse.

Róisín worked with Dian Cécht, doing her own exercises. She spent a great deal of time speaking with him, explaining the modern technology of medicine and healing, surgery and therapy. He seemed excited about the possibilities. He then taught her about the herbs and poultices, the magical uses of them, and how to imbue her own healing into the remedies.

On the afternoon of the seventh day, Dian Cécht boomed out a request. "Take me to a modern healing place. I want to see these wonders for myself."

Komie glanced up from the periwinkle she'd just brought back to life and exchanged a glance with Róisín. That seemed like a very unwise expedition, but Róisín looked thoughtful.

Komie let out a snort. "You realize you'll frighten half the patients into heart attacks if they see you, right?"

Dian Cécht lifted his chin. "They do not need to perceive me. I shall remain in Róisín's mind and see what she sees. That will keep my presence a secret from the common folk. But I wish to watch you put my lessons into action with truly ill or injured people."

The common folk. The elitist phrase grated on Komie's nerves.

Róisín pulled out her phone. "Let me check the visiting hours in Limerick. I think I know someone there we can ask for a tour."

Komie insisted on joining them. Luckily, Macha agreed to give her the afternoon off training. Komie wasn't certain what she'd do if Macha had argued.

Komie:

A male voice intruded. "Komie? Komie wake up. Are you okay?"

Komie batted away the voice. "You aren't Macha."

The person cleared their throat. "No, I'm definitely not Macha. I'm Colin. Do you remember me, Komie? Colin Byrne? Can you open your eyes?"

She tried to obey, but they seemed stuck shut. She shook her head, but something restrained it. Komie reached out with her hand, but only felt dirt, more dirt, endless dirt. Would she ever again feel anything but dirt? Black, rich soil that went on for miles. Deep into the ground. Never seeing the light of day.

"Komie! Caoimhe says you've been asleep for two days. You need to wake up. I have tea and soup. You must eat."

Her hand gripped something soft. A thing other than earth. Cloth? Was that the word? Yes, cloth. Fibers. Clothing. Bed clothing. Sheet.

She clutched at it as if she'd never felt something so luxurious in her life. The air smelled delightful. Savory and salty. Her mouth watered. She opened it to speak, but only a croak escaped. A frog. Didn't she meet a frog a lifetime ago? A farmer. A farmer who'd argued with Macha.

Her eyes flew open, and she gasped. *Macha.*

Struggling to sit up, she flailed, unable to move. "I must return to the farms."

Colin held her down. "The only thing you must do is rest. Maybe go to the loo, but that's all. Do you understand? You looked like death when we found you on our doorstep. How did you even get there?"

Komie shook her head, still in a daze. "I didn't, not under my own power. I was at a farm, helping the crops grow. The next thing I knew was waking just now. Macha must have delivered me here."

Colin's eyes grew wide as he drew back. "Macha? The actual Macha? She manifested?"

"Oh, she manifested, no doubt. I wish to all my ancestors she hadn't. I don't know if I'll survive more of her attention."

As Colin fed her spoonfuls of broth, the warm liquid trickled down her throat. Komie savored the luxurious sensation of hot food. When had she last eaten? She couldn't recall ever eating before.

A large black bird landed on the window, chirping quizzically. Komie stared at it. The crow looked odd. It cocked its head to one side, regarding them both, before flitting away.

Komie shivered, remembering the raven on Macha's shoulder. Did the birds spy for her? Why would a goddess need spies? She must be getting paranoid.

Once she finished her broth, Colin allowed her to rise. She needed the toilet and craved a shower. He wasn't happy about letting her shower alone, still so weak from her exertions. As a compromise, Fiona waited outside the bathroom door, in case she needed help.

Despite her determination, her ablutions took longer than she expected. Just the act of lifting her leg into the tub took more energy than she had. Her muscles whimpered in pain with every movement.

When she finished her shower, dried, brushed her hair, and dressed, she needed another nap. Fiona eyed her as she emerged, giving her a frank assessing look up and down. Finally, with a narrowed gaze, she crossed her arms and nodded once. "Da said that if you want to rest again, you can. But we're gathering tonight for stories, if you want to come."

Komie adored their stories, so reminiscent of the campfire tales of her people. At the same time, her body begged for more rest. "I'll come for a little while, but I'll probably have to leave early."

Fiona helped her down the stairs into the sitting room. Colin jumped up to help her into a recliner. He propped up the footrest as she rocked back. Michelle brought her tea as Liam and Hugh fed the fire. A perfectly homey, relaxing room.

Her mind still buzzed with Macha's power. She rubbed the goosebumps on her arms, despite the cozy warmth of the hearth.

Colin settled into his chair. "I'd just begun to tell the story of Macha. Would you like to hear it?"

Curiosity warred with dread in her mind. "Very timely, certainly. Thank you, Colin."

He drank from his cup to wet his throat. "There are several tales of Macha, and perhaps even several Machas. However, she's widely regarded as being one of three sisters known collectively as the Morrigna. She is a goddess of sovereignty, war, horses, and yes, fertility of the land."

Liam poked Hugh, who giggled and poked his brother back, until Fiona knocked Liam on the head with a newspaper. They both glared at her. Michelle hid a smirk as she picked up her crochet project.

"The Macha I will tell you of tonight married an Ulster farmer named Cruinniuc. This man's first wife died, and Macha just appeared at his house one day. She moved in and took care of his house, lying in his bed, and basically, becoming his wife."

As he spoke, Colin's voice took on a regular rhythm, much like the storytellers of her own people. His voice soothed her mind, and her eyelids grew heavy, almost like a guided meditation, a tribal chant, or white noise. She took a sip of tea to remain awake. Komie wanted to hear all she could about this goddess, especially if she would be working directly with her.

"As long as Macha lived with Cruinniuc, his wealth increased. His cows gave more milk, his fields grew more grain, and his chickens laid more eggs."

He stopped to pour more tea into his cup. "The time came for the men of Ulster to attend the king's festival. Macha warned Cruinniuc to speak of her to no one, and he promised to keep quiet. However, as men can be prone to boasting, he didn't keep that promise. During a chariot race, he blurted out that his wife could run faster than the king's horses.

"The king pounced on Cruinniuc's boast, and told him he must prove it, upon pain of death. Therefore, he told Macha, who was now heavily pregnant, that she must run against the king's horses and win. If she did not run, or if she runs and doesn't win, Cruinniuc will be killed."

Komie snorted, trying to keep her eyes open. "Men never know when to shut up, do they?"

Colin flashed her a half-smile. "That is patently true in this story. Macha ran the race, and she did indeed win. However, as soon as the race is finished, she went into labor, and delivered two twin boys on the finish line. For her humiliation and betrayal, she cursed the men of Ulster to be as weak as a woman giving birth at their time of greatest need."

Michelle let out a laugh. "And that comes back to bite them later, so it does."

"Aye, it does. But this curse isn't just for the men there on that day. No, this curse plagues the men of Ulster, their sons, and their sons' sons, and so on for nine generations. The incredible weakness lasts for five days, the length of a woman's monthly bleeding. Now, the place where Macha gave birth, a great burial mound called *Emain Macha*, lies near Armagh in the north. The name means Macha's Twins. It's one of Ireland's ancient sacred spaces."

Komie was certain she'd heard that placename before. "Is that one of the areas where Róisín discovered no cases of illness?"

Michelle nodded. "One of them. It's a grand man-made hill with a ceremonial structure underground, which someone burned and filled before burying the whole thing shortly after they built it."

"It seems," Komie sipped her own tea, "that this particular goddess has absolutely no patience for fools or bragging men. I can't say I blame her. And you said she's a fertility goddess? Perhaps that explains her interest in me. But she's even more abrasive than her *draoi*, Caoimhe. So far, I've bitten back my defiance, but I don't know how much longer I'll hold my tongue against her sass."

Colin frowned. "It doesn't sound like a good idea to sass a goddess, Komie, or those dedicated to her."

"Well, sass may not be the right word. But I do need to work on setting my boundaries. She doesn't understand human limitations of the flesh or soul. I highly doubt she has anything resembling human compassion."

"Human compassion is just that, human. When dealing with the Fae or the Gods… how can we possibly judge them by our own standards?"

Michelle made a rude sound, concentrating on her crocheting.

Komie grinned at her. "I'd say, if they wish to work with us, they must follow our standards."

Colin's eyes grew wide, and he sat up in his chair. "You're going to force a goddess to sign a Code of Conduct?"

With another sip of her tea, Komie shrugged. "I can try, can't I?"

Max:

By the time Max recovered from the level of intoxication he needed to fly, Ash had reconnoitered the location, drawn up a map, and outlined a plan.

They spread out a map on the table in a rented flat. "Here's the service entrance, and deliveries are brought in every Tuesday and Thursday. We'll dress in the uniforms I got yesterday. Your job is to create a distraction. Maybe a whirlwind to scatter the catering supplies as they're loading them from the truck?"

Max nodded. "I can do that. Then what?"

"Then we follow this hallway, turn left, and down three flights into the records department. After that, we'll have to search, but we're looking for personnel recruitment. That should be along this wall, unless they've moved things around."

"Brilliant. So, we may know where it is, and we may not. Then what? Carry the boxes back on our heads? And you know my talent is useless inside, right?"

"No. First, we won't need boxes. Perhaps a half dozen files, tops. Those will fit into our backpacks. Second, we don't need to escape the same way we went in. We won't need your talent then. That's where my talent comes in."

He raised his eyebrows. "Are you ready to tell me what that talent is, precisely?"

Ash gave him a half-smile. "I can tunnel through rock as easily as a hot knife through butter. The walls here are hewn from the bedrock. I can't push through concrete, but rock is easy. That's why I'm the mission lead."

Max gave a nod of grudging respect. "Right. Then what?"

"I close the tunnel behind me, and we emerge over here, in the park."

"And no one will notice us burping up from the bloody ground like a ripe pimple?"

They shook their head and rolled their eyes. "Not where I'm bringing us. It's hidden behind a line of bushes. We have careful scouts. And one more thing…"

Max lifted his eyebrows.

Ash pointed to their chest with their thumb. "*I* am in charge on this mission. If I give you a command, you obey. No questions, no dithering, no faffing about. Am I clear?"

Max clenched his jaw but knew the chain of command. "Sure, fine. Crystal. I've been on a mission. I know how it works. When do we start?"

Ash placed the rolled-up map into a tube. "Just about closing time, about four. By the time we're in and rifling through the files, everyone will have gone home. If *someone*," they raised their eyebrows at Max, "falls flat on their face, then no one'll be around to hear."

"I won't be falling on my face, luv, rest assured."

Ash held up a half-full bottle of rum. "Unless I give you this before we go."

Max waved his hand in dismissal. "Rum? Make it whiskey and you might be right."

"Whatever your preference, I'll have supplies on hand for after. Call it your carrot for a good job. Let's get dressed and in position."

After they reached the rear of the red-brick building, Max and Ash watched from behind a phalanx of rubbish bins. Four different delivery vans pulled up to the supply entrance and unloaded, each worker wearing a jumpsuit uniform like theirs, but blue rather than khaki. As each finished, the driver walked inside for twenty minutes before emerging.

"That's the time we need to enter, just after the driver does. Far enough behind that he doesn't notice us, but close enough that anyone observing will assume we're with his company."

Max tried to peer into the doorway, but the wall blocked his view. "And no one is checking names against a list?"

"Correct. We'll carry our boxes, so we look busy. People don't interrupt deliveries. They assume anyone with a box is supposed to be there. Once we're in the docking bay door, keep it shut with the wind. That way, people will be focused on that and not us."

Max glanced at the prop boxes. They held canteen supplies like coffee and sugar, in case of a spot inspection. He didn't have a great deal of confidence in his own ability to lie his way out of a sticky situation. He hoped Ash had that talent. Some voice in the back of his mind told him everything would be fine, but he ignored that, and worried as much as he wanted to.

As the catering van backed into the docking bay, three men dressed in khaki jumpsuits like Max and Ash emerged and unloaded dozens of boxes. When the caterers finished, they walked into the building with a clipboard, presumably to get the bill of lading signed by receiving.

Ash rose and picked up their box, walking with all the confidence in the world. Max followed suit, keeping his eyes on their back. As they shut the small walkway door next to the loading bay, Max sent a mental command to the local winds. They'd agreed to play along, though they'd copped a surly attitude. Still, they didn't need to be thrilled, just obedient.

The door slammed shut with a bang, and everyone glanced in that direction. Ash looked back, shrugged, and kept moving forward as others ran to the door to try to pry it open.

Through the dock, through the storage area, and into the hallway. Not one person even looked up as they passed. By the time they reached the stairwell into the basement, Max's confidence had grown to the point of cockiness. *This'll be a bloody cakewalk!*

Just as they entered the records room, Ash grabbed his shoulder and yanked him into a dark corner. He almost protested when they put a finger to their lips for silence. Max made himself as small as he could against the wall and held his breath as footsteps approached. Once the person passed by, he let out a shaky sigh.

When the coast cleared, Ash led him out again, turning down the first aisle. Dozens of open steel shelves held cardboard office boxes filled with files. He let out a low whistle. It might take days, even weeks, to search through all these.

Ash whispered, "Hush!" as they jabbed him in the ribs. He let out a huff of air but made no more noise. A door shut somewhere, and they both froze, waiting to hear if anyone entered. When no footsteps came, they kept moving.

Ash counted aisles as they walked. One, two, three, four. They turned down one and stopped halfway through, reading the labels on several boxes. Finally, they let out a soft breath, reaching for a box on a high shelf. Max scrambled to help them lift the heavy box.

Once they placed it gently on the concrete floor, Ash glanced up. "Grab the one next to it. We'll need files out of each."

They flipped open the first box as Max wrestled the second one down. Another door closed, the sound echoing against the walls. Freezing, Max glanced at Ash. They shrugged when no footsteps came and kept flipping through their file box.

Max opened his box but had no idea what he was looking for. Ash didn't look up but whispered, "Any file that says PHAE on it. I've got the personnel files."

"Right." Max knelt beside his box and glanced at the first file, but it only had a series of letters and numbers. So did the next one. No patterns popped out, nor did he find anything with PHAE as he worked his way through the box. He did notice one with Tiberius Wilkinson's name and pulled that one.

"Hey! You!"

Max's head snapped up. A young man in a guard uniform pointed at them and reached for his hip. Tensed for a weapon, Max breathed again when the man pulled out a radio.

Ash shoved a folder into his hands and leapt from their crouch toward the man, evidently intent on tackling them. Max quested for any winds but here, deep inside the bowels of the building, only a bare whisper answered his call.

Yesssss.

"Oi, mates! Can you knock this guy out?"

Nothing answered him. *Damn.* His biggest advantage was completely useless down here. He'd only be useful once they escaped.

Ash tackled the man, but more footsteps ran toward them. After wrestling the security guard to the ground, they turned and mouthed, *Run!*

Max didn't want to leave them, but the order came crystal clear. Ash had command and had made him promise to obey. He gripped the folder Ash shoved at him against his chest with the one he'd pulled and backed away. How would he escape without Ash's burrowing power?

He rushed toward the records room door. Before he touched the handle, the door flew open, and he scrambled behind a shelf. Once the footsteps pelted past him, he stole a glance. Two more guards ran to Ash's spot. Then, with perfect nonchalance, Max strode out of the records room, tucking the files into his jumpsuit.

Three more guards rushed past him, paying him no attention. Without Ash's talent of burrowing through rock, he had to exit the way they entered, out the docking bay door.

He kept his ears peeled for any commotion, hoping Ash managed to get away on their own. If they were captured, he might find a way to help them escape. However, as he got further away from the records room, and closer to his own safety, that hope dwindled.

Max had been in the service. He knew the mission trumped personal safety. That didn't mean he had to bloody well like it. He barely knew Ash, but they'd been solid.

By the time he calmly walked out of the warehouse and into the London streets, his fists were clenched so hard his hands ached.

Ash had given him drop off instructions, and he followed them to the letter. No sense in making their sacrifice be in vain. He carried the files to Hyde Park and handed them off to the waiting PHAE operative. Once he finished, he could breathe again.

No, he couldn't breathe yet. Even though he'd completed the mission, he still had a moral duty to find Ash and rescue them. Nothing in his briefing forbade it, and there was no way he'd leave a mate behind. Even if they'd just met. Even if they'd strong-armed him into this mission. Soldiers of any stripe followed a code.

Returning to the building docking bay, Max watched and waited. He observed the comings and goings all evening, until the warehouse went dark. Even then, he peered into the windows, hoping to find someone inside. Someone he could beat up to rescue Ash.

Max didn't know if they were still inside, or the PEM blokes had moved them while he delivered the files. He had to operate under the assumption they were, because otherwise he had no chance in hell of rescuing them. So, he watched and waited.

He asked the winds to alert him if anyone opened the doors. Then he settled down for an uncomfortable and stinky nap behind the rubbish bins. A few false alarms woke him, from a stray cat to a stumbling drunk, but no one entered or left in the night.

As the sun burned through the morning fog, the winds shook him awake. Max struggled to his knees to peer from his hiding spot, rubbing the sleep from his eyes and stifling a mighty yawn. There, held tight by four burly guards, was Ash. They looked like they'd had a rough night, with a swollen eye, several burgeoning dark spots on their face, and a vacant stare. Their escort dragged the aboriginal Unhidden to a waiting car.

This would be Max's only chance. "Now, mates! Now!"

A whirlwind spun around their five captors. They wobbled on their feet, halting their progress. Ash glanced up in alarm, shaking their head as their eyes grew wide.

What? Did they not want rescue? *Bloody hell.*

He called the winds back and stared at Ash. A small smile formed on Ash's face as their captors forced them to their knees. While Max was trying to puzzle out what was happening and what he should do, a guard looked around wildly and shouted, "That's another of them! They're attacking!"

Another slapped his hand on his hip. Next to his radio, this one carried a gun. Highly unusual, maybe even illegal, for a security guard in England. Max swallowed as the man spoke into the radio. "An attack? Is that confirmed?"

"Confirmed! You know our orders. Do it!"

In slow motion, the guard pulled out his gun, placed it on the back of Ash's neck and, with the muzzle angled down, fired. Ash's eyes rolled back and faded into glass.

Chapter Nine

"If you spend your time hoping someone will suffer the consequences
for what they did to your heart, then you're allowing them to hurt you a
second time in your mind."
– Shannon L. Alder

Hiroki:

After they finished their tour of each county, Hiroki, Ciara, and
Masaaki returned to the Dublin bunker. In the end, he'd enjoyed giving
the speeches, though he still had qualms about the half-truths he'd been
instructed to give. He sat in his office for a much-needed decompression.
Just as he finished his lunch, Ciara came in.

After a bit of small talk, Hiroki brought up the subject that kept
nagging at the back of his mind, the news they'd heard about Joel's possible
torture. When Ciara refused to answer, Hiroki clenched his fists as he glared
at her. "I don't understand it. We did good work on the tour! Everyone
responded to my speech! What went wrong? Why do you keep evading my
questions about Joel?"

Ciara paced back and forth. "No one's denying you did well. More
than well. You exceeded our already very high expectations. However,
circumstances have changed. Bintou is only just back from caring for
Martin. She's fragile, and she needs rest before we do anything more."

"I am very sorry for her loss, of course. But we are different people.
I can still do things! I'm not fragile, and I don't need to rest."

With sad eyes, Ciara pursed her lips. "No one says you do. However,
please remember, Martin was more than just a colleague to many of us. He's

been my friend for years, back before all this Unhidden stuff came about. We used to make videos together, for fun, for entertainment. Trying silly stuff. People would watch and laugh. I miss those days, and I miss Martin."

She glanced at a photograph on their bunker office wall. A bucolic scene of the west coast, a steep cliff with a sliver of sandy beach below. Sheep dotting the green fields. Ciara let out a long sigh. "Look, why don't you put this out of your mind? I told you before there's nothing either of us can do to help Joel right now."

He crossed his arms, glaring at her. Where had he gotten the gumption to be so bold? Perhaps the successful tour bolstered his confidence. "You said you had a plan. Back before Bintou got sick, you said you'd help."

She shrugged and looked away. "Like I said, things change. I can't do anything to help him now. I just don't have that level of authority."

Hiroki slammed a hand on the table. "We need to do *something*. Even you said they weren't treating him right."

Ciara leaned on the desk and scowled at him, barely six inches from his face. "Look, I can't help. And when it comes down to it, he's killed a lot of people. People who were my friends! Maybe this is the only way to get the information they need. Technically, it's not against the law!"

Clenching his teeth, Hiroki matched the taller woman scowl for scowl, despite fear bubbling inside him for his insolence. "It may not be against Irish law or PHAE law, but it's against human law."

She threw her hands up and paced again. "Fine! Then *you* do something about it."

He tensed his shoulders. "I have less power than you do in PHAE. I don't even know where they're holding him."

"If I tell you, will you stop pestering me?"

Hiroki glanced up, his eyes wide with eagerness. "Tell me."

Ciara pursed her lips. "He's in Mountjoy Prison, in Dublin. But don't think it'll be easy to see him. It's not maximum security, but the wing he's in has been closed down for years. He's the only one there. And there's Hafsia."

He furrowed his brow. "Hafsia? I am unfamiliar with this word. Is it Irish?"

"Hafsia is his interrogator. She isn't anyone to trifle with. If you do anything, be careful of her."

Ciara left, her heels clicking along the hallway as Hiroki digested this information. He had no conspirators to discuss his plans with. Bintou was mourning Martin, and it would be dishonorable to intrude upon her grief. Masaaki had been sent on an assignment with Paul.

Hiroki had to figure out a way to rescue Joel by himself.

When he slipped into bed that night, he didn't sleep. Instead, his head swirled with dozens of plans, none of which would work.

Joel had killed hundreds, perhaps thousands of people. He'd destroyed a city. He'd nearly killed his own sister, though he couldn't have known she'd been so close. Joel had been a double agent, betraying the trust the PHAE had put in him. He deserved to be punished and locked up forever.

But the PHAE had not yet enacted a policy for capital crime. Masaaki had checked the records to confirm it. That didn't mean they'd kill Joel for his crimes, but that didn't mean they wouldn't, either. And since the PHAE hadn't signed the Convention against Torture with the United Nations, legally speaking, they might use any techniques they wished to extract information. Ciara told him Hafsia's talent was compelling the truth. A complementary talent to his own, extracting a response rather than impelling belief.

If he planned a rescue, he'd need help. Would Bintou help? Masaaki? He didn't want to involve any of the Byrnes, as they'd be too loyal to the PHAE to help a prisoner of war escape. If he used his persuasion power, he could create an entire army to rescue Joel, but he refused to use his talent for this. Hiroki couldn't justify that amongst friends, no matter what Max might believe.

Joel was a Prisoner of War. His grandfather had been a prisoner of war in World War II. Captured by the Soviet Union, he'd been sent to a

Siberian work camp. When they finally repatriated him to Japan, he was a broken man. His grandfather never spoke of his time in Siberia, but the eternal shame of being captured alive haunted him for the rest of his life.

No matter how despicably the American man had acted, Hiroki couldn't let Joel be tortured like his grandfather.

First, he'd speak to Masaaki when he returned with Paul. If Masaaki agreed to help him, then and only then would he recruit Bintou. If he actually convinced both of them, without his talent, that Joel deserved to be freed from his torture, then they'd form a plan.

If he couldn't get them on board with his mission, then perhaps the mission was based on false empathy, and Joel truly did deserve to remain in prison.

The next day, when they returned, Hiroki filled Masaaki in on his thoughts. After some deliberation, Masaaki agreed his plan had merit. Together, they decided to bring Bintou in on their conspiracy.

They walked down the hall together, but Paul pulled Masaaki aside for a question before they got to Bintou's door. With an apologetic wave, his friend left with the Irishman. With a sigh, Hiroki hesitated before he knocked on Bintou's door. The Malian woman might still be too mired in grief to help or to care.

Was Bintou even inside? He listened at the door. He heard someone speaking, so she must have a visitor. He hesitated again, but Hiroki didn't want to waste time if each day meant Joel had to endure more torture.

He knocked, and footsteps approached the door. When it opened, he didn't see Bintou's smiling face. Ibrahim stood with a confused expression. Hiroki had met the Malian antiquities expert several times, but he'd thought Bintou detested him.

The other man shook his hand and turned his confusion into a wide smile. "Hiroki! Please, come inside. I just started the kettle. Would you like some tea?"

Bintou glanced up as he entered the bunker bedroom, her face still etched with grief. She sat at her desk and gave him a bare nod. Ibrahim poured them all tea and brought biscuits. Once Hiroki added honey to his tea, he didn't know how to proceed. He hadn't counted on Ibrahim's presence, but it would be incredibly rude to ask to speak to Bintou alone. Her current state might not be the best to receive his suggestion. Perhaps it would be best to simply drink his tea and leave.

Ibrahim took a biscuit and bit into it, crumbs falling on his lap. As he brushed them away, he asked, "Have you a new project for Bintou? Something to work on would be quite beneficial."

Bintou glanced up long enough to narrow her eyes at the other man, but then she returned to staring into her cup.

Hiroki cleared his throat, Ibrahim's choice of words giving him an idea. "I had not intended to, but I could certainly use some help on an upcoming, uh, plan. It's something Masaaki and I have begun. Would you be interested in joining us?" He turned to the Malian woman with his eyebrows raised.

She shrugged and cupped her hands around her tea. "It might be nice to keep my mind off…other things."

Ibrahim clapped his hands. "There, you see? This is exactly what you need. Hiroki, will you excuse me? I have business I must tend to. I didn't wish to leave Bintou alone, but if you have a scheme to discuss with her, my conscience is clear."

He drained the rest of his tea, brushed off his trousers, and rose. After giving Bintou a tender kiss on her forehead and squeezing her shoulder, he gave Hiroki a thumbs-up and strode out the door.

The room grew quiet once he left. Bintou took a sip of her tea.

Hiroki cleared his throat. "I thought you were not friends with Ibrahim any longer?"

She spoke in a monotone. "He has offered me comfort when I needed it."

He stared at his own tea, unsure how to open the discussion, but Bintou saved him the trouble by asking, "What are you planning? Do we have another presentation to prepare?"

Hiroki shook his head. "No, this isn't an official project. Nothing the PHAE has assigned to us. This is a more personal quest."

She glanced up, a flicker of interest in her eyes. "Something not sanctioned by the PHAE?"

"I would imagine not. It's about Joel."

Her eyes widened. "Have you found out anything more about him?"

"I found out where he's being held."

She swallowed and shook her head, staring at the table. "He's killed so many people, Hiroki."

His heart sank. He'd hoped she'd be more open to helping him. "Does that justify torture? Ciara told me some very disturbing details, and I am not comfortable with the techniques being used."

Bintou glared at him, her eyes glittering in the fluorescent light. "Who are you to dictate what the PHAE do with their prisoners, Hiroki? Are you their mother? Their conscience? Are you the avenging hero who can do no wrong?"

Hiroki pulled back, surprised at the vehement attack. "Of course not! But I do have a conscience, and torture is something I feel very strongly about. Humans should not do such things to other humans. My grandfather was tortured after the war. Such practice is evil."

Bintou narrowed her eyes. "And you are required to fight evil wherever you find it? You aren't the only person in this organization. And you are far from a physical fighter. Your powers lie in persuasion. Wouldn't it be more logical for you to speak to those in charge, to make your case to them?"

He dropped his gaze. "I cannot use my powers to influence like that, Bintou. It would be an abuse."

She let out a derisive laugh. "An abuse. Perhaps if people were less worried about using their talents when they were really needed, people wouldn't be dying across this country right now. This is what happens when we let honor overcome common sense. Don't you see that? If you want to make change, a real change, you must become that agent of change. You need to use your talent and take a position of power in the PHAE."

The conversation had skirted too close to his words with Ciara earlier for his own comfort. "What do you suggest?"

She leaned forward, a twinkle in her eye. "Something Paul mentioned yesterday gave me an idea. Let's prepare your application to be the next Head of Unhidden Defense."

Hiroki:

Ciara was thrilled with the idea, so Masaaki, Bintou, and Hiroki worked long into the night to prepare talking points, slides, and a speech to present his qualifications for the position. Hiroki doubted any of this would work, but when they discovered they needed to present his application the next day to get into the first round of candidates, he dug into the project.

Would he be comfortable using his powers to persuade the upper echelon of PHAE to his position? Even if he used his powers, would they work? He knew someone in the group had the talent to suppress other Unhidden's powers, but he didn't know who. What if they were in the room?

His own confidence fluctuated between gibbering fear and talent-fueled self-assurance. Masaaki and Bintou worked out the language while he dozed, despite liberal use of coffee and sugar. Despite the caffeine, anxiety sapped all of his energy.

Eventually, he put his head down on his arms. Masaaki's voice blended into Bintou's and formed a strange lullaby.

When Masaaki shook him awake, he let out a shout. "What! What?"

Bintou chuckled. "We've got a draft. Read it and share your thoughts?"

Rubbing sleep from his eyes and taking a sip of his now-cold coffee, he wrinkled his nose. "Give me a minute." After he relieved himself and washed his face and hands, he only felt half-asleep.

Hiroki nodded as he read the bullet points, appreciating the nuance they brought out with precise phrasing. "You two make an excellent team. You don't even need me to convince people."

Masaaki might have blushed, but his paper-white skin wouldn't show it. He cast his eyes down and poked his toe along the floor. "You're the one who delivers them, Hiroki. You put your talent into it for a perfect weapon."

A weapon. A tool of destruction. An implement of fear, intimidation, and conquest. Hiroki didn't like the idea of being a weapon, but he couldn't argue against the analogy. He planned to use this speech to catapult him into power. Power that the PHAE treated Joel, and anyone else they took into custody, fairly. What could he call himself but a weapon? Why did it matter that he only wanted that power to help someone else? A tool to get him what he wanted.

Such responsibility both filled him with terror and with a manifest purpose to make the world a better place.

With a deep breath, he read through the speech again, and stomped on his qualms about using his talent for this.

When Ciara came for them, Hiroki's power surged through his body, making his blood and skin tingle with confidence he knew wasn't real. He strode behind her, Masaaki and Bintou almost treading on his heels. As they reached the conference room, his talent made him turn and glare at them. He needed his space to complete this task.

Masaaki dropped his gaze and took two steps back, but Bintou scowled. No matter. Hiroki must perform now. The power surged once again as he stepped to the podium.

A semi-circle of people dressed in suits stared at him. For a bare second, his legs itched to flee, but his talent took a firm grip on his fear and suffused his muscles with strength. As the tingling spread through him, he felt as if he could lift the entire building over his head and let out a barbaric yawp of power. Instead of a yawp, he launched into the exquisitely crafted speech, locking gazes with each of the ten PHAE representatives in turn.

"And as an organization, the PHAE has a solemn responsibility to act within the commonly accepted norms of world society. Without attention to this responsibility, our enemies can easily paint us as unworthy. They can use this as a weapon to block our efforts at carving a space of our own on the world stage."

He stared into the eyes of the member on the far right. Their brow furrowed in confusion, so Hiroki spoke directly to him with the next point.

"In order to defend ourselves against those who are intent upon destroying us, we must first define ourselves. We are the Protectorate for unHidden Assistance and Education. But what, in everyday practical terms, does this mean?"

The man wrinkled his nose. Hiroki shoved aside the final scrap of misgivings and pushed his power through his words, visualizing his talent as water sprayed through a firehose.

"It means that we, first and foremost, support and foster those who demonstrate Unhidden talents. That's a grand goal, and worthy. But how do we achieve this goal? What is our plan for this year? For the next five years? Do we even have a plan?"

The next person in the semi-circle, a woman with her gray hair swept into a severe bun, nodded with his questions. He gave her an encouraging smile and looked to another.

"And once we have established our goals, how do we protect those goals, our organization, and most importantly, our people? For isn't this the very core of what we must do? Protect each and every one of us." He tapped the podium with each word of the last sentence.

Hiroki thought of Joel, imprisoned less than five miles away. He detested what Joel had done and didn't care about him personally. But if he didn't secure this position in the organization, what happened when someone he *did* care about was in PHAE custody?

As he finished his speech, he gauged about half the assembled PHAE leaders responded positively to his words. The other half frowned or scowled.

Ciara led them out to allow the board to discuss his application for the Head of Unhidden Defense, but he already knew the answer. He'd thrown everything he had at them. It hadn't been enough.

The talent still buzzed along his nerves as they returned to their office. Bintou turned on the teakettle while Masaaki plopped into his chair.

Ciara closed the door behind them and gave him a bright, polished smile. "That was fantastic, Hiroki!"

He lowered himself into his chair, clenching and unclenching his fists to return circulation to his fingers. "It didn't work. They'll vote against me."

The Irishwoman patted him on the shoulder. "Sure, and you can't know that. It'll be grand. They've got no one else interested in the job. Well, except for Paul, and he's less qualified than you."

Her phrasing made Hiroki glare at her. With realization, Ciara glanced down. "I'm sorry. I didn't mean it like that. I mean—"

"No, you're right. I am unqualified. Why did I think I had any chance at such a position?" Hiroki sprang to his feet and paced, his shoulders tense. "I left the only job I was qualified for. I abandoned my family, my home, and my career. For what? To be rejected by *gaijin* for a job I don't even want?"

Frustration bubbled up through his still-tingling hands. With a bellow of impotent rage, he punched the door to the bathroom.

Hiroki expected his fist to hurt. It didn't. He didn't expect the door to implode. It did.

Shattered splinters showered the four of them, as Hiroki stared at the damage. Instant disgrace doused his white-hot fury. His hands stopped tingling as he ran out of the office.

The empty hall echoed his humiliation and beat him with it as he escaped.

Hiroki:

After his rage finally subsided, Hiroki returned to his cell and locked the door. He wanted no company. They called it a room, but it was merely a cell with the bare essentials. Yes, a cell, though they weren't imprisoned. Sure, they could leave the tunnels now, but Ciara asked them to remain. The hotel where they'd had rooms had been destroyed by the bomb, so they were imprisoned here by circumstance rather than by force.

As he washed his face in the basin, he noticed a white envelope on his cot. His curiosity piqued, he picked it up. When he turned it over, he dropped it again, backing up several steps. He recognized his father's precise handwriting.

Hiroki both craved his father's acceptance and dreaded any communication from him. He stared at the envelope for several minutes before gathering the courage to retrieve it. With shaking fingers, he broke the seal on the airmail envelope. His father's precise, black lettering covered the seal in perfect kanji.

He used the good stationary, which meant this was an official correspondence. After he swallowed his heart, Hiroki read the letter.

Hiroki:

You are a dishonor to your family name. We have struck your name from our family registry. You are done.

The letter dropped from his fingers, fluttering to the concrete floor. Hiroki's knees no longer worked. He collapsed to the ground, all muscles in his body refusing to obey him.

He didn't cry. How could he cry? That would only further dishonor his name. Instead, he hugged the cold floor like a life preserver, the only thing keeping him afloat on an ocean of disapproval.

Waves of horror swept through him, pulsing with the chill of the concrete. His world shrunk to just this space, this small area around him. Nothing else intruded into his misery.

Countless ages passed before he noticed a sound. Someone pounding on his skull? No, on the door. A voice cried out, forming words he didn't recognize. They yelled again, but finally left him in peace.

Peace? He had no peace. Peace requires acceptance. Peace requires family.

Instead, he clutched tight to a maelstrom of disappointment. Everything he'd ever done in his life became void. Nothing he'd accomplished mattered.

Again, pounding poked into his desolation. This time, more than one voice shouted. Was that his name? He didn't have his name anymore. His father had taken it.

Still, tears refused to fall. He let out a silent scream of agony, anything to relieve the intense pain.

The pounding shifted to scratching. The voices stopped crying his name and whispered worried words.

With shaking arms, Hiroki pushed his body away from the comforting cold concrete. He sat with his back against the edge of the cot. The cold metal cut into his spine. He relished the discomfort. He watched the door as the scratching resolved into a click, an exclamation of victory, and a creak as it opened.

Masaaki peered into the room, his eyes searching from side to side, before his gaze fell to Hiroki, sitting against his bed. "Hiroki? May I come in?"

This man used to be his friend. But he used an invalid name. He could be Hiroki no longer. His father took his name.

His friend stepped inside, with Bintou close behind him. They perched on the bed, on either side of him. Masaaki placed a hand on his shoulder. "You should have something to eat. Ciara brought stew from the canteen. Will you come with us into the office? She even fetched that brown bread you like so much."

When he didn't move, Masaaki and Bintou exchanged a glance. With a shared nod, each one put a hand under Hiroki's shoulders, lifting him to his feet. They propelled him into the office. He stumbled to a chair just as Ciara arrived with a tray with bread, butter, and jam.

The Irish woman's face lit up with a polished smile. "Ah! There he is. Here, you must be starving. I'll prepare a bowl, and you get your first choice of bread. Bintou, can you pour the tea?"

Hiroki lifted his head, staring at Ciara. He threw his head back and screeched, his fists pounding the table. Masaaki's can of Coke fell over, spilling all over the table and floor. The three of them stared at the Japanese man as he howled in incoherent fury. Several people poked their heads in from the hallway, but Ciara shooed them away with a wave of her hand, shutting the door with a firm click.

Masaaki placed his hands on his friend's shoulders, but Hiroki leapt to his feet, shrugging the comfort away. He paced back and forth, growling with each step, his fists clenched and his eyes tearing from the strain.

Bintou put out a cautious hand on his forearm, but Hiroki whirled on her, fire in his eyes. She pulled back, her eyes brimming with hurt.

Masaaki exchanged a glance with Ciara, but she only shrugged. "Short of a tranquilizer dart, I've got no clue."

When his voice finally fell to a cracked whisper, Hiroki whimpered in the corner, curled into a fetal position. Bintou placed a warm blanket over him, tucking in the edges. She pushed a pillow under his head. Ciara and Bintou both left, leaving Masaaki to watch over the grief-mad man.

After rocking to himself for an endless time, Hiroki slowly grew aware of his surroundings. Masaaki sat at the table, eating a piece of brown bread and butter. He glanced at Hiroki, standing when he realized his friend had come to his senses. "Have you returned to us?"

"I have returned."

His heart remained as cold as the icy floor. He had no intention of ever letting it warm again.

Bintou:

After Hiroki stormed out, Bintou helped Ciara clean while Masaaki hurried after his friend. She'd never seen the Japanese man so agitated, but she understood his frustration. Over the last week, she'd considered the therapeutic method of hitting something to satisfy her own anger several times. But smashing a wall, even if it might make her feel better, wouldn't bring Martin back. Neither would slapping Ibrahim, though that thought occurred to her a few times, as well.

Once they'd swept the splintered wood into the rubbish bin, Ciara sat with her forehead cradled in her hands. "I shouldn't have said that. Why did I say that?"

Bintou wrinkled her nose, but Ciara couldn't see her. She'd cringed when Ciara spoke but had no words of wisdom. They'd all been lured here under one pretense or another. Bintou had burned her own bridges coming to Ireland. She'd never be able to return to her old job. Not that she wanted to. Her old boss, Oumar, had turned into such a horrible misogynist. She never wanted to work with him again.

Unconscious bias was a terrible thing in the workplace. Ciara had just exposed her own bias. Sure, Hiroki wasn't really qualified to be the Head of Unhidden Defense, but no one better had applied. Bintou still believed he'd make a brilliant head of a communications-oriented department.

Remembering her old job, Bintou ached to be part of the academic world again. Not the misogynist supervisor who'd tried to bully her into a position she didn't want, but the sensual feeling of ancient manuscripts in her hand, the odor of old papyrus and ink, of crumbling scrolls and hidden lives. How her life had changed, helping write speeches for a Japanese man in Dublin. A far, far cry from the halls of learning in Sankore Madrasah.

Did *she* have unconscious bias? Bintou had never considered herself prejudiced, but she just thought about working for a Japanese man with disdain. Perhaps she had some self-discovery to work on. She made a resolution to herself to examine her thoughts and amend them as needed.

The teakettle whistled, so Bintou dropped in bags to steep. Ciara still held her head at her hasty words. With pursed lips, Bintou decided Ciara needed some medicinal help. She had to sniff back tears as she retrieved Martin's flask from the filing cabinet. After doctoring Ciara's tea, she kept the flask. It didn't matter that it contained whiskey which, as a Muslim, she couldn't drink. The flask had belonged to Martin, something she could keep to remember him.

She pushed the tea toward Ciara, who lifted her gaze long enough to register the offering. She took a sip, raised her eyebrows at the addition, and gave Bintou a grateful smile. "That's a welcome surprise. Thank you. I absolutely needed that."

"I may not be permitted to imbibe, but I understand its medicinal value." She pulled out her tablet and stylus. "What is our next step?"

Ciara rubbed her temples with her eyes screwed shut. "Right. Let me think. If Hiroki doesn't get selected, then we can ask whoever *is* selected to help us."

"And that's likely to be Paul? Or had someone else applied for the position?"

Ciara shook her head, touching her temples again. "I don't know. I'm not privy to the selection committee's workings, so there may be thirty-seven applicants, for all I know. But with the current chaos, I doubt many people are paying any attention to politics. Paul and Hiroki are the only two who I know have applied."

A knock on the door made them both glance up. Masaaki entered with sad eyes. "He won't listen to me. I've never seen him this upset. Not even when he earned an A rather than an S in History."

Ciara wrinkled her brow. "An S?"

"The highest score. An A is only eighty, ninety percent."

Bintou let out a snort but then tapped her tablet. "We need a plan. Have you any ideas?"

Masaaki sat in his chair, wrinkling his nose at the teapot. "Is there Coke?"

Ciara waved toward the fridge. The Japanese man pulled out a can, snapped it open, and took a long swig. When he came up for air, he opened his mouth and let out a big "Ah!" before pulling his chair in to the table. "What have we got so far?"

Bintou:

After Bintou finished her phone call with Colin, she pursed her lips and glanced around the room. They'd been on speaker through his report about Róisín and Komie's encounters with ancient Irish gods. It sounded like the tales of djinn and ifrit. Strange gods making bargains with modern people. Humans seldom came out ahead in such deals. Occasionally, they got lucky and found a Djinn who worked kind deeds. Very occasionally.

Would she accept such a bargain? To work magic with an ancient god? The Q'uran didn't permit such dealings. Any commerce with witchcraft was strictly forbidden. Muslims must rely on Allah and Allah alone to keep them safe from sorcery and malicious spirits. Even talismans or charms to keep them safe were forbidden. And yet the Catholics carried such charms, dedicated to their saints. They carried their sacred crosses like shields against evil.

That didn't keep Róisín safe from her ancient god. She always wore her gold cross and despite that talisman, this god contacted her, and she evidently accepted his help. The pagan god had evidently taken Róisín as an apprentice, despite her strong Catholic faith. Bintou appreciated the strength of Róisín's faith. That cross should have protected her against any evil god.

Perhaps faith wasn't such strong protection. Or perhaps these ancient gods weren't evil. Bintou wasn't sure she could rely upon this simple logic to apply to her own faith. She turned to Ibrahim, as he'd listened to the phone call, along with Masaaki and Hiroki. His eyes sparkled with excitement while Hiroki looked worried.

"What do you think of this, Ibrahim?"

Ibrahim's eyes grew wide. "I think this is exciting! Imagine, living in these momentous times."

Well, he'd be no help. He always did have a problem reining in his enthusiasm. She turned to Hiroki to get his take on this development. The Japanese man clenched and unclenched his fists. "Should we tell the others about this?"

Bintou furrowed her brow. "The others. Do you mean Ciara and Paul? Or the rest of PHAE?"

Hiroki shrugged, staring at his clasped hands. "Any of them. Is this something that we should keep secret? Or do they deserve to know?"

Shaking her head, Bintou dropped her gaze. "I don't think that's our call to make. Michelle and Colin have been our mentors. If they wished to inform the PHAE about these encounters, wouldn't they call them directly?"

Ibrahim slapped his hands on the table. "How can we keep this quiet, though? This is tremendous news. With the gods at our back, how can we not be victorious?"

She stared at him, confusion prickling into irritation. "Victory? Over whom? The disease? The PEM? The rest of the world? Not everything can be framed as a battle, Ibrahim."

He waved his hand. "Oh, I don't mean it to be a battle. You're putting words into my mouth. What I mean is, we can be victorious in establishing the PHAE as a legitimate power in the world. One that cannot be destroyed with smuggled bombs and sleeper agents. One that should be entrusted with determining how our people are treated and governed."

Bintou narrowed her eyes. Sometimes he made sense, and sometimes she wanted to slap him.

Masaaki pulled another Coke from the fridge. "I think we should tell Ciara and let her decide. She's been our advocate from the beginning. I trust her to do right by us all."

Bintou rose, ready to go find the Irish woman, but Hiroki waved her back down. "I shall fetch her. We can tell her together. One of us might remember parts of the conversation others do not. The details will be important."

As he left the room, Bintou wondered how Martin might have taken this news, but when tears threatened to close her throat, she deliberately thought about something else. Shopping. Rainbows. Fiona, the youngest Byrne child, with wide eyes and a sunny smile. Anything but Martin.

When Hiroki returned with Ciara, the other four sat around the table in silence, unsure how to begin. Ciara cleared her throat. "Well? What is it? I've an important meeting soon. The Taoiseach herself has requested an update on our progress."

Ibrahim cocked his head. "The Taoiseach? Truly?"

Hiroki asked, "What is a Tee-shock?"

Masaaki finished his Coke with a chuckle, crushing the can and tossing it into the rubbish bin. "The Taoiseach is like the Prime Minister of Ireland."

Swallowing, Bintou steeled herself. "Ciara, Colin called from the Byrne farm."

The tall Irish woman raised her eyebrows, sliding into an empty chair. "Oh, is he feeling better? I'd heard he got quite ill."

"Yes, he's much improved. Róisín's healing has been effective. But we called you here to discuss a different matter." She swallowed again, glancing at Ibrahim. He liked talking so much, he should relate the difficult news.

A wide grin spread across Ibrahim face. "Róisín and Komie have both been contacted by powerful entities."

"Entities. Worldwide corporations? A government? The PEM haven't contacted them, have they?"

Masaaki's face lit up with excitement. "Not the PEM, Gods! They've talked to actual, real-life, gods!"

Ciara sat back in her chair, crossed her arms, and leveled a cynical look at them both. "Gods."

Hiroki nodded vigorously "It is true. Gods. Not ancestors, but true gods, with incredible powers. One helped Róisín heal Colin when her own powers were insufficient. His name is Dian Cécht. And then the other one, a war goddess, contacted Komie."

Ciara's shoulders tensed. "A war goddess? The Morrigan?"

Bintou waved her hand. "No, that wasn't her name. Something with fewer syllables. Like the tea. Matcha?"

Ciara turned pale and she gripped the arms of her chair. "Macha. Macha contacted Komie? She has nothing to do with the harvest." She let out a humorless laugh. "Unless you mean the harvest after a battle. She severs the heads of the slain. They call those Macha's acorns, or Macha's harvest."

With a shrug, Ibrahim said, "We don't know why she contacted Komie. Maybe she has other reasons. However, they absolutely spoke to each of them, and have agreed to be their apprentices."

"Apprenticed. To Macha. None of you are making sense." Her phone buzzed. She glanced at it, her face almost as pale as Masaaki's. "Feck. That's the Taoiseach. Wait here."

Ciara hurried out of the room, her heels clicking away on the tiles. Bintou, Ibrahim, Masaaki, and Hiroki shared a tense silence. After a few moments, footsteps approached with a low murmur of conversation.

When the door opened again, an older woman in a pale blue power suit accompanied Ciara. "May I present Taoiseach Éadaoin O'Kelly?"

They all jumped to their feet. Hiroki straightened his spine so much, he looked in pain. Ibrahim flashed his most charming smile. The Taoiseach shook all their hands and gestured for them to sit. She sat on the edge of the table while Ciara stood, neither taking the fifth chair.

The Taoiseach had a strong, gravelly voice. "Ciara tells me you have some exciting news for the PHAE. What is it?"

Róisín:

As they approached University Limerick Hospital, Róisín chewed her lip. Could she really channel ancient magic? Or would she burn her own power out? She was glad Dian Cécht had agreed not to manifest physically. With social media and gossip running wild already, who knows what the world would make of ancient Irish gods come to life in the modern day?

Instead, he and Macha secured a farmhouse outside the city and sent Róisín and Komie to the hospital with strict instructions. She felt his presence in a corner of her mind, like someone riding in the back of a taxi, watching but barely speaking.

Komie put a hand on her back. "You'll be wonderful. You have the support of your teacher and I'll stay by your side. I promise."

With a grateful glance for the native woman, Róisín squeezed her hand and took a deep breath before opening the hospital's double doors.

They'd debated whether to mention the god's help with her talent, but Komie argued against it. "Why share more information than they need? How are they to know your talent is being augmented?"

"But I don't want to take credit for more than what I do myself."

The native woman cocked her head, pressing her lips together. "It will take longer to convince them that the gods exist and are willing to help, won't it?"

Róisín had to admit the truth of that. And so, they determined that Dian Cécht's assistance would remain private information. Not a secret, as she detested keeping secrets. If someone asked, they'd explain, but they wouldn't volunteer such information up front.

This hospital had no bomb victims from either Galway or Dublin. However, patients with respiratory illness filled the wards. From the epistemology reports, they must be dealing with more than one epidemic. It seemed every patient presented with different symptoms. While some survived, many died. Róisín still thought her initial diagnoses had been right, but no one had been willing to believe her. She just hoped they'd finally started testing.

Komie gripped her shoulder, and she swallowed her fear. The harried receptionist glanced up, peering over her glasses. "May I help you?"

Róisín took a deep breath. "I'm here to help with the epidemic. May I speak to your staff physician or attending?"

The woman pursed her lips. "May I ask who is calling? We're rather busy just now."

"Yes, I'm well aware of that. I'm an Unhidden healer with the PHAE. I assisted in the Galway hospital since the bombing."

The receptionist punched a few buttons on her terminal and picked up the phone receiver. "Dr. Neal? Yes, I need you down here immediately. Yes, I know. No, this can't wait. Very well."

Róisín tried to regulate both her breathing and her heartbeat. She felt like a complete imposter, striding into a hospital to take over healing duties. She'd trained as a veterinarian, not a doctor. She shouldn't be here, trying to heal human patients.

The urge to run away made her legs twitch, but she kept them still, locking her knees until they stopped shaking. If Komie hadn't stayed with her, she might have given in to the impulse.

The doctor entered, her black hair pulled into a huge bun. Komie stood by Róisín's side, a silent rock bolstering her confidence. A tingle spread across her skin, a sensation she associated with Dian Cécht lending his power. She took a deep breath. "Dr. Neal?"

The doctor spoke in a soft Jamaican accent. "What may I help you with today?"

"I'm Róisín Byrne, and I have an Unhidden talent for healing. May I accompany you on your rounds, to offer my services?"

Dr. Neal studied her and Komie, raising her eyebrows. "I'm certain you realize we are in the throes of an epidemic. We're limiting visitors at this time."

Róisín straightened her spine and tried to channel her mother's self-assurance. "I'm not a visitor. I'm a healer."

"Have you credentials to present?"

The PHAE had a plan to create certifications for Unhidden talents, but they'd halted that program with the bombings. "I have veterinarian training. I've also been helping patients in Galway since the bombing. If you like, you can contact Dr. O'Shea at the Galway University Hospital. He can attest to my skill."

The doctor's eyes narrowed slightly. "I know Dr. O'Shea. I'll give him a call. Please, have a seat until I return." She gestured toward the bank of uncomfortable plastic seats along one wall. Komie led Róisín to sit as the doctor disappeared through a set of double doors.

A myriad of possibilities ran through Róisín's mind, but they had no cohesion. Just flashes of patients, the tingle of power, and the dead coming to life. Passages from the Bible chided her for playing God. She clasped her cross close to her chest and closed her eyes. *I pray for such discernment to not only make wise choices, but in the course of it all, to know I can trust Your guiding hand.*

Komie placed a hand on her shoulder. "You'll be fine. There can be no true conflict between the Irish gods and your God. They obviously exist. Wouldn't your God have created them as well as humans?"

Róisín couldn't fault the logic, but the puzzle pieces didn't fit into her minds-eye visual of her faith. But then again, generations of Biblical scholars argued about that faith without firm conclusions, either. Rules shifted as attitudes transformed, belief evolved, and power changed. She wasn't certain what shape her faith formed, just like hundreds of thousands of others throughout history.

As Dr. Neal returned, she wore a pinched smile. "Dr. O'Shea waxed poetic about your talents. I suppose I'll have to let you come. Please, follow me."

Komie gripped Róisín's arm. "Are you good from here? Do you need me by your side?"

She hugged the older woman. "I'd love to have you with me, but you should return to your...mentor. I'll be grand. Thank you."

With one more squeeze of reassurance, the other woman left. Róisín took a deep breath before following Dr. Neal through the double doors.

The doctor led her through two full wards of patients before they came to their destination. The Neonatal Unit. Róisín swallowed again and sent another silent prayer to God.

"Enough of that."

She halted, thinking someone in the hospital had spoken to her, but it was Dian Cécht's voice in her head. *Do my prayers to Christian saints bother you?*

"You do not need their help now. You need mine. If you wish to do what you've come to do, ask for my help, not theirs"

Róisín didn't like that one little bit, but he hadn't asked her to eschew her faith completely, just not pray while he was in her mind. She could comply with that, at least.

Dr. Neal brought her to an incubator, a haughty expression on her face. "This child was born yesterday, premature at twenty-four weeks. She has a fifty percent chance of surviving. Can your healing help to improve that chance?"

The tiny baby looked no bigger than her hand, red and unmoving, covered in wires and bandages. Her nameplate read "Rose." Róisín's own name meant Little Rose. Her eyes prickled with tears. Suddenly, Róisín didn't care which God helped her. She needed to do what her talent allowed. What Dian Cécht's assistance allowed.

Please, then, help me with this child. Give her a stronger chance to survive.

"I will help. Place your hands on her head."

Róisín glanced up at the doctor. "May I touch her? It will help with the healing."

Dr. Neal frowned and looked around. "Nurse? Help this woman scrub up. She must touch the patient, and we need to ensure she's as sterile as possible." She turned back to Róisín. "Will you be able to work your talent through gloves?"

"The plastic in the gloves hampers my power."

Róisín stored away this information, turning to Dr. Neal. "The gloves make this more difficult."

The doctor grimaced, but the nurse scrubbed her hands and dressed her in a gown. Her heart raced, but she might use that energy toward healing.

234

She placed her hands through the armholes in the side of the incubator. The armholes hampered her range of motion. With a tentative touch, Róisín placed her left hand on the child's forehead.

Now what? Do I just heal like I normally would?

"Start as you have done in the past. I shall guide you as needed."

She'd never healed a baby so young before. Children, yes. Many had been hurt in the explosion. But a toddler survived without an incubator. This wee thing seemed so incredibly fragile, as if a stray breath could steal her life. A butterfly wing. A morning's frost. A wisp of a cloud.

Róisín drew her power through her body as always, the tingling rushing through her blood and bones, her legs, chest, and out her arms. As it reached her fingertips, tiny sparks showered the baby's head. The nurse gasped and the doctor shushed him.

Little Rose waved her tiny hand. Róisín's power flowed into the child, gently at first, then stronger as she gained more confidence.

Suddenly, her power flooded through. Her vision blurred and her knees buckled. The tingling cranked to electric buzzing through her arms. The miniature sparks turned almost into flames. She yanked her hands from the incubator, afraid to hurt the baby.

"Do not stop. The human child needs more healing."

It won't hurt her?

"It will not hurt her."

The doctor murmured behind her. "Has something gone wrong?"

"No, no, just adjusting the power. Give me a moment." She shook her hands to get feeling back into her fingers.

Róisín steeled herself and placed her hands back into the incubator. When her finger brushed Rose's forehead, the bright flames returned. She clenched her arm muscles to keep from pulling back. Dian Cécht's magic flowed through her as a conduit for the god's power.

The buzzing itched her skin, bones, and blood. She ached to scream and scratch, to rub her skin, but she couldn't. She must heal this wee baby.

She must give little Rose a chance for a full life. To keep her attention focused, Róisín hummed and clenched her teeth.

Finally, when the muscles in her arms twitched and jerked, Dian Cécht's power sputtered to a trickle. She could finally withdraw her hands. Her entire body felt like a used wrapper, utterly empty.

The baby opened her deep blue eyes. Both the nurse and the doctor gasped. Róisín's vision swam with gray. She collapsed to the tiled floor.

Komie:

As the evening wound down, Komie managed to get Róisín to rest once more, but an emergency call came in just as she shut her eyes. The Irish woman jumped up and strode to the door before Komie caught her arm.

"Róisín, the hospital has dozens of doctors and nurses. You need to rest so you can help the others. Don't you see that?"

Róisín pulled her arm away. "Yes, of course they do. But I can help so much more with my magic! Don't you see that?"

"I see that. I also see you using yourself up."

Her expression turned hard. "You aren't my mother. I've got one of those, and she gives me plenty of guilt. I don't need another dose of that, thank you very much. Now, you'd best return to Macha. I can't imagine she gave you a long time to come visit me."

Komie let out a sigh as she watched the younger woman hurry down the hall, then left the hospital reluctantly. She still didn't like it, but Róisín was right. She must allow her to try this on her own.

Now, Komie must face her own mentor, another part of her reluctance. A teacher whom she hadn't wanted. She'd been touched by Anú, a gentle, mother goddess of growing things and the earth. This Macha, she seemed all sharp edges and anger. Komie felt working with this entity would be a difficult challenge.

She'd worked with people she didn't like before. But when it came to her power, she preferred to work in a comfortable space. When working with the earth, she was vulnerable. She focused on the earth, not her external body. Komie had no trust in this Macha.

"I do not require your trust. Merely your compliance."

Komie glanced at the sky. "I'll thank you to keep out of my private thoughts. If I have a question to ask you, I shall ask it aloud. Is that clear?"

"That is clear. However, your condition is not accepted."

The native woman crossed her arms, glaring into nothing. "Then we will not work together. Have you another, less demanding entity I can work with?"

"No. You will work with me, or you will receive no assistance from us."

Komie let out a deep breath. "Working with others requires respect. If you cannot offer such respect, then you do not deserve such respect in return."

"You have strength. I respect strength."

"Then do you agree to my condition?"

"Very well. I shall only read your outermost thoughts. Will that suffice?"

"Only with my express permission. Now, do you have my first assignment?"

"Not far from here. Would you prefer to walk?"

What else would she do? Komie had no car. But she didn't want to ask this goddess what other options she offered. She was pretty sure she wouldn't like the answer. If the next place was close enough to walk, she should stretch her legs. Walking in Ireland was much more pleasant than walking in the Arizona desert.

With Macha's instructions and a flashed image, Komie walked several blocks away from the hospital to a nearby sugarbeet farm.

Without Colin to introduce her, it took much more to convince the farmer of her helpful purpose. However, when she suggested he call the PHAE for verification of her abilities, he did. Once he verified her name, he welcomed her with open arms.

His wife brought her tea and scones as she walked the paths between his six fields, gauging his property and their relative growth. "Are you having any problems with this year's crop? Anything you'd like me to concentrate on?"

Mrs. Thomas shook her head. "No, indeed, everything's coming up nicely this year, despite all the furor on the news. Are you really able to make things grow faster? What a blessing that must be. Have you always had this talent?"

She grinned at the talkative woman, who stayed by her while her husband returned to mucking out the cow byre. "I have, but my abilities have grown stronger lately. Speaking with the land is part of my native tradition, back home."

"And where's back home, if I may ask? I have some cousins who immigrated about ten years ago. Maybe you've met them."

Komie smothered a chuckle. "Upstate Maine, near Moosehead Lake. My ancestors have lived near Mount Kineo for several thousand years."

The woman's eyes grew wide. "Oh, my! Yes, well, you are certainly part of the land, then. No, my cousins moved to Chicago. I doubt you've run into them."

As the woman chattered on about her cousins, Komie tuned her out and started with the nearest beet crop. She pushed her hands into the damp, black earth, sensing the growth within, vibrant and fecund. These were good keepers of the land. They kept the soil healthy and strong. She liked them.

"Use your power as you normally do. I wish to observe your process."

Komie's spine straightened at the commanding tone, once again wishing Anú had agreed to help instead of Macha. However, a goddess helped her, even if she wasn't one of Komie's choosing. She must be grateful for the assistance.

She drew the power from the land, drawing in the tendrils of growth and feeding them into the questing roots of the nearest plants. Above the earth, the greens vibrated and stretched, popped and twisted. The farmer's wife behind her gasped, her chatter falling silent.

When Komie let out her breath, her energy flagging, she glanced up at Mrs. Thomas. "That tea would be most welcome now."

The woman scrambled to pour her a cup, her hands shaking as she handed it over. Komie smiled and took the hot beverage, drinking deep to nourish her body and soul.

"Interesting. Perform again."

Komie glanced up. "If I don't rest in between sessions, I will pass out. I must ration my strength."

"I grow weary of your human frailties. You will not pass out."

With a sigh, Komie handed the empty teacup to Mrs. Thomas, whose eyes had turned wide when Komie conversed with thin air. She couldn't hear the responses, but Komie obviously spoke with someone.

The native woman walked to the edge of the next field and repeated her process. Her body resisted, not wanting to use her last scrap of energy. Without warning, power surged through her body with such vigor, the earth ejected her hands. She fell backward.

Komie's head buzzed with power, dizzy and disoriented. She clutched at the ground for something stable.

"Insert your hands again."

So much power made her dizzy. It felt delicious but also dangerous. At the same time, Komie wondered how much power she could channel.

Digging into the earth, Komie shut her eyes tight. The earth buzzed, tickling her fingertips as it always did. She drew the energy through her hands and into her body, then out into the roots. They wiggled as they grew, like a film sped to show a day's growth in one minute. They grew as much as they would have in two weeks. Buzzing grew to humming, and the energy flooded into her body. Plants grew so much, bright green showed on the stalks.

The hum morphed into a drone, then a persistent throbbing of electric energy.

"Now."

The torrent of power that burst through Komie sliced across raw nerves. Fire laced every inch of skin. She arched her back, screeching like a dying wolf. Mrs. Thomas stepped back, crossing herself and mumbling prayers to Mother Mary.

Despite the agony, Komie kept her hands deep in the earth. Her hands clenched tight around the loamy, black soil. Her eyes, now blinded by the intense force, gazed sightless into the heavens as she screamed again.

"Ah, yes. That is lovely."

Komie collapsed, the cool soil caressing her like a long-lost lover. But she didn't pass out. Macha kept her promise. Though she ached for respite, Komie remained conscious.

She stumbled to the next field. And the next. After completing the process a third time, Komie dragged herself out of the farm and peered down the road. Instead of walking to the next one, she planted her feet and crossed her arms. "I need to rest before I perform again."

"You do not."

She raised her eyebrows. "I absolutely do. I will not allow you to wring me out like a dishrag."

"Your body has the energy it needs to continue."

"Maybe my body does, thanks to your bolstering power. I feel like I've drunk a gallon of espresso. But my mind and my soul require rest as much as my body. If I ignore those needs, I will go insane long before my body collapses."

A tickling buzz scratched the back of her skull. As she rubbed it, the tickling shot out to the rest of her body.

"You will do four more. Then you may rest."

"One more."

"Two."

She let out a deep sigh and trudged to the next farm. And the next. At each farm, Komie introduced herself and knelt beside the field. To the wondering eyes of the farmer, she dug her hands into the soil and poured out first her own power, then Macha's, until she was utterly drained.

As Komie stumbled toward the next farm, she wanted to beg Macha to let her rest. But she refused to beg, even to a goddess. Macha gave her energy, strength to perform as a conduit. Her soul ached for the rest her body no longer craved.

How could she get a goddess to understand her soul needed rest?

Komie lost count of how many farms she helped that day. She didn't even know if these farmers wanted to bring in their harvest so soon. At least she helped the country. Macha didn't seem interested in the benefits. The goddess seemed more intrigued with how much power she could push through Komie.

So far, they hadn't found a limit, and that frightened Komie in a way nothing ever had. Not when her husband died. Not when the messenger approached her house in Arizona, bringing news of her son's death. This endless anticipation and exhaustion felt like a punishment of the gods. One where the foolish mortal dared to defy the eternal ones, only to be cursed to an eternity of forever striving for a goal. Just as he reached his goal, it would be snatched out of their grasp.

Prometheus brought humans fire and lived forever cursed. All she did is grow some crops. Should she be so punished?

The newest farmer peered at her with narrowed eyes. "My crops? Why, they won't be ready for another month. Why would I have hands for harvesting? Have you been out in the sun too long, pet?"

Komie sighed, and in a flat voice, explained her purpose again. It had become a droned chant, with no inflection. "I'm from PHAE, the Protectorate for unHidden Advancement and Education. I have a talent for making things grow faster. I'm here to make your crops grow. If you have people to harvest it, the produce can be ready today. Are you interested?"

The man just shook his head and backed away. So far, the farmers had been interested, even helpful. This one might take some more convincing. Or she'd just move to the next one.

"No. I will speak with him."

That perked Komie's attention. Would Macha manifest physically again?

"Hey, did you bring someone else? Who's that?"

Komie turned to see a figure approaching. Taller than many men, perhaps six-and-a-half feet tall, the woman strode with strength and purpose. Her black braids fell to her waist, and the enormous raven stood on her shoulder, letting out an imperious caw. Her pale white skin almost glowed against the overcast sky. Navy blue tattooed spirals adorned her cheeks. She wore a gold-spiral belt around her white tunic's waist and leather bracers studded with bronze on her forearms. A red, white, and black checkered cloak billowed from her shoulders, despite the lack of wind.

The farmer blanched and took a few steps back.

"You will allow this human to attend your fields."

The farmer froze in place, his mouth open. The only sound escaping his mouth sounded like a hoarse frog.

Macha strode forward, shoving the farmer aside. Komie followed in her wake, nodding thanks to the man.

When she finished the promised farms, Macha allowed her to rest. The farmer grumbled, but let her curl up in a guest room, filled with tacky plastic knickknacks. Komie fell instantly into a deep slumber. However, Macha roused her after only an hour. As she grumbled awake, she made a mental note to negotiate for a minimum time in the future.

And so, she continued, from farm to farm, and field to field. Komie might have rested in between sessions, but she couldn't remember sleeping. The days, farms, and pain all melded together until every waking moment distilled to a dream from which she could never emerge.

Joel:

Once Carlos fell asleep, Joel crept out of bed, collected a few useful items, and stole from the room. Not that he had anything against the guy, but Joel preferred to work alone. And in truth, why should he trust his rescuer? He might be taking him into a worse situation, the old bait and switch. Get the victim to trust the rescuer, then betray them. It *had* been nice to hear an American accent again, though.

He thought about searching for Anna, but his sister had blown the whistle on him in the first place. She'd do it again, with her inflated sense of morality. No, he had to remain a free agent.

At least Ireland was an English-speaking country. If he was on his own in, say, Vietnam or Nigeria, he'd have a harder time surviving. But he'd be fine here. He'd have to find a place to lay low. Then he'd figure out how to contact the PEM.

His hand slipped into his pocket, where he'd taken cash from Carlos' wallet. He'd had about fifty Euro, so Joel took forty. It didn't seem right cleaning the guy out completely, but that forty Euro would keep Joel going for a bit. It would keep him from starving.

He never wanted to be starving again.

Joel hadn't been given instructions for after his mission, other than to do as much damage as possible and stay quiet about it. The latter had been a bust. That Hafsia woman drew every detail from him, and he felt like a wrung-out towel. It didn't seem fair that the PHAE had a lie-detector talent. Worse, someone who could force another to tell the truth. There must be international laws against that somewhere. But there were international laws against starvation and torture, and they already proved they didn't care about that.

In payment for the pain Hafsia caused him, his determination to help the PEM jelled. If he could find a contact, he'd double down. The PHAE had no business with power. He wanted to take them down. That would show Anna and her oh-so-precious PHAE.

Joel strolled down the house-lined street. He had no idea where he was, other than somewhere near Dublin. Each house looked attached to its neighbor, with tiny fenced-in front yards brimming with flowers and bushes. Picturesque and quaint, something out of a postcard. Joel wanted to vomit.

Joel wished he still had his phone, but they'd taken that immediately. His fingers itched to look things up as soon as he thought of them. Back at the hotel room, he considered taking Carlos' phone, but that would make him easily tracked. Besides, it seemed rotten to steal both cash and phone. Cash got him food.

As he turned the corner, the aroma of something fried beckoned him, and his mouth watered. He grinned when he spied a food truck with meat pies. While he wanted to order one of everything, he restrained himself to one pie. The soup and bread Carlos bought him last night had made him queasy. The rich meat and pastry might upset his starving stomach. Joel didn't want to throw anything up. No sense in wasting the bounty of food.

Food, delicious food.

Before he bit into the treat, Joel breathed deep of the aroma of his buttery fried pastry. It burned his hands, but he didn't mind. He nibbled at the edge as he found a bench to enjoy his bounty.

The pie still steamed, and he didn't want to burn his tongue. He studied the square as it cooled. Thirty-some people milled around the park. He spied a church spire jutting out of the next block. A few taller buildings peeked above the house roofs and trees.

He bit into the soft part of the pie, closing his eyes as he savored the rich, meaty juices. He licked hot grease as it dripped down his hand. His stomach roiled, so he stopped, to allow it time to recover before taking another bite.

A half hour later, his stomach still wasn't happy. He'd only eaten half the pie, but there was no way he'd waste the bounty. He wrapped it in the napkin, grimacing at the grease stains. Still, he didn't even think of tossing it. He'd carry it until his stomach behaved and he could finish.

Joel headed toward the tall buildings. Downtown meant people. People meant a chance of finding someone he could talk to. Someone in the PEM.

As he turned a corner near the financial center, he spied protesters carrying signs. A glimpse of one allowed him to read the words, *"Freaks go home."*

Exactly what he was looking for. A grin spread across his face. Now he had an action plan.

Joel:

"Hoi, mate, watch it! You almost knocked me over!"

Joel flashed the other guy a smile. "Sorry, man! Just reading your sign."

The blond man furrowed his brow and looked at the sign he held, with the words *"Freaks Go Home!"* in messy red letters. "Yeah? My banner? What about it?"

"I agree with it."

As the other man raised it up again, above the others, shook it a few times, and then glanced back at Joel. "You want one for yourself? They've got a few extras over at the check-in table."

"That would be great. Thanks!"

He threaded through the crowd, jumping to see above the sea of heads, cursing his short stature, trying to find the table. Usually, they had a bunch of water bottles, a PA system of some sort to give directions or lead chants, some sign in sheets, and a stack of flyers for anyone who wanted more information.

There! He spotted a glimpse of a folding table to the back. Joel ducked down, winding through the sweaty bodies until he escaped the crowd.

Once he got to the table, he nodded to the Asian woman sitting behind the stack of flyers. "Someone said you might have an extra, uh, banner for me?"

"Sure! I've a few right here. How about," she turned around and came back with one. "How about one that says *Pure Humans Only?*"

He gave her a charming grin. "Perfect! Thanks. I'm Joel, by the way."

"I'm Yasmin. Here. Have you signed our roster yet?"

He did so as he took one of the flyers, folded it and placed it in his pocket. "Thanks, Yasmin. Do you hold rallies here regularly?"

"Every few days. We've got a schedule on our website. I've got the QR code if you want to grab it with your phone."

He put on a pitiful expression. "My phone got stolen along with my baggage last night, I'm afraid."

"Really? Was it one of them, do you think?"

"Pretty sure. There was some strange goo left in my hotel room. I knew better than to call the police. They're all in the PHAE's pocket, right?"

Her face lit up as she gave a knowing nod. "You were wise. Hey, if you're in a hotel, that means you aren't local, right? Do you need a place to stay?"

He glanced around, but no one else was within easy hearing. "I need a place to stay and a place to work. Got any ideas?"

Yasmin gave him a half-smile. "We have plenty of work for those who know what's really going on. I can hook you up. In fact, I have a treat for you."

That sounded intriguing. "A treat above a place to stay and a job?"

"Way above! We've got a visitor coming in tonight, and you'll get to meet him." Her voice fell to a conspiratorial whisper. "Tiberius Wilkinson will be there for a special dinner. Can you believe it? He's come in from America on a private yacht. They won't let him through the airports. That stupid fake quarantine they've put on everyone is keeping him out, but we know better."

She gave him a wink, and he returned it, his face flushing warm. "Yes, yes, we do."

Róisín:

After Dr. Neal went home, Róisín tossed and turned, but sleep eluded her. Her mind kept racing with case details, faces, and charts.

Over the last week, she worked on healing each baby in the Neonatal Unit. Every time she grew low on power, Dian Cécht filled her up, like a car at a petrol station. With the god's help, she'd healed or strengthened twenty babies.

She still hadn't quite reconciled her Catholic faith with accepting help from the ancient pagan god, but every time she saw the pink of health fill the cheeks of a previously pallid child, she knew she must be doing something good in the world. Something pure, something helpful, something beautiful. That had to earn her some amount of grace, didn't it?

Weary of trying to sleep, she rose, pulling a sweater over her scrubs. She padded down the dim, quiet halls. The Children's Ward lay beyond the Neonatal Unit. Instead of babies, this ward held toddlers through teenagers. They might have broken bones, chicken pox, cancer or anything in between. None of them had the plague, though. Róisín hadn't seen that many cases here.

That was one reason they chose Limerick Hospital instead of going back to Galway. Dian Cécht wanted her to practice on a wider variety of issues, from injuries to illness.

Most of the children slept, but she spied one with a torch under the blanket, flicking back and forth. He must be reading. Róisín suppressed a grin. She'd done the same growing up. She'd always thought she was fooling Mam, but she now realized her torch had never run out of batteries, no matter how much she used it.

She moved to the child's bedside and glanced at his chart. Brian Gallagher. Ten years old. Lymphoma. She'd never tried to cure anything so serious. Her throat caught. With Dian Cécht's new power, how could she not try?

The boy must have heard her footsteps. The blanket dropped and the torch went dark. She chuckled. "Don't worry, I won't turn you in. I used to do that myself. What're you reading?"

He narrowed his eyes. Despite in the low light, his bald head shone. Reluctantly, he showed her a comic book.

With a chuckle, Róisín picked it up, reading the title. "Batman, huh? Do you like superheroes?" She offered the comic back to him.

Brian held it close to his chest. "My dad's a superhero. He's in the guards. He puts the bad guys in jail, just like Batman."

"And what about you? Do you have any superhero powers?" She wiggled her fingers like she was doing magic, making him giggle.

"No, but I'm hoping a radioactive spider bites me in here. Do you think it could happen?"

Placing a hand on his thin shoulder, she clenched her jaw to keep the tears in. "Sure, and anything's possible. I'm Róisín. What's your name?"

He dropped his gaze, staring at his blanket. "I'm Brian. But my friends call me Bri."

"I'm pleased to meet you, Bri. How long have you been here?"

He shrugged, his breathing shallow and pained. "It seems like forever. But my Mam says I've been here for a month. They keep sticking me with needles and feeding me medicines, so I can't sleep like I used to."

Róisín pulled up a chair. "I can't sleep, either. I did a lot of work today, so my mind is running like horses on a racetrack. Would you like some company?"

He smiled shyly. "Sure. My sister visits sometimes. You remind me of her. My mom hasn't come much. I think she cries on the way here. Her eyes are all red."

How would she feel, as a mother, watching her child go through cancer treatments for months? His skin looked so translucent it seemed blue in the dim light. She placed a hand on his arm. His skin felt thin and dry. "Want to hear a secret?"

Bri nodded, his smile growing.

Róisín glanced back and forth, as if ensuring no one could hear, and then whispered, "I have a superpower."

The boy's eyes grew wide, but he let out a giggle. "You're just teasing me now."

"No, I swear! I do. Want to guess what it is?"

He narrowed his eyes. "You're in a hospital. Is it something about sick people?"

Róisín's face broke out in a wide grin. "You're too smart for me! Yes, it is. I can heal folks."

Bri lost his smile. He pulled his arm away. "No, that's not real. You're lying to me."

Róisín placed her hand on his chest and locked gazes. "Would you like me to try to heal you, Bri?"

"Yeah, yeah. Very funny." The boy grimaced and stared at his sheet.

"I promise, I'm not fooling around or lying. I really do have power. I can't heal everything, but I might help."

For a bare second, nothing moved. No one breathed, coughed, or snored. Then Bri nodded, his eyes wide again.

Róisín placed her other hand on his stomach. She closed her eyes, drawing deep for the healing power, as Dian Cécht showed her. Would the god be paying attention? Would he help her? Her previous confidence in God's grace crumbled as she prayed.

Power surged through her like a firehose, the recoil almost throwing her backward. Electric force flowed through her arms into the boy's body, lighting him with healing energy. Bri's skin sizzled and cracked. His hair stood on end like a dandelion gone to seed.

The boy arched his back, his mouth open in a silent scream. Afraid of hurting him, Róisín tried to pull her hands off him, but she couldn't move them from his body. Dian Cécht and his healing power had control of her now. She'd been relegated to a conduit for the god's purpose, like so many times over the last few days.

With a final cry, she snapped back to herself, her hands sliding away from Bri's chest. He slumped in his hospital cot, panting and hoarse while her knees buckled. She grabbed tight to the cot's railings to keep on her feet.

He breathed more easily than before. His skin looked ruddier and healthier. When his eyes blinked open, he glanced around, as if amazed by his surroundings. "What did you do?"

Róisín cleared her throat. "I'm hoping that I helped to heal you, but we won't know for certain until I can find a doctor to run a CBC."

Bri searched the dim room, as if previously hidden doctors would pop out from behind a curtain, but most of the patients in the ward still slept. Róisín thought they had made enough noise to wake at least a few. Maybe Dian Cécht kept them slumbering while his magic worked through her.

She couldn't deny her thrill when an apathetic baby cried with a healthy set of lungs. And now, as Bri looked around himself with renewed interest and energy, Róisín's heart surged with pride. He looked ready to run down the hall and find a doctor to test his white blood cell count.

As he swung his leg over the edge of his cot, she stopped him with a hand on his shoulder. "Whoa, cowboy. You shouldn't leave the bed. You're still all hooked up, remember? Let me go find a doctor for you. There should be one in the lounge."

His grin would have looked natural on any child, full of mischief and hope. She couldn't help returning it and adding a wink. As she walked down the hall, her footsteps echoing in the quiet space, her gait bouncing. How much of her joy was from healing Bri, and how much from the power that still crackled in her fingers? She touched the doorway as she turned a corner. A spark flashed from her fingertips.

Despite her joy, Róisín still had misgivings about being a conduit for this ancient magic. Aside from her lingering horror at working with a pagan god, she felt like a vessel shaped into his needs, discarded the instance she was no longer of use. At least his purpose corresponded with hers, the need to heal the helpless.

She halted with a horrible thought. What if he gave her a task against her conscience? Would she have the strength to say no? Did she have that strength now? She'd just have to make that decision if it came. She pushed open the lounge door.

She spied one resident, an intern snoring on the couch. Róisín frowned, debating the wisdom of waking anyone in the middle of the night, much less a feral intern. Still, he could run tests. She doubted she could convince Bri to sleep again.

She placed a hand on the intern's shoulder. He startled awake, his eyes wide with terror. When he scrambled away from her, Róisín felt horrible for waking him. Sweat dripped down his dark cheeks. Had he been having a nightmare?

The man spoke with a Nigerian accent. "Who are you? Is there an emergency?"

Róisín held her hands out, smiling to calm him. "No, I'm so sorry, no emergency. I need a doctor to run a CBC."

His eyes darted to the corners of the room, his muscles still tense. "No emergency?"

"No emergency."

He closed his eyes and got his breath under control, wiping his face with his scrubs. "I do apologize for any rudeness in my words. I do not sleep easily. I hope I did not upset you."

She sat next to him, her head cocked. "I'm not upset. I shouldn't have woken you. I know interns don't get much sleep."

The man grinned, sticking out his hand to shake. "I got very little sleep even before my internship. I am called Ekon. Waking to such radiant beauty makes me believe I have died and gone to heaven. What is your name, lovely flower?"

Róisín flushed as she shook his hand. "I'm Róisín, which means little rose. I've been healing in the Children's Ward. I'm very pleased to meet you, Ekon."

After a brief explanation, Ekon agreed to run the CBC and other labs on her patient. He went to the emergency department to get them run quickly. As they waited, Róisín asked Bri about his life before the cancer.

"I used to play hurling. I was on the team. If I'm really healed, do you think I could play on the team again?"

She patted him on the shoulder. "Sure, that's a possibility. Especially for a superhero like you."

Bri reminded Róisín of her brothers, Liam and Hugh. She didn't want to imagine either of the twins lying in a hospital bed for months.

When Ekon returned with the lab results, his brow was furrowed. He studied Bri's chart, shaking his head. "I just don't understand this. Are you sure he doesn't have a twin? You are not playing a prank?"

A grin split her face as she turned to Bri. "Does that mean his cell count is normal?"

The Nigerian man shrugged. "As normal as someone without cancer gets. Is he on a new therapy?"

Bri's face lit up. The hope he must have suppressed shone out. Róisín hugged him tight, trying not to let tears of joy leak. If she started crying now, she'd never stop. "It worked, Brian! It worked."

He clutched her close, even when she began to pull away, so she hugged him more tightly. How many nights had he lain here, unable to sleep, imagining his short life over?

Ekon left to fetch a resident while Róisín rubbed Bri's back. "What's the first thing you want to do when you get out?"

He scrunched up his nose, considering his options. "I want to eat pizza! They won't let me have any here. I want to go swimming, too. At the beach! And run along the sand with my dog, Bru."

She grinned. "Bri and Bru?" They shared a giggle as he nodded.

As Ekon the intern returned with a doctor in tow, Róisín retreated with a final squeeze on Bri's hand. She'd done what she came to do and should leave Brian to his new life. Now she let her tears take over. No one noticed as she disappeared toward the ward door.

Róisín loved helping Brian. She treasured that warm feeling close to her heart for hours. The healing felt like a sweet wave rushing around her. Like honey dripping through her veins. As more doctors converged on Brian's bed, she escaped into the next ward, searching for another patient to help.

One girl's chart said she had a broken rib. That should be easy enough to heal. Róisín might not be able to fully heal a broken bone in a single session, but she could speed along the natural process.

She laid hands on the sleeping girl. The child twitched but didn't wake. The healer didn't need to call on Dian Cécht for this work. His power flowed anyway, a sweet river and a wave of pleasure. Róisín shivered as the dregs poured into the patient.

The next bed held a younger child, three years old. The sides of his bed were raised to keep him from falling out. As she read his chart, Róisín wrinkled her nose. Kidney infections could be painful. Easy enough to fix, with Dian Cécht's help. She closed her eyes as the delight coursed through her body and into the patient.

She worked her way down the ward, healing each patient with growing enjoyment. Róisín could grow to love this work, not only for its own sake, but for the joy she felt as the magic coursed through her body, from the healing god to each patient, reveling in the delight and power.

Chapter Ten

"Endings are abstruse, mystic and unreal.
They are but depleted beginnings purposed to be substituted with newer
ones."
– Chirag Tulsiani

Komie:

Komie needed a break. Macha had wrung her dry again, forcing her into a grueling pace. She'd rested her body, but her mind needed a different respite. On top of that, through her lessons and practices, Komie hadn't stopped worrying about Róisín and her work at the hospital. So, when Macha set her to another task, she balked. "Tomorrow is soon enough. I must take a break."

The goddess wrinkled her nose, her eyes flicking to the tree branch Komie had been encouraging to grow in a spiral. **"A break? What is breaking?"**

"A break. A rest. I need to regain my energy."

"You have slept your required hours last night."

"Yes, but my mind needs time to rest as well. I will be no good if you don't allow me that."

The goddess pursed her lips and the ever-present raven cawed from the lamppost. **"Very well. You will have this evening to rest your mind, as you request. But I expect you to be available for your first assignment at sunrise."**

Before Macha could change her mind, Komie called a taxi to return to the hospital. After she paid the driver, she squared her shoulders. A crowd of angry protestors milled around the entrance. Komie paid little attention to their signs, but they seemed more passionate than the normal political dissidents. When she read the signs, her blood chilled.

"Arrest the freaks"

"Get rid of the Unhidden"

"Humans only!"

"No Unhidden, no disease"

They wanted the Unhidden arrested, dead, or just gone. They blamed the illness on those who just wanted to heal them. Her worry about Róisín cranked up several notches.

Komie swallowed against the urge to convince this band of protestors of her kindness. Her need to be liked warred against her sense of self-preservation. She was one woman alone. Hiroki had the skill in persuasive speeches, not her. She had no chance to sway a mob. To try would be dangerous, and would keep her from helping Róisín, besides.

A sharp pain in her shoulder made her spin. One red-faced man glared at her, his wooden sign clutched like a weapon. She glared back in her best grandmother scowl. He narrowed his eyes but turned away.

Another protester poked her side. She whirled to find three women. Komie didn't know which poked her. All three scowled, one with thunderous hatred in her green eyes.

A punch in the kidneys made her double over. Someone kicked the back of her knee. She stumbled but kept her feet. When she stood straight, she planted her feet wide, anger surging through her blood. How dare these people attack her? She, who had spoken to the gods of their own land.

Her anger reached into the earth, calling upon the growing things to help her. The call faded into a dying scream. Komie tried again, frustration fueling her effort. Another failure. After a third attempt, she realized inert concrete pavement blocked her powers. The earth couldn't heed her cry. Even the dirt beneath the concrete couldn't break through that barrier, no matter how loud she called.

Exhausted and defeated, she stumbled through the crowd, reaching the edge without further incident. As she breathed more easily, she gave thanks that her magic hadn't worked, and she hadn't surrendered to her rage. Vengeance was unworthy of a tribal elder. Komie resolved to do better in the future.

After she entered the hospital, Komie let out a sigh of relief. The protestors still milled outside, but their angry words were muted by glass doors. She turned her back on them, peering down each hallway, searching for Róisín. This hospital wasn't large, but the endless wards reminded her of an ancient labyrinth, designed to befuddle the logical mind. If she were smart, she'd inquire about Róisín at the front desk. However, her stubborn streak convinced her to find the healer on her own. She'd relied too much on other people since coming here. Once upon a time, in the woodlands of Maine, she used to be more self-sufficient. She could set up a summer camp, gather her own food, build a fire, and tan leather. She'd grown too reliant on modern conveniences, and it showed. Komie should be able to find one woman in a single building.

An intern passed, nodding in greeting. She nodded back but strode with purpose so they wouldn't stop her. People would assume she belonged here if she moved with confidence. She held her head high, walking swiftly.

Finally, after peering down a dozen corridors, Komie spied her quarry. The Irish woman had just turned a corner into a children's ward. "Róisín!"

When the younger woman turned, Róisín's face lit up. She gestured at Komie. "Come with me, I'm on a mission!"

As Komie followed the healer into the next ward, Róisín opened her arms wide. "I've been busy today. Every one of these kids are going home. Maybe not today, but soon."

Her eyes widened. "Every one of them? That's impressive. And it sounds like a great deal of work."

Róisín gave an insouciant shrug. "I enjoyed it."

Komie peered at Róisín. Though she smiled, something haunted the back of her eyes. "When's the last time you slept?"

With a half-smile, she waved her hand in dismissal. "Oh, some time yesterday. I took a nap. But with so many people in the hospital, how can I sleep? I can make a real difference here. Dian Cécht has helped me so much. Without him, I'd have burned out hours ago."

The older woman scowled. "You look burnt out now. When's the last time you ate?"

Róisín clearly had to search her memory for the answer but gave up and shrugged. "I don't feel sleepy or hungry."

Pursing her lips, Komie grasped the younger woman's arm. Her skin felt thin and hot. "And you wonder how drug users get addicted. Hmph. Come with me. I'll find you a place to sleep."

Róisín pulled out of her grip. "No, I can't sleep! Not yet. The children need my help."

Komie searched Róisín's eyes. The Róisín she'd come to know, the gentle woman with quiet wisdom, hid. This new Róisín, this frenetic, anxious woman, seemed like a stranger living in Róisín's body. How much was due to fatigue? And how much due to the god's interference?

With a shudder, remembering the feel of Macha's hand on her soul, Komie stepped back. "Very well. Do what you must. But I'm staying with you. When you crash, you'll need someone to catch you."

"Ekon's helping me. I think he's formed a crush on me." Róisín's expression sparked with mischief and a hint of manic.

"Ekon?"

"A cute intern."

"As admirable as that may be, I don't think an intern with a crush on you is going to assess you with objective judgment. If you won't rest, then let me at least feed you before you dive in again."

After fetching soup and sandwiches from the cafeteria and making Róisín sit still long enough to consume her lunch, Komie allowed her to return to the Children's Ward. The young man, Ekon, did indeed dote on her. She had three or four other observers, both doctors and nurses. Róisín must have already built a healing reputation. Several took notes as she approached the first patient on the right.

This toddler, perhaps aged about two, barely moved in her cot. The chart said her name was Angela. For a moment, Komie didn't see this Irish child. Instead, her own granddaughter, Tansy, gazed back at her. Komie clenched her jaw and swallowed. She never wanted to imagine Tansy in the hospital.

Róisín glanced up at her audience. "Her chart says she has a skull fracture."

Ekon nodded eagerly. "Her mother told us she was jumping on the bed and fell, hitting her head on the table."

Replacing the chart, Róisín shook her hands for dramatic effect. Then she placed them on the girl's head, closing her eyes and tilting her own head back. The gathered medical personnel held their breath as Róisín worked her healing.

Komie scowled as sparks crackled along the healer's arms, arching into the child's temples. The toddler moaned and clenched her tiny fists. Her face contorted in pain. As the girl was in obvious distress, Komie stepped toward Róisín, ready to pull her hands away. She couldn't allow the Irish woman to torture the child.

Before she could interfere, Róisín lifted her hands and bowed her head, as if in an evangelistic prayer meeting. The surrounding doctors and nurses let out their breath.

The little girl opened her eyes wide, staring at the surrounding adults. Fear glimmered in her face as her gaze flicked from person to person. Ekon walked up, putting a hand to the girl's cheek. "It's alright, sweetie. You remember me, yes? I helped your mother when she arrived."

She gave a tentative nod. "I remember you. You have a singing voice."

Ekon gave her a wide grin. "Yes, you said that before. Now, how do you feel? Does your head still hurt?"

She placed a hand on the back of her head, still bandaged from her wound. Testing the spot, she shook her head. "It doesn't hurt anymore!"

Ekon glanced up. "When she came in, she cried so hard she could barely breathe. We tried to keep her awake for the concussion, but she fell into a deep sleep. We couldn't rouse her."

One nurse gasped and another clapped. Róisín spun, taking a bow and basking in the admiration for her efforts.

Komie furrowed her brow. Róisín had always been modest and soft-spoken. Now she looked like a stage magician performing for the crowds. Komie would definitely have to keep watch on the younger woman.

Max:

Chaos swirled in his head as Max called the wind and flew away. He screamed with rage as he rose into the sky. The guards watched him, but he didn't care. He had to get the hell away from here. What had he just fucking *done?* He'd gotten Ash killed with his own idiocy, is what he'd done.

When would he ever learn? Anytime he tried to do something to help, he just made it worse. He'd gotten Qacha captured and taken away. He'd gotten Ash executed. And Trina… Max let out another howl of pure frustration and rage.

The icy wind tore at his clothing. Up, up he rose, into the thin clouds of the morning. His breath came harsh and painful, but still he howled like a wild animal.

When he couldn't feel his hands, his feet, even the skin of his face, Max came to his senses. *"Fuck!* Right, then. Bring me down, gently, mates. I need a drink like I never have before."

As he rushed toward the ground, Max searched for some landmark, but didn't recognize anything in the rural area. The winds had taken him so high, so far, he'd drifted from London. He might be back in Ireland. Hell, he might even be in France, for all he knew. Still, any place there was a pub would be grand.

The local winds didn't have any practice landing him, but he didn't come to that realization in time to slow his fall. He slammed into the hillside, thankful he landed on soft bushes and not jutting rocks or asphalt. Still, he sprawled for several minutes, catching his breath, before he could move.

He flipped over on his back, staring up at the sky. Ash's face flashed through his vision at the moment the bullet went through their head. Over and over, on instant replay. Shutting his eyes made it worse. This image would join his last memory of Trina, with her burnt skin flaking off in his hands. A constant highlight reel of his worst failures.

The only way to erase such things, even temporarily, was to sink into the oblivion of drink.

Max struggled to his feet and glanced around. The wind had dropped him in a village along an unpaved, one-lane road. Hedgerows marched along each side of the road, making the path wide enough for only one vehicle.

To the left, nothing but hedges filled the view. To the right, several buildings clustered around an open square. He moved toward this cluster.

He spied picnic tables with enormous umbrellas outside one building. At the very least, a restaurant where he could get a drink. At the very best, a proper pub.

His shoulders tense, he strode into the building, noting the enormous bar. A feral smile crept across his face.

When Max staggered out hours later, the sun had sunk low on the horizon, hidden by hills and trees. He never even asked the landlord what town he was in, but at this point, he didn't care. Facing the sky, he opened his arms wide. "Right. Let's go up, mates!"

Pointing his hands like Superman, Max let out a delighted, drunken laugh as the winds lifted him into the twilight. He soared up and down, riding the thermals like a bird of prey. Land below him winked in and out. Time disappeared as he played in the clouds. When he finally descended, green showed once again in the sunrise, a patchwork quilt of farms.

Despite the rising sun, black clouds gathered as he sped through the icy air. The winds made him swoop and howl as he played through the storm. Thunder rumbled and he laughed back.

Lights flashed and he chased them like fireflies on an autumn night. He let out a howl of pure intoxication and triumph, his arms pumped above his head like a champion. The storm growled again, and something slammed into him. The air whooshed out of his lungs, and he croaked out, "what the hell was that?"

We do not know.

"Sorry, I wasn't asking you, mates. It hurt!"

Again, something struck him, his entire body crackling with energy and pain.

"Stop that! Whatever, whoever the hell you are. Clear off!"

The ground rushed toward him. He threw his arms up to cover his face just before he hit.

Max woke, wet. Rain pelted his face. He opened his eyes, blinking as the water stung them. He moaned as he put his hands on his head. Every muscle in his body ached, full of tingling agony. "Ugh! What the hell!"

This wasn't a hangover. He knew that pain better than most. This was more than just hitting the ground, though that would have been enough. His body had been beaten and bashed a lot over the last few days, but still, there was something more. Had he been struck by lightning? Max supposed that's what he got for playing in the storm. *Bloody brilliant idea, that.*

With great effort, Max pushed himself to his feet. The sun had long since set. He must have been knocked out for a while. He stood on a hillside. He spied a line of pine trees uphill, and a village downhill. With a deep sigh, he brushed off his jumpsuit and stumbled toward the buildings below. He slipped on the wet ground, falling on his butt. "Goddamned rain! Stop bloody falling on my bloody head!"

Finally, after the latest string of invective, the sky boomed in answer, "**No.**"

Max glanced up, his eyes widening. That hadn't been thunder. That had been a voice. Not in his head, either, like when the winds answered him. This had been an actual voice, telling him no. A voice large enough to fill the sky.

Max swallowed and glanced up. "Were you talking to me, mate?"

"**I am speaking to you.**"

He turned while looking at the sky. Blackness stared back. No moon or stars penetrated the dark clouds. "Who're you, then?"

His answer was a booming crack of thunder. His hair stood on end and his head pounded. A thick fork of lightning struck the ground at his feet. Max danced back, rubbing the hair on his arms down. "Fuck! What the fuck was that?"

"**That was me. You are insolent.**"

"Well, that's me to a T, mate. Uh, I'm Max. Do you have a name?"

"**I am Taranis.**"

The name didn't sound familiar. Max tried to remember if Colin's stories back at the Byrne farm had mentioned a Taranis, but he drew a blank. "Right. Taranis. Well, pleased to meet you, I guess. What are you telling me not to do?"

"**You have invaded my realm.**"

Fuck. Just what he needed. A jealous god angry at him. That just made his night so much better.

Anna:

Waves lapped at Anna's feet. Well, what used to be feet. They'd become covered in scales, sparkling iridescent in the sun as Anna sat on the beach. She wiggled her toes, watching the prismatic colors glimmer. Her skin finally stopped itching, but that might be from spending most of her time in the water. At least they hadn't fused into a mermaid tail. As much as she adored all things marine, losing her legs would have been too high a price. The little mermaid had paid a high price to turn from a fish tail to legs, stepping on knives, in the original tale. She didn't think she could handle that much pain.

She'd told *him* that. Either he'd listened or that hadn't been her path to begin with.

Scales covered her arms and legs now, and a little bit under her belly. Her hips grew smaller scales, almost snake-like, tapering to a point near her waist. The rest of her body remained human skin.

Anna rarely saw humans once she'd found this cave with its white-sand beach. Seals swam nearby every day. Their barks frayed her nerves, and sometimes she screamed at them to shut up. *He* told them to bring her fish, which she cooked over a campfire. She ate seaweed washed along the shore, clams, and oysters.

Seals, fish, even dolphins and whales visited her sea cave, but not humans. Anna didn't really miss people. She missed tea, though. And she'd kill for some cheese and bread.

Maybe if she swam along the shore, she'd find a nice older woman, living alone in a cottage. The woman might be willing to serve her tea and soda bread, and not ask any questions about her scales. Anna chuckled at this unlikely scenario.

A low moan rose from the sea. That moan heralded his visits. Sometimes it meant he'd be there in a few minutes, sometimes in a few hours. Anna didn't know if the water moaned, or if his voice traveled through the ocean, or if the sea creatures moaned on his behalf. She hummed back, indicating she'd heard his message.

She glanced at her hoard. Three fish, several scallops, and an eel. When he came, she must offer him a meal, for politeness' sake. He rarely accepted, especially if she'd cooked it but the proprieties must be maintained.

Voices drifted from above her. Human voices, not his. Curious, she swam into the bay and peered up to the cliff above the cave.

Three boys sat, dangling their feet over the edge. Teenagers. Suddenly, her heart ached for human company. At the same time, anger surged through her blood. This was *her* place. Not theirs. They needed to go away.

One scrambled to his feet, pointing at her. "Hey! Ken, d'ye see that?"

His companions craned their necks to see past the rocks. The second boy's eyes grew wide. "The Selkie Girl! Old Tam told me about her."

The third boy let out a piercing wolf whistle. "Damn! She's gorgeous! Hey, sexy Selkie Girl! Give me a kiss!"

His companion shoved him on the shoulder. "You'd have to go down there, ya numpty."

He gave a startled glance to the boy, then down at the rocks, and shrugged. "Grand! Stay there, Selkie Girl! I'm gonna come give you a sexy time!"

Anna's rage grew white-hot. How dare they invade her home? How dare they make catcalls and reduce her to a sex symbol? The tiny part of her mind that held tight to her talent let loose. Power flooded through her body. She let out a song.

Not just any song. An intoxicating call. An invitation to wreak havoc upon her tormentors. A siren call.

The boy who'd whistled at her clapped his hands to his ears and cried out. His companions did the same. All three fell to their knees on the sharp rocks. Blood seeped through their fingers. Their faces contorted with intense pain.

The boy who called her Selkie Girl scrambled to his feet and ran, his hands still over his ears. The first one escaped, too. The one who cat-called her did not.

He crumpled into an unconscious pile on the rocks. His body slid down, down, into the water below. The splash made her smile, but then she frowned. Why should she celebrate his death?

The water swirled and mist formed, which heralded *his* arrival. She waited for him to emerge.

The waves rose into a huge, amorphous bubble, bursting to reveal her mentor, the Irish god of the sea, protector of sailors. *Manannán mac Lir.*

His bluish skin glinted in the morning light. He wore no scales, but his skin still shone with water which never dried, even in harsh wind. His long black hair, beard, and mustache hid bits of braided seaweed, draping over his muscular chest.

Manannán lifted the still unconscious boy from the water. Carefully, he placed the boy on the shore, well up from the high tide mark. **"This one will live. He will be a sailor, devoted to me and my realm."**

His tone made this a commandment, not a prediction. The boy didn't stir, but Anna had no doubt he'd survive. Relief flooded her veins. She hadn't really wanted him to die, but her rage still pulsed. She must learn how to control such urges.

"You have been sorrowful."

Again, a statement of fact rather than a question. Anna gazed up at her mentor and nodded.

"What would ease your sorrow, child?"

Anna couldn't answer. She didn't know. Tea and bread and cheese were banal things to ease the bone-deep grief she held like a talisman. She didn't miss humans as a rule. But she ached to see certain people. Did she miss her brother? Carlos? Brendan? Her scowl deepened. Brendan had used her. Still, she'd been happy at the Byrne farm, if only for a few days.

They wouldn't like her now. She'd turned half sea-creature, something out of Colin's legends. Anna stared at the water's surface. She rarely spoke in front of her mentor, but he read the nuance in her body language.

"As you desire. Have you practiced yesterday's lesson?"

Anna swallowed, steeling herself for a tiring day. She took a deep breath, stood on in the water, and raised her hands toward the west. Pulling her power through her feet, the crackle of energy flowed along her body and out her fingers.

She formed water into an oblong shape, like a pickle. She drew the back end out twice to form a dolphin's rear fins. Then the front, bulbous nose. Last, the dorsal fin.

She glanced at Manannán and received a nod of approval. Then, with a deep breath, Anna gestured for the dolphin to swim through the air. It bounded up and down in a circle. She clapped her hands and laughed with delight.

Yesterday, Manannán had taught her how to draw the ocean up into herself and craft delicate sculptures of pure seawater. Four times she tried, without success. But today, she did it, better than she'd imagined.

"You have a basic understanding of this lesson. I am pleased. Now, for the next."

As she cycled through several exercises, refining her touch to a fine point, Anna wondered at the lessons' purpose. She'd asked him yesterday, but he ignored her question. Did she dare ask again? Or would he get angry? She didn't dare risk angering a god. Still, she worked better with a goal in mind.

A goal. That reminded her of Joel. He'd had a goal, and that goal had killed hundreds, maybe thousands, of innocent people. Did he still live? Did the PHAE have him in custody?

Brendan's face flashed into her memory, but she shoved that away. She didn't want to think about the Irish man. Her heart still stung with betrayal. What right did he have of being jealous of Carlos? And where did Carlos go? Was he still in the B&B? Or had he gone to Dublin?

As she formed an intricate Celtic knot with a thin line of water, a seal barked and clapped. Anna gave her audience a sad smile.

Maybe she needed people again, even if she didn't want them.

Anna:

Someone called her name, fading words dancing on the sound of the surf. Manannán never needed to call her name. She simply knew when he wanted her, and the command sprang into her mind without warning, so she must obey.

But this must be a human voice. Her name sounded odd to her own ears. Did waves distort the sound? Maybe a voice she barely remembered? Or had she just not heard her own name in so long, she no longer recognized it?

"Anna!"

There it was again. Curious, she swam out from her cave to seek who dared call her. She'd developed quite a reputation amongst the locals. Everyone now knew to give her plenty of room. No one came near, especially not after she sang at those boys. The one *he* saved did survive, but she wouldn't have been very sad if he died. He'd been cruel to her.

She crafted waves to carry her around the sandy beach. Anna must see the whole cliff face without being seen herself. There, a figure stood on the shore. Dark clothing, dark hair. Brendan had dark hair, but much longer. Nevertheless, he seemed familiar.

"Aaaanna! Where are you?"

Something in the lilt of the voice, the accent, niggled at her memory. She'd met this person. Were they at the Byrne's farm? That time seemed a thousand years ago. Even a week ago felt like another lifetime. Each wave of sea water washed away the tether to her landbound life.

"Aaaanna! Please, I need to see you!"

The voice wended its way into her heart. Dark, curly hair. American, like her. The man at the B&B. The name whispered in her mind, with his accent. Carlos. Her memory of that visit flooded back, reminding her of being human. She'd asked him about her brother. Did he discover where Joel went?

Without thinking of the consequences, she swam back toward the beach. Anna called seaweed to weave into a garment, a flowing dress to keep prying eyes from her body, her scales, her skin.

She rose from the waves like Aphrodite, wrapped in brown, purple, and green seaweed, her hair streaming with seawater. Carlos spied her, and scrambled down the cliff, almost falling as he jumped to the sand.

Anna would not have been pleased with his fall. He hadn't hurt her or teased her. He'd been kind to her. He'd made her smile once upon a time.

The flood of nostalgia made her long for a human embrace. Male arms. Arms to protect and cherish her. Arms to make her feel human.

Carlos slowed, looking her up and down. In anyone else, it might have been a leer, but his expression seemed sweet. His smile deepened as they locked gazes. "Hey, you. I've been searching for you."

Brendan should have looked for her. He's the one she'd spent so much time with. Why didn't he search for her? But Carlos had found her, and she wanted to be held by human arms.

Without speaking, she wrapped her arms around him and melted into his hug. His arms felt much warmer than the ocean's embrace.

He kept hold of her for an endless time. When she let out a deep sigh, he stood back, hands still gripping her shoulders. "It's really you. You're the Selkie Girl. I heard tales about her all up and down the coast. I figured it might be you, so I came looking."

Her voice cracked on the first word she'd spoken in days. "Why?"

Carlos' brow furrowed. "Why? Why not? You're a friend. You might have been in danger."

A friend in danger. Anyone would help someone like that. She turned away, but he held tight to her shoulders. "Hey! Okay, I didn't mean it quite like that. You're more than a friend. At least, I'd hoped you'd be. But you were with Brendan?" The last sounded half comment, half question.

Her shoulders tensed. "I'm not with him now. We argued. I left."

"That must have hurt." Carlos pulled her back into a hug.

It had hurt deeply, a fact she only now let herself understand. Tears burst out as she pressed her face against Carlos' chest. She cried more than she had in weeks.

"C'mon, let's watch the sunset. You can tell me what you've been doing, and I'll catch you up with my news. Deal?"

"You really came to find me?"

With a squeeze of her hand, he grinned. "I did. But I should have brought you some clothes. What is this, seaweed? You'll start a new fashion trend."

Anna let out a snort and grimaced, feeling more human by the minute. "I doubt 'sea hag' is a look anyone wants to copy."

He touched her nose with a finger. "A siren by any other name would sound as sweet. Now, I've got updates on who's done what. Where would you like me to start?"

As Carlos shared news from the world and the PHAE, Anna gazed at the horizon. Manannán's interest in this person pulsed through her. He didn't seem upset with his presence, at least. Maybe he'd allow her to have a land-bound friend.

Something Carlos said penetrated her fugue. "What? Komie did what?"

"She signed on as an apprentice to Macha."

Anna didn't know that name. Did Manannán know her? She'd ask at their next lesson.

Carlos drew a shape in the sand. Circles within circles. "So, I have a question for you."

Raising her eyebrows, she cocked her head. "So? Are you going to ask or just hope I read your mind?"

He let out a low chuckle, ducking his head. "Will you come back with me?"

Anna drew away, sudden fear at returning to the land prickling her skin. "I can't. I have duties here." The sand felt rough against her feet. Her heartbeat sped up. Panic rose in her throat.

She didn't want to make decisions like this. Choosing was hard. Working with Manannán made her feel like she was back in school, without any major decisions to make.

Anna wanted to run into the water, but that would be rude. It felt good to talk to Carlos. He made her laugh, and the only one to laugh with her the last weeks had been the seals. Several of them basked on the beach, posing like stone statues in the setting sun.

Carlos knelt next to her, still holding her hand. "Anna, please. We need you. Besides, I have news about Joel."

At her brother's name, she sat up straight. "Joel? You found him?"

With a sheepish grin, he shrugged. "Well, I did, and I didn't. I found where they held him. In Mountjoy Prison, Dublin."

Anna narrowed her eyes and pulled back a fraction. "Held? Past tense?"

Carlos looked up to the left and bit his lip. "Yeah, well, he broke out."

Joel had gotten free. Now he'd be a fugitive from the PHAE, an organization she technically still belonged to. "How did you find out?"

"Well, I was sort of with him at the time."

Anna stared at him. "You broke my brother out of jail? Why? I didn't ask you to do that! I just wanted to find out where he was!"

Carlos fell backward on his butt and held up his hands. "Whoa, whoa! Hey, I'm sorry! I thought you'd want your brother free from torture! How was I to know you wanted him to starve to death?"

She couldn't think. Her mind swirled with too many new ideas, too much information. "Torture? Starving?"

"Yeah. He said this woman pounded him with questions constantly, with truth-telling Unhidden power. He only got a few bites of food, a few sips of water. He looked like death warmed over."

"Oh." Anna stared at the waves lapping her feet. Too many emotions crashed in her mind, and she couldn't pick any of them out as valid. "What happened after you got him out?"

"First, I got him some food, water, and a place to sleep. He hadn't had any real rest in weeks. When I woke in the morning, he'd disappeared."

"He's gone? On his own?"

Carlos gave a shrug. "Well, yeah. He's a grown man. He'll be okay. Your brother seems to have a deep well of sarcasm that'll get him through most things."

With gritted teeth, she said, "Yeah, he's pretty talented at being a prime jerk. He's had *lots* of practice."

A seal at the end of the beach clapped and barked. They both burst out laughing, the tension draining. "Jerk or not, he's free now. And that removes some of your worry, right?"

Anna wrinkled her nose. "Sort of. I mean, he deserves punishment. And I'm the one who turned him in. But starvation? Torture? That's not what I wanted. I guess it's better that he's free than that." She swallowed and stared at the waves again.

A darkness grew on the horizon, blocking out the setting sun. A storm across the ocean. She shivered, and Carlos put his arm around her shoulders, hugging her tight. "I've got a blanket in the car. And a thermos of tea. Oh, and I brought sandwiches, too."

Tea and bread. She gave him a half-smile.

Komie:

Komie got Róisín to rest for a bare two hours in the doctor's lounge before Ekon knocked. The young intern had become Róisín's personal assistant, besotted by her healing abilities, and he looked as exhausted as Róisín did. "Hello? Is she awake yet? We're ready for her in the burn unit."

Komie returned a fierce whisper. "No, she is not. She is getting much-needed sleep and will remain so for some time. Go away for at least two more hours."

Róisín moaned and rubbed her eyes, sitting up on her elbows. "I'm awake, I'm awake! I can do more. Let me wash my face."

The native woman pushed her back down on the cot. "You will not. I insist that you rest longer. Your body will fail if you keep pushing it. Believe me, I know this from first-hand experience."

Shaking her head, Róisín flung her covers off. "Dian Cécht gives me all the energy I need. I'll be fine."

Komie drew the covers back up to Róisín's chin. "No! The human body needs sleep for more than just physical recovery, girl! It needs to recover mentally from the stress of the day, and you're putting yourself through far more stress than normal."

Róisín glared at her, angry lines marring her expression. "I said, I'd be fine. I already have a mother. I don't need another. Or a grandmother." The healer pushed past Komie, flashing Ekon a saucy grin. "Lead on, MacDuff! And damn'd be him that first cries, 'Hold, enough!'"

She shot one last resentful look over her shoulder as she shut the lounge door.

Komie clenched her fists and pounded them on the cot, a wholly unsatisfying expression of frustration. She didn't want the child to burn completely out. Yes, she did an incredible thing, and the god fed her energy. But as Komie learned from Macha, the gods had no true understanding of human frailties. He'd use her like a tool until only an empty husk remained.

Which could kill her, and Róisín couldn't heal that.

With a deep sigh, Komie pushed up from the cot, her knees creaking. Her back ached, too. Her own fatigue threatened to take her down. She daren't ask Macha for help, as she'd abandoned the goddess to come here. That act would have consequences as well, but she couldn't think about that now. She must find a way to help Róisín.

Komie only had to follow the shouts of encouragement to the burn ward. Róisín gathered a large audience now. Doctors, nurses, interns, and even family members watched as she attended each patient. Her theatrics had increased, with lightning crackling from her fingers and sing-song humming. Whether these were a natural result of the power coursing through Róisín's body or effects added for drama, Komie didn't know or care.

Róisín stood beside the hospital bed of a man bandaged from the waist down. He'd been caught in a chemical fire and burns covered much of his skin. A doctor made him sign a hasty release before he backed away, allowing the healer room.

The healer removed several bandages. Komie didn't think bare skin was necessary for the healing, but only to cater to the growing audience. This would increase the possibility of infection, if her healing didn't work.

Róisín raised her hands, humming a solemn tune, head back and eyes closed. She looked like an evangelical preacher calling for manna from Heaven. And perhaps that's what she did, asking for the gods' help. Her voice held a monotone as she called out, "Dian Cécht, Healer of the Gods, hear my plea. Visit your power upon this man, take away his pain. Make his skin whole."

Sparks flew from her fingers as she lowered her arms. They got larger as she came closer to the man's chest. His eyes grew wide, and he squirmed, trying to get away from this madwoman.

274

As her hands touched his body, his muscles spasmed, his back arched, and he cried out. The long, painful wail bounced against the hospital walls. It ended in a whimper as she did it again, and again, each touch punctuated with his anguished screams.

The audience watched, as rapt as if witnessing gory gladiatorial games in a Roman arena.

Finally, the skin exposed by the peeled bandage looked whole again. Still, he screamed. Dr. Neal pulled off more bandages, and they saw that his skin was, indeed whole, from the waist down. All of it. Even his belly button.

The doctor's eyes grew wide. Those closest to the burn victim, close enough to see that detail, staggered back. The doctor peeked under the man's gown and backed away, horror on his face. "All his skin is sealed shut, even…"

Róisín's face still glowed with triumph and the god's healing energy. She lowered her hands, nodded once to her audience with regal dignity, and strode to the next bed.

Her eyes shone with orange light which had nothing to do with her humanity. Komie followed, hurrying to catch the younger woman. She pushed her way through the crowd of on-lookers, elbowing one young nurse and shoving aside another. Finally, Komie reached the front line around the newest patient's bed, standing next to a handsome doctor she didn't recognize.

A young lady, very pretty, with flaming red hair, with burns on both arms and across her torso. Róisín raised her hands again. Komie froze, unsure if she should stop the healer. She glanced back at the previous patient. Several doctors swarmed around him, preparing him for surgery to repair the overzealous healing effort. He might be lucky. They might repair his sealed bowels quickly, though he'd never be the same.

Still, he'd been spared months of painful healing from his burns, and scar tissue across his lower body. Would a reconstructed penis and anus be sufficient payment for that? Only he could tell for certain. He ought to have been given the choice.

Róisín hummed, singing that wordless melody. The memory of it tugged at Komie's mind, but she couldn't place it. It had the cadence of a nursery rhyme or a lullaby. Something both soothing and disturbing. Róisín lowered her arms, chanting again for the god's assistance. The young burn victim before her screeched in utter agony.

The new doctor put out his hand. "Róisín? You're hurting her."

The healer shook her head and continued to sing, her volume increasing.

"Róisín, please!"

Komie couldn't take it anymore. Róisín had gone mad with her power. She might do something even worse to this young woman, all without meaning to, just by allowing Dian Cécht free reign with his powers. Komie grabbed Róisín's arm and yanked her away. The Irish healer didn't budge. She felt as solid as a rock, with no human weakness. Her skin felt like carved marble, not pliant flesh. Human flesh.

The native woman pulled again, placing her feet under her for leverage. "You need to stop!"

Róisín ignored her efforts. One of her followers shouted out, "Hey! What are you doing? Leave her alone!"

An intern grabbed her waist. Another joined him. Soon, four people jerked Komie away from Róisín. She lost her balance, and they dragged her along the tile hospital floor. "Róisín! Stop! You're hurting her!"

As more of the gathered medical personnel pulled Komie away from Róisín, the healer stopped her work on the young burn victim. She twisted her head, without turning her body at all, an unnatural pose. She looked like a broken mannequin. As she glared at Komie, a horrible smile crept across her face.

A triple-echoed male voice issued through her lips as her eyes shone with that ethereal orange light. "I do not answer to you."

Róisín:

What time was it? Did it matter? Róisín didn't even know the date. Her consciousness ebbed and flowed like ocean waves. Flashes of memories danced in her mind, darting between darkness and light, with shades of gray playing in the background.

Had she imaged Dr. O'Shea's arrival? She seemed to remember his lovely voice during the last healing, when she'd healed that woman's burns, when they took Komie away. The older woman had meddled too much, but she had been sorry to see her leave. No matter. She'd gotten lots of healing done in a very short time.

Dian Cécht had taken the driver's seat as they worked through each ward, and all she could do was watch as he worked his magic on patients. He questioned the purpose and effectiveness of each modern piece of equipment while she explained in her mind. He inquired about their medicines and what maladies could and couldn't be healed with modern science. Then he healed patients with those maladies.

Surrounded by the growing audience, Róisín strode to a victim of the recent plague. Through her eyes, Dian Cécht peered at the patient's face. "This is not one illness."

The surrounding audience perked up at the triple-echoed male voice. Ekon wrinkled his brow. "What do you mean? Can you diagnose them? We've worked for weeks trying to determine the cause."

Róisín held her breath, mentally, wondering if her original theory, proposed so long ago in Galway, was correct. Dr. O'Shea had dismissed her idea out of hand, and it would feel gratifying to be vindicated. She glanced around to see if she had imagined his arrival after all, but there he was, standing behind her.

"Dr. O'Shea! I thought I heard your voice earlier."

He looked at her with sad eyes. "You've changed a lot in a very short time, Róisín."

She waved off his criticism. "I've healed a lot of people, and that's what matters."

Dian Cécht cleared her throat and spoke through her lips. "I recognize both diseases. One is known as the Black Bane, and the other a common enough plague."

Dr. O'Shea's eyes grew wide. "Black Bane. Isn't that Anthrax?"

She'd been right. Róisín sighed at the hundreds, perhaps thousands of lives that might have been saved if he had just listened to her theory in the first place. But he'd dismissed it and sent her away. And now look at her, healing patient after patient with the help of a god. She straightened her spine, full of righteous indignation.

Murmurs of "anthrax" and "plague" ricocheted through the crowd.

With Róisín's lips, Dian Cécht slipped into a condescending smile. "It is a disease more common amongst kine, but humans *can* fall into its clutches."

Everyone stepped back from the patient, despite the fact that they were gowned and gloved, with face masks, as per pandemic protocol. A few stepped farther away from the group, and one left the ward. Ekon looked uncomfortable as he shifted his gaze from Róisín to the patient.

Dr. O'Shea cleared his throat, taking a tentative step forward despite his pale face. "Can you heal him of both maladies?"

With an enigmatic smile, Dian Cécht nodded. "Róisín tells me that many of your people are afflicted with this plague."

Gripping his clipboard, the doctor nodded. "We've been fighting it throughout the country. It's spread to twenty percent of the population, an alarming rate in just a few weeks."

"I can heal them. However, I am limited to one place and time. This human's body will be unable to host me much longer. The strength is almost gone."

Ekon's stared at the god in Róisín's body. "Gone? You must let her rest!"

With a cocked head, Dian Cécht asked, "Which is more important? This human's health or that of your people?"

Dead silence greeted his question. Dr. O'Shea swallowed. "Of course, our people are more important. However, can we find a way for you to help without killing Róisín?"

The smile Dian Cécht now wore grew sly. "Who else do you offer?"

Everyone glanced around, unwilling to offer themselves. Ekon glanced at Róisín, terror clear in his eyes, and straightened his spine. "I volunteer, if I am acceptable. Róisín must be allowed to recover."

The god considered Ekon for several long moments, cocking his head at the Nigerian intern. He narrowed his eyes and crossed his arms. "Very well. Prepare yourself. But we will need more than one host. Eire is a large island and holds many people to heal."

Róisín's body glowed with a light so bright, no one could look at her. That light sparked and crackled as if she'd grasped hold of a bolt of lightning. She screamed, arching her back and gripping her head. Her scream choked into silence as she fell to her knees.

Just as Dr. O'Shea grabbed her hands, the crackling light leapt to Ekon's body. His spine stiffened, and he cried out in an animal howl as Dian Cécht settled into him. He let out a triple-voiced chuckle as Róisín collapsed in a limp heap to the tiled floor.

When she finally woke, she lay in a darkened room. The sheets felt harsh against her bare skin, like when she had a fever. Stretching, she tried to recall the last thing she did.

She'd gotten used to losing time. Dian Cécht had taken over chunks of her life, and she retreated to the back of her mind. She sensed no trace of the god of healing now, though. The absence made her heart sink. Had he abandoned her? Was she no longer an acceptable apprentice? How had she failed him?

Anger, frustration, and despair all warred within her. How could he leave her? She tore the sheet off her body. In the dim light, she noticed she wore scrubs. A hospital. Flashes of memory of healing flooded in on her. Róisín held her head, but the images didn't stop. They pounded upon her mind in painful staccato, more and more memories pelting her soul. How could she escape the pain?

She moaned and stumbled from the dark room, blinking in the harsh hospital light. Everything hurt. Her muscles, her head, her throat, she had to get away. Beeps and buzzes taunted her, like children on the playground.

Róisín shoved through several sets of double doors before finding the exit. It beckoned to her down a bright, empty hallway. She ran for surcease from stimuli, aching to see the blue sky above her.

When she finally emerged from the hospital, driving rain stung her face. She stared up into the gray storm clouds, laughing and dancing in circles at her freedom. Her arms stretched out as she gave a manic laugh. Raindrops fell into her mouth.

A new power rushed through her, despite having no patient to heal. She cackled at this sign of the gods' favor. Perhaps Dian Cécht wasn't with her now, but she wielded some sort of godly talent, even without his grace.

The energy gave her stamina and the urge to run, away from the hospital with its horrible stench and pain, away from the people who judged her and found her wanting. Away from people, any people. She sprinted down the main street, through the line of angry protesters, away from the hospital, and toward the green hills. Róisín needed to be in the countryside, not in the oppressive city. She wanted to feel the loamy soil between her toes, to smell wildflowers and fresh-cut hay.

The absence of Dian Cécht's mind slammed her, a sudden pain of bereftness. Róisín stumbled, skidding along the road on her stomach. She scrabbled along the gravel, groaning from pain in both her body and her heart. Something else infused her, something powerful, magical, but with a different taste. Another god? Her own power flooding the empty space? It insisted she rise and run. She jumped to her feet.

Róisín's laughter grew desperate as she ran further from the city. She loped through the suburbs and smaller villages. Farmhouses flanked her, but still she ran. Her feet didn't even ache, her nurse's shoes giving her plenty of support. Murmurs called on the wind, behind her, into her ears, then further away, beckoning her forward.

When Róisín reached a hilltop, she spun around with her arms out, her face toward the sky. Soaking wet, the scrubs clinging to her body, she felt more alive than ever before. Sparks flew from her fingers as her healing power discharged with nothing to heal. In the distance, the river played hide-and-seek in the rainy mist.

This urgent new power drew her west toward the ocean shore, calling her name, whispers in the corners of her psyche tugging at her focus. Dodging a herd of sheep, jumping over a fence, through a beet field. Why were they already ripe? They shouldn't be ready for months.

She shoved aside the idea and heeded the call. Her name tickled and teased the countryside. She followed the breeze along the road, hugging a cliff. Then she ran along the rocky shore, out to a series of caves along the Shannon.

Róisín slowed, her energy finally flagging, as she peered into a cave mouth. She still heard her name in her ear, first on one side and then the other, tiny voices, as if mice spoke to her.

A human moan floated across the sand. Róisín tried to shake her head to clear it of sparks and crept to the entrance.

The interior looked inky-dark, but something shuffled inside. Her head still buzzed and swirled, but she stepped in. After her eyes adjusted to the gloom, she spied something in the back. It moaned again.

Her healer instinct kicked in, and she knelt by the form. Placing a hand on one hump, energy crackled where she touched their warmth. They were alive, whoever they were. Tentatively, she pulled down on the shoulder to see their face.

The world kicked sideways. "Max?"

Bintou:

Bintou hadn't been to this room, the largest in the underground bunker beneath Dublin. The group of thirty PHAE officials sat in two semi-circles. Most of them wore black or gray. The room had a dry-erase board on one wall above a wooden lectern. Ciara stood at the lectern, gripping the edges.

Bintou sat with Masaaki, Hiroki, and Ibrahim while Ciara spoke with intensity. Ciara had asked them all to attend to back up her claims, if anyone should ask more details, as they'd heard the original phone call. "We have verified testimony from a trusted member, Colin Byrne. He swears both Nokomis Nicholas and Róisín Byrne, his own daughter, have been not only contacted by the ancient gods, but that these gods have lent their power to the women, to amplify their own Unhidden talents."

One older woman shook her head. "I don't understand what you mean by *lent their power*. Can you elucidate?"

Ciara glanced at Bintou and Hiroki before answering. "I could, but my explanation would only be a guess. I suggest you either call upon those directly affected, Róisín and Nokomis, for more detailed explanation. I can, however, expand upon the effects."

Bintou clasped and unclasped her hands throughout the presentation. She shouldn't be so nervous, so inadequate. This felt like her first job interview, or her oral exams at school. Not knowing what she might be asked, or if she had the information to answer, gave her a great deal of anxiety.

Ciara stepped out from behind the lectern, interlacing her fingers in front. She paced along the line of PHAE officials. "From what Colin has reported, Róisín has been able to, with Dian Cécht's assistance, heal an entire ward of premature infants at University Hospital Limerick over two days."

The same woman asked, "What do you mean by healed? Preemies aren't ill or injured. They're only born early."

With her head cocked, Ciara stopped walking. "Correct. She helped their lungs grow, reduced their jaundice, and improved their strength. Most of the infants even gained body mass of up to ten percent. Many have been moved out of the Neonatal Ward, as they no longer need incubators."

Some whispered to their neighbors, in excited tones. A tall, bald man stood, his arms crossed. "What proof do you have of this implausible claim?"

Bintou caught her breath at this disrespect. He'd come so close to calling Ciara, and by association, them, liars.

Taking a deep breath, Ciara opened her hands. "Mr. Dillon, I invite you to call UHL yourself if you disbelieve me."

Someone called from the second row. "What about the American woman? What has she done?"

"Nokomis has brought ten fields, including beets, soybean, and potato, from seedlings to eminent harvest in the same two days. She will prove an invaluable asset to our food supply in case of further attack or the need for quarantine."

More murmurs swept across those assembled. The bald man stood again, his face turning red. "And they think whoever they spoke to are gods?"

Ciara glanced toward Hiroki and Bintou before answering. "Yes. While we have no way of verifying their actual divine status, they have demonstrated god-like powers, far and beyond anything our Unhidden can do."

This settled a silence across the murmurs, and then the silence grew uncomfortable. The same man then asked, "And what do these so-called gods want of us?"

Ciara pursed her lips. "They haven't made specific demands in exchange for their assistance. However, Colin Byrne mentioned that they wished to scale up the healing operations. To that end, they've requested volunteers to act as conduits to their power, much as Róisín Byrne has been doing in Limerick. They've asked our permission to recruit said volunteers."

Dillon shook his head. "I don't like that. I don't like that one bit. We need to stop their interference immediately, whoever they really are. They could be spies with esoteric technology. They could be Unhidden talents themselves, for all we know, someone working for the PEM."

Ciara shook her head. "Mr. Dillon, The PEM wouldn't hire Unhidden. They think we are mutant abominations, slated for extermination or imprisonment."

He glared at her. "They were quick enough to hire that Taylor boy to bring bombs into Galway. May I remind you that *you* recruited that particular Unhidden into PHAE, and now thousands of people, both Unhidden and regular citizens of Ireland, have lost their lives. You're assuming way too much about the PEM and their capabilities, Ms. Doherty."

Chastened, Ciara dropped her gaze. Bintou had never seen Ciara so unsure of herself. The man might be rude, but he had a point. Joel's bombs had killed thousands of people in Galway. Only Anna and Max's quick work saved Cork from a similar fate. Another agent smuggled a bomb into the port of Dublin, though it didn't make it to the more populated city centre. But the fact remained that the PEM weren't afraid of terrorist tactics or killing innocents to implement their plans.

Three loud knocks echoed through the silence. Ciara turned toward the door, but a PHAE official rose before she could move. He opened it a crack and spoke with someone in words too low for Bintou to hear.

The man turned around. "We've been asked to present this information to the *Dáil*. I'm not sure how they found out about it, but it would be unwise to delay."

After much murmured discussion, the PHAE officials filed out of the room, with Bintou and her group trailing. Ciara led them out of the back door to the tunnels and into the noisy streets of Dublin above.

It had been days since Bintou last saw the sun. She lifted her face to greet the shining orb, to bask in its warmth. Unfortunately, this being Ireland, usually only gray skies and misty air greeted her. Still, breathing fresh air rather than the stale atmosphere in the bunker felt like a delightful release.

They only had to walk two blocks to Leinster House, where the *Dáil*, the Legislative Assembly of Ireland, met. Bintou wished she'd known they'd be presenting to the *Dáil* today. She'd dressed nicely, but to be paraded in front of a country's government with no warning kicked her anxiety into high gear.

She clenched and unclenched her hands as they trekked to the government building. She'd never been prone to such distress before coming to Ireland. Her confidence cracked into a shattered thing, torn to shreds with each crisis.

The road past Leinster House was crowded with people. So immersed in her own distress, Bintou barely registered their chants and signs. Angry, red faces shouted epithets as they passed. Bintou shrank away from their rage.

As soon as they spied Masaaki, whose paper-white face declared him as unmistakably Unhidden, their voices rose in renewed frenzy. The crowd surged toward them, harm intent on their expressions. Ciara hurried their group across the street and into the gated entrance.

Something hit the back of her head. Bintou cried out, "Ow!" and turned to see who threw it. The sea of fury rushing toward her turned her blood cold. With wide eyes, she scrambled to join Ciara. Flashes of childhood fears intruded on her mind. Her heartbeat raced and her face dripped with sweat.

Once they got safely inside, Bintou worked to regulate her breathing and mopped her face dry. *I'm safe now.* She chanted it like a mantra but stole several glances over her shoulder as they escaped through the huge wooden double doors.

The gray, stone building didn't seem large from the outside. Three stories on a central square, with flanking ancillary buildings. They marched through three echoing hallways, with a legion of oil paintings of *Taoisigh*, presidents, and *Teachtaí Dálaí*, the Irish equivalent of senators, known as TDs. Another set of double wooden doors opened to reveal the assembly room of the *Dáil Éireann*, the Irish lower house.

The assembly room had a semi-circle of seats on one end, with a bank of seats in the mezzanine on the other end. Almost two hundred seats in all, most were filled with government representatives. Visitors stood in the center, like performers in a circus. Bintou didn't like being on display, and she very much wished she could hide in the hallway.

Luckily, she hadn't been asked to present any information. Ciara answered questions from the Taoiseach and the assembled *Dáil*. Several ranking members of PHAE added to her data. Then it fell to wrangling between the lawmakers of Ireland.

One member of the *Dáil*, a junior *Teachta Dála*, his black hair mussed and sweat beading on his face, stood. "How do we know these so-called gods will be able to help us?"

Across the aisle, a female TD laughed. "The ancient gods of Ireland? Do you not remember the tales? They have more power than we can imagine."

The original speaker shook his head. "I never cared much for the 'auld stories.' More important than *can* they help us, *why* do they want to help us? What're they getting out of this arrangement?"

The woman, her gray hair tied in a bun, glanced toward Ciara. "Well? What are their conditions?"

Ciara stood with her spine straight and shoulders back. "They have offered to help. They have demanded no price for their help, except for the volunteers to help their healing campaign."

Letting out a snort, the woman shook her head. "You never make a bargain with the Good Neighbors without knowing all the terms."

Murmurs swept the room, sprinkled with a few giggles and several solemn nodded agreements. Ciara took a deep breath. "I would suggest that we invite one here as a spokesperson, to answer any questions the *Dáil* might have. I'm afraid any intentions or nuance might be lost if the PHAE acts as their mouthpiece. As the governing body of Ireland, you deserve direct answers."

That set off another round of murmurs, though most sounded like agreement.

A young, dark-haired man jumped to his feet. "This is ridiculous! We can't believe these people talked to actual, living gods, can we? Logic dictates that this is some elaborate wind-up!"

Hiroki rose, turning to him. "And are the bombings a wind-up, TD Fitzgerald? The plague that is even now spreading across this island? Are these all part of some amusing prank we're playing on the people of Ireland?"

TD Fitzgerald sat again, a defiant frown still on his face.

The gray-haired TD stood again. "Ciara, you suggested bringing in a representative. Would they be willing?"

Ciara nodded. "I believe they would be willing to do so. Do I have permission to request one?"

The Taoiseach stood, her hands gripping the podium. "I think we must decide that without you. If you will excuse us, we shall deliberate."

The four of them exited from the room full of mute tension. As they left the building, Bintou tensed, but the protestors had moved down to the other end of the block. They hurried back to the bunker entrance and down to their rooms to await the decision. They ate their dinner, take-away Indian food, in nervous silence. Bintou didn't even taste the biryani spices she loved so much.

At first, this decision didn't seem so momentous. However, the more Bintou thought about it, the more she worried. The government of

Ireland debated accepting help from their own ancient gods. What would gods do if rejected? How much power did they actually wield, and how sensitive would they be to rejection? Bintou had studied many religions for her degree in ancient cultures. In no religion, except perhaps Buddhism, did the gods take rejection kindly.

She chased the last few grains of rice around in her dish with her fork. Masaaki excused himself to read, while Hiroki fell back into morose introspection, something he did more and more often. Ever since he received that letter from his father. Ciara stayed with her, but she stared at her dinner as well.

Every sound outside the door made them glance up, eager for news. The evening turned to night with no word, so Ciara left for her own room. She gave Bintou a bare smile as she left, the lines around her eyes stark in the fluorescent light.

Bintou struggled with sleep. Nightmares of angry, vengeful gods filled her dreams. Not those from this land, these ancient Irish gods, but those of her own faith. Furious djinn destroyed entire cities from an unintended insult or rained down fire and pain upon an innocent family.

An insistent knocking dragged Bintou from her troubled slumber. By the time she wrested herself from a tangle of sweat-soaked blankets and pulled her robe on, Hiroki had answered the door. His voice murmured and the door closed again.

She washed her face before poking her head out into the common room. "Hiroki? Who was that? Have they sent word?"

He stared at the door. "They have. They will invite a representative of the ancient gods to speak before the Assembly."

Bintou swallowed, trying to process that data. The gods would be heeded, so they shouldn't be angry. For the first time since Colin called yesterday, Bintou breathed more easily. At least they had a chance now.

Bintou:

Ciara told Colin a spokesperson for the gods was invited to speak at the Assembly. Colin promised to pass on the invitation to Róisín and Komie. They would then inform Macha and Dian Cécht of the offer. Then they waited. She had grown to hate the waiting.

Masaaki played a monotonous, silly game on his phone, something with beeps and buzzes that annoyed her. Hiroki stared at the wall. Ciara made unusual cocktails for them to try, making some without actual alcohol so Bintou could partake.

Bintou tried to read the Irish historical novel she'd borrowed from Ciara, but the words kept dancing off the page. The story wasn't at fault, nor the author's writing, but her own worry about future events. Escapism wasn't a sufficient distraction. How could she read about the heroic age of Ireland when the entities who created that age might walk amongst them?

Now that the Assembly had agreed to speak with the gods, her feeling of doom eased, but there was still a chance they'd insult the gods. Her anxiety swung between a certainty that the gods would destroy everything out of sheer pique, and a delight in witnessing this miracle in her own time.

Bintou hoped they weren't like the capricious Djinn, causing mischief and pain in human lives for millennia. Djinn would someday answer to Allah for their cruelties, and some of them realized this, so acted kindly toward humans. Did the Irish gods answer to a higher power? Perhaps this Anú, Komie's earth goddess? She'd also heard of the Dagda, a father god to them all.

Words on the book's pages blurred. She gave up reading again. She'd done this a dozen times today. Every time someone walked down the hall, or a phone buzzed, Bintou glanced up, in case it was news.

She barely ate. Her weight had dropped off the last few weeks, and her clothing fitted poorly. Not that she had any desire to go shopping in a bombed Dublin. Sure, some places escaped damage, but who could she ask to accompany her? Ciara had her duties to the PHAE, and seldom left. Hiroki and Masaaki weren't what she'd call shopping partners. Shopping alone didn't hold as much appeal, as she loved shopping with friends.

Bintou wished Róisín or Anna had come to Dublin. Either would be fun to shop with. Her throat caught at the notion that Martin might have taken her shopping, if he'd survived his illness. But he hadn't. Suddenly, shopping with friends seemed like a banal thought, so ephemeral in the grand scheme of life.

She escaped to her bedroom, taking her novel with her. Masaaki didn't glance up from his game, nor Hiroki from his despair. Ciara stared at her own phone, sipping a festive, orange-colored cocktail.

After she placed the novel on the dresser, Bintou pulled out her nightstand drawer. Grief pricked her eyes as she spied Martin's flask, long since emptied. She clutched it to her chest, imagining his smiling face, his musical accent, and his delightful laugh. The way he gazed into her eyes when he spoke to her. A tear slid down her cheek. Of all the things she'd endured since she left Mali, Martin's death would always be the worst.

Just as she got ready to change into her night clothing, a knock startled her. Ciara's voice came through. "He's here."

Her heart fluttered, thinking for a crazy moment that Martin had come, but that wasn't possible. "He? He who?"

"The gods' representative."

Bintou swallowed hard. She placed Martin's flask carefully back into place and shut the drawer. Using a damp cloth, she wiped her face dry. She wouldn't miss this show for the world, even if it courted disaster. *To meet an actual god!*

Tales from her childhood collided in her head as they walked down the empty hallway in silence. Ciara led the way, with Hiroki bringing up the rear. They emerged from the bunker, the cool twilight deepened with cloud cover. Bintou rubbed the pebbled skin on her arms as chilly air surrounded them.

The short walk to Leinster House cleared her mind and heart.

Before they entered the courtyard, they had to once again thread through the line of protesters outside. The raging people held their hateful banners like weapons, demanding that the PHAE leave Ireland, that the Unhidden go home.

Their angry shouts made Bintou shiver. She'd been caught in a violent protest as a child in Cairo. Only her parents' quick action got them out unscathed. This line of angry people filled her with anxious fear. Despite the government's assurances that they kept control of the country, these people didn't believe them.

Bintou didn't believe them, either.

Mindful of their last experience, Masaaki kept his head down and wore a hat to hide his paper-white face. Despite that, someone spied him and shouted. One shout turned into several as the protestors crowded around them.

One protester with fury distorting his face grabbed Bintou's sleeve. She jerked away and the fabric ripped. Another man clutched her arm, his fingers digging into her muscles. With a whimper, she pried his fingers away as her companions disappeared in the crowd of people.

Wrath-filled faces surrounded her. Panic rose in her throat, and her stomach churned. Flashes of the Cairo riot drowned her. "Help me! Ciara! Masaaki!"

More hands clutched at her. She crossed her arms across her chest, lowering her head to protect her face. Someone hit the back of her neck with a sign. Another person kicked her in the calf, and she fell to her knees. Bintou covered her head with her hands as more kicks and blows rained on her.

Someone yanked her to her feet. Glancing up, she breathed with intense relief as Masaaki pulled her to her feet. "This way!"

Through the gauntlet of signs and fists, he drew her to the courtyard gates, shutting the iron barrier firmly behind them. Bintou gave in to a heartfelt shudder.

After navigating several hallways, they entered the meeting place. Every seat in the hall was filled. No one wanted to miss the chance to meet a real god, or to expose them as a hoax. A range of wonder and disbelief showed on the surrounding faces.

Bintou joined those standing in the back. She spied Ibrahim, who gave her a silly grin. She answered with a solemn nod. Other than Ciara, none of them held any official status, even in the PHAE. Ranking members of their organization sat in the center arena, with one chair left for their expected visitor. "Chair" was underselling the grand piece of furniture, which would look at home in a throne room, carved cherry wood and plush velvet.

They waited. Low conversations whispered through the ranks. Most sat silent, eager for what they were to see.

Footsteps echoed down the hall. Bintou gripped her hands together as everyone else held their breaths.

Silence almost smothered them as the double doors flung wide, revealing a powerful young blond man with broad shoulders, breeks or trousers, a bright red belted tunic, and a multi-colored checkered cloak. His bare chest had curly blond hair, and his skin glowed with more than just a sunny disposition. He positively shone. A gasp swept through the assembly.

The newcomer glanced to the right, then to the left, and strode into the center. With his hands on his hips, he puffed up his chest. "I am Lugh Lámfada, spokesman of the *Tuatha Dé Danaan*."

He flung his head back as he spoke, his hair cascading like a romance novel cover. Bintou had to stifle a giggle. Masaaki elbowed her in the ribs. Someone in the assembled legislators chuckled.

The Taoiseach cleared her throat and placed her hands on the podium. "I'm afraid, sir, that we cannot understand you. Some of us do speak modern Irish, but you seem to be speaking Old Irish, which only scholars speak now."

Realizing her time to shine had arrived, Bintou stepped up. "Pardon me, Taoiseach, but I understood him perfectly well. I offer my services as a translator. I can tell you what he said."

As she translated his introduction, the leader's eyes widened, and she gestured for Bintou to join her. Stepping to the podium, Bintou addressed the visitor, and translated the Taoiseach's words into Old Irish.

"We, the people of Ireland assembled here today, welcome you, Lugh Lámfada, as spokesman of the *Tuatha Dé Danaan*. We offer our hospitality."

A secretary scurried up with a tray containing a cup and a scone. Lugh raised his eyebrows at the trembling young man, took a sip of the drink and popped the entire scone into his mouth. Then he downed the rest of the drink.

Once he finished eating, he let loose a loud, booming laugh. It echoed off the wooden walls. "Ha! It seems my brethren were mistaken. Hospitality is still held sacred in this land. This is good!" He opened his arms wide, turning back and forth to face all assembled.

A grin crept across Bintou's face. This man's laughter proved infectious. She appreciated his attitude and the looks of sheer horror painted across the surrounding faces.

The tall, bald man sprang to his feet. "Why are you willing to help us?"

Lugh crossed his arms over his massive chest and peered at the man. "Why shouldn't we help you? You are our children. Our kin. Our blood."

A younger woman with blond hair stared at him with wide eyes. "Will you heal those with the plague?"

The god gave her a wink and a half-smile. "That is already being done, my lovely child. And more to come." She sat down with a blush.

The Taoiseach cleared her throat. "What do you ask for in payment for your assistance?"

He gave a solemn nod. "All things come with a price. We ask for your goodwill and your welcome. You are our people, the humans of Ireland. We wish to be amongst you once again."

One by one, legislators asked questions, and Bintou translated in both directions. She wished she possessed Hiroki's talent to smooth out the harsh edges, but he was numb to the world, staring at the god without really seeing him.

A middle-aged man in an old-fashioned tweed jacket raised his hand next. He spoke in modern Irish "Why now? What kept you away before?"

Lugh cocked his head, waving Bintou's translation away. Evidently, he understood. "Why now? Because our blood is alive once more! These Unhidden, these humans with Fae powers, are our direct descendants. The blood of the gods sing within their veins! Even within this lovely dark woman beside me, her blood hums with ancient notes. I can almost taste it myself!"

He licked his lips. and grabbed Bintou's waist, pulling her into a bear hug. The god gave her a hearty kiss on the cheek, then let her go. She cleared her throat and straightened her blouse. Her cheeks burned hot.

Lugh's words made Bintou's mind race, interfering with her work. How could she be descended from gods? Especially *these* gods? Her family had lived in Mali for thousands of years. Perhaps some trader from Rome, someone with Irish blood, visited in ancient times? She had read accounts of traders from Venice and Sicily all through the Middle Ages. She'd translated their travel journals at the university. Suddenly, it didn't seem so outrageous that she might have a bare thread of lineage from this lonely island perched on the edge of Europe.

More questions bombarded her for translation, so she shut her private thoughts away. She must concentrate to keep up with this shining god.

A young man, his clasped hands clasped with nervous energy, asked, "Will you help us fight off the people attacking Ireland?"

The room fell into hushed silence. All eyes turned to Lugh, eager for his answer. Bintou's mouth turned dry as she translated, but halfway through, the Taoiseach interrupted her. "No. We have not agreed to request military help." The woman glared at the young man. He sat, his gaze dropping to his feet.

Bintou turned to the Taoiseach. "Should I translate that as well?"

She shook her head. "We don't wish to even open that door. Not yet. Perhaps not ever."

Lugh raised his eyebrows, waiting for her words, but she opened her hands. "We have no more questions, honored visitor."

"Very well. Has this *tuath* accepted me as a liaison for the *Tuatha Dé Danaan*?"

The Taoiseach answered through her translation. "The assembled *Dáil* of Ireland and the Protectorate for unHidden Advancement and Education accept your embassy as a liaison for the *Tuatha Dé Danaan*."

He clapped his hands with a beaming grin. "Excellent! Begin the celebration feast!"

Chapter Eleven

"The supreme art of war is to subdue the enemy without fighting."
– Sun Tzu

*Latest **CNN Update:*** *"We come to you today from the city of Waterford, Ireland. On the ground, our reporter, Tom Ballin, has an update on the unrest in the city.*

"Word has gotten out that the Dáil hosted an unusual guest last week, a man claiming to be the ancient Irish god, Lugh. As you can see behind me, there are protests around the City Hall. Similar protests are being held at all major cities in Ireland and Northern Ireland. A few smaller groups have gathered to welcome the ancient gods. Several incidents have erupted between the two groups."

"Tom, fill us in on who Lugh is supposed to be."

"Diana, Lugh Lámfada, or Lugh of the Long Arm, is the closest equivalent the Irish have to a sun god. He's good at all the skills, from blacksmithing, to singing, to hunting. He was a king of the Tuatha Dé Danann, and we still use his name in the Irish word for August, Lughnasa."

"And there's an August festival of the same name?"

Tom nodded. *"That's correct. His mother was* Ethniu, *from whom Ireland derives its Irish language name of* Éire. *And he killed the big baddie of the* Fomorians, *Balor. Most people in Ireland are familiar with the legend of* Cú Chulainn, *Ireland's most popular legendary. He's Lugh's son."*

"Tell us about the protesters there."

With a glance over his shoulder, Tom turned back to the camera. "These are mostly religious groups who object to the government negotiating with pagan gods."

"And do they believe this man actually is an ancient pagan god?"

"That's what I'm here to discover, John. There are also a few groups of doctors and nurses, protesting the rumors that hospitals are now using magic to heal the sick and injured. If what we're hearing is true, there's an interesting alliance being formed in several cities, such as here in Waterford."

Bintou:

The next few days passed in frantic preparations, meetings, and consultations. Bintou barely slept as she was needed to translate for all of them. Lugh had now spoken to the *Dáil* multiple times. On his last visit, they'd discussed the resources on hand and how those resources could be distributed to best help the gods heal Ireland.

The god requested hundreds of humans to infuse with Dian Cécht's healing knowledge and power, so they could spread quickly across the country. While the government practically salivated at the promise of a rapid remedy to the crisis, they seemed less keen on handing over humans, even volunteers, to the gods' control. The Catholic church warned against reliance upon pagan gods almost daily now.

For once, Bintou agreed with the government and the church. At the same time, she realized that if Martin were still alive, she'd have volunteered herself immediately and without any qualm to help deliver this pagan healing power to him, no matter what strings might be attached.

After Lugh's latest speech, the Taoiseach let out a deep sigh. "Yes, we are absolutely dedicated to eradicating this illness as quickly as possible. The basic fact remains that we only have fifteen volunteers. We must ensure each and every volunteer has all the facts at their disposal before they agree to help. I refuse to compel people or allow them to make uninformed decisions. That's not how we do things in this society."

Lugh placed his hands on his hips. "Do you have no slaves? No criminals bound to service? Has your society eradicated all evil people?"

Bitter laughter rang out in the hall, making Lugh's smile quirk.

The Taoiseach shook her head. "Even criminals are not forced to do things, dangerous things, acts against their will. They have basic human rights. And no, slavery is no longer legal in Ireland."

The god crossed his arms, glaring at her. "Then what is your solution? If we have fifteen people, where should they begin?"

Several *Teachtaí Dálaí* rose, shouting at the same time. "Dublin!" "Limerick!" "Belfast!" "Galway!"

Waving them back into their seats, the Taoiseach read from her notes. "We have determined those city centres with the highest percentage of plague victims. Our priorities are Dublin, Galway, Belfast, Waterford, and Limerick. Following them, we must concentrate on Cork, Wexford, Athlone—"

A young man jumped up. "What about Letterkenny?"

She lowered her glasses, peering over the top at him. "Will you please remain in your seat, TD O'Donnell?"

"But we need him!"

Once again, Lugh cracked a smile, winking at the young man. "It is gratifying to see someone so eager to work with me. I'm afraid you are not quite what I crave." The god turned to Bintou with a sensual smile. Bintou dropped her gaze when she finished translating, her cheeks growing warm. TD O'Donnell sat with an uncomfortable expression.

The Taoiseach resumed her list with a glance at the TD. "Letterkenny, Drogheda, and Westport. Once those areas are healed, we shall create a new list and redeploy our resources at hand. Throughout the plan, we will work hard to employ new volunteers to replace those who tire. We will not allow the volunteers to be abused into a state of exhaustion. Each volunteer is permitted to quit at any time with no questions asked."

No one seemed satisfied with the plan, and Lugh had warned them the healing process took time. It wouldn't come fast enough for the protesters outside or the news media. Lugh insisted on the right to reject any candidate presented. He also asked that Bintou come along as his translator until he learned modern Irish, but Bintou knew that the request had the force of a demand. How could she say no, with the country's population at stake?

Memories of her last tour across Ireland brough back painful images of Martin's death. If she turned down Lugh's request, she might endanger thousands of people. Maybe hundreds of thousands. No amount of personal pain justified such selfishness.

She wished they hadn't needed help from the gods. But their own talents proved to be inadequate. They must have the gods' help to pull out of the pandemic's deepening spiral.

Perhaps if they'd only been infected with anthrax, or only pneumonic plague, they could have survived. Perhaps not. Or they'd diagnosed it more quickly and stop the spread in time. They'd never know now.

Bintou had to admit, the protesters had one fact right; this never would have happened if the Unhidden hadn't made Ireland their headquarters. If the PHAE never formed, the PEM wouldn't have resorted to biological warfare.

They had no proof the PEM planted the plagues, unless that verification had been extracted from Joel. But all circumstantial evidence pointed to the PEM as the guilty party. Who else would have the means or the motive? Once they got the plagues under control, the PHAE Board of Directors would have to decide what they might try next.

No one believed that the PEM would give up. Not Bintou, not Hiroki, not Ciara, not even Masaaki, with his bright outlook on life. If this initiative failed, there would be another attack, another invasion, another operation to destroy PHAE and all the Unhidden. Eugenics at its worst. Bintou shuddered, horror filling her imagination.

And if the PEM returned, this time with stronger military firepower, could the PHAE avoid asking the gods for military help? What would the cost of that help be?

After the large meeting concluded, Ciara, Masaaki, and Paul met with Bintou in a smaller conference room to discuss what had been agreed on. After a half hour, Hiroki rushed in and turned on the television mounted in one corner. "You must see this."

Ciara started to object but when the CNN reporter's face faded, and Tiberius Wilkinson's replaced them, she shut up and stared.

The Texan gripped his podium with both hands. "We are *tired* of these people taking our jobs." The crowd cheered, and the speaker waited for the sound to fade.

"We are *tired* of these people corrupting our children." The cheers rose to a higher level.

"We are *tired* of these people, these freaks of nature, taking over our world!"

The crowd rose to their feet, stomping and whistling. Hiroki estimated there must be thousands, even tens of thousands. He spoke at some sports arena, probably in Texas. That may be far from Ireland, but Hiroki's skin pebbled with goosebumps at every word. He recognized true charisma, someone who could sway a crowd with their words, and this man had more natural skill than Hiroki had, even with his Unhidden talent.

"We will drive them out of our homes, out of our schools, and out of our cities! We will take back what is ours. Take back what they've stolen from us with their unnatural powers! We will take back our world!"

Ciara stood and turned the television off. "We don't need to watch that disgusting man."

Hiroki shook his head. "How can we fight him? He's getting too popular to ignore."

"We don't fight him. He's in Texas, not here."

But hadn't the PEM already attacked Ireland? They'd only started recovering from that attack, and only with the help of the gods. What if they attacked again?

Hiroki:

Bintou opened the door, waking Hiroki from a doze. He blinked several times, trying to focus on his computer screen.

The Malian woman came around to see his progress. "Have you had any luck with the campaign materials?"

He shook his head. "Nothing seems to work. Anything I write sounds like empty promises and platitudes. I can't make it sound sincere."

She placed a hand on his shoulder. "I thought Masaaki was helping you? Where'd he run off to?"

With a glance to the door, Hiroki shrugged. "He and Ibrahim went off to find something. I didn't hear what."

Frowning, Bintou bent closer, peering at the screen. "Maybe this word should be 'assurance' rather than 'declaration.'"

Hiroki blinked up at her. "Very well. I will change it."

She pointed out several other phrases to refine, until he pushed back from the keyboard. "Perhaps it would be better if you write this." Keeping his jaw clenched tight, he stalked from the room. He didn't slam the door. His father would have done so. Instead, he kept his pace even and escaped from Bintou and her oh-so-helpful suggestions.

Hiroki had no interest in the tasks PHAE asked him to complete. Each assignment became an irritation to scratch or brush away. Why should acceptance at PHAE be of any importance to him now, when his own father had disowned him?

All this fuss over the Irish god's performance at the *Dáil* disgusted him. Japanese gods wouldn't be so arrogant, bragging and strutting around like a prize bull. His favorite of the Shinto *kami* had always been Omoikane, the god of wisdom and intelligence. In a way, Hiroki followed Omoikane's path now, performing as a diplomat.

An idea struck him. Perhaps he could ask the advice from his own gods? Omoikane's advice might be exactly what he needed right now. And if the Irish gods could manifest in this world, why shouldn't the Japanese *kami* do the same?

The notion grew in his mind as he walked, first becoming a desire and then a requirement. He'd need some tools, if he wished to attract the god's attention. He didn't wish to return to their office and face Bintou's optimistic face and grammar suggestions. Instead, he sought out Masaaki's room.

His friend wasn't inside, for which Hiroki was grateful. The room looked more like an American teenager's room than the living space of an adult Japanese man. Posters of rock bands stuck to the wall, several empty Coke cans littered his desk, and when Hiroki peeked into the sleeping chamber, the bed looked buried under a pile of mussed blankets.

Wrinkling his nose at his friend's messiness, he stepped into the bathroom, searching for a small hand mirror. Masaaki didn't have any incense, but he had candles. Finding a lighter, Hiroki emptied the paper bag from yesterday's food delivery, keeping the leftover rice. He gathered these items, along with a metal bowl and a spoon, and placed them carefully into the bag.

Now, he must find a quiet spot where he wouldn't be disturbed. The bunkers emptied as more repairs were done to the buildings above, but many PHAE members remained in the tunnels. He needed to find an abandoned office or meeting room where he wouldn't be disturbed. Better yet, the bedroom of someone who had left.

With a flash of inspiration, he sought out Martin's room.

He'd shared a suite with Ciara, similar to the rooms Hiroki shared with Bintou. But when Martin died, she'd moved into Paul's second room. Now, this suite sat deserted, dark, and achingly empty. Exactly how he felt inside.

Hiroki had never actually performed a Shinto ceremony. He'd watched his parents many times, as they kept a Shinto shrine. He helped maintain the altar in their home and attended birth and wedding celebrations. He'd only been to Buddhist or Christian funerals.

He dredged his memory for the required ceremonial steps. First, he must purify himself. He washed his hands and face in the sink. While the first affirmation of Shinto was to hold fast to tradition and the family, Hiroki hoped his rift with his father wouldn't cause the *kami* to shun him. The second affirmation, a love of nature, was close to his heart, despite being entombed under the city. The third affirmation, personal cleanliness, was his favorite. Finally, he would perform the *matsuri*, the final affirmation, and give honor to the *kami*.

The rice had dried from yesterday, so it was similar to the uncooked rice often offered to the *kami*. A twinge of guilt at offering used food almost made him abandon his purpose, but he squared his shoulders and took a deep breath.

Hiroki cleared a space in the center of the room. He turned off the overhead light and lit the vanilla pillar candle. After bowing twice in respect, at ninety degrees with a straight back, he clapped his hands twice and sat cross-legged.

He struck the upturned metal bowl with the spoon, purifying the space with the sound of a bell.

As the sound died, he presented the rice. He ate a small bite, holding communion with the *kami*. He chanted passably, despite having no musical talent.

Then he intoned the ritual prayer, as he'd heard in other ceremonies, calling upon Omoikane as his protector, with a sincere heart.

As Hiroki chanted and stared at the bright candle flame, he bowed his head, keeping his hands together at chest level. Flame flickered on the edge of his vision, like stars winking in and out of clouds on a stormy night. Hiroki concentrated on the candle, but the distractions finally got too much. Movement to his right caught his attention.

A figure stood shrouded in the darkness. Hiroki fell back, his eyes growing wide as he dropped his gaze out of respect. "Are you Omoikane?"

"No, he has little power here. I am *Oghma*."

Hiroki:

As Hiroki stumbled back to his own room, his mind spun with both the possibilities the Irish god, Oghma, had shown him and the plans he must make. The god talked nonstop. But what else did he expect from a god of knowledge and communication? Oghma seemed like that one student who had researched a subject for years and someone finally asked him to explain it in great detail.

For now, he had work to do. First, he must speak with Masaaki and Bintou about Lugh and his proposals. His mind swam with the things Oghma suggested he discuss. But when he approached his room, Paul rushed down the hallway. "Hiroki! We've got a situation. Ciara needs you."

With a longing glance toward his door, he followed Paul down the hallway, up the stairs and out onto the street itself. The streetlights twinkled in the misty fog, making them feel otherworldly, like something out of a suspense movie. Hadn't it just been lunchtime? He must have been in with Oghma longer than he thought. He clenched his fists as they crossed the near-empty streets. "Where is everyone?"

Paul looked around and shrugged. "Most folks are staying home after the quarantine announcement. You'll still see a bunch of PEM assholes in front of Leinster House."

Stopping in his tracks, he stared at the Irishman. "Quarantine? I heard of no quarantine."

Paul waved his hand in dismissal. "They just announced it an hour ago. Everyone is to remain home except essential workers. A one-kilometer walk is allowed once a day. The government's really trying to keep this plague to manageable levels, but if you ask me, it's far too late. Too many people are sick to keep it contained."

Hiroki hadn't seen much of the illness since he returned from his speaking tour. Had he helped spread the sickness to every county in this land? Bintou had fallen ill during the trip. She'd recovered, but then Martin had fallen ill, and he died. Hiroki had particularly liked Martin, but Bintou fell in love with him, and she hadn't been the same since. She cradled his old flask like a good-luck charm.

When Leinster House came into sight, Hiroki narrowed his eyes at the line of protesters carrying signs. Why did these people ignore the quarantine? He peered at the words in the dim light.

"Mutants go home"

"No Frankenvirus!"

Each face looked angry, eager to visit violence upon him and those he cared for. As they walked closer, the crowd surged toward them. Paul glanced back, pulling Hiroki forward. "Don't mind them. The bloody bastards are here every day."

"But what do they want?"

"They want you to go away. They think you brought the sickness."

"Me? From Japan?"

"Not you, personally. You, me, all the Unhidden."

Hiroki forgot to walk, staring at the protesters. They got closer, but Paul yanked his arm to keep him moving forward. In truth, they *had* brought the sickness. This whole mess dated from when they came to Ireland. The bombing, the PEM, none of that would have happened without the Unhidden. Hiroki swallowed back guilt.

His blood chilled as they skirted around to the side entrance. Flashes of memory made him stumble, images from the mob who had attacked him back in Tokyo.

Something cracked on the back of his head. He whirled as the stone clattered at his feet. He swallowed against the surge of fear that roiled his belly. A man stared at him with such intense rage, Hiroki stumbled into Paul, clutching his arm. The angry man snarled and reached for him, but Paul pulled him away.

As they entered the building, Hiroki drew his power around him. He might not need it, but if the situation was serious, he wanted to be ready. He enjoyed the tingling sensation through his arms and fingers. When he first realized the tingling meant his power was working, it felt annoying, almost painful. Now, it energized him and gave him confidence he never felt without it. It prepared him for performing. Despite the elation it gave him, it seemed like he was always performing, always wearing some mask, some face other than his own.

Hiroki followed Paul around a corner. In the large, mostly empty meeting room, he spied Ciara sitting with Binto and two others. The Malian woman waved to him, and he nodded back. Her cheerful expression fell to a frown.

Ciara gave him a grim look. "I'm glad you're here, Hiroki. We're working on this treaty between the *Dáil* and the *Tuatha Dé Danann*, and we need help hammering out the details. The *Dáil* wrote it up, but your wordsmithing would really be a boon. Then Bintou can translate it into Old Irish for Lugh."

He furrowed his brow. "Colin didn't mention Komie or Róisín needing translators. Why does this god need one?"

She shrugged. "Maybe gods have different talents for learning new languages, like humans. Maybe that those called for recent rituals have learned the modern version. I don't know the answer."

Letting out a huff, Hiroki twisted his mouth. "Or Lugh is pretending not to understand."

Bintou and Ciara exchanged glances. The Irish woman nodded slowly. "We'd considered that possibility. Short of calling a god a liar, we can't do much about that. In the meantime, we need to assume everything requires translation and be cautious of whatever we say in any language. But first, we need these documents worked on. Can I leave you to the job?"

Hiroki eyed the thick stack of papers. "I suppose we have a great deal of work to do." He spied a snack and drinks cart. He prepared a cup of tea and a sandwich before returning to the table.

Bintou handed him the first section. "If you refine this chapter, I'll take a break, and then translate after as you refine each section. We've been in meetings for hours and my eyes ache."

Hours. And the sun was already setting. Hiroki glanced at his phone and calculated over six hours had passed. He must have meditated longer than he'd realized. That information shook him more than meeting a god had.

As Bintou rose to refill her teacup, Hiroki examined the first page of his task. He cringed as he read the opening paragraph.

He took a deep sigh and grabbed a pencil as Bintou interrupted him. "Hiroki, about earlier…"

He held up a hand. "I don't wish to discuss it."

She stared at him, her eyes wide. He returned her gaze with cool confidence. Hiroki wouldn't allow the earlier discussion to color his reactions, but neither would he allow sentimentality to affect him. His father's rejection left him determined to keep his emotions in check.

Bintou sat and placed her hands flat on the table. "I'm worried about this entire situation. I don't trust these gods. And I don't trust their effect on us."

Hiroki merely blinked, his jaw clenched.

"I'm certain they've got an ulterior motive. Some grand plan they are using us for. I just haven't figured out what it is."

Glancing at the agreement, Hiroki tapped the first page. "Have they made any requests or demands from us?"

Bintou shook her head. "Not yet. They've offered to help us heal, and they've offered to help us fight off any invaders. We accepted the former but not the latter. For now."

"Is there not a truism about not accepting gifts from the Other Folk in this country?"

She dropped her head into her hands, her elbows propped on the table. "Of course. Most cultures have similar cautionary tales in their lore. History is full of tales of foolish people accepting gifts without asking the true cost."

How much had it cost him to move to this country? His job, his friends, his father's approval. Not that he'd ever earned the latter. He'd barely begun to prove himself as an adult. Then, at the first opportunity, he'd derailed his entire life to chase a dream.

What would his father think of him working with gods? Would it change anything? Both his parents honored the *kami* with deep-felt piety. They maintained their household Shinto shrine. They made pilgrimages to the larger shrines, with gifts for the *kami*. Perhaps, if his father saw that the gods accepted him, he would do the same. The cynical part of Hiroki chided him for foolish notions. He couldn't even properly call a Shinto deity and ended up with an Irish god instead.

"If we'd had their help earlier, they might have saved Martin. And yet, we can't let them dictate terms. It's vital that we spell out every detail."

Hiroki didn't follow her vacillating views. "We need their help. Is there not also a saying about not looking a gift horse in the mouth?"

When her eyes grew wide, he realized how rude that sounded. He shook off the urge to apologize. His words were not wrong, and he was determined to change his habit of apologizing for everything.

Bintou let out a sigh and stared at the table. "Yes, there is a saying about that from the Trojan War, involving a wooden horse filled with soldiers. A lesson in hidden betrayals."

He clenched his jaw. Was she being deliberately obtuse? "This isn't about Trojans. It's about us, in the modern world. People are dying, and the gods are offering to heal them."

Shaking her head, she jumped to her feet and paced again. "But is their help worth it? Who knows what they'll ask for in return? And we aren't asking for military help now, but what if there's another attack on Ireland? How will we resist asking for their help then?"

"You worry too much, Bintou. You're acting silly."

She spun to face him, her eyes sparking with anger. "Silly? You're calling me silly? How can you not see the danger?"

Hiroki rose to face her, his face set in stony stillness. "I am calling you silly. Your arguments are distracting me from my work. You will no longer speak of this."

Her lips became a thin line as she narrowed her gaze. "Are you using your power on me?"

Taking a deep breath, Hiroki felt his fingers and muscles tingle as he repeated, "You will no longer speak of this."

Qacha:

Somewhere, in the darkness, the screaming stopped. Blessed silence caressed her ears, cool and comforting, an absence of tortuous noise. Qacha let out a sigh and, for the first time in too long, fell into a deep, healing sleep.

When she finally wrestled from slumber's embrace, her eyes cracked open with reluctant curiosity. Unfamiliar surroundings. She examined the space with cautious eyes. A round room made with wicker and thatch. Wooden shelves and table. A woolen blanket, itchy against her tender, fresh-healed skin.

Healed? When had she healed? She'd borne deep burn scars from Galway, itchy and painful. Now her skin felt smooth as a baby, despite the trace-work of sullen red glowing lines along her veins.

Buzzing bees. Someone hummed a song. A bird called for a mate.

Her muscles didn't even ache as she swung her feet to the dirt floor. She wore a simple garment, a long piece of off-white cloth with holes for the head and arms, sewn up the sides.

Had she died? Was this some Western afterlife, a religious concept of paradise? Or just another illusion from her madness? Something skittered in the shadows.

She jumped back on the bed as the recollection of creatures in her cell returned to haunt her, despite the bright daylight. A cat meowed. Or not a cat. Something didn't look right in the fuzzy gray creature who wound its way from under the bed.

She placed a tentative foot back on the floor, and the not-cat skittered out the door. A female voice exclaimed. In a few moments, a physically imposing figure appeared in the doorway, wiping her hands on a smudged cloth. "Ah! You've woken. Wonderful. Would you like something to drink? I have ale or water."

Qacha suddenly had a more powerful thirst than anything she'd ever felt before. Her parched throat and lips ached for a drink. The woman poured two ceramic mugs and handed her one. Qacha took an experimental sip, not quite ready to trust this person. Cool, crisp water never tasted so good in her life. She took a deeper drink.

"Now, do take it easy, child. You've been dry for a long time. A few sips now, and a few in a while, aye?"

Child? Qacha was far from a child. She would be forty-five next year, yet this woman appeared to be barely thirty. She narrowed her eyes at her hostess and took another sip of water, trying to figure out why this powerful woman looked familiar.

"I imagine you are wondering who I am, and where you are, is that a fair guess?"

Qacha nodded once.

"You can call me Brigit. I brought you here yesterday."

"Where is here?"

A wide grin cracked her face. "This is my home! I've a lovely garden outside. Would you like to see?"

Qacha swallowed. She'd not seen the daylight in how long? That cell had become her entire world for days, weeks, however long she'd been held prisoner. She got to her feet and strode to the door, eager to be outside.

Bees buzzed in the sunlit glade, surrounded by honey-sweet flowers and dappled sunlight on a path into the surrounding woods. Even Qacha had to let out a smile at this bucolic beauty.

"This is my haven, my retreat. You may stay here as long as you would like, to heal."

That reminded Qacha of her injuries, and the new-healed skin. She rubbed her arm and looked at where it used to be decorated with dark-red lines along her veins.

"Oh, yes, I had a bit of work healing your scars."

"You healed me?"

Brigit sat on a stone bench. "Of course, I did. That's one of the many talents I have."

"Talent. Are you one of the Unhidden, then?"

She let out a booming laugh, echoing through the glade, making several birds take flight. "Unhidden! No, I am not one of your Unhidden. But our blood does run in their veins, so I suppose you could stretch the definition."

"And what do you want with us?"

She let out another laugh, and Qacha wasn't certain if amusement or contempt colored Brigit's voice.

Joel:

Joel clasped his hands tight to keep them from shaking. It had taken him a dozen meetings to gain this audience, and he didn't want to fuck it up by looking too nervous. Nervous was a danger sign, a giveaway that he wasn't ready for another assignment.

He gritted his teeth at the memory of his first debriefing. They'd been amazed that he returned alive from his mission. He still didn't think they believed his story about Hafsia and her truth-compelling Unhidden talent. But they must have thought he did well enough, because here he was, about to meet with Tiberius Wilkinson.

Joel had seen him on the news, of course, and in interviews on the right-wing talk shows. He had such incredible charisma, a mere look could brighten the gloomiest agent's day.

And here he was, the gloomiest agent. But he'd survived a suicide mission, and that had to count for something.

The door swung open, and Joel jumped to his feet, but it was only the secretary leaving, still writing something on his ePad. The other man barely glanced up as he walked to his desk. Joel glanced from the open door to the secretary, wondering if he should enter or wait.

"Joel Taylor?"

He knew the voice. When he looked back at the office door, Tiberius Wilkinson himself stood in the doorway, a charming smile on his face.

He clenched his fists to keep his hands still. "That's me!"

"C'mon inside, Joel. I understand you've a rather amazing story, and I'm eager to hear the details."

Anna:

Carlos and Anna fell into an awkward silence after they finished their tea and sandwiches. Sitting in a car seemed surreal and uncomfortable. He lent her a pair of swimming trunks and a jacket. She still wore her seaweed gown beneath. Anna stared out to sea from the cliffside parking lot. Dark storm clouds gathered in the distance.

Carlos tapped the steering wheel. "Well, it looks like it's going to rain soon."

"Mm-hmm."

"We should head back to the mainland."

"Mm."

He cleared his throat. "Would you like to stay at the B&B? You're welcome, you know. Always."

The wind picked up, rocking the car. The back window, slightly open, whistled. Carlos pressed a button to shut it and the whistling stopped.

Anna's eyes remained glued on the squall. That way, she didn't have to meet Carlos' gaze. "I shouldn't leave. Not now."

"Why not now? We need you." He cleared his throat. "As much as I hate to say this, Brendan needs you."

Brendan. He'd gone all jealous on her, and she didn't want that kind of cheap manipulation. Joel had done that enough for a lifetime. Brendan could rot for all she cared.

That made her turn, anger boiling in her blood. "What do you mean Brendan needs me? If he needs me so badly, why did he send you to fetch me? Why didn't he come himself?"

Rubbing the back of his neck, Carlos ducked his head. "Ah, well, Brendan isn't exactly able to do that just now."

Anna crossed her arms, glaring at him. "And why not?"

"He's…well, he's sort of sick. I just found out, but he's been sick for a while. I thought you'd like to know."

Her anger drained away. The plague had Brendan. Her heart felt hollow, and her rage at his jealousy seemed petty.

The first drops slapped the windshield. In a few minutes, water sheeted across the glass, drumming loud. The water beckoned her. By instinct, Anna grabbed the door handle.

Carlos gripped her arm. "Wait, don't leave."

Anna glanced back at him, then at the storm outside. The turbulence called to her, a whooshing within her ears, as if she held a conch shell close. Whispers of the sea. A fraction of a literary quote floated into her memory. *Men were deceivers ever, one foot in sea, and one on shore. To one thing constant never.*

Was Manannán calling her home? Pulling on the door handle, she slipped into the downpour, the delicious coolness caressing her skin and scales. She danced in the deluge, tilting her face up to catch drops in her mouth.

The car door opened and closed, and Carlos ran to her. "Anna! We need you!" His dark eyes danced with worry.

"The sea needs me. Manannán mac Lir needs me."

Carlos grasped her hands, his skin warm and comforting. Her own blood grew chill with seawater. "Look, I don't know what went on between you and Brendan. But even if you can't forgive him, we need you. *I* need you. Please?"

"Need me? What the hell do you need me for?"

He stared down at her hands, her tiny iridescent scales glistening in the sun. "I just do. I can't stop thinking about you. It's like you're haunting my thoughts."

Anna's heart skipped as she threw another glance over her shoulder at the white-capped sea. Something disturbed the surface, a white whirlpool. Her hands clutched more tightly to his human warmth as she faced the ocean. Waiting.

The wind whipped the disturbance into a waterspout. The base grew, rushing toward them. Carlos stepped back, but she kept a tight grip on his hand.

The ocean rose in a great wave, taller than the cliff. Fish and seals fell from the edges, tumbling into the water below. The wave formed into a giant man, his blue-silver skin glinting in the storm. His eyes flashed with lightning, as his white hair whipped wild in the gale. **"You would take my student from me."**

Carlos' eyes grew wide, and tried again to pull away, this time trying to drag her, too. She didn't let go of his hand, nor did she step away from the towering sea god. As much as she adored the sea and valued Manannán lessons, she couldn't let him hurt Carlos. Her heart would not allow that.

Despite her wariness, she stepped between them. The god could kill Carlos without a thought. She lifted her chin high, though her jaw ached from tension. Carlos whispered, "Anna… be careful."

Anna shrugged it off. She mustn't let Manannán witness her weakness. Nor could she let him harm Carlos. The sea god had the power to push her aside, but he wanted her as an apprentice. If he pressed his claim, such a show of power would damage their fragile understanding. She hoped. With a swallow, she squared her shoulders. "This is something I need to do."

Her gaze remained locked with Manannán's.

"I have chosen her."

Carlos stepped beside her, though she could smell his fear. "Anna's still human, and we humans need her, for now. We'd like her to help the PHAE until the crisis is over."

"She has much to learn yet."

He swallowed and stole a quick glance to her. "There's a human man who…" He caught his breath. "A man who loves her, and he's very ill. A visit from her would help him."

"She is not a healer."

"That's not what we need her for. We already have healers. We need her there to help him want to live. Even if Brendan wasn't ill, she'd be invaluable to the PHAE for herself. She's loved and cared for. But it doesn't matter how much we need her, or how much you need her. What matters is what she wants. It must be her choice."

Pain stabbed through Anna's heart, despite the delicious water surrounding her. A memory of her human life tugged at the edges of her soul. It called her back to mortality, to the routine of humdrum life. Recollection of a sweet smile, a shared laugh, a soft kiss. A single name thrummed through her mind. *Brendan.*

Would she ever fit back into that mold? Could she return to a mundane human life, even if she wanted to? Or would she forever be an outcast, always different, eternally alien?

Manannán's lessons thrilled her. The things he taught excited her sense of mystery and wonder. Despite the god's power, he taught her beautiful, delicate techniques. Arts no one else could teach her. She yearned to feel his power coursing through her veins, to relish in the delight of the ocean.

Anna wanted to scream. How could she decide? This was her home now. This was her family. The seals and the fish and Manannán. His blood sang in her body. She couldn't turn her back on him. And yet Carlos' pleading smile made her sigh. The memory of Brendan's embrace wrenched at her heart.

With all her strength and confidence, Anna gazed into Manannán's lightning-filled blue eyes. "I wish to go. I vow to return when I'm done."

Her entire body tensed with anticipation. Would he allow her to leave? Would he force her to stay? Would he lose patience and destroy them both?

The ground beneath her feet rumbled with his answer. **"You are dedicated to me."**

She willed herself to be strong and straightened her spine. "And I appreciate that. I do not wish to leave your tutelage, but I also have an obligation to these humans. I don't wish to break my promise."

The sea god's gaze bore into her, and then shifted to Carlos. For a horrified moment, she thought he would strike Carlos down with a flick of will, leaving nothing but a shadow. Instead, the sea god let out an almost human sigh. The rumble of Manannán's blood vibrated through her. **"You have my permission to leave for one month."**

Anna let out a deep breath, relief flooding her. She bowed her head to the sea god. "One month, and I'll be back."

Róisín:

Róisín held her breath as she flipped Max's body, thankful he felt warm, even though the cave was chilly. He moaned again, in the throes of whatever illness or madness or injury he'd suffered. The waves outside punctuated his moans. She traced her finger along half-healed burns on his arms and chest. His face looked red with windburn, even on his sun-darkened skin. What adventures had he been on?

While her fingers still crackled, this energy felt different. Dian Cécht's healing energy had a warm, sweet taste. This power seemed cooler and crisper, like cold grapefruit juice instead of hot apple cider. Róisín didn't know if she could heal with this new power, so she relied on her own talent, unwilling to experiment with Max's life.

Pushing aside his singed shirt, she laid hands on his battered chest. He pushed her away, but he had little strength. Pulling up through the ground, her talent suffused his skin, bones, and blood. His groan turned into a long, low growl, like a train going by. It tickled her ears as it hummed through the dank cave.

She missed her audience from the hospital, and Dian Cécht's hot apple cider power. That brought Dr. O'Shea to mind, with his ice-blue eyes, but she had no time for romance just now.

Whispers surrounded her, but they were a far cry from the intoxicating adulation she had soaked in before, and she ignored them. Right now, she must concentrate on healing her friend.

Max had always been a puzzle to her. Acerbic and outright rude, he nevertheless intrigued her, and she had made it her purpose to try to help him. While he stayed at their farm, she'd been able to gently heal his dependence on alcohol without him noticing her healing touch, but as soon as they separated, he'd evidently fallen back into his old habits. She needed time to heal him more deeply, his mind and his memory, not just his body. That would take time and perhaps more magic than she actually possessed. Maybe she'd need Dian Cécht's help for something so intense. But Ireland's healing had priority, so that must wait.

He shivered, dislodging her touch again. His skin felt icy. What had done this to him? Or who?

Once again, she pulled in her power and spread it through him. The crackle returned, but the magic fought against her, bucking and jerking instead of flowing. She shoved her power against the resistance, like ramming a concrete dam, unable to get her healing flow into his body.

A crack formed, a small opening where her healing oozed into Max. That trickle grew wider, forming a steady drip. She poured her power into that crack until she'd used up all her energy.

Exhausted, Róisín sat back on her heels. Max turned on his side, hacking and coughing, propped up on one elbow. "What in bloody hell are *you* doing here, Róisín?"

She gaped at him. "I just saved your life, and *that's* your first question?"

Max closed his eyes and let out a deep breath. "Sorry, luv. It's been a rotten week. But how did you find me? I don't even know where I am, except in the middle of fucking nowhere."

"I just left University Limerick Hospital, and some voice in the wind called me. Maybe your friends? I followed them here. Did you ask them to do that?"

He shook his head, pushing himself into a cross-legged position with a grunt. "Not me, luv. I haven't spoken to the wind in days. Near as I can tell, I've been right out of my head. I don't remember much, not after I got into a row with some bastard thunder god."

Róisín narrowed her eyes. "Thunder god?"

"Aye. Bloke called himself Taranis. Bloody pissed, he was. Claimed I invaded his realm. He banged me up good, worse than any bar brawl I've been in. Worse than in Vietnam. I mostly stayed in my plane then." His expression turned bleak, and he stared out of the cave mouth. "Bloody bastard tossed me about on the wind like a lost balloon. Then he slammed me into the ground a few times for good measure. Just my luck, I fell into a campsite firepit. That's where I got these damned burns." He held up his arms.

It was all Róisín could do to keep from giggling at that imagery. "What did the campers do?"

With a shrug, he rolled his eyes. "I don't bloody well know, do I? They scattered to the four winds. I don't imagine they have blokes falling out of the sky on a regular basis here. I certainly don't want to ride that roller coaster again." He brushed his arms and the half-healed burns.

"Stop touching them. You'll get an infection before I have a chance to heal them."

He pulled away from her. "You've done enough, girl. I don't need more coddling."

Róisín scowled at him as she reached for his arm. "You need healing, Max. I'm a healer. You must let me help you."

Jerking his arm away. "No! I've had enough of your meddling. You're just like a woman."

She clenched her teeth. "Max. You know, you really need to get over this idea that all women are evil. You're better than that misogynistic crap, I know you are."

He mumbled, "You know nothing of the sort. I'm a right bastard, and too old to change."

She reached for his hand, not for healing, but for comfort. "You aren't too old to change. You are never too old to change."

His gaze rose and their eyes locked and for a moment, nothing existed but the two of them. He looked frightened, and Róisín gently flowed some healing magic into his mind. Something to soothe his jagged anxiety, his old fear, his prickly self.

Max cleared his throat. "Do you hear voices? Or am I still a stubbie short of a six pack?"

"I heard shouting earlier, but they didn't sound close." As she spoke, a murmur of voices penetrated the sound of waves. "Yeah, I still hear them. Maybe there's a match or a festival nearby?"

Max raised his eyebrows. "During a bloody plague? Humans are stupid, but not that stupid."

She followed his gaze to the shore outside. "I think you'd be surprised. Humans tend to be self-serving."

"Such cynicism from the Optimist of the Century? The world's gone wonky!"

The voices grew loud enough that Róisín rose, helping Max to his feet. She spared a glance at his burns, but they looked much improved. She grasped his hand, infusing more power into his body. If they faced some danger, he'd be of more help if he was fit.

"Don't waste the dregs of your energy on me, luv. I'm sound enough."

Róisín set her mouth into a thin line. Without Dian Cécht bolstering her power, her power was limited. Flashes from the hospital came to her. She didn't remember much, but she couldn't deal with that now, as the voices got even closer. Individual words filtered past the waves. They shouted about fairies, magic, and God's vengeance. This might turn ugly.

Max jumped to the far corner of the cave. He picked out two stout sticks, driftwood from the ocean, and handed her one. This cave must fill at high tide. "We shouldn't stay in here. There's no way out."

He nodded, and they stalked forward, clubs in hand. As they reached the mouth, Max mumbled under his breath, "Alright, mates. Give us some help now, aye?"

The wind kicked up as they emerged. About fifty strangers stood along the beach, blocking the trail, their hair fluttering in the breeze. She glanced to the other end of the beach, but it ended in cliff. Unless they could swim or fly, they must fight their way out through the mob. Some carried torches. All looked angry.

Maybe Max could fly, with help from the wind? She was about to tell him to escape when she turned back to stare at the crowd. With a shock, Róisín recognized a man in front. "Joel? What's going on?"

Instead of answering her, he held his torch high, turning to face the others. "I told you about these two! I've seen them do magic with my own eyes. What's more, they're the ones who brought the plague on us all! It's *their* fault!"

The people behind them chanted, "Burn them! Burn them!"

Róisín glanced at Max, panic rushing to her heart. "This must be a joke, right?"

The Australian man's expression turned grim. "I see people from last night's campfire. They must have witnessed Taranis knocking me about."

She wiped her sweaty hands on her scrubs. "But why's Joel leading them? He's Unhidden."

Max shrugged. "A dollar says he didn't tell 'em about that part. I know it ain't your style, luv, but I suggest we rat him out."

Róisín had to admit they were in a rough spot. But she still couldn't bring herself to do that. "You do it."

He flashed her a wry half-smile. "With pleasure! Oy! You lot! You've got something against these Unhidden talents, do ya?"

A roar answered him, with brandished torches. They stepped closer, while Max and Róisín backed toward the cliffside. "Well, that bloke there is just as much a mutant as we are! If not more! And if there's anyone to blame for the plague, he's the one!"

Joel let out a belly laugh. He shrugged, palms up, and glanced at his mob. "Are you going to believe a pair of charlatans? He'll spout any lie you might be gullible enough to believe. Remember how I told you about the propaganda they've got the Japanese guy saying? These are his friends! It's all snake oil lies!"

With a shout, they surged forward. Róisín tried to calm her racing heart. She gripped her club tight, wishing she knew more than the rudiments of martial arts. Why hadn't she gotten her black belt? Max had been in the air force and probably more than his fair share of bar brawls. He'd be able to hold his own, but he'd want to protect her.

As the closest attacker lifted his torch, she swung low to crack the club against his knees. He cried out, falling over while clutching his knee. The next man held both hands out as he crouched, like a wrestler. Róisín stepped to one side. He followed, diving toward her waist. She skipped to the other side, knocking him on the back of the head.

He stumbled, but quickly regained his feet. Two other attackers joined him. All three charged at once. She knocked one in the nose with the heel of her hand, blood spurting on her hand. Another grabbed her knees, knocking her over. She fell hard, the wind knocked out of her.

A fourth man shoved a nasty-smelling cloth on her mouth. She kicked his shin and tried to spit it out, but he clung tight. He tied it so hard, the fabric bit into the sides of her mouth. Someone tied her hands behind her back. Three people lifted her as a cheer spread through the crowd. She grew dizzy as she breathed whatever the cloth had been soaked in.

Joel's vile smile chilled her to the bone.

In her mind, she shouted with all her strength. *Dian Cécht! Help me!*

No answer came. Could she use her healing power to hurt? The notion disgusted her, but what choice did she have? Vague memories of dead lions and live jackals flickered in her shattered thoughts. But the gods could help her become a live lion. She'd felt powerful like a lion when the god's power flowed through her. She could be like that again, if she just unshackled herself from these moral manacles.

Stealing herself, she pushed her power through the man clutching her arms. Instead of the warm, clean healing energy, she pulled twisted, ghastly power from the earth. Black, foul-smelling rot flowing through her arms and into her attacker's body. The man behind her grunted but held fast.

She felt filthy. Would she rather be filthy or alive? She tried again, pushing harder, concentrating on the tendrils flowing up into the veins of his hand, into his arm, hot and pulsing like a fever.

Another grunt rewarded her efforts as he tied her to the tree. After he broke skin contact, her power lost control over him and the oily evil dripped from her fingertips back into the ground. Tears of rage and frustration burned as Max shot into the air. His words faded as he got further away. "I'm sorry, Róisín! I'll bring help!"

As he disappeared, she screamed, "Max! Don't leave me!"

Chapter Twelve

"Any human power can be resisted and changed by human beings."
– Ursula K. Le Guin

*Latest **CNN Update:** "We come to you now with news in Ireland, where local rioting has increased across the country. Protesters call for the so-called Unhidden Talents to go home. They blame a recent country-wide epidemic of unknown origins on these individuals. While we have not been able to discover any conspiracy to support these claims, fears have spread like wildfire across the land.*

"According to a statement from the Taoiseach, their Prime Minister, Ireland's first priority is the health of its people. Anything else must take second place until that's achieved. To that end, they've closed the borders to outside visitors and enlisted the help of a group of expert disease consultants. The government has been negotiating with this group for several days and have reported progress in a hospital near Limerick.

"While we have no details on this group of experts, the government spokesman assures us they have a great deal of experience with this disease and the technology to heal. They are asking for volunteers to help the distribution of their measures. No word yet on what they are looking for in these volunteers, but we assure you, we'll share more updates when they become available."

Max:

Max's mind spun with shame and fear. He hated leaving Róisín with the mob, but the wind only half-listened to him now. He'd asked the surrounding wind to lift them both away, but they refused. That bastard Taranis must be interfering. So instead, he took the next-best option, and flew himself away. He should be able to find some help and come back to rescue her.

Her captors carried her away from the beach to the cliff above and tied her to a tree. If they meant to harm her immediately, they wouldn't bother securing her. That meant he had some time.

Other than 'somewhere along the River Shannon,' he had no clue where they were. He'd have to land, get his bearings, and then find help. He directed the winds to carry him along the single-lane road until he spied a cluster of buildings. The wind dropped him gently in front of a pub, deserted at mid-morning. Max let out a snort, that the winds knew his habits so well. An old man sat on a stool outside, smoking a pipe.

Max reasoned that a town this size might have one or two policemen, but he needed a larger city if he wanted a force strong enough to quell a mob and rescue Róisín. Still, every minute counted. "Oi! What town is this? What city is closest?"

The man chewed his pipe stem, pulled it out of his mouth, and spat to one side. "Yer in Paradise, man!" Then he let out a cackle and slapped his knee at his own wit.

Confused, Max glanced around. It certainly didn't look like a paradise. A ramshackle auto repair shop had the sign, "Paradise Auto Lot," and Max got the joke. He forced a fake smile. "That's a good one, mate! Tell me, what's the closest city?"

The old man jerked his thumb over his shoulder. "Head east and ye'll find Limerick."

Limerick! They were close to the Byrne farm. He'd seen that from the air. He ought to be able to find it again. He waved to the old gent before the wind picked him up again, and he followed the inlet coast.

A few minutes later, he spied the farm, with its ornamental garden and red roof. As he spiraled in for a landing, he frowned. The place seemed deserted. That didn't bode well. He needed someone's help. Time grew short. Who knew what they'd done with Róisín now?

Someone walked in the house. Flinging open the back door, he spied Komie making tea. "Komie!"

Startled, she turned. "Max? What are you doing here? I haven't seen you in weeks!"

"No time to explain, I need help. Is anyone else around? Someone with offensive talent?"

She shook her head. "No one but me. Fiona started coughing, so Colin and Michelle took her to the doctor. We'd hoped Róisín would come home from Limerick, but—"

"Bloody hell! No, Róisín isn't there. Damn! I wish you had a useful talent."

She crossed her arms, glaring at him. "Mind your tongue, Max. My talent is incredibly useful."

He paced the kitchen, clenching his fists. "I didn't mean it that way, woman! I mean useful to get Róisín away from her attackers. That's what I'm trying to tell you. She's been captured by an angry mob."

The native woman placed her teacup on the table, her lips set in a thin line. "A mob? Where? Can you get me there?"

"What will you do, then? Ask them to sprout roses on their heads? This is why I need someone with a different talent!"

Steel flashed in her gaze. "I can help. Get me there."

Max stared at her another moment before nodding. "We'll have to hold onto each other. The winds are being picky about which things I ask them to do. Especially lately."

She looked him up and down, from his charred and ripped clothing to his unwashed and unkempt hair. "If it will help Róisín, so be it."

Komie held him tight as the winds lifted them. They didn't rise very high, just skimming the roofs of farms along the shore. Their toes brushed the tops of the trees. As he passed docks along the river, Max suddenly realized he might not be able to find Róisín again. It had been a beach, but where?

His heart raced as they skimmed along the riverbank. People pointed up at them, but he didn't care. He just needed to save Róisín. He really hoped Komie wasn't lying. She refused to explain, but the woman had never boasted about her talents. He hoped whatever she could do would be enough.

There! He recognized the beach, covered in footprints. His gaze travelled up to the cliff, searching for people. Clumps of thick trees carpeted most of the shoreline.

Then he spied the mob, in a clearing surrounded by rhododendrons. An enormous single hawthorn tree grew in the center. The sun rose bright and hot.

They surrounded Róisín. Rope bound her waist and feet to the hawthorn tree. That made his heart catch in his throat. She was alive, but this didn't look good at all. It reminded Max of tales of witches being burnt at the stake. His hope soared when he realized no wood had been piled at her feet. Róisín looked alert and unhurt.

The winds glided him and Komie into the back of the crowd. Several people turned at the motion. "There he is! And he brought another of *them!*"

The mob rushed them, but Max held his hands up. "Hold up there, mates. No need to be vicious. What's your beef, then?"

Joel elbowed his way to the front. "Our beef, as you so colorfully say, is that everyone's getting sick. The sickness came after these Unhidden talents arrived." He turned to face the crowd. "What's the best way to get rid of the plague?"

The man next to Joel raised his fist. "Get rid of *them!*"

"Kill the magic bastards!"

"Burn them like witches!"

Max's heart grew cold at the anger, frustration, and desperation in their voices. *They really believed this crap.* Joel had them whipped into a right frenzy.

He crossed his arms, glaring at Joel. "And how, exactly, do you think that'll work, mate? You think that if we brought some infectious disease with us, it'll just disappear if you kill us? Where'd you get your medical degree? Bloody Disney World?"

A few chuckles echoed through the crowd. Did he have a chance of turning them? Laughter was powerful stuff. "Right, so say we go away, like you ask. When we leave, then what happens? The virus just fades away, and everything returns to normal?"

Mutters ran through the group.

Joel let out another laugh. "Don't let him pull his tricks on you. You know they have speaking magic, right? They've got that Japanese guy on broadcast every week, with touchy-feely speeches to *make* you like them. It's more magic!"

Max bared his teeth. Hiroki was a weird dude but didn't deserve to be painted like a cheap manipulator. He ached to punch Joel straight in the teeth. That might not be wise or diplomatic, but it would feel so bloody good.

What could Joel do? Something with water, like Anna. He glanced at the ocean, a potential supply for whatever Joel might whip up. If he provoked the bloke, and he fought back with water, that *might* convince his pet lynching mob that he was Unhidden. That he lied to them all.

Max stepped toward the American man, his fist clenched. As soon as he moved, the crowd surged around him. They looked ready to kill. So much for his diplomacy skills.

Komie raised her arms. "Halt! You will not harm us." For a wonder, they all obeyed, exchanging confused glances.

Joel stepped forward. "Don't be afraid of her! All she can do is make plants grow. She's no threat. But she might have mutated her plants into a spore to make us sick!"

Grumbles grew as the crowd considered this. Anger mixed with fear on some faces. One man looked about ready to rip her apart with his bare hands. He let out a growl as he stepped forward.

Komie planted her feet wide and with her arms still raised, boomed out a chant.

> *"I call to you, Red-haired Queen,*
> *Lady of sovereignty*
> *I call to you, Woman of the Sidhe,*
> *Who runs swifter than any horse,*
> *I call to you, Battle Goddess,*
> *Who gathers heads as trophies,*
> *Fertile plain, racing mare, battle crow,*
> *Macha, be with me now."*

The rhododendrons surrounding them rustled. A few on the edge of the crowd gave nervous glances, but the rest brandished their protest signs. Komie repeated her chant, her voice growing strident, louder, commanding. Even Max backed away from her.

On her third chant, her arms crackled with energy, actual lightning traveling up and down her body. The sky above swirled with dark clouds, rumbling and sparking with their own lightning. A funnel cloud formed above the Native American woman.

Joel stared up with a deepening frown. A hint of fear flickered in his eyes. Behind him, ocean waves crashed against the shore. Was he calling the sea? Maybe Max still had a chance to punch the bloke's lights out. A crackle of energy tugged his attention back to Komie.

Max's eyes grew wide as she clenched her fists, lowered her arms parallel to the ground, and out to her sides. Then she opened her hands and threw her head back. She let out an inhuman laugh in several harmonic tones, deep and vicious. He felt that laugh in his bones. It echoed in three voices, louder than any human voice.

His eyes darted around the clearing, his blood growing cold. The rhododendrons crept closer. Others dropped their signs, glancing wildly around, but they found no escape. The plants hemmed them in. The one entrance to the clearing lay behind Komie and Max. That would soon be closed off, too.

A woman broke from the herd to dart past them, toward this escape. Out of the thunderous clouds, an arch of lightning struck the ground in front of her. She skidded to a halt and backed away, naked fear clear on her face.

The triple-booming voice surrounded them. **"You dare harm one of mine?"**

For the first time since Max had met him, Joel looked terrified. Still, he had to appreciate the bloke's moxie. Anna's brother's wide eyes darted back and forth, trying to identify the source of the voice. "Who are you? Show yourself! You won't fool us with your tricks! This is more of your pagan magic!"

The voice laughed.

Now, the rhododendrons hemmed in the group so tightly, they had to huddle near the hawthorn tree, where Róisín was still tied to the trunk like a sacrifice. Max wanted to edge through the throng to free her. With a hopeful upward glance, he nixed that idea, too. It wouldn't be the wisest thing to ask the winds to lift him up into a raging thundercloud. Had it been Taranis, or one of the other gods? He might be reckless, but he wasn't *that* bloody reckless.

A form coalesced before Komie, at least six feet tall. At first, only bright light shined from it, but it faded to reveal a woman with broad shoulders, leather armor, and an enormous black raven perched on her shoulder.

She stood with her feet apart, like Komie's, facing the crowd. **"You have insulted those under my care. You will pay."**

Now, the crowd backed away as one. Some only now realized vegetation trapped them. One tried to push through the rhododendron, but only succeeded in slicing his arms. Joel stood his ground, facing the goddess, who could only be this Macha person he'd heard about.

Komie dropped to her knees, shoving her hands into the dirt. The vines around the clearing crept out and encircled the ankles of every attacker. Some tried to rip their limbs from the plant's grasp, but the woody vines held fast.

Max swallowed his fear and inched closer to Komie. She hadn't been lying about being able to help, nor did she need his protection. Perhaps he needed hers. Her eyes glowed with an inhuman light, as bright as the sun, and Max wished he was anywhere but in this clearing.

Macha let out another chilling laugh, and the rhododendron vines yanked each of the mob from their feet, including Joel. The vines wrapped them into thick bundles, unable to move. Some shouted. Others cried. One screamed until the vine covered his mouth. He continued to struggle, but the vines curled around his torso and legs, holding him fast. The entire mob was trussed up like flies in a spider's web, ready for feasting.

Max wanted to throw up, but he clenched his jaw. He crept around the edge of the circle to Róisín. The lone hawthorn still peeked above the mess of rhododendron vines. He must get to her before the goddess took notice.

When he finally got through to her, Róisín looked horrible. No longer the lovely young woman, barely thirty years old, tall and willowy with honey-blond hair. Now she had deep lines around her face, worry wrinkles and faded skin. A lock of hair at her forehead had turned snow white. Her eyes looked raw red with prolonged crying. She let out a silent cry for help, the sound dying on her lips.

He touched Róisín's shoulder when Macha called out. **"Halt."**

Max spun to see Macha striding toward them, stepping on top of the bound mob. **"You will not release her. She belongs to Dian Cécht."**

Max stood straight, his shoulders back. "Then he can come and untie her. Now. If not, I'm pulling off these bloody ropes."

Macha narrowed her eyes, glanced into the sky, and nodded. **"Very well. I will allow your insolence this once. But Dian Cécht is on his way."**

He bent to untie the rope immediately. Max didn't want to wait for Dian Cécht. From what he could tell, that god had wiped the floor with her. Róisín looked completely strung out. He didn't like that. Not one bit.

As Max untied the last knot, Róisín fell into his arms. She felt like a rag doll, barely weighing a thing. He glanced at Macha, who glared at him with judgment. *Well, she can bloody judge all she bloody liked.* He wasn't going to let these jobbos get their claws back into Róisín. Not after how they'd treated her. Ignoring the glaring goddess, he turned to the native woman, her eyes still glowing. "Komie, can you get back on your own? I need to take Róisín home. She needs rest."

"I'm fine. But I don't think the gods want you to leave yet."

"I'm bloody well leaving whether I'm granted permission or not!"

He called on the winds to lift him, Róisín still in his arms. They swirled, and he rose three feet before he slammed into the ground again.

Luckily, he fell first, shielding Róisín from the impact. She didn't even groan. He struggled to draw breath as pain flooded his body.

That other voice boomed, the one called Taranis. **"You will not leave."**

Another shining figure appeared next to Macha. The blonde bloke, that healer who'd wrung Róisín to a limp rag. Rage swelled up within Max. He gently laid Róisín down and climbed to his feet to face the new arrival.

Dian Cécht strode to Róisín. Max called on the wind to help him as he shoved the man's chest with all his might. The god didn't move. *Bloody hell.*

His eyes glowed red as he considered Max. **"You have attempted to injure me. That is not permitted."**

Max swallowed his fear and pushed on. "Look, mate, you can do what you like with me, but leave that poor sheila alone. She's a good person and doesn't deserve this abuse. You've almost killed her!"

Another form appeared next to Dian Cécht. This one had gray hair filled with storm clouds, his lined face suffused with rage. That must be Taranis, the bloke who'd been messing with his winds. One more god formed on the other side of Macha, a blue man with streaming waves for hair. Max tried to move, but he couldn't even wiggle his fingers.

The blue god placed a finger on his lips. **"These humans have been our conduit, and we should garner their respect. There is much to learn in this new age."**

Macha turned to him, scowling. **"They have no respect for us. We deserve their worship and honor. They are humans, Manannán! *We* are the gods."**

The sea god shook his head, bits of seaweed shedding. **"We must *earn* their respect, Macha. Human or not. While iron no longer repels us, other things in this world do. We need their help, even if you don't wish to admit that."**

Taranis clenched his fists, thunder booming around his head. **"No! These modern humans are arrogant and insolent. This one is particularly insolent. He's invaded my domain more times than I can count. He steals what is mine. This one, I can remove."**

He grabbed Max by the front of his shirt, lifting him into the air. No matter how hard Max wiggled, twisted, or struggled, he couldn't get away. His arms flailed, trying to get close to the thunder god's head, with no luck. Even Taranis' hand felt like cold marble, unyielding and impervious.

Taranis' mouth curling into a snarl. He growled as his grip on Max's shirt tightened, almost cutting off his breath. Now, his limbs lay limp at his side, unable to move at all. His heart pounded in his chest. This god hated him and would snuff him like a fly. Was this the end of everything? He sent one last heartfelt plea to Trina to forgive him and shut his eyes.

When nothing happened, he opened one. Dian Cécht laid a hand on Taranis' arm. **"No, don't kill him. We can still use him."**

Max didn't want to be used. He didn't want any of them to be used. He tried again to move but failed. He could clench his muscles, but nothing else. At least he could still breathe.

Manannán shook his head. **"We must work carefully. Brigit's almost killed one in a fit of pique and a considerable lack of wisdom. It could endanger our relations, despite Lugh's questionable charms. We must proceed with caution. We've worked hard for a millennium, and our efforts are finally coming to fruition. We dare not squander our chances with unwise tempers."**

Taranis rumbled, sending peals of thunder across the sky, and Max shivered. He never wanted to meet this bloke in the clouds. Taranis brandished the limp Max like a prop, flinging him about as he gesticulated in anger. **"I don't *want* to wait any more, Manannán! I've waited long enough. I'm not meant to wait. I'm meant to destroy!"**

Macha stepped an inch away from the thunder god's face. **"If Manannán says do not destroy, then you will not destroy. Don't forget, Taranis, you are not a native god. You are a blow-in."** She gave him an impish grin. For a moment, Max's mouth fell open. The gods liked puns?

Taranis dropped Max and clenched his fists, his face growing red with rage. He leaned toward the goddess, his eyes sparking. However, Macha was prepared for him. Max couldn't even tell what she did, but a moment later, Taranis lie on his back with Macha's staff at his neck, a feral smile spreading across her face. **"You will listen to Manannán's judgment. He ranks us, at least until the Dagda arrives. Do you understand?"**

Before Taranis replied, Dian Cécht placed his palm on Max's forehead. He wanted to shout, to scream, to punch the son of a bitch straight in his mouth, but his body refused to obey him. His vision faded to black.

Caoimhe:

The Irish Draoi, a priestess of the old gods, stood on the gallery of the Waterford lighthouse. She loved this city, perched on the southwest corner of Ireland. This was her home, her old stomping grounds. The place where she'd grown up in the ancient traditions. The land itself was of her blood.

And she'd be damned if she'd let these bloody bigots steal it from her. She stroked the sword she'd brought with her for this duty station. Others had brought more modern weapons, but most of them used ancient ones. Crossbows, swords, daggers, even slings. She preferred the steel blade that had been wielded by her several-times great-grandfather in the 1798 Wexford rebellion.

Caoimhe had gathered a passel of other Draoi, priests, hedge witches, new age practitioners, conjurers, and anyone else who could wield any sort of true power. Pushing aside her distaste at their commercialism, she pulled in the "popular" druid groups in Ireland and Wales. She'd even managed to snag Morgan, a visiting American witch who worked with the Good Folk. Their knowledge and power would be a boon to their defenses.

After working up a duty roster for defending the coast, Caoimhe stood at her own station atop the Waterford lighthouse, gazing out into the distant ocean. From the PHAE reports, the PEM had already tried water attacks a few times. One had been foiled in Cork, but the Dublin initiative had breached their defenses. They'd tried to bomb Belfast, but the attack had been minimized with quick thinking by the locals.

Now that their new leader, that Wilkinson man, had started riling up the masses again with his hate speech, Ireland was again in the crosshairs, so they had to be vigilant. Waterford seemed an obvious target, being closest to mainland Europe. The anger flowed through her at the idea of her island being attacked. If she could wield her own power to protect it, she would. And if she needed to call upon help from the gods, she would do that, too.

Caoimhe was no stranger to the Irish gods. She'd worked with Macha, in many of her guises, for decades, and like the goddess, did not suffer fools lightly. Now that she'd finally met the physical manifestation of her patron goddess, Caoimhe wanted to show the world what Macha could do.

Just let them come at her. They'd learn.

No sooner did this thought cross her mind than something tickled her web. Not here, in Waterford, but much further down the coast. The Shannon Estuary? But where? That was a huge area. She concentrated her perception, trying to find the bright points along her security web. Something glowed bright on the headland past Limerick. Much too bright to be her normal watchers. Who was stationed there? She tried to remember, but the names slipped out of her mind like sand through her fingers. Damnit, she'd never been this scattered before.

Another tickle, this time north of Dublin. This was no fluke. Was it a false alarm? Caoimhe grabbed her phone and looked up the list of names. Who was there now?

A man named Hughes. She didn't know him, personally. But she'd call him to find out what happened. His phone rang, but no one picked up. Cursing, Caoimhe tried the Limerick location instead. Nothing. She dialed the next person up the river.

Four phone calls later, her worry grew so strong she had to clench her teeth to keep them from chattering. Where had everyone gone?

Finally, one of her phone calls connected. "Hello? Hello, Colin, is that you?"

The line crackled. "Caoimhe? What's going on?"

"Something's hit the shore near you, up near Belfast, and in Dublin. Something bad, and lots of it. I need you to go see what's going on."

"That's pretty vague. Can't you be more specific?"

"No, I feckin' can't! Get your arse down there and find out what's happening! And report back immediately! If we need to call reinforcements, we need to know now."

As she hung up, she gripped the lighthouse railing so tight her hands ached.

Another hit tickled her senses, something up near Belfast. She cursed, knowing that she had no direct numbers for anyone along that coast.

A web of protection was fine, but no one was communicating. What the feck good was it to have a network if none of the nets were working?

She needed to wait now, and she detested waiting.

Komie:

The ocean stirred behind her. Despite her exhaustion, Komie spun to face this new threat, whatever it was. A rumble on the surface of the sea, and then it disappeared up the river estuary. She turned to the gods arguing over Max. "Manannan? I understand you are a sea god. Can you see what just went by?"

Halting their conversation, the sea god turned to her, and for a moment, Komie steeled herself for an attack. However, he only gave her a nod before he dove into the ocean.

A moment later, he emerged. "There is a vehicle below the surface. You call them submarines."

Komie's blood chilled. The Irish didn't have any submarines, as far as she knew. The PEM had some, and they'd attacked once before. Were they trying again? It must be so. Panic gripped her as she blurted out, "They aren't ours! The PEM is attacking again!"

A slow smile spread across Macha's face as she exchanged a glance with Taranis. Moving to crouch next to Max's unconscious body, Komie did her best to shield both Max and Roisin from whatever these two dangerous gods did next.

Macha turned to her. "It seems you are in need of some help, Nokomis. Do you now request our assistance?"

She knew this was a dangerous thing, to ask the gods for a favor. Hadn't the PHAE set up some sort of network to warn them of an attack this time?

Komie was damned if she would give in to this sort of strong-arm pressure. She hated bullies. Her daughter-in-law had been a bully, and Komie let that bitch push her away from her only grandchild. She wouldn't let these bullies steal her new home away.

There had to be a way she could stop that submarine. Could she make the trees grow enough to form a barrier? No, even she didn't have so much power. Or she could make the ground itself swell? Only with the gods help.

Even as she considered and rejected a half-dozen plans, the vessel went past her and further up the estuary. She was running out of time.

Then her gaze fell on a willow tree whose branches brushed the river surface. There were plants underwater, kelp and other seaweed. All she needed to do was tangle the propellers. Did modern submarines even have propellers? She had no idea.

Komie dug deep into herself to pull on her power. Down, down, into the earth of the cliff she stood upon, where the gods stood, watching her, waiting for her to fail.

The tendrils of power pulsed with deep green light, into the soil and under the riverbed. She found countless river plants and seaweed, all willing to heed her call. They grew up and out, at a faster speed than she had ever managed before.

But the submarine didn't stop.

She tried again, pushing more power through the riverbed, straining with every breath, every muscle of her body to throw up a wall of tangling weeds and to stop that invading vessel.

But the submarine didn't stop.

Komie tried once more to make the river plants grow, but they couldn't grow any more. They had used up their own power, their own resources, choked off from river traffic and pollution. Komie's own strength, already drained from her earlier use, just wasn't up to this task.

She fell on the grass, utterly spent. Just as she let out a defeated breath, her phone buzzed.

Komie pulled out her phone and tried to call Colin, but it just rang. Then she tried Ciara's number. After a moment's hesitation, she dialed Caoimhe's, bracing herself for the caustic woman.

Finally, after six rings, the line clicked. "Caoimhe here. Who's this? I don't recognize this number."

Trying to calm her beating heart, Komie answered, "Caoimhe, it's Komie. I've got a situation here."

The other woman barked, "Tell me the details."

With a glance around to the others, Komie tried to get all the information in short sentences. "I'm on the Shannon estuary. We just saw a submarine go by. I tried to stop it, but I wasn't strong enough."

"Who else is with you? Why aren't they trying? You don't have good offensive magic."

Komie wanted to call out the insult to her power, but there wasn't time. "Max and Roisin are with me, but both are unconscious. Manannan, Macha, and Taranis are here. I know the gods have offered to help us fight against the PEM should they invade again, but I don't have the authority to say yes."

Static crackled in the silence before Caoimhe answered, "I have three other people calling me with news of intrusions. I don't know if they're all submarines, but I will bet every dram I've ever drunk that this is a coordinated attack."

"I don't have any way to stop the one here. Max is completely passed out. Roisin wouldn't be able to help even if she weren't unconscious. What do I do?"

"What the feck do you think you should do, Komie? You're not an idiot. I'd never agree to teach you if you were an idiot. Even you should see that you need the gods help now, whether the fecking government puts their rubber stamp on that or not!"

Komie clenched her teeth against an angry response. "Fine. I'll tell them you authorized it."

"You do whatever you like, Komie. I've got to deal with the other intrusions."

She clicked off the line.

Komie stared at three gods. They all stared back, waiting for her decision. She was a peaceful woman, and detested personal violence. At the same time, she understood that her opinion wasn't the only one that mattered. The entire country of Ireland was in danger, and she had the power to help save them. Or at least, this corner of it.

"Yes. We would like your help to neutralize this threat."

If Komie hoped her phrasing would make any difference, she was quickly disabused of that notion.

Macha gave a slow, wicked grin, turned to the river estuary and lifted her arms. Manannan did the same. Taranis joined them. Out of the dark water, a submarine rose, five, ten, twenty feet into the air.

It fell back into the river with a tremendous splash.

Frowning, the gods tried again, this time lifting it thirty, forty, fifty feet. The metal submarine wavered in the air, dripping water and shaking. And, as the gods flung their hands to the left, it sped toward the cliffside, smashing into the rock.

The metal may have been strong enough to guard against pressure in the depths, but it couldn't resist being smashed against a cliffside. It crumpled into scrap with a sickening sound. A siren wailed and then silenced with a horrible whimper. Men screamed. Komie shut her eyes and her ears against the noise, knowing she'd just condoned violence against other humans, but what else could she have done?

Her phone rang again. She answered to Caoimhe's voice, "Well? Did you get their help?"

She answered in a deadpan voice, "I did. The submarine is destroyed."

"Good. So are the others. Evidently your gods passed the word around faster than anyone can credit. Congratulations, Komie. You just saved Ireland."

She may have saved the island and her people, but at what cost?

To be concluded in **All's Fae That Ends Fae.**

Bintou's world is grim. Her allies are divided.
Can she be the voice of peace and prevent their utter annihilation?

Can she help her people put their differences aside
in the name of survival?

Buy **All's Fae That Ends Fae** to prepare for storms brewing today!
https://www.amazon.com/gp/product/B0B6Q2ZS1Q

Thank You!

Thank you so much for enjoying Much Ado About Dying. If you've enjoyed the story, please consider helping others find Róisín, Hiroki, and the rest of the Unhidden by leaving a review.

If you would like to get updates, sneak previews, sales, and contests, please sign up for my newsletter.

Monthly Newsletter Signup and homepage:
www.greendragonartist.com

Other Books by This Author

See all the books available through

Green Dragon Publishing at

www.greendragonartist/books

About the Author

Christy Nicholas writes under several pen names, including Emeline Rhys, CN Jackson, and Rowan Dillon. She is an author, artist, and accountant. After she failed to become an airline pilot, she quit her ceaseless pursuit of careers that begin with the letter 'A' and decided to concentrate on her writing. Since she has Project Completion Compulsion, she is one of the few authors with no unfinished novels.

Christy has her hands in many crafts, including digital art, beaded jewelry, writing, and photography. In real life, she's a CPA, but having grown up with art all around her (her mother, grandmother, and great-grandmother are/were all artists), it sort of infected her, as it were.

She wants to expose the incredible beauty in this world, hidden beneath the everyday grime of familiarity and habit, and share it with others. She uses characters out of time and places infused with magic and myth, writing magical realism stories in both historical fantasy and time travel flavors.

Social Media Links:
Blog: www.GreenDragonArtist.net
Website: www.GreenDragonArtist.com
Facebook: www.facebook.com/greendragonauthor
Twitter: www.twitter.com/greendragon9
Instagram: www.instagram.com/greendragonartist9
TikTok: www.tiktok.com/@greendragonauthor

Lightning Source UK Ltd.
Milton Keynes UK
UKHW010821121222
413794UK00004B/288